The Merkids from the Lost Continents of Atlantis and Lemuria

By Katherine Snitker

authorHOUSE®

AuthorHouse™
1663 Liberty Drive
Bloomington, IN 47403
www.authorhouse.com
Phone: 1-800-839-8640

Published by AuthorHouse 1/6/2013

ISBN: 978-1-4772-8905-1 (sc)
ISBN: 978-1-4772-8906-8 (e)

Library of Congress Control Number: 2012921136

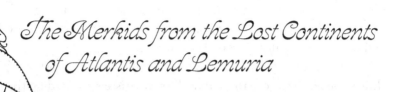

The Merkids from the Lost Continents of Atlantis and Lemuria

The story begins with seven shooting stars rocketing through the darkness of outer space across the Universe towards Earth.

It was the seven sisters traveling through the galaxy to a new world. They were leaving the star cluster known as The Pleiades in the constellation of Taurus. They were headed to this new planet to begin a settlement, to colonize and start new life. Once they arrived on Earth they settled on the one land mass or continent, a true Garden of Eden and called it Lemuria. Later it would become known as the Motherland of Man. The people who lived there just called it Mu.

The seven sisters and the first Beings of Light were pure spirit energy but they learned and adapted over time to take on physical bodies, which enabled them to reside on the Earth's heavier astral plane. Much like the earliest deep-sea divers had to put on heavy outer gear to be able to walk on the Ocean floor. This transition into physical body was considered the birth of mankind. All people had a memory of who they were and where they had come from. In the beginning they were able to enter or leave their body at will.

Unfortunately over thousands of years in their heavier physical bodies and as they used their psychic abilities less and less they started to forget their spiritual and galactic origins. Soon they stopped returning to spirit completely: most men were beginning to care more for their physical senses than their spiritual souls.

As men settled and started new colonies they became even more removed from their spiritual base, too busy or too tired to devote time to spirit. Life was a struggle with catastrophic events happening that literally tore Lemuria apart. Man was becoming greedy and proud of his things, at this point in history Atlantis was the largest and greatest of the colonies, so before the true path and spiritual ways were all forgotten and lost, their history was written and encoded on tablets and seed crystals by their leaders.

A total of seven seed crystals and three sets of tablets carried the history of Lemuria, from its humble spiritual and galactic beginnings into the birth of mankind, to the continent's time of growth and prosperity and later it's several, separate destructions.

Just before the final destruction of Mu, where most of the land slipped beneath the ocean's water, the seven sisters divided up the tablets and seed crystals: each would carry the history of Lemuria with them to their next homes. With their followers, each sister traveled to one of Earth's seven most sacred chakra/vortex locations and began seven new colonies. Lemurians had always been more concerned with their spirit and souls and that of the new planet they had settled. So after arriving at their final destinations, each sister hid her seed crystal for safe keeping, afraid that past mistakes would once again repeat themselves. They decided it was better if man didn't remember everything from his past.

Halfway around the planet, Atlantis, now a separate continent was still the greatest of Lemuria's first colonies. It had fared far better than Lemuria only experiencing minor damage from the troubles that led to the end and final sinking of most of the land known as Mu.

With Lemuria gone it was Atlantis that ruled and led the world. For many, many centuries it grew and prospered leading the way forward, to much advancement for mankind. Atlantis had always been more advanced than Lemuria and many of its people were less spiritual because of their technology. It was all the advanced technology of Atlantis and greed, that helped lead to its end and final disappearance, also into the belly of the Ocean like Lemuria.

After the final destruction and sinking of Atlantis both once great continents were gone and soon all but forgotten. Over eons of time words of Lemuria and Atlantis became legend and myth; proof of their history and existence long buried and forgotten except in the hearts of seven sisters, their tablets and the seed crystals.

The sisters and their followers began the seven religions and tribes of today's world leading their people forward into a newer, once more spiritually grounded world with seven new continents.

Man and time marched on.........................

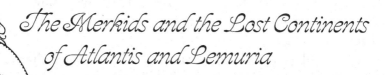

The Merkids and the Lost Continents of Atlantis and Lemuria

One day by chance, in this new world, two young girls came upon two figures playing in the water off the Gulf Coast of Florida. They appeared to be just another two children playing and enjoying the late afternoon surf. Kat and Becka, the two girls were walking on the beach searching for shells to take home when they saw the other two children. There wasn't anyone else on that end of the beach that afternoon and as they looked around, the two on the beach could see they were the only ones in sight, of the two in the water. The four of them, all appeared to be about the same age, maybe ten to twelve years old. The two playing in the water were a boy and a girl, and they didn't seem to notice the two girls approaching them on the beach.

"Look Becka do you see those two kids?"

I asked as I pointed in their direction. They were playing in the surf, splashing each other and laughing. I didn't think that they had seen us yet as they were having so much fun and seemed to be so in that moment of joy and fun they were creating. Suddenly the girl jumped up a little and flipped her body as if to dive into a wave and we saw it. We both saw it and we looked instantly to each other and then back at the scene in front of us. She had a tail, or at least it looked like a tail, just like a fish. Had we really seen a fish tail on that girl or were we just imagining things?

We looked at each other again. Becka said,

"Did you see what I saw?" as I was saying the same thing.

"Did you see what I saw?"

We both looked back just as the boy did the same thing and he had a fish tail too, just like the girl. Well maybe, we thought, it was a costume? It looked like we were looking at two mer-kids. One was half fish, half

- 3 -

boy and the other half girl, half fish. The tails looked pretty real from where we were. Were we dreaming or was this for real?

I couldn't stop myself as I ran a couple yards closer trying to get a better look, then I abruptly stopped; I was lucky I didn't get whiplash, from the sudden halt I made trying to get that closer look. Were my eyes deceiving me? I moved to the waters edge a little more slowly this time and stopped again. I didn't want to scare them away and I wasn't sure what to say to them.

Becka walked up behind me and she called out very calmly,

"Hello there, don't be afraid. We'd like to meet you."

They both froze on the spot, then only turning their heads to look our way. You could see they were surprised. They must have thought they were all alone out there and then suddenly, there we were. They looked at us like we were some kind of aliens. They seemed a little afraid at first and then they both looked a little curious; like two little kittens who got stopped playing in the middle of a game of tag and what ever caught their eye and stopped the game, seemed suddenly very interesting to them.

They said something to each other but we couldn't hear what they said or how they sounded. They looked back at us then she left his side and swam in a little closer towards us. It looked like she started to say something and you could tell she wasn't sure about what she was doing, she stopped and looked back to her friend and then turned back towards us again.

"We won't be afraid if you aren't afraid. We won't hurt you, so please don't try to hurt us."

As she finished her last words she looked back to her friend again and he started to swim in a little closer too.

I blurted out,

"We don't want to hurt you we just have to know, was that a fish tail we saw when you dove into the waves a minute ago?"

She giggled and as she did, she flipped her tail up out of the water and made a little splash, with it.

"Yes, you saw our tails and scales but we don't always have them, only when we're in the water. We are able to walk on land just like you. It's just when we enter the water our scales come out and we get our tails back. If we have to travel for very long distances we even have gills and can breathe under water too," she stated.

Well, this was totally blowing our minds and more than just a little!

This was like some fairy tale or maybe a dream. Becka and I were both shaking our heads in wonder.

"You're both like that? Where did you come from? Are there more people like you? What do you call yourselves?"

I was talking fast again, asking too many questions but I wanted to find out a lot of things, right now.

"Before I can tell you any of those things I must ask and get your sworn oath, what ever I tell you, will never be repeated by the two of you," she said.

"Oh we swear. We promise we'll never repeat what you tell us."

I answered her first and then Becka added in her,

"I swear too."

The boy swam up next to the girl, and then together they both started to come in closer. He looked a little different from her, not like sister and brother at all. He actually looked like he had some Asian blood from his ancestors but from a long time ago. She looked a little more Polynesian. She was dark haired and so was he but their features were different.

"Come meet us half way" the boy called out.

We stepped into the surf and started towards them. As we got closer to them we could see their tails were split in the middle. They actually had what looked like two scaled legs with fins on them instead of feet. When they put their legs together it looked like one complete fish tail.

The boy said,

"We're from Atlantis, the buried continent south of here. We call ourselves Atlantians."

Well let me tell you, even in my dreams I had never heard anything like this before. I thought my eyes might pop right out of my head. Becka and I both knew Atlantis had been destroyed a very, very, very, very long, long time ago. How could they be from a place that didn't exist anymore? I said as much to him too.

"How can that be? Atlantis was destroyed way before recorded history even began?"

They started to explain.

"Although a large portion of the continent and the cities fell beneath the water some of our people were able make preparations for such an event. As much of the land mass went beneath the oceans, the main city was saved under a protective shield, powered by our giant crystals. Many people survived the last of the destructions; while some of the others, from other far cities made it to land again, in other farther away locations. We have survived all these thousands of years with the help of our crystals and the shield that has been our protection. Over those years, the shield has grown many layers of coral and reef that has helped to hide and protect us from detection, by your world. Atlantis is buried far beneath the surface and has long, deep passages into it. If you did not know the way and the signs, you would never be able to find your way in. My name is Shi, my brothers and I am working towards a cure for the ills of our people. The only reason we have ventured out to your world, is to find if possible, botanical specimens that were used in the ancient times by our people, to work towards that cure."

"My name is Mu and it was my ancient Family head, Cyrus who helped to build and design the shield that has protected us for so long. We are here now to find some of the specimens that Shi just mentioned. We know these plants would always grow at vortex locations but there are thousands of them around the world. We have been trying to find them but so far we haven't had any success. Bach told us to come to this location today. Do you know of plants and could you help us?" She was so humble and sincere in her plea for our help.

Becka and I were almost in shock. Could any or all of this be true? What had we stumbled upon here at the waters edge? Atlantis still out there, with people living in the capital city; it was almost too much to try and take in. But they were there, right in front of us and we could clearly see their tails here in the clear waters of the Gulf of Mexico. If aliens had landed and jumped out of their space ship, I don't think we could have been more stunned.

"Becka and I don't know much about many plants. We help her family in the garden so we do know how to plant and harvest but that's mostly fruits and vegetables that you eat. What kind of plants are you looking for?" I asked them.

Becka spoke up then,

"If we had a picture or could see what the specimens looked like we could look them up for you and find out if they are still growing in our area."

Mu said,

"We could take you with us to the city and show you pictures and see if you could help us."

She said it like it would all just be so easy.

"How could you take us? We can't swim as far as you and we don't have any gills to breath under water like you. Besides it would take a long time and we'd get in trouble for being gone, our parents would never let us go with you," Becka told them.

"It would be easy" Shi said "We have masks you can wear and we would be able to take you so you wouldn't have to swim, you would just be along for the ride. Plus I have a way to make time stand still for certain periods of time in your world, time is just an illusion of your world, no one will even know that you are gone. I know the powers of the universe and can do many such things. You would be back before you know it and no one would know you had ever left. I guarantee it! My brothers are working on the cure and we must find what they need before it is too late. The ills of our people have killed all the elders and there is only the younger of us left. If we don't find the cure, our people will vanish from our world and Atlantis will truly die."

Becka was getting that look on her face, the one my Dad would get when he was going to say no to me. I jumped in and told her,

"We have to go Becka they need our help. How can you even think of saying no? I don't want to go without you and I'm not missing a chance to see Atlantis. This is more than a once in a lifetime thing and who would ever think we would get a chance like this one?" I took a deep breath and continued, "They're here and they say they can do it. I believe them. I'm going, and I know you'll regret it if you don't come too! Please Becka, say you'll come too. I don't want to leave you behind for this."

She was quiet for a couple minutes and had the most thoughtful look on her face. Finally she said,

"Okay we'll go but if anything goes wrong Kat, you're never going to hear the end of it!"

She turned and told them,

"We'll go with you and we'll try to help you, any way we can. I just hope we don't get in trouble for this and I hope you can do what you say you can do."

We hadn't noticed until just then, they both had pouches tied around their waist and they each opened their pouch to pull out something that looked like a mini snorkel mask, they were made from shells and looked like something my Nana might have made.

"Here are your masks, they are worn like this" Shi said and he started to demonstrate how to wear it.

They handed us the masks and Mu said,

"You don't have to worry about running out of air, the crystals and plant cells inside will produce a continuous supply and they never run out. The masks will make the necessary adjustments to your air levels, as your body needs them to allow for the different depths we will swim through, on our way into Atlantis. All you will have to do is take hold of our waist straps and we will do the rest."

Mu pulled some small things that looked like crystals from her pouch.

"Here" she said, "You'll need these too. They are amplifiers that will enable you to communicate with each other as well as protect your inner ears during our travel back to Atlantis." She explained how to use them with a short demonstration. Them she handed us each a pair to use.

"How will they let us communicate with each other? They just look like ear plugs made out of crystals to me." I asked Mu as she handed me my pair.

"They will work much like your radio, they will receive the thoughts of anyone in our group while we are in the water. The ocean water and wave movements act much like sound waves that will carry our thoughts from crystal to crystal. You should find it helpful and we can talk you through each step of our journey this way."

"Don't be afraid," Shi added, "we will take good care of you. When we get closer to Atlantis we will have to go deep towards the ocean floor and we must go through several caves and dark tunnels to get to the inner passage way back up. It will be the most frightening part of the journey for you, but trust us, it won't last too long and you will be able to make it."

Becka and I both looked at each other. Well, maybe this wasn't as good an idea as I had first thought it might be. Caves and dark tunnels under water? Becka was looking at me like she wanted to say, ' What have you gotten me into this time?' The look of fear and backing out, was clearly written across Becka's face and I wondered if mine showed the same. I forced myself to take a cleansing breath and tried to feel brave again.

"They said we'd be okay. I trust them. Remember, we're going to Atlantis!! It'll be worth it, no matter what!" I whispered to her. How could anyone be talking to two merkids with fish tails and gills and not believe whatever they were telling you?

"Okay" we said, "we trust you and we believe you. Now lets go before one of us changes our mind." They turned so we could take a hold of their waist strap. Becka took Mu's and I took hold of Shi's.

"Put your masks on and we'll go," he said.

As they started to lean into the water we did the same and we were off. Our bodies were gliding easily through the water next to them. They gave us a minute or two to get use to the mask and then they signaled they were going to go just a little deeper under the surface. They took us deeper in gradual little increments, only a few feet at a time as we adjusted to this new environment under the surface of the gulf waters.

I remember thinking this must be what a dolphin feels like gliding through the water. We were traveling pretty fast it seemed and they swam with ease, even with us in tow. I didn't feel like we were slowing them down at all but never having done this before, I had no idea what they could do. Maybe this was slow gear for them.

It was amazing all the sea life we were seeing and swimming with. It was like being in one of the attractions at Sea World only a thousand times better. You could reach out and touch some of the fish and they were right next to you, not in some pen or pool. They didn't even try to swim away from us. It was like they knew we would never hurt them and they were happy to swim along with us. It was fascinating to see so many creatures so up close and personal. I looked towards Becka and she looked as awe struck as me. We were both pretty busy, looking in all directions, trying to see everything.

Suddenly I heard what sounded like Becka's voice saying,

"I can't believe all this. I've never seen anything so beautiful there are starfish and corals and more kinds of fish than I even knew existed."

"Is that you Becka?" It was the thought that just popped into my mind.

"Is this what Mu meant when she said we'd be able to communicate? Can you hear me?" I thought.

She immediately answered me.

"Yes I can hear you. Did you hear my thoughts about the starfish and coral we just passed?"

"Yes." I told her, "but I still can't believe I can hear you. WOW, what a mind blower this is!"

We passed manatees and a few sharks that we saw at a distance. Once three dolphins actually came up and swam next to us for a while. I reached out and touched one and so did Becka. What an adventure the two of us were having. The colors and the textures of it were intoxicating to the senses. I felt like Alice in Wonderland again and I didn't want it to end.

The further south we got the colors of the water became lighter and brighter. Suddenly it was lime green, turquoise and almost powder blue all around us. Becka and I were ogling and awing over just about everything we saw and passed by. The fish changed only a little, they were more colorful here in the Caribbean. Little fish with yellow stripes swam by and around us by the thousands. I could feel the currents helping to move us towards our destination as we started to swim a little more to the east as we left the coastline of Florida and the Florida keys.

I never gave a second thought to anything we had left behind us. I was in such wonder with all that I was seeing and feeling. What a ride this had become. I think what I was feeling what the astronauts must feel something like, when they're in outer space and look back down on the world and the rest of the Universe. I couldn't imagine that much of anything else could beat what I was feeling right then and the journey was just beginning.

Soon we started to swim deeper and more to the south again. At least I thought it was the south. I was so amazed with how easy the snorkel like breathing gear and crystal earplugs worked. They seemed so simple in their design and yet they enabled us to make this trip and open this undersea world to us.

The water was getting a little cooler but not cold. It lost only a little of it's jewel tone color as we went deeper and deeper. Soon we started to swim and work our way around and under massive boulders and reefs. At least a lot of the stones looked like giant blocks, as if some huge structure had fallen and the blocks had tumbled here and there at random, leaving little crevices and tunnels to swim into and through.

"What do you think of those blocks of stone Becka?" I asked.

"Those are some of the ruins of Atlantis from the second destruction." Mu answered.

"Wow!" was all I could think.

"Soon we will pass over some of the accession temple ruins as well. They will be more recognizable." Mu added.

What other marvels could we expect to see this day? It was really something to ponder while we made our way through these slightly darker waters.

It was beautiful to see all the different corals and shells that had grown onto the rock and other places were bare where only seaweed swayed in the water's current. The deeper we went, the darker it got.

This was only the second time a little panic started to creep into my thoughts, first it was the sharks and now all this darkness starting to blind me. It was making me question the intelligence of this decision and I had to rely on blind faith as the darkness totally overtook our surroundings.

I wondered if Becka was scared and hoped that we hadn't made a poor decision, trying to help Mu and Shi. Of course they all heard me thinking my scary thoughts.

"You will be fine. Try to relax as we enter the darkened tunnels do not panic or be afraid. Think about a place where you feel safe and picture yourself there." Shi told us.

Becka Jumped in and reassured me.

"Yeah, I'm okay Kat. I'm a little nervous but I'll make it. Don't worry about me. How about you? Are you okay?"

"I'm okay," I answered back.

We seemed to swim for a very long time, back and forth, a little up and then a little down. We were winding in all directions and I had lost the sense of what was up and what was down.

Just as the doubt was starting to creep in a little deeper and a little more than just nervousness started to over take my brain, I heard the words.

"We are almost through the worst of it. It won't be long now."

It was Mu announcing our progress. We had made the deepest part of the entry and had turned and started back up to the surface again. It started to get a little lighter and I could see again. Becka looked as relieved as I did, just to be able to see again. The total darkness was a very eerie feeling and it wasn't easy to deal with. I guess it was a good thing neither of us was claustrophobic or we might not have made it through that part.

It was still a while before we could look up and see we were getting close to the surface again. Many times there were options, of which cave to swim into and we wondered how they knew the way, so well. We would never be able to find our way out without them. That alone was a scary thought. Lets hope that nothing happened, where we would have to deal with anything without their help, until we were back home again.

Now when we looked at Mu and Shi they were smiling at us. I think that they were happy to be getting help in their search for a way to save their world, their friends and families.

Mu said,

"We are happy to have your help in our quest to save our world and the last generation of Atlantians. You need not worry. We will take the best care to keep you both safe."

There were steps to the right as we neared the waters surface and they took us over to the landing next to them. Mu and Shi started up the stairs, as they moved up to the top stair and started to stand erect, their tails and the scales just started to almost melt away or retract. I was thinking," Wow," could you do that again? It looked like melting to me anyway.

We were out of the water and apparently they couldn't hear my thoughts anymore. I was kind of glad. It was really eerie and strange to have people hear your, every thought. You had to be so careful and try not to let your thoughts wander too much.

They both had human legs now, just like us and all the other kids, who now surrounded us. I was happy to be getting back on dry land. As exciting as that trip had been, there were a couple times I thought, I would almost peed my pants: especially when we saw the sharks and the last part of the passage into Atlantis when it was so dark and scary.

That was certainly something to think about! We just came through the entrance to the lost city of Atlantis, on the sunken, lost continent of Atlantis. This had to be the most incredible moment I would ever have in this lifetime. I was starting to feel a little like Indiana Jones; what was going to be around the next corner and what other wonders and sights were out there waiting for us to take in?

As we stepped up to the main level at least another 40 to 50 kids came running over and surrounded us. There was nothing but kids. Then I remembered, Mu and Shi had told us, all the elders were gone and only the young were still here. That brought back to mind the reason we were here. They needed help and they needed it as soon as possible or else they would all perish. That was a sobering thought, as my dad, would've said.

Looking around I couldn't help but think of the Disney movie I had seen called Peter Pan: Never, Never land was a place where only children lived. They were all looking at us as if we were movie stars, or some royalty from another world. Actually we looked basically, exactly like them but they knew that we were from the outside world so they all crowded in close to see us.

Mu started to introduce us to some of the others.

"This is Bach."

He was a dark skinned boy, his hair was done up in what our world called cornrow braids and he wore a colorful skirt like clothing with an African design, very primitive and bold.

"Cato,"

He had a little lighter skin than Bach and was dressed differently. He wore his hair loose with a few thin braids on the sides that had beads on the ends of the braids. His clothing looked more like something I saw in the movie The King and I, kind of a ballooning draped fabric that turned back up from the knees and tucked in at the waist. He had on a short vest-like top on as well.

"Mume'

She had a very Polynesian look and her top reminded me of a Hawaiian wrap-around. Her bottoms looked like what we called leggings. Her clothes were both bright and very colorful. She had tiny little seashells in her hair. They looked like they were holding her thin braids at the ends.

"Ling,"

She looked Asian and she had on simple clothing that made me think of a Chinese girl, wearing silk pajamas.

"This is Umm, Da, He, Varr, and Aki".

Each of the boys, were all different looking and dressed differently too. She turned and gestured toward another small group.

"This is Isis, Ru and Ra. We'll meet the others another time."

The two of them looked somehow more Egyptian to me. Their clothing seemed more like what you would see in the old hieroglyphs. All of the kids had on clear bright colors, even though their clothes seemed a little different they all seemed to mesh and blend a little together. Most of them wore sandals on their feet or no shoes at all.

"What interesting names and clothing," Becka said.

"You think so? They are very ancient family names from Lemuria like mine and the others are from here in Atlantis. As for our clothing, we are all individuals and the only common ground our clothing has is that the colors balance out, reflect and enhance our auras. The stones and gems we wear help to amplify our auras as well. Each of us has our own vibration. We use color and gems to fine-tune those vibrations that in turn also help each of our chakras to work at their highest level. The spiritual body is the true temple, not the physical. Now, what was it we heard you call each other? How should we address you? "Mu asked.

"I'm Becka, which is my nickname or short for Rebekha and this is my best friend Kat, which is her nickname. Kat is short for Katherine."

Once all the introductions were over with, Mu asked us to follow her, to go and find Shi's brothers. We walked through the arrival area and as we went through some hallways and up more stairs, we came to a room that opened to a large terrace that was open to the sky. It was surprisingly bright, as if the sun was shinning. What an unbelievable place this was. With just the first glimpses of light on the city of Atlantis and I was taking in my breath. Becka and I both walked to the short front wall of the terrace in front of us, to look around at our surroundings. It was absolutely breathe taking.

For as far as the eye could see, the view that lay before us was a tropical paradise with lush beautiful trees and plants everywhere. It looked like every description of every Shangri-La, paradise and the Garden of Eden ever described, all rolled into one. Mere words couldn't begin to describe the world we suddenly found ourselves in. There were hundreds of terraced gardens with cascading plants and flowers. I had never seen anything like it. Was this where the idea for the hanging gardens of Babylon, that the history books always talked so much about, came from? The buildings all seemed to have patios, terraced areas like the one we were standing on at every level. At the upper levels all of the buildings had more of the pyramid shape to them .The buildings appeared to be built back into the hillside. I couldn't believe it, a hill in a sunken city, on a lost continent. Could I begin to really believe it all, that this was really Atlantis?

"How does the sun shine down here under the sea? "I had to ask.

"It is not the sun as you have in your world. It is the energy and light of the crystals that we rely on here. It is in every way, as nurturing and life giving as your sun is to you, with none of the harmful solar rays to deal with. Our world is surrounded by a geode of giant crystals: they run everything here from the warm waters of the falls and ponds to the lighting and the clean air. Crystals are the soul and spirit of this planet and our world. They are the source of everything life giving; the air we breathe as well as the light and vibrations that sustains us. Do you not remember this? Has your world so out grown it's past history and knowledge? We are the same in spirit as the crystals. They are the vibration and magnetic frequency of life. Doesn't your generation realize this any more?"

I was dumbfounded the way Mu answered us and surprised at how it all sounded so simple. She said it with such a matter of fact attitude, I wondered if she thought we were stupid not to already know or remember it.

The trees were as tall as the buildings and so full and lush, even more so than the ones we had seen back home. Was the light from the crystals superior to our sun? This was such an interesting place already. So many things to draw your attention, many of them were in some ways, the same as back home and in other ways so different. If this is the way the world use to be, I wish that it hadn't changed. Everything just seemed so much more established and virginal at the same time. How could I begin to find the right words to describe all these things I was seeing with my old earth eyes?

There were birds flying here I had never seen anything like them back home. They were similar to parrots in our world but I don't think I had ever seen any as large or with the colors these had. They were beautiful turquoise, lime green and magentas. The birds and the flowers here, both seemed a little larger than the ones back home. So far the few flowers I could see, from the terrace where we stood, they were definitely more exotic than the ones I had ever seen back home. I wished again I had my camera with me so I could take pictures. I was seeing way too much, to be able to remember it all.

When I looked down, I saw the biggest cockroach; it must have been at least 8 to 9 inches long and was fatter than a cigar. That was a little scary. Mu saw the look on my face as I tried to get away from it and she giggled.

"All of God's creatures are loved and honored here in our world. Each has a purpose and a reason for being. Don't be afraid, they won't hurt you or interfere with your life, just be careful not to step on one or damage it."

This was more than a little different from our world. I could hardly believe what my eyes were seeing and I could tell that Becka was feeling the same way. We both kept looking in every direction and pointing out new things to each other. We were getting so caught up in this new world we found ourselves in, we almost forgot we were on a mission.

Shi brought us both back to the moment when he said,

"There will be time later for you to stop and appreciate all that Atlantis has to offer. Now we need to find my brothers and take care of the task of showing you the plants that we need. Come with us now please."

He headed towards another open archway and we followed. The other kids all headed back to what ever they were doing when they heard of our arrival. It seemed that each had a job or a chore that they preformed, just like the adults in our world.

We left the arrival building and headed up the walkway following behind Shi and Mu and we were once again looking in all directions taking in this amazing and wonderful place. As we walked along, one of the boys walked by us, with the strangest looking animal on his shoulder. I had to ask,

"What kind of animal is that?"

Mu looked back and said,

"Oh that's Pookin and that's his pet Zimmer. It would be the ancestor to your Lemur monkeys, which grew larger over the centuries. Our zimmers all stay very, very small. Often the zimmer travels around, just hanging onto Pookin's hair at the back of his neck, where it is well hidden from sight. He must have been aware that strangers were here and that there was something new to see. They are very curious and sensitive creatures that can sense very small changes in the energy and thought waves around them. The fact that he didn't hide from your curious eyes means he feels no danger from you. You must have a pure heart as well, for him to be so trusting."

Wow, here was an incredibly small creature and even he could read my mind. I didn't know if that was good or bad. Could Shi and Mu read our minds. I had to wonder what talents did they have that we weren't aware of yet. So far, they were pretty amazing people and we barely knew them.

The next thing that caught my eye was a purple bird the size of a parrot that was landing, on the wall of the courtyard we were just passing. The tail looked a little like our peacocks, it was so beautiful, and the colors in its feathers were almost iridescence. It reminded me of something I had seen on the Discovery Channel once before. It was a bird from the Amazon Jungle and was very rare.

Becka pulled on my hand and I turned to look her way, to see she was staring off into the distance. I looked in the same direction and I saw what had caught her attention. It was a Temple of some sort. It looked a lot like a pyramid. That surprised both of us I guess. I always thought the first pyramids were built by the Egyptians or the Aztecs, who would have thought we would see one in Atlantis? It was without a doubt, the biggest, grandest building or structure in the area. How could I have missed seeing something so over-powering and large? It must have been all the colorful, smaller things and I couldn't see the forest for the trees, kind of thing.

Now it felt like my eyes were glued to the pyramid. Suddenly it seemed like I couldn't see anything else. I was trying to take in the details of the carvings that adorned it. I would have liked to ask Mu to tell us about it but just as I thought I might ask, Shi said we needed to follow them into the building we had just reached.

My head was swimming from all the new things to see. Everything here was so different, so beautiful, so interesting and so strange all at the same time. I didn't know how I could ever tell anyone about what I was seeing today, first we had promised not to, but even if I could, how could I put it into words? It would be like trying to explain heaven to someone, if you hadn't been there yourself, you could never fully understand much less appreciate the beauty described.

As we followed Shi and Mu, I was starting to watch how their legs worked. They were every bit as good as Beckas' and mine and there was no evidence of the scales that had been there earlier when they had their tails. I think my brain was in over load. With all the other things that were here to look at and try to take in, why would their legs suddenly interest me so much?

We climbed a few stairs and then made a hard right to enter another room with a baloney and terrace. There were three boys all sitting at a desk and they seemed deep into a discussion as we entered. One looked our way. He looked so much like Shi I thought he has to be one of his brothers. The three at the desk had several very large books opened on its surface. As we got closer, I could see the pictures of botanical specimens that must be the plants they would need for the cure.

"These are my brothers, Chou, Wu and Chen."

Now the other two looked up at us, as if they hadn't heard us all come into the room. All three brothers looked like Shi but didn't have the green eyes that he and Wu had. Chou and Chen's eyes were brown and they looked a little more Asian with their darker eyes. Shi and Wu's green, eyes would almost glue your brain in place, they were mesmerizing, holding you in their spell. It was as if they were somehow exotic and hypnotic all at the same time. I wondered if they could read my mind like the Zimmer could. Even considering where we were at the moment, there was something very, other worldly, about those eyes.

Shi explained to his three brothers how we had met and that we promised to help in their search for the plants they needed. He explained how we promised to use our Internet to find the locations for the plants they needed. Then he explained, he had promised us pictures, so we'd know what we were looking for. Quickly the three of them started turning the pages of three of the books currently on the desk. Each in turn showed us a picture of a different plant.

"These we must find and have our formulas tested long before the Guardians return to Atlantis. They will expect us to have these cures in place; we cannot jeopardize their health and wellbeing. Plus if we are to save our people and still be here for their return, we must work fast. There is little time left for our generation. We know that these plants would all grow in sacred places that should be at the Gaia chakra points or vortex locations. The trouble is, there are hundreds, maybe thousands of lesser vortex locations around the world. It is also very important that they be collected at the right phase of the moon in these vortex locations. The strength of the plants has to be at its highest level. We truly need your help and assistance. I hope that your Internet will find the answers for us. There just isn't time to check every vortex. You are our last hope." Chou told us.

I couldn't help it, it was my nosey personality and I had to ask.

"Who are the Guardians? Where do they come from? When do you expect them to return?"

It was Mu who answered me.

"The Guardians are from the Cygnus Constellation, they pass by your world on their visits to ours. Surely you know of them? They are one source of life in this world. They are our most ancient ancestors from the very beginning. Living here we have all adapted and adjusted to millions and millions of years, of change but they are our source and our Guardians. They are the original Children of Light."

Again this was way too much information to digest. Just being here seeing all this and knowing we could try to save the most ancient part of history, now we're finding out on top of everything else that we are descendants of Extra Terrestrials. I couldn't even begin to take it all in. Better to pocket this topic for now and get back to business. I had to shake my head to try and clear it and get back on track. This other search, was here and now. I'd try to focus on that and let the Guardians topic wait for another day.

I asked them,

"Is there anyway you could make us copies of these pictures so we can take them with us? We'll be able to look them up on the Internet if we're going to recognize them we'll need to be able to see all the details and be sure of what we're looking for."

Shi stepped forward and as he picked up a blank piece of what looked like paper or maybe papyrus. He said,

"I can do this for you. I have the mind power to do this. It will only take a few moments."

With those last words, he held the first piece of paper to this third eye at the center of his forehead. He closed his eyes and a look of concentration came over his face. He slightly nodded his head forward to the paper and when he pulled his head and the paper apart, the illustration was there on the paper in full detail, no line or detail left out.

"Wow, how did you do that? I mean I think I saw a demonstration of something similar on television once. That kid could do it, but his picture was on Polaroid film, like what they used to use in cameras. He used his mind to make the picture appear. How did you do it? Did you use your mind too?" I asked.

"It is a simple thing. I merely pass the magnetic energy of the image from my minds eye to the paper and the energy attaches itself to the paper creating the images. All here could do it. Some are better at it than others. We have full use of our minds, we live a life that keeps our minds and bodies clear, without blockages of the spirit energy. We are one with the universe and capable of doing many things like this. Has your world been away from the true path so long that you have no memory of these things or how to do them? We knew you had polluted your world and the oceans but we didn't know if it had affected your essence. Is the vibration of your spirit so low, that you are unable to do this?" he asked.

WHOA!!!! That was a big pill to try to swallow.

I think I was having a brain freeze, these things he was saying. There was a time when all people could use their minds to do what ever they wished? I knew in my heart of hearts, what he said was true. I always knew somewhere in the back of my brain that there was a time when I was all. A time when I was everything and I could do, or be whatever I could think or dream about being or doing. His words seemed to awaken in me a deeper knowing and understanding and I knew he was right. Everything he was saying, I could remember. There had been another time and place for me too when I did these things and more, much, much more.

Shi brought me back to the present moment again as he handed me the first of several pictures that he mentally copied for us to take home. When all the copies were made, there were seven pictures that he folded and placed into a special pouch so we'd be able to take them under water with us for the swim back. The pouch would keep them all safe and dry.

While all this was happening. I saw Becka step a little closer to the wall. She placed her hand on it and closed her eyes. I think she was remembering too, maybe a way to read, with her mind the history of this place. She seemed not to notice the care that Shi was taking with the pictures. I wondered if she felt what I was feeling or if she was lost in her own thoughts. It was as if being with these kids was lifting up our own energy and we were able to tap into a higher knowing some how. Was this the Universal Consciousness that we were experiencing? Was this place, in the center of a world vortex? Was the energy here more in tune with the universal energies of the galaxies?

Would Becka and I ever be the same again after having been in this place? I think clearly, the answer was no, how could we ever be the same two kids after seeing and experiencing Atlantis?

"It's time, we need to go now. I only planned to hold the forces of your time for so long today and we are quickly coming up to that point."

Shi was keeping his promise to get us back before we were missed. As we walked back to the arrival building I kept looking in all directions. I wanted to remember everything, not forget a single detail. There were so many buildings I wondered what was happening inside their walls: what great mysteries were we missing by not going into each one of them? This place, it was a busy city and there were so many treasures here that we hadn't seen or uncovered yet. I wanted so much to stay and see and feel them all. Shi said maybe next time we could stay longer. Next time!!!! To think we might revisit this world. My mind and emotions were spinning, like a vortex. How could I let go of this adventure and go back to our old normal lives again?

The way back home seemed far less scary than the trip here. The worst was over first and the best of the colors and undersea sights were the last things we'd get to see. It was as if, only minutes had gone by not hours, when at the shore line we handed back the snorkel like breathing gear, the earplugs and took the pouch of pictures from Shi. We agreed to do our research and return to this same spot in three days time.

As we watched the two swim away, the last things we saw were the tips of their tails. We turned and looked at each other. I don't know who pinched whom first but I think we were both in total shock and awe. Were we just daydreaming? Did this all really happen? Could we both be hallucinating, and could we hallucinate the same thing? I finally asked Becka,

"What were you thinking or feeling when you put your hand on the wall and closed your eyes?"

I don't know why of all the things I could have asked, why I asked her that question. But I had been wondering since I saw her do it and I was dying to find out. Had she felt anything like what I had been feeling?

"I felt that being with them was somehow making me see more clearly and I just got the feeling that I could tap into the secrets that the building held. It was like I could see and hear all the centuries of history pour into me. I could see and hear, as well as feel the emotions, of all the violent destructive things that took place over the millions of years of Atlantis's history. I also felt and experienced the good, great things that made its as great as it was. I wish I could just hold your hand and let you feel it all too. I should have tried that when we were there. It might have worked then. I think I should try to write down some of what I saw and felt. No one would ever believe us even if we tried to explain what we just saw. I felt like all the things that had ever happened were there on the walls, as readable and viewable as a DVD. Like the magnetic frequency of history had been imprinted on the energy of the stone and I just tuned in like on a radio station. It was so unbelievable Kat."

I looked down for the pouch Shi had given me. It was there, the proof that we had been there, seen them and it was all real. Oh dear God, it was real. Now we have a real mission. We looked at each other and just started to race back to the house. We would need to do a lot of research and we only had three days to do it all. Time was ticking and we had to get busy now.

We were sorting out the drawings and trying to find a way to search the Internet for the names or species of the plants the merkids needed to find. Who knew there were thousands and thousands of plants in the world, maybe millions? I certainly never knew there were anywhere near as many as there seemed to be on just the first site we visited. What had we gotten ourselves into?

"How are we ever going to find these when there are so many plants to look through? I never dreamed it was going to be this difficult. What are we going to do Becka? We're going to need a lot more people helping us."

Mr. Mac heard me talking to Becka and he came over to see what we were up to.

"You girls got some new project going? What are you looking for and what's the problem?" he asked.

"Oh granddad, Kat and I promised a couple friends we would help them find where these plants grew and now we're realizing what a giant search it's going to be. We don't even know where to get started. I think maybe we promised something we might not be able to do."

Mr. Mac was looking down at all the drawings we had on the table. He moved a few pieces to be able to see more of the drawings and finally he picked one up and as he looked at the picture, he started to rub his chin, like he was thinking or maybe remembering something.

"I think I've seen this one before girls. A very long time ago but I think I'm right. When I was In Machu Picchu I think I even took a photograph of a plant just like this one. I remember they said how rare it was. Back in the day I was something of a want to be botanist. You know, I bet it's the same flower. I'll see if Ellen can dig up my old photo album and we'll just check it out. Here, I'll be right back." He handed Becka the drawing and headed to the back of the house to their rooms. We just looked at each other. Was it possible Mr. Mac was going to help us solve our problem? Who would have guessed Becka's grandfather would be able to help us? It wasn't five minutes later and out he came photo album in his hands.

"Here, look I'll show you what I'm talking about." He sat the album on the table in front of us and started thumbing through the pages, finally stopping at one. It was a black and white photo, the detail wasn't perfect but it sure looked like the drawing we had.

"Wow Mr. Mac, that's incredible. I can't believe it was so easy for you to recognize something you saw and photographed so many years ago."

I was so excited that he was able to help us find and recognize the first drawing and plant. Well, he hadn't exactly said what the plant was called but at least he knew where it grew.

"Do you remember what they said it was called?" I asked.

"You know Kat I can't say that I remember what it was called but it only grew high in the mountains around Machu Picchu. I remember when I was climbing and saw one: I decided that I had to have a picture of something so rare. I considered the photo a real treasure to get to bring back with me. Interesting how I just found your first specimen and actually was able to get you started. Makes me wonder if these others are as rare as the first. Maybe if you look up sacred plants of Peru you might find it. The natives there considered the flowers very, very special and used it in their most sacred ceremonies.

If you can't find it there, check on rare plants of Machu Picchu. One of those should get it for you."

He started looking at the other drawings and picked up another and said,

"I think I might know this one too. I think this looks like something I saw in Bali. The Balinese Natives used a plant like this in some of their medicines. I remember gathering it up and helping them grind up the leaves for some healing potions they made. I don't have pictures of it but try looking at plants that grow in the mountains on Bali. I'd say you're looking for sacred plants from the different native cultures from around the world or possibly just some of the oldest ones used by the first medicine men."

"Thanks so much Granddad I don't know what we would have done if you hadn't come along and seen the drawings. At least now we have a starting point and you may have solved the biggest part of the puzzle for us. We'll start by looking up sacred plants and see what that brings up."

"Well, I'm glad to have been of some help girls. You know as a young man I was something of an adventure-seeking traveler. I can't imagine whom you're helping that you'd have such old and rare drawings. I dabbled in archeology a little when I was younger. Even this paper looks very ancient. I'd like to meet the people who own these pictures."

"Sounds like you were something of an Indian Jones when you were younger Granddad?'

"Yeah you might say that... a regular Indiana Jones. Maybe some time you'll bring your friends around for us to meet, I think I'd enjoy talking with them.. Well, good luck girls, don't stay up too late with your project."

As he left, he picked up and took the picture album with him. We saw him turning the pages as he walked back to him room enjoying the memories all over again

"Can you believe we got this lucky? Who would have ever guessed that your Grandfather would know two of the drawings? He's actually seen two and even had a picture of the one. What are the odds on that happening?"

"I think you're right about that one, talk about luck. Okay lets get to work, start googling 'sacred plants' and lets see what comes up. Maybe we'll get even luckier and find some of the other plants tonight before we have to go to bed."

Luck wasn't with us again that night. We searched so many sites and finally gave up about ten o'clock. We packed up the pictures and headed to Becka's room and her bed. I dreamt all night about plants and think I must have been searching even in my sleep. It was so wild that it was Mr. Mac who solved the first mystery and got us on track with our search to help the merkids.

We spent all our spare time for the next two days searching and trying to find another lead. We enlisted the rest of the kids to help us. Ronnie and Cookie volunteered to go to the library and check their reference books. Bunny and Amy each took a picture and tried looking for just the one plant. Becka and I tried to research the last plant and find a match to the picture Mr. Mac said he thought he remembered in Bali.

We met the merkids at the appointed time on the beach. They were already there waiting for us when we arrived. It was a beautiful, quiet morning without another soul anywhere along the shoreline. The sun had just come up and the newness of the day was electric. We felt electric. We still couldn't believe this had all really happened. When we saw them we raced to meet up, splashing the water as we ran into the shallow waves.

We were so excited that we had found at least one of the plants and possibly a second. We just needed a little more time to finish our research and that's what we told them. They were happy and our excitement became contagious. We were all talking at once and it was hard to keep up.

Finally Becka said,

"Wait, wait a minute. I think we need to decide what to do next. What do you two think we should do?"

Mu spoke first,

"I think this is something we need to talk to the others about. I think it is something they should all have a vote in. Nothing has ever been as important and it is a matter of our life or death."

Shi raised his hand to get our attention and said,

"I agree. I think Becka and Kat should come with us. Without their help we still have many issues beyond our resources. I think we must all go before the group. Maybe once we can discuss it with my brothers, take a vote, we can make a plan. It will mean another trip to the city. Can you leave now?"

"We have the whole day. We told everyone we were coming to the beach for the day and then going to the mall to do some shopping until dinnertime. Nobody will miss us. Until then." I told them.

"As long as we can try to do all this without having to lie to our parents I can deal with it and I'm ready too. Lets go so we can get back."

Becka seemed a little concerned about this trip. I don't think she'd ever done something like this without telling her mom and Gram about it. I could tell it was bothering her. I grabbed her hand and said,

"It'll be okay Becka. Remember why we're doing all this. It's for a very important purpose, something way bigger than you and me. I know your mom and Gram would understand."

She smiled and we nodded our acceptance to Mu and Shi. They handed us the breathing gear and earplugs. As soon as we put the earplugs in and we were able to put our masks on, the four of us slipped into the water. The trip didn't seem as long or as scary as it had the first time. The wonderful things were just as spectacular as before during our first swim into Atlantis and I wished once again I had my camera.

"Capture your memories in your minds eye Kat. It's a picture you can pull up anytime." Shi told me. Well I was doing that, so hopefully Shi was right and I'd always be able to remember all of this.

This time, we seemed to get there in far less time. I guess I wasn't as scared and I was busy gawking at everything again. There wasn't the wondering like what we went through the first time we came. I was getting used to this.

We didn't waste any time once we arrived. We joined Shi's brothers and all the others as they gathered for a group discussion and vote. There was a large gathering building near the center of the city. The building was one we hadn't been in before. It was impressive and had a grand entrance. The columns inside were huge. They climbed high to the ceiling at least 20 feet over our heads and they had to be at least 3 and ½ feet across. I couldn't tell how many kids were there but the building was filled to capacity. If I had to guess I would have said there was hundreds of them there for the meeting. They were a serious group and as it turned out very democratic in their way of governing and deciding their futures. Once the dust settled from all the talks, they voted and it was decided that a group of us would go to Machu Picchu to locate the first plant. Wow. How did it all get decided for Becka and me??? We didn't get a vote!

I looked at Becka and asked her, "Who do they think they are? Do they think they get to decide all this for us? I didn't hear anybody ask us what we thought."

"Try to relax Kat, we'll have to talk with them. I'm not so sure about all this either. I just know I don't want us to blindly go do something that will back fire on us. I want to help them anyway we can but I'm not so sure about all this. I have to confess I'm a little worried."

I had to ask some questions. I approached Shi and asked,

"How do you think we can be gone long enough to travel half way around the world? How can you make that work? How long can you affect time? How long would it take us to even get there? How would we go? I mean how would we get there? What's this going to cost?"

Mu spoke up, "We have traveled for many centuries through the Under World passageways. They are mostly waterways that move under and along Earth's Dragon lines. I'm sure in your world they are called something else, if you even know about them. Most of the passageways have been damaged from earthquakes or volcanic eruptions over time but there are many we can still use. We can get there much faster using them rather than going around by the oceans. With control of time on this side we can do many things and still get you back to your beach with time to spare. We promise you. None of it will cost anyone anything, except time."

I couldn't help but ask a few things and point out a couple things to them.

"I need to know more about these Dragon lines and the under world passageways. How long would we be in darkness? How long would a trip like that take? I mean we both want to help you all we can, any way we can but this is sounding like a major undertaking and this is all so new to us. Frankly I have to tell you it sounds pretty scary and I think we're both worried about what we're saying we'll do. This idea of going half way around the world underwater, in some old cave or passageway, in total darkness is pretty frightening to both of us. It might be old hat to you but it's pretty major scary stuff to us."

Becka spoke up and added,

"This is a really big leap of faith for us to take with you. Maybe we should talk a little more. I think we need to understand and hear more about what the trip there would be like. Are you absolutely sure we won't be missed back home? I couldn't go if it meant my folks would worry about me or be concerned about us because we didn't get home on time. I think we just need to understand a little more of the details."

Shi stepped forward and spoke.

"I can understand your concerns and why you question us. You are not use to our ways or abilities. Trust me when I say we can do all the things we tell you we can. I can alter time and we could be gone for weeks, in your world it will be as if time hardly moved at all. It would be as if it had only been hours to your family and friends. There are much of the spiritual and psychic worlds and their energy that you have no true knowledge or understanding. The Universe is a much larger place than you can begin to even dream of. There are hundreds of Earth out there in the Universe and many other peoples.

Our talents and abilities are more advanced than yours but trust me when I say you would be safe and we will take very good care of you. It appears we need your help and I ask you both with an open heart, filled with love for you and all mankind, to please help us. This is something bigger than you or us. We must save our race and protect the future arrival of the Guardians. This is something we must do even if we have to go without you to do it."

Becka and I looked at each other trying to read each other's mind. What would we do now? How could we not go? Not help? It was already too late for us to say no. Becka spoke first but she spoke for both of us.

"It's okay Shi, we will go and do what ever we can to help. My grandmother has always told me "love, family and friends are the most important things in life." You are our new friends and we do love you all.

Lets make plans. What can Kat and I do? Let's just hurry up and do it before one of us gets cold feet."

We spent what seemed like hours to me, making plans and deciding who would go. It was decided that besides Becka and me, Bach, Shi and Mu would go.

Bach and his sister Sheba were the best mind readers and they would be able to keep us all connected with the kids back in Atlantis, while we were gone. Sheba would stay in Atlantis while Bach was on the journey with us. Both Bach and Sheba were something like American Indian shaman plus they were superior psychic readers. They were the most spiritual and psychic members in the community. Kind of like a psychic's psychic.

Once the members of the group were decided on it didn't take long to get ready. There wasn't much to do or get together. I wondered about food and had to ask.

"What will we do for food? Please tell me you eat and get hungry."

It was the first time I heard Mu laugh since the first day on the beach, when we saw her and Shi playing in the water.

"Yes we eat Kat: probably not as much or as often as you and Becka do. Mostly we eat fresh fruits and vegetables. Each of us will leave with our own food supply. Yours will be packed with the same energy reserves as ours. If you are hungry now I could have something brought for you? Would you like to eat before we leave?"

Becka spoke up,

"I would like to have something to drink and maybe something small to eat. What kinds of fruit do you have?"

"What would you like? I think we have much the same here as you have up above? Would you like apples, oranges, plums, pears, raisins or dates? We have melons or berries. What would you each like?" Mu waited to get our request.

"A couple oranges would be nice and some water to drink, if it's not too much trouble." Becka told her.

Mu sent one of the other kids off and they returned with our snacks. We watched as they all hurried here and there getting things ready for our trip. Almost before we could eat and drink our water they had things finished and were set to go. It was probably good that we didn't have too much time to think about things.

One thought and one word kept going though my mind....BELIEVE.

I had to believe this would work out and the trip would be a safe and easy one. Mostly I had to believe that Becka and I weren't going to get in big trouble for what we were doing to help our new friends. We knew we were doing the right thing for all the right reasons but nobody back home would ever have believed us if we could have told them. There were times as I looked around myself I wasn't sure if I could believe everything I was seeing with my own eyes either.

As we got our little pile of gear and food I wanted to ask, "Is this all there is?" I looked at Becka. She was looking at her pouch too. I tapped her on the arm and whispered,

"Do you think this is it? How could this little bag of fruit keep us going for what might be weeks? Maybe I should say something to Mu and Shi. Maybe they don't eat as much as us but I don't think this could last me two days much less the time it might take just to get there."

Becka whispered back,

"I'm sure they know what they're doing. Let's try not to fret Kat. I don't think we'll have to worry about starving. Maybe when you're in time bending mode, you don't get very hungry."

So I decided to be quiet and just hope we wouldn't starve on this journey. We were going to leave Atlantis and make our way to the Yucatan Peninsula walk inland to a sinkhole or Cenote near Chichen Itza (chee-chehn-eet-sah). Then we would travel the under world water passageway to the coast of Peru and continue the journey from there.

Mu explained that many of the sinkholes around the world were the beginnings or ends of dragon lines and the under world passageways. That was our destination now, a sinkhole near Chichen Itza. From the coast of Peru we would have to hike from the shore to the mountain top ruins of Machu Picchu.

I wasn't too sure how all this walking and hiking would go. The swimming part was easy, the merkids did all the work and we were just along for the ride. I was hoping that maybe somewhere there might be a bus. Becka and I both had some money in our pockets maybe we wouldn't have to walk all the way, bus tickets in Peru couldn't cost too much could they? I'd just have to hope if we found one and tickets didn't cost too much, that they'd take American money.

Adventure #1
Peru

We left Atlantis and wove our way through the same caves back out to the Caribbean and started swimming towards Mexico. The water began to turn to the most beautiful royal or medium blue color I had ever seen. I was used to the turquoise blue, emerald and lime greens of the Caribbean but this was unexpected to me. I wondered if this was what was called Azure blue? It seemed to me if there were Mayan and Aztec Indians who lived here maybe this could be their Azure blue color. I'd have to check that out when I got home.

We swam through the Caribbean to the area around the North end of Cancun Mexico. We made landfall in a disserted area along the beach and started to walk inland towards Chichen Itza. Both of us had read and seen pictures of the Famous Mayan ruins in the Yucatan region of Mexico. The pictures had been a marvel of engineering and craftsmanship with all the carvings each building had. When you read about the astronomy involved in the placement of the buildings and how the Indians studied the heavens it just made you wonder what pointed them in the directions they moved their lives towards. Also it was a wonder to me how did so many original tribes of people all have such similar beliefs and similarities in how they said things started and worked in this world? They all couldn't be wrong, could they?

Back home, Gram was probably right when she said the real truths were all simple truths. That's why so many people all held the same beliefs, all around the globe at the same time. She said there was a time when all people lived by the intuitive side of their nature and people just knew things. If the truth about life was that, all life is energy or the God force, that we are all connected to each other and every other living thing and if that energy was all around us and inside us and every one of us could read and tap into that energy or God force; then it would explain how sometimes several people invent the same things at the same time. Or why so many people write the same kind of stories, or movements happen when people unit under a certain thought, desire or cause.

I was really letting my mind wander with the thoughts of early man and seeing the Mayan ruins and what brought them to build such an empire. For the hundredth time I wished I had my camera. The only consolation I had was that I would be able to capture the memories forever in my mind and at least that was something pretty spectacular. I couldn't wait to see and touch the stones that built such a place and wonder again at the people who put it all together.

It was a rather dry and sparse area that we found ourselves walking through. Not a lot of trees mostly some grasses and agave looking kinds of plants. It seemed like a long walk and a few times the flies were becoming pests, swarming around our heads and bugging us like we were horses or cows. No one talked too much, I think we were all looking and taking in the terrain, lost in our own thoughts of the Mayans.

Finally it was Becka who asked Mu about the ruins and if they had ever been there before.

"I believe we are like you in this respect, we have read the energy of the Mayans stories over time and there were times the Guardians may have told our people things about them but we have never been to their villages or towns. We have always stayed more to ourselves in the hopes of protecting our world from yours."

Shi spoke up then,

"We have always picked up on what has happened in the upper world. Our readers are always tuned into the life force. It is the same as receiving radio waves and signals from your world. Explaining things to you when you have forgotten so much is not easy. Its like bending time some things are easier to do than to explain. Bending time between the two worlds is easy for me but to explain to you how it is done is difficult and complex. I hope for now you can just believe and accept what we can do."

"Oh, we are amazed at what you can do." Becka told him. "Everything about you since we met on the beach is amazing and wonderful. We still can't believe that we are here with you and have been to Atlantis. No one would believe us about all this but we gave you are promise and we would never tell, I just meant even if we told them, they wouldn't believe us. This is something you have to see to believe. In our world they say Atlantis is just a legend and never existed."

Quiet returned to our group as we walked on. Walking wasn't my favorite thing to do in life but seeing the country and the scenery around us proved interesting and kept me from being totally bored to death. The flies were annoying but that was the only negative thing so far we'd had to deal with.

We walked for what seemed like days before we got close to Chichen Itza. The scenery was changing and trees were starting to pop up. I could see the top of the ruins above the trees before we got there. I jumped a couple times as we were walking through the trees, as Iguanas would suddenly dart away from us. What ancient looking creatures they were and to see them in their natural habitat was a trip. Some were larger than others but when one would run to get away from us it seemed to startle both Becka and me. I think I was worried about snakes and hadn't even thought of seeing iguanas. This was definitely a lot different than back home. I even started to feel a little like and Indiana Jones myself, hopefully there wouldn't be any temples of doom up ahead.

As we got where we could finally see the clearing with the first ruins, we slowed down to get our bearings and to give Bach a chance to read the compound area. We entered the ruins from the south east corner where the first building we passed had seven door ways on it's west side and it had many strange writings or glyphs on it. There were other visitors there today so we fit in and just looked like more tourists.

The next impressive structure was the Observatory according to Bach. He told us how the Mayans studied Venus and felt it's importance was even greater than the Sun in astronomy. It even had a domed top on the building and looked like our modern day observatories. He added,

"The Mayans were known all through history as precise calendar makers and astronomers. Although they were deeply concerned with astrology they believed that astronomy and their calendar work came from a deep discipline of mathematical origins. Always the Mayans used architectural alignments to reflect the constellations above. Their sacred calendar is based on the cycles of the constellation called the Pleiades.

The Mayans understood that they came from the Pleiades and they wrote about that relationship in their sacred books. It was in the consciousness of the great, great, great grandmothers and grandfathers that this information was passed down. They were told the Universe comes from the Pleiades and there is proof in your world today. Man now knows that stars are born there."

Bach was able to read everything it seemed and could pull up information anytime. He was a pretty interesting guy to be around because he was like a walking Universal Encyclopedia, Almanac reference source or every subject under the sun.

As we walked farther towards the north we passed some of the ruins that just appeared to be mounds and a few blocks of stone, not restored ruins or buildings. What a shame, it made me wonder what they had been and why they didn't last as long as the other buildings had. Next there was a small group of ruins pointing towards one of the local cenotes that we heard had dried up. I wanted to touch everything and dream about the person or people who had carved the stone or put it in place. What a wonderful time it must have been when they were building all of this. You could almost hear the ancient echo of the stone being chipped and carved. This was so much better than going to amusement parks or museums.

As we left the first portion of the ruins we walked through a wooded area and as we entered the next open ground the giant pyramid Temple of Kukulkan stood like a warrior before us. It was so impressive with all the steps and serpent heads at the bottom of each side. The steps were high for a step up and then short for the space you would place your foot as you climbed. I could only imagine they were of small body structure more like older children. They certainly had to have small feet to maneuver those steps with any ease or comfort.

I wanted to climb the Mayan pyramid before me but Bach and the others said there was no time for it now, besides they stopped letting the public climb the pyramids years ago. We had more important issues at hand. So we only shirted around the pyramid but it did allow me to make a few more observations of my own. All four sides had the same set of stairs and serpent heads adorning them at the top was the temple with it's squared off enclosure. Bach said it was a leaping off chamber used only by the most attuned souls.

As soon as I could pull my eyes from the massive step pyramid I turned and saw what Bach said was the Venus Platform. Off towards the right of that was the Temple of the Warriors and it was rather striking building too. We weren't walking too close to the other ruins because of our timetable but Bach also pointed out to the far left the Ball Court. That brought more pictures to my mind as I remembered the movies I had seen where they showed the games they played in that sports arena. What an incredible place this was and had been.

Some of the ruins had great Mayan carvings of serpent heads, eagles and jaguars; some had panels of great carved sporting or war scenes. I had never seen so many ancient things outside of a museum before. This was the most unbelievable place I had ever seen and all I could do was walk by and look. Maybe on the way back we wouldn't be in such a hurry, I could always hope so anyway. As we walked on past all the ruins we followed a path back towards the sinkhole, our entrance into the under world.

Mu started to tell us a little about the sinkhole,

"The name Chichen Itza means, 'at the mouth of the well of the Itza", The Itza means wizard of the water."

"Before it was named Chichen Itza some called it by other names but the translation meant 'Seven great houses.'" Bach added in.

Then Mu picked up where she had left off with out little lesson in geography,

"The rivers of the Yucatan all run underground so it is a natural place for a settlement here where the two cenotes were found. We'll work our way over to the water and wait until there are no people around before we go in. We'll be on our way shortly. Do you wish to eat or drink while we wait?" Mu asked us.

We all decided to have a little water and some figs while we waited for a few people to leave the area. The Sinkhole was considered a sacred place and they would have frowned on us going in. So we ate and drank and waited. It wasn't long before we were there by ourselves and we just slipped into the water and down under the surface, to the caves below. I was so surprised to see so many pieces of pottery and bones on the floor of the hole and in towards the different cave entrances.

Mu reminded me the cenote had been a place of sacrifice and offerings. Keeping ones thoughts to one self was impossible when underwater with the crystals in your ears. It wasn't long and we were away from the light filtering down through the water and into the caves.

The passageways weren't as dark and frightening as I had thought they would be. Shortly after we left the main cave going into the Peru entrance we entered another cave or grotto and it seemed lighter and the water was the prettiest green color. It was like some kind of iridescent reflective metal on the walls of rock or sandstone. I wasn't sure actually what I was looking at.

"The mineral you see on the surface of the coral and rock is what helps to illuminate our way." There was Mu answering my thoughts.

Not being so dark, it was more interesting to watch and be able to see all the things we were passing. There were fishes, corals and seaweeds just like in the oceans and gulf and so far, no scary monsters to deal with. No strange creatures, form the deep, I think if anything had suddenly jumped out towards us I might have lost it. Not being in total darkness may be the one thing that helped both of us to make this journey.

Trying not to think about exactly where we were may have helped me to deal with what we were doing. I mean, if you really thought about it, could you deal with being in the middle of the planet, traveling in a water passageway that goes who knows where? Not to mention not knowing when it would end or if it might have been a dead end; we could have been lost forever trying to find our way out. Suddenly I was thinking we must have been out of our minds to blindly follow these kids into the depths of the under world. I was sure I was awake but maybe not because the thoughts in my head felt like a nightmare.

"You must learn to conquer your fears Kat. The underworld is not a scary place full of monsters. You should have the conviction of your decisions and not let fear creep into your mind this much. "Shi was right. I didn't know if I was going to get used to this thought communication thing. You really did have to be careful what you thought when everybody could hear whatever popped into your head.

Things like this could only be happening in some bazaar kind of nightmare. Never in my life had I questioned myself as much as I had in the last week of my life, since the encounter on the beach with these kids. Never had I ever seen such wondrous sights or discovered such incredible places either!

I was never so happy to see blue sky and sunshine overhead as when our heads broke the surface of the water in the Pacific Ocean on the coast of Peru. We had to be careful the jagged, rocks and shoreline were the roughest I had ever seen. When we first broke the waters surface all I could see was soaring cliffs and rock everywhere. Peru was looking like the most rugged land I had ever seen. I felt like we had landed on some other planet and we were in the sea of despair. I looked as far as I could see in either direction, there didn't look like there was a way to get beyond the cliffs. I couldn't help but wonder what do we do now? It looked like an impossible task to get to dry land from here. How many hundreds of miles would we have to go to find a beach where we could get on land again?

Shi called out to us,

"We must be very careful the rock is very sharp and the current is strong. I see a small way through. Stay close and follow me." With his last words he dove back into the water and we all followed him. I hoped this wasn't the blind leading the blind. I hadn't seen anything that looked like a beach or anyplace we'd be able to scale up the cliffs to a real landing. The short spot of beach he found was more like a steel gray gravel yard. We all made it in without a scratch and worked our way from the small patch of beach up the hill to level ground. I was so amazed. How did Shi see this and recognize it as a way to get to land safely?

As I got my first real look at Peru I was in total awe. The Andes Mountains were in the far distance. They stood tall and grand just like in the special I had seen of then on the History channel. Where we stood now looked more like the far side of the moon. There was sand and rock everywhere. It almost seemed like we were entering the Sahara desert, not the western coast of Peru. What a strange land this seemed to be at first glance. I couldn't help but wonder what other surprises it would hold for us, as we began this journey to Machu Picchu and the ancient city of the Incas.

Becka and I weren't sure what the next step would be. Bach and Shi started to walk towards the town we could see a little farther up the hillside. Mu turned to us and said,

"Let's go girls. It's going to be a long trip, we better get started."

Mu sounded more like her old self. I wanted to ask her how she was feeling now but she didn't seem in the mood to talk. She immediately turned and followed the boys. I was worried we might stand out once we actually got into the town. The people here seemed to be dressed so brightly with coats, shirts and skirts of so many colors. The first few people we passed didn't seem too concerned with us or really take much notice of us. At least they weren't looking at us like we were aliens!

The town up ahead of us was old but very colorful. One building was a bright royal blue with white trim, another was yellow, a third was gold with white trim and even another was red. We passed through what seemed like a town square with a fountain in the center. I kept thinking,

I hope there's a bus or some easier way than walking to get to Machu Picchu. We hadn't asked what our next step would be but maybe it was time we started asking. Becka and I did have some money. Maybe we could buy bus tickets and save our feet for later when we needed to search for the plant we came for.

"Mu" I asked, "Do you know how we're suppose to get to the ruins? I mean do we have to walk? If we could buy bus tickets wouldn't it be faster getting there?"

"We'll have to speak with Bach and Shi. They may not think it's safe enough to take a bus. What is a bus?"

Becka and I both chuckled a little and smiled to each other. Becka answered her, explaining the concept of public transportation. We called to the boys and they waited while we caught up. Once again Becka explained the possible idea of us all taking the bus to get there sooner. After a couple minutes of discussion the boys decided it sounded like a firm plan with great merit. So now the chore was to see if we could find a bus station. Bach seemed to know almost exactly where to go. We didn't walk much longer, just a few turns and he led us right to the bus depot. It was like he knew all along about buses and where the depot was located. Mu explained it was his ability to read more than just minds. I guess it pays to travel with a psychic's psychic. Bach was an amazing person. Now it was just the matter of finding out how much the tickets would cost and if we had enough money to buy them.

We really got lucky. We had just enough to get round trip tickets on the bus for the five of us and a couple dollars left over. We all seemed excited about the up coming bus ride. The three of them had never been on a bus before and really didn't know exactly what to expect. Becka and I were just glad we didn't have to walk the entire way. From here at the coast it was hundreds of miles to Machu Picchu. I couldn't imagine the two of us being able to make it, no matter how much we wanted to. I'd never even walked 10 miles before.

It wasn't too long to wait. Again we were lucky to have arrived just minutes before the bus would pull out for it's long trek to the Andes. There were people with children, one man with chickens in a coop, a woman with a medium sized dog in her lap and a couple other tourists like us. When we got on the bus Becka and I let Mu and Shi shit at the window seats and Bach sat in front of us at a window too. This it would seem would be a similar adventure and ride for each of us. Not one of us had ever seen Peru or been in the Andes. Plus for the three of them it was their first ride on a bus.

I should mention the bus was nothing like a Greyhound bus from back home. This looked like something from before the last World War. It was really old and beaten up. I guess that explains the cheap price of the tickets. You get what you pay for. This looked like it would be more of an adventure than we had all signed on for and I could tell as soon as the bus pulled away from the town. My biggest worry was if the bus could make it all the way or would we get stranded somewhere along the road in the middle of this desert that stretched out in front of us. I said a little prayer hoping that the road wouldn't disappear as we entered the vast sand pit in front of us. Was this really Peru or some other world? I wasn't sure but hoped it was Peru.

The ride was not a comfortable one by any means. We were jostled in our seats, many times bumping into each other and occasionally hitting heads. The natives seemed to be seasoned riders and didn't seem to have as bumpy a ride as the five of us. They seemed somehow glued to their seats.

The desert seemed to go on forever. I wondered if the driver knew where he was going and prayed he did. There were times the desert was nothing but sand dunes for miles and miles and nothing else in sight: just one rolling wave after another of golden sand. Some areas there were rock and sand intermixed. More than anything else it was hot. I didn't think it could get this hot and for sure I never thought I could ever get this hot. We were all dripping wet from the heat and the closeness of the other riders. The body odor of a couple of the people was pretty strong and made me glad that the bus basically had no windows. I couldn't imagine being so hot and having to be cooped up with the entire body odor thing too. I could even smell the chicken poop. It was a good thing we all had strong stomachs.

I was never so relieved as when we started to leave the desert behind us and started to climb into slightly higher elevations and cooler weather. I couldn't begin to dream or imagine how we would have walked through that desert. Driving through in this bus was torturous enough. I wouldn't be looking forward to the return trip either.

It seemed like forever riding in the bus before the driver pulled off the road and said we could get out and walk a little or use the bathrooms if we needed to. It would be a short break and then we'd get back on the road.

That is if you could really call this a road. I never saw so many potholes and ruts in any road I had ever seen back home. I wasn't sure if it truly qualified to be called a road versus a trail. I voted for trail and hoped it didn't get any tougher to travel over than it already had been.

We all seemed exhausted from the heat and all the jostling around for the last three hours. I think I must have bruises on my bruises. I know my rear end sure felt numb and I was thrilled to get off that bus seat and be able to walk around. The merkids all looked as worn out as we did. I couldn't wait to hear what they thought of their first bus ride. I kept thinking, wouldn't they be surprised after this to get to ride somewhere in an air-conditioned Greyhound bus with restrooms in the back. At the little rest stop we were able to refill our water and use the outhouse that was there on the side of the rest area.

We talked to the driver who spoke very good English as a second language. We tried to find out how many more hours of driving this would take. He told us it was just a little over 200 miles but with the bus only able to do about 40 miles per hour and sometimes less in the mountains, the trip usually took him about eight hours. The winding Mountain roads were slow going.

The most important thing about being on the bus was, not having to try and figure anything out for our selves. I would have been lost trying to find the way, I'm sure. I'm also sure that Bach would have probably been able to figure things out. He seemed to be able to read everything. Mu explained to us that he could read the energy of people, animals, places and things. So there wasn't anything he couldn't read or try to figure out. I guess that explained how he could find the bus depot so easily in the little town we'd just left.

The merkids were actually enjoying the ride. They of course had nothing better to compare it to. It did beat the alternative of walking even for Becka and me

Bach said it was a very interesting invention but not one he thought would be useful in Atlantis.

Back on the bus we were a little more refreshed for the second half of the trip. As we climbed into the Andes we could feel the temperatures drop. The smells were still there but without all that heat it was easier to deal with. A little breeze picked up and we were actually comfortable. The kids were taking in all the scenery and pointing things out to each other much the same way Becka and I were doing. The Andes were the biggest mountains I had ever seen and they were impressive. I remembered seeing a special on them called the Dragon backs of South America. Other wise I never would have known that they were still growing and getting taller each year. I couldn't imagine what it would be like to watch a mountain grow.

As we climbed higher into the Andes there were a few times when the road seemed narrower and I tried closing my eyes so I didn't have to watch and feel scared out of my skin. This was such a small bus and the road didn't seem anywhere near as wide. The road up here was a trail and not a very well taken care of one either. Looking down the side of the mountain you could see how easily you might fall to your death. One tire too close to the edge and you could imagine the frightening plunge the bus would take. I couldn't think about it, I was already holding on as tightly as I could. I'm sure Becka was ready to pry my fingers from around her arm. She was the something I was holding onto so tightly.

Finally we reached a real road again and the way wasn't so frightening to me. Some how I felt more secure just because it looked more like a real road again. The trip was coming to an end soon and we had a lot to get accomplished. I wondered how much time had passed back home and how much longer we'd be gone trying to help our friends. Said another little prayer that we'd get home without being put in lock down for the rest of our lives.

Finally we were there. When we got off the bus I was surprised by how many people were here. We didn't stand out so much now. There were tourists from all over the world. We decided to find some rest rooms, have something to eat and refill our water supply again before we set out on our search.

"I feel like I've been sitting for days instead of just hours." Becka commented. "I'll be glad to have a little something to eat too."

Mu looked at both of us and said," It was most helpful getting the bus ride. We thank you both for having the funds to pay for us all to ride it saved us a lot of valuable time. Now we must prepare for the true journey and find the plants we need."

"You're welcome for the rides, all of you. It was our pleasure to be able to pay for your tickets. Now we will do our best to help find the sacred plants you need. Let's eat and get ready," Becka answered her.

The boys seemed lost in their own conversations again. They were talking like they couldn't agree on something when Shi spoke up.

"Bach is concerned. He picks up that there is a gate and a fee to pay to be able to enter the ruins. We had not been prepared for this paying to get in."

I reached into my pocket and Becka did the same with her pockets. We pooled our money to count it and see how much we had left. If we were lucky we'd have enough.

"I think maybe we have enough to get all of us inside. Let's eat and then go see how much the tickets cost." I suggested.

We sat together and ate a little more out of our food supply. Our bags were filled with raises and dates, some nuts and a lot of other dried fruits. Surprisingly I wasn't starving even though we had only eaten a couple times and each time, just a small snack of fruits with water.

After eating we all followed Bach from the parking area towards where he said the gatehouse would be. Again he knew which way to go because he had read the area. From where we had been sitting you couldn't tell which way to the gate because the trees hid it from our view. As we saw the gate the merkids fell back behind us. We approached the little window where you could get your ticket and saw the entry prices on the board next to the window. It looked like we were less than a dollar short of being able to get all five of us in. As we recounted our money and double-checked the prices, Becka spoke up and said.

"I'll wait here while the four of you go in."

"No I'll stay here and the four of you go." Mu said. "You have done so much to get us here, you should be the ones to go in. I'll wait here for you."

Before we could finish fighting over who would stay while the others went inside, a short red haired lady walked up and heard us discussing our problems. She said,

"I don't usually do things like this but I think today should be the exception. Here I'll make up the difference for you. That way you can all go in to visit the ruins. I have come many times to see the ruins. Each time I have found it a new and wonderful adventure. No one should come this far and not be able to go in."

"Thank you so much ma'am. We really appreciate this. I guess we spent more than we thought we had. Thank you again. We can't tell you how much this means to us."

I almost couldn't shut up. I was so surprised by this strangers help. She couldn't know how much it meant to us right now. We had so much to try and accomplish this day and not getting in all together would have upset the whole thing. I was really hoping that Bach would be able to read the area and we'd be in and done in no time at all. Staying together was very important to all of us.

Gram always said be good to strangers, they could be your next friends. We all thanked her one more time, took our tickets and then entered through the gateway. We were all so excited.

As we walked away I found myself looking back at our mystery benefactress. I couldn't help but wonder she looked like someone I had seen before. She really looked familiar to me.

"Becka, do you think that could have been someone we've met before? She sure looks familiar."

Becka turned to look back at the red headed lady and turned back towards me.

"I don't think we know her. What would anyone we know be doing here?"

I kept walking towards the ruins. I kept looking back. She sure looked like someone I thought I knew.

I think we all figured that Bach could read the ruins and know where to find the plant we were after. He didn't seem to pick up on the plant and we found ourselves roaming around. I was so in awe of the ruins and where we were. I told Becka,

"Can you believe this? I can't. I think I must be dreaming. I'm in Machu Picchu, Peru. These ruins have been here, lost to the world for hundreds and hundreds of years. Plus, can you believe we're someplace your grand father has been when he was just a little older than us? That all just boggles my brain."

"I know Kat, I'm pretty much is awe of the place too. Everything about today is totally unbelievable isn't it!"?

"Where do you girls think we should start looking? I thought you said the grand father took pictures here and you could find that spot?" Mu asked.

Becka answered her,

"We don't know exactly where Mu, but he told us a general area. We'll have to try and get our bearings first. We haven't ever been here before. Plus it's been over 40 years since he was here. He did show us on a map where he took the picture. It should be towards the other end of the ruins and up a little higher past the Sacred Rock.

"Let's begin." Shi suggested and so we did. We started walking to the far end of the ruins. I couldn't help but look at everything along the way. There were walls and stonework that was all around us. I had read many things about these ruins. What was most interesting was that almost all places where ruins still stand all have a few things in common. The fit of the stones is almost a perfect fit, sometimes not the width of a piece of paper that will fit between the stones. Many times the bigger stones weight 30 to 90 tons each. No man today can explain or say how the stones were put in place or even how they were cut with such precision. I have begun to notice that usually all of these sacred ruins and places are built on or near vortexes.

I kept pointing out to Becka the things we read about before we came. I loved being able to see in person the things we saw pictures of. I could almost see the Incas who lived here when this place was thriving. We had also read on one Internet site that Shamanic legend says, when a person who is sensitive psychically touches their forehead against the Intihuatana stone at Machu Picchu, it will open them up and they will be able to see the spirit world. Now that was something Becka and I wanted to try. Maybe it was only a myth or crazy legend.

Becka and I both believed there was always some truth in legends and myths, no matter what many adults would say about it. We both agreed if we got the chance to try it out at the Intihuatana Stone, we'd see for ourselves and we would definitely give it a try. I wondered if Shi would be willing to humor us with another favor when we got up to the stone. What could it cost to just spend a couple minutes to find out?

We were working our way towards the back of the ruins and we were approaching an area called the 'Three Windows'. There wasn't one of us that weren't totally absorbed in checking out the ruins. Each of us was touching and exploring with our eyes everything we passed by. The boys were right in front of Mu and Beck and me were right behind her when she touched her right hand to a mark on the wall.

"Look at this." she said.

Suddenly the whole world seemed to be moving. At first I think my brain and body went into shock. What's happening? I never had anything like this happen to me before. I had never been in an earthquake but the way the ground was moving under our feet, I couldn't imagine that this was anything else. We started to grab a hold of each other and tried to brace our selves against the rock wall when the large rock slab under us moved completely out from under us and we were falling into darkness.

We must have dropped at least ten to twelve feet straight down. Landing hard almost knocked the air out of me. I heard Becka cough, as the dust exploded all around us, and she called out,

"Are you okay Kat? Is everybody here? What just happened?"

Shi's was the next voice I heard,

"We are here. I'm not sure what just happened or where we are. Bach what do you sense?"

He answered,

"I don't sense it was an earthquake. It didn't have the energy of a quake. I didn't feel it coming. I know we are under the ruins but I am a little confused. It's as if we entered another doorway. I feel like I am reading another place, someplace older and stronger than Machu Picchu. Maybe it is a cave or a place that was used in some sacred manner. I feel very pure, extremely strong energy."

"I can't see my hand in front of my face." I started to cry out. "How are we going to find our way anywhere in this darkness?"

"We have beam crystals in our food pouches. Do you still have your pouches?" Shi asked.

Before I could locate my food pouch in the darkness, Shi was pulling out and putting his beam crystal on his forehead. Suddenly there was light. It wasn't much more than a flashlight would have given us but it was light! Halleluiah, I could see. I think I lost 20 pounds of fear as soon as that little bit of light illuminated the cave or whatever it was we were in. Next Mu and Bach got their crystals on while both Becka and me were digging ours out of our bags.

HOW WONDERFUL!! I don't know what I would have done if we didn't have light. I wasn't good in total darkness. Plus who knew what kind of snakes or animals might be in here with us. If something was going to get me, I wanted to see it coming. Thank God for the crystals and that the merkids thought to bring them. Who knew that beam crystals even existed? I was so relieved to have light. With all five of us wearing the crystals the cave became fairly illuminated. I felt so much safer now, even though we were lost deep down in some hole in South America, at least we weren't in the dark anymore. I hoped this wouldn't turn out to be one of those rabbit holes like in the story of Alice in Wonderland, because I was starting to get some strange and creepy feelings myself. You could bet on one thing, if I found a table with a little bottle on it that said, "drink me" I wouldn't be doing it!!!

"Is everyone is okay? No one broke anything did they? Are any of you girls hurt?" Shi asked and we all did an inspection to be sure. No broken bones and only a couple minor scratches, nothing to worry about for now. "Okay then, Bach thinks we should go this way. He's reading the energy and feels it stronger from this direction. Let's follow him."

He wouldn't get any trouble from me. I was anxious to get out of this place and get back to our search of the ruins up above.

"I'll follow you anywhere just as long as you get us out of here." I blurted out.

Becka added, "I'm with Kat, lets just find the way out and get back to our search. I don't want to have to try and explain all this to my parents or grand parents. But I want to get back to be able to be with them again." There was a little catch in Becka's words and I could tell she was worried and close to tears thinking about her family. I didn't want to start thinking in that direction or I'd probably be ready to cry too. How had we gotten ourselves into this mess? I'm sure Becka was thinking, how did I get her into this mess. She said the first time we traveled with the merkids, that if anything went wrong she'd make sure I never heard the end of it. I hoped this wasn't going to be one of those kinds of times.

We kept walking for what seemed like a couple miles and we started to feel a little current of air moving through the cave or passage way, whatever it was. The only thing that really added to my worry was it seemed like we were going down hill a little. Deeper into the mountain wasn't what I had in mind for getting out of this place.

Both Mu and Shi said we had to put our trust in Bach, he was never wrong about anything. So now as we went deeper under the ruins I tried to be brave and think about seeing the light of the sun again. It was hard not to think about every movie I had ever seen where bad things happen in caves and dark places. Places usually full of weird and ancient creatures that liked to eat humans. Not to mention the places like this, where they got smaller and tighter and a person could get stuck, unable to go forward or backwards. I was having all kinds of nightmares and I wasn't even asleep. Man oh man I needed to see the sun shine soon.

We started noticing on the walls of the passageway veins of what looked like gold. They were running through the cave on both sides and even overhead. The further we walked the larger and wider the veins seemed to get. Bach started to slow down and at a narrow place up ahead he stopped completely.

"What is it Bach? What do you see?" we all started to ask at the same time.

Before he answered, we all rushed forward to see for ourselves. It was hard to see it all but you could tell it was some kind of small village or town or maybe a city. With the little light we had we couldn't see it all. I couldn't guess how far it worked through the cave or cavern. I wasn't sure what this place was. I couldn't tell if it was man made or some work of nature where someone just happened to build a city. The veins of gold were incredible, ranging up to twenty feet wide inside the cavern and there were at least four of them. Our crystal lights were reflecting off the veins and it seemed to increase our light as we stepped through the narrow opening into the city. Wow. I could hardly believe my own eyes. Was this one of the Under Worlds the merkids talked about or ancient myths spoke of? Could people really have lived in this place? For what reason would you want to build a city so deep inside the mountain? We had heard and read many times of the legends of the people in the underworlds, about how they tried to escape the turmoil of the worlds' floods and other natural events by going underground. I never expected to be inside one of those places.

As we started to walk closer to the buildings you couldn't help but wonder who built this and when did they do it? I wasn't talking about some little mud huts. This looked like a real town or city.

Becka looked up, then around at it all again and spoke, "Could this be the Lost City of Gold that so many legends talk about?" She walked over to put her hand on one of the veins. "Have you every thought anything like this was possible Kat?"

Before I could answer her. She asked,

"Mu did you all know about this place? Did any of you know it was here?"

Mu was the first to answer her.

"We know of many things in the Under World but I did not know of this place. We have many legends too. But this City of Gold is not one I have knowledge of."

Shi said,

"If this is part of Lemuria, that might explain it's being here. Many things were lost to the upper world when it sank. Even I don't understand all that happened back then."

Finally Bach started to talk.

"The energy tells me this was once a most sacred place. It was begun back in the time of Lemuria and the beginning of mankind. I can tell you it was built by one of the seven sisters when they separated and started the second generation of the seven colonies. This was a very sacred place. Even more so than Machu Picchu was in it's time. The Inca sensed the positive energy of the place and that is why they build above it. I do not know if this is the Lost City of Gold you asked about. It is definitely a City of Gold and it must be the richest site of gold the Earth has. The energy here is very strong and very rich. Let's explore a little more as we try to find our way out."

We started to walk and look at all the buildings. I wondered if there would be plates on the tables or pottery and cookware. As we looked into the first few smaller buildings you could tell they were homes. I was worried and didn't want to come across any skeletons. I didn't want to see any but thought for sure there would be some and tried to be ready each time I walked around a corner or through a doorway.

The homes weren't real large but roomy enough. There was pottery, tables and chairs and even a few artifacts here and there. A few things were made of gold but there was also many things made of stone. This was both eerie and incredible. To think I could be walking through a city from the time of Lemuria. Whether it was the Lost City of Gold talked about in legends didn't matter. We were walking someplace where man had walked before but probably not for the last 15 or 20 thousand years at least. I wanted to touch everything and was afraid at the same time to touch anything for fear it would disappear or turn to dust.

"I keep thinking this is the most incredible thing I've ever seen and then something else happens and I think the same thing all over again. How about you Becka? Are you taking this all in? I feel like it's some magnificent display at some Museum. Can you believe we're here seeing all this and it's REAL?"

"I feel the same way Kat. I can easily accept this is Lemuria too. I am in such wonder at being here, knowing it could be a part of history that no one else has had the chance to see or discover before us. Just thinking we're the first ones since way back then. It's almost too much to take in. It's hard to wrap my mind around it all."

Mu stepped up behind us.

"I can tell you without any doubt, this was once part of Lemuria. There was the time of the floods when the first destructions came that many people went into places like this and sometimes even further under ground. My ancestors handed down many stories through the generations telling of just these kinds of places. I can imagine Cyrus the first head of our family lived in a place like this and I have heard many stories of it and the floods that forced them underground. Even for me, this is amazing. I can still feel the coming home vibration here. Come on let's move on. There's so much more to see."

The boys were further ahead of us and we passed by a couple more homes to catch up with them.

Shi started to point ahead of us.

"Look." was all he said.

Immediately even in the dim light, we all saw what he was pointing to. There up ahead we could all see the most amazing building. Every square inch looked like it was made from gold. It looked like it was part pyramid and part altar. It shined and shimmered. It was something you couldn't miss once you got a little deeper inside the cavern. The cavern had to be the largest one on Earth and it looked like some magnificent natural, gold veined cathedral. We walked closer and started to inspect the golden structure.

It was round in basic structure with a top that looked more like a pyramid. I was the first to touch it. I put my hand on the serpent head to the right of the steps. Oh what a feeling. It was so cold to the touch I felt like my fingers almost froze to it. There was a searing sensation in the palm of my hand. I wished I could read its energy. I wanted to be able to experience its history, to know what it was, how it was used and who was the last person to stand here.

It was hard to tell what this building was. It could have been anything from a wedding chapel to a sacrificial altar. Who knew what these people were like? They may have been very spiritual and loving or they could have been fighters or even worse, they could have been cannibalistic. History taught us that many tribes early in the history of man were very primitive and aggressive.

"Bach, can you read the energy of this place? Please touch this place and tell me what it was." I begged him. I was anxious to know what happened here. My mind was reeling. I was touching something from the beginning of time. It was such an awesome moment for me. I just had to know more.

Bach stepped forward and he placed his hand on the serpent's head on the other side of the steps, across from me. He closed his eyes for a few moments. He took a deep breath and he exhaled slowly through his mouth. I watched and held my breath waiting to hear what he would have to say.

Bach finally opened his eyes and dropped his hand. He turned and looked toward me as he spoke.

"This was a place of great awakening. It was constructed of gold to help raise the energy vibrations of the people who entered. Gold this close to the source has one of the highest and purest vibrations of Earth. It was a temple, a place for those who were reopening to the spirit of the soul. They came here to realize their psychic-self. Mu has been here before. I can read her energy, from that other time. This was a wondrous place that gave joy and spiritual bliss to all who entered. This was the place where two people would meet, to look into the eyes of the other and discover a true meeting of their spirits. When civilization reined here, it was a world of believers who knew true hearts with love over-flowing for all. It was an extremely high spiritual vibration that is mostly lost to today's world. Does that answer your questions and curiosity?"

"Wow." Becka said.

"Yeah, I agree. WOW. I don't know how I knew. I just knew it was someplace of great spiritual importance. I wish I could experience it now."

'Come on girls, we need to keep moving. This isn't getting us our of here or getting our search for the sacred plants accomplished. We need to find our way out of this place." Shi tried to usher us away from the Altar and on our way.

Now it seemed with every few steps we were discovering something more interesting than the last. The buildings were a little larger here compared to the first homes we saw. It seemed they were more impressive in size and grandeur. Maybe they were buildings of the governing party or places where they held meetings of a larger scale. As we walked into and through the next structure it felt as if it was some sort of museum. The artifacts we saw were so simple and placed in positions of importance. Not all of them were made of gold. Some pieces were crystal, some looked like emerald and many were made of stone with precious gems inlaid. This was definitely a step through the doorway into the past. I wanted to touch and feel everything. I wanted to ask Bach to read them all and explain them to us. I felt the need to know more about this place and what happened here so many thousands of years ago.

"Everything is so incredible Kat. Do you feel as overwhelmed as I do? I can't imagine who made all these things. I could stay here if I wasn't so worried about getting out and finishing our search. I would love to understand it all. Do you really think we could have lived here so long ago? Does it feel like home to you?" Becka asked.

Mu spoke up and told her,

"I can imagine having lived here before. I know it was my home before. I know who I was and I think you're starting to understand who you were. There is a vibration that I feel coming from both of you. It feels as if we are all one, the three of us. I can feel it. Can you?"

Surprised by her words, all either Becka or I could say was "Wow."

How could our brains keep processing all that was happening? It was one thing meeting the merkids and the first trips to Atlantis. Next it was the search for the sacred plant but now having so many dramatic things happening to us: our fall into the past, including finding this cave and cavern, this City of Gold that we're exploring, how much more could happen before our brains just shut down on us? I mean I really wasn't sure if I could handle too much more. Then Mu starts talking about the three of us being one??? Oh my word, what next? I was starting to feel like a walking zombie or someone on autopilot. Thinking and processing all this was screeching to a halt inside my brain.

"Come girls, we need to keep moving." Shi called to us again. No matter which building we walked into there was something equally as surprising in each one of them, as the last we had been in. Another structure was filled with what seemed like some sort of ceremonial masks. Some looked like birds and wild beasts mixed together to create very imposing creatures. Some seemed very Incan and others a little more out of this world. They were mostly all made from gold. Some had inlaid gemstones, emeralds and rubies. Apparently these things were abundant and as Bach told us, they all had a vibrational value that would enhance the vibration of the wearer.

When we entered the next building I was holding my breath, waiting to see the treasures it would hold. As we walked into the inner circle of the center of the structure I had to let it out as I was amazed a new, at the wonder of the things I was seeing. The pillars were in a circular pattern and each one seemed to be made from a different natural gemstone. I couldn't imagine ever a ruby or emerald the size of what we were looking at. The pillars were approximately ten feet tall and two feet across. There was nothing connecting them at the top. They stood there as tall giant guards while we walked in among them. I had to touch each one of them and Becka and Mu were doing the same thing. It was like if we touched them, we'd know we weren't dreaming. Could they possibly be real? Who would have ever thought that rubies or emeralds could have grown this large anywhere in the world?

Bach started talking again,

"Everything these people did was meant to enhance the spiritual value of the vibration each person resonated to, in the attempt to make soul ascension again before death. They knew who they were and they tried to bring back the old ways of leaving their physical bodies at will. It was a goal all tried to achieve and most did relearn how, within these walls. The power of the gemstone pillars are much like gold in that they carry a very potent and strong vibration and the vortex pattern helped them to raise the vibration enough to achieve their goals. Lessons learned here could later be achieved without the extra help of this temple. With practice, once the way was learned it could be revisited at will. The power of the gemstones greatly helps in lifting any ones level. Can you feel it? Look, hold your hands out like this. See if you too can feel the higher energy." He held his arms out from his body and held his palms up as if to receive the energy from the pillars.

I almost fell over backwards. There he was, Bach was standing there but I could also see him, or at least a shadowy image of him slightly rising from his body. Was I seeing things, or imaging this? Many, many things, wild and crazy had happened since we met the merkids but this was the most bazaar of all of them. His image only lifted about a foot from his body and then it returned. Holy cow.

As soon as Bach's spirit returned to his body, he seemed back to his regular self and put down his arms. I asked,

"Can I try that? Please?"

"Certainly." he said and stepped back out of the way.

I stepped into the center of the pillar vortex area and lifted my arms just the way he had and put the palms of my hands up to face the energy of the giant gemstones. I could feel a tingling on the surface of my palms. I closed my eyes and took a deep breath. I tried to see and feel myself lifting up out of my body the same way Bach's had done. I sensed that I was vibrating at a higher level but I didn't feel as if my body was rising the way Bach's had. I just felt the finest little tingling all over my body. Suddenly I heard a scream and the words,

"Kat, come back, you're going too far!!" It was Becka's voice and I opened my eyes to see what she meant. My whole body jerked and I felt a splitting headache for the next couple seconds after that. It was so intense I couldn't even open my eyes for a minute.

Becka rushed up to me, grabbed my arms and asked me,

"Did you feel yourself leaving? You raised up higher than Bach did. I was afraid you might not come back."

"Holy cow Becka. I couldn't tell what I was doing. I only opened my eyes because you yelled at me. Do you want to try it?"

"I think I'll pass Kat. We better try to get out of here. I don't know how much longer we have before everybody at home starts to miss us and we don't know how to get out of here yet. Maybe we better stop looking at everything and just try to find the way out."

Shi stepped up and said, "She is right, we need to move on."

"Okay, I'm ready. Lets go." I answered them both as I tried to shake off the little pain I felt in the center of my forehead.

We passed by many more wonderful buildings and followed Bach again until he stopped outside what looked like some kind of crystal entrance. The steps and outside of the structure looked like they were growing off the side of the cavern. It was definitely a door or gateway to go deeper into the mountain. Bach wanted to go inside. He said he felt it was the way out.

Becka and me were a little leery about going inside. This one was different from all the other structures we had entered so far. This one was going inside the wall of the mountain and you couldn't see where it ended. What if we walked into some place we couldn't get out of? Or if the floor started to move like the one up above had done and gotten us into this mess? It didn't look like something that was man made. Who knew, maybe that would be a good thing. Maybe it ended on the outside of this hidden city and the mountain. This could be the exit, the way out. I was ready to be out of here and on our way home again.

"Lets go Becka, where else can we go? What direction? Bach has been right so far." I tried to get us both talked into following Bach one more time.

"Okay Kat. Let's go. Let's just get this over with, I want to go home."

I could feel the temperature raise just a little as I followed the rest of them into the crystal opening. Our beam crystals suddenly seemed to be brighter or they were reflecting their light onto something that was bouncing the light back at us. For just a couple seconds I couldn't see. We were all blinded. It was like the sun reflecting off the water or some shiny object in our world. As we all stepped a few feet apart and tried to adjust our eyes, we could see we were in what looked like a giant, colossal crystal geode with a flat crystal floor. Bach and Shi took their beam crystals off their heads and placed them back in their pouches. That helped with the intense light that had blinded us. I looked down, my eyes wandered to the very center of this place to what looked like a circular pattern or mosaic design on the floor. What an interesting design. It was like a crop circle design I had once seen on the Internet. It had seven circles and they were forming a pattern of a vortex spiral with the circles getting smaller or larger whichever way the spiral was turning. It was all circles within circles, within a larger circle.

At first I was so busy adjusting my eyes and noticing the floor design I didn't see any of the things more at eye level. I almost ran to them as I saw what looked to be seven crystal skulls on the tops of separate crystal spikes. They were lined up in a semi circular line against one side and there was another strange looking crystal in front of the skulls at a level just below them, about 30" off the floor.

"DON'T TOUCH THEM." Mu yelled at me as I had my hand out towards one of the skulls. I froze and slowly turned my head to see where Mu was standing. She moved quickly and came up next to me.

I almost couldn't believe my eyes. I saw the most beautiful colors all around everyone. It was the first time I had actually looked towards any of them since we walked into this place and became momentarily blinded by the light. Their colors were bright and see through with a pulsating dance like movement to them. Could this be their aura? I was totally mesmerized for a few seconds until Mu spoke again.

"You don't know what could be attached to the skulls, it's better we don't touch them." She almost whispered the words, as if she didn't want to disturb them or wake them from their sleep. Well, that thought just about made my eye balls pop out of my head. I just knew at some point this whole adventure was going to turn into something like the creature from the black lagoon, or the alien things that would suddenly start popping out of us and we'd all die or be eaten alive. I put my hand down and stepped back away from the skulls.

Becka got my attention when she called me over to the other side where she was standing. The colors dancing around her were the purest greens and blues with just a little purple and pink. I was so busy looking at the colors dancing around her she had to get my attention again.

"Look over here Kat. What a beautiful necklace." As I got closer she added, "Have you ever seen anything like this before?" It was very similar to the design on the floor, all the spiraling circles with jewels hanging from the bottoms of the smallest circles. It was made from gold and had to be one of a kind. It was a very unique piece and looked to be of the finest craftsmanship, even by today's standards.

"Is anybody else seeing all the colors dancing around us? Are these colors our auras?" I had to ask because no one seemed to be noticing all this magic but me.

"Are you seeing our auras Kat?" Becka asked me. "Since we walked into this place I noticed the colors seemed to get a little clearer and brighter. I always see auras so I guess I didn't notice that you could see them too."

"Your colors are so beautiful Becka "Look at the others, they're so similar to yours. Some how I would have though any one from Atlantis would have different auras than ours. You know, some wild or strange colors we'd never seem before. Look at all the purple colors around Bach. I've never seen such perfect tones or colors before."

"What sort of place do you think this was Bach and is there something about it that it allows me see your auras?" I had to ask. It was so different from anything we had seen so far and the crystals that were here had to be as old as time itself. They were like fallen trees they were so long and so big around. It must have taken millions of years for them to grow this big. I couldn't imagine that there could be another place like it.

Bach closed his eyes and was silent for a couple minutes. We all watched and waited to hear what he would have to say. When he opened his eyes I saw a tear drop down his cheek before he spoke.

"This was the portal of one of the original seven sisters of Lemuria. It was the link to her old world in the Pleiades. It was a place where she could reconnect to the stars and the other worlds beyond. It was her sanctuary and her home. I believe Mu was that sister, in that time. The energy of their auras is identical and that is not possible. Auras are like your fingerprints and no two are exactly alike. Through each lifetime, all your different incarnations, your aura is always changing colors and symbols but the energy is always the same, as it is your soul, your eternal fingerprint."

Whoa. This made me look at Mu in a whole new light. Becka and I both had read that some people believed the seven sisters from the Pleiades were the first Beings of Light who became the first people to live on the Earth. Mu had told us when we first met she was a descendant of Cyrus, one of the main leaders of Lemuria who later, helped to save the city of Atlantis.

Now we were hearing that she was actually one of his ancestors. What a twist of fate. Could our time with the merkids ever be boring??? We had moved closer to Bach, when he was speaking and now that he was silent we were starting to notice our surroundings again. The whole area seemed to be made of crystals and everything in the space almost completely made out of crystals too. What was it about the quartz crystals that made this a portal and how did the sister connect to the other worlds? I wondered if she left this place or just her spirit would depart and leave the physical body behind. It was a little warmer in this room and I could feel little beads of sweat start to drip from my hairline.

We each seemed to be lost in thought as we were inspecting the area, looking for another way out. We were looking for anything that might look like a door or panels that we might push to get out. Or even anything that looked like a handle or pull that might open the door or gate we couldn't actually see yet. We were all feeling a little warmer and taking drinks of our water to try and cool off.

"It looks hopeless to me." I told them all. "I can't see any way out but the way we came in. Now what are we going to do?"

Bach spoke up again.

"I know this is the way, I can't read just how it works yet but I am certain this is the way out. Please be quiet and let me concentrate."

Back behind us and totally unaware of what she was doing, Mu reached out to pick up the necklace that Becka had pointed out to me just minutes ago. The moment she removed the necklace from it's display something happened. None of us realized what she had done and the minute we all turned to see what sound had just drawn our attention, Mu hid the necklace in her clothing. None of us had seen what she had done or that the necklace wasn't where it belonged. The sound however was the sound of the entryway closing shut. All of us including Mu noticed that.

"Who did what?" Becka asked. We all looked at each other and nobody had anything to say except, "it wasn't me!" Becka especially gave me the evil eye like she was making sure it wasn't me who touched or pulled something they shouldn't have.

I looked back at her and said, "I told you it wasn't me, I didn't touch anything! I swear."

"Well, now what are we going to do?" She asked the room in general. I could feel beads of sweat starting to gather and roll down my forehead and neck.

"I think it's getting warmer in here since the door closed and it was already warm in here." I said.

Mu stepped toward the rest of us and pulled the necklace from inside her clothing. "I'm afraid it might have been me who made the entryway close. Apparently I took the necklace from its display. I wouldn't have done it if I had known the way out would close. I couldn't help myself. I almost didn't even know I had done it until I moved and felt the necklace move under my shirt. I'm so sorry. I'm not a thief really I'm not. It just felt like it was mine and I wanted it back."

Bach spoke up again, "I believe we are going to have to find the way out soon, the heat from the crystal energy is building quickly and we will not last long if the temperature keeps rising with the entryway closed. Drink what's left of your water sparingly. I think it's time for me to connect with Sheba and see if there's any way she can assist us. Maybe she will remember something to help us find the way out of here. Maybe some legend or story handed down in through the generations in Atlantis." With those last words he became silent again and you could tell he was communicating with Sheba. He looked like a wave had poured over him. Something like a trance.

I looked at Becka and she looked like she was close to having the tears spill from her eyes.

"Don't cry now Becka, you better hold onto whatever moisture you still have inside your body. Bach will think of something I'm sure. Besides, I'm sweating enough for both of us already."

We all kept searching while Bach stood motionless, mentally connecting with Sheba. He had to come up with something. One of them had to. This couldn't be the end of us, could it? It was getting pretty hot in here, even worse than the desert we had to ride through to get here and that was pretty darn hot. We were all starting to wind down and I felt like I was losing my strength to keep standing.

As I wiped the sweat from my brow, I sat down and looked over towards Mu. I started thinking. If she were the sister who used to live here, she would know how to get in and out wouldn't she? If this were her home, she would know where she left the key wouldn't she? I looked to Becka and said,

"If Mu was the one who lived here, shouldn't she know how to get in and out? Maybe we just need to pick her memory and she'll be able remember the way out. What do you think?"

"I think it's worth a try Kat." She turned to Shi and asked him, "How can we help Mu to remember the way out? There should be something we could do to help her remember. If she was that sister and she lived here, she could get us out."

"Good idea you two." He turned to face Mu and asked her, "How can we reach back into your memory and find the key to get out of here?" Now none of us except Bach had the strength to stand up. We were losing it, being totally drained of our energy. Never in my life would I have thought that heat alone could push us all to the ground, unable to keep standing. We were slowly dying and I think we all knew it.

I made the suggestion, "Why couldn't we hypnosis her? Couldn't we regress her to that lifetime and ask her how to get out?" That seemed pretty simple to me.

"Not a bad idea Kat.' Becka said and then she turned and asked," Do you think we have that much time Shi?"

Suddenly Bach opened his eyes and looked to see where we were standing.

"I believe Sheba has been able," surprised that we were no longer standing, he looked down to where we were now sitting and continued, "to find a clue for us. There is a story of Astral Gateways back in the time of the first floods. They tell of a crystal key that opens the way back into man's world. It is an escape for only a privileged few as most never wanted to return to the turbulent Earth of those times." I looked over where the crystal skulls were lined up and then, once again to the separate crystal that was placed just below them, all by it's self. Could that be the key? I think all our eyes had landed on that spot. We were losing our strength and there wasn't going to be much time left, to find the way out. Soon we wouldn't even be able to move. It was as if we were being cooked in a pressure cooker and every ounce of water in us had been baked out. Soon we would dry up and turn to dust. I didn't like the picture that thought painted in my head.

"But what do we do with it? Even if it's the right crystal and we don't have too many choices, what do we do with it? If we lift if off it's base and something worse happens? Then what?"

Becka looked at me and said,

"It probably won't matter. I don't think we have much time left. I feel like I'm dying. Like I'm never going to see my parents or grandparents again. They'll never know what happened to us or where we died."

Bach, who was still somehow standing, managed to walk to the crystal, pick it up and carry it to the middle of the inlaid design in the center on the floor. He turned it and placed the pointed end into the center circle on the floor.

Suddenly there was a strange sound. The crystal seemed to slip right into the floor and lock in place. As it slid into place, the crystal wall in front of us started to drop away like a Moat gate. How did he know? How could he read the crystals and know what to do?

Fresh air rushed in and I thought my throat would close up from the cool air that touched it as I took a deep breath for the first time since we got locked in here. The moment I let my breath out I noticed a pattern had appeared on the crystal walls all around us. There were signs much like ancient letters projected on the walls. They seemed to be coming from the large crystal in the center of the mosaic pattern on the floor. The crystal was clear and I saw no sign of the encoded message it was projecting onto the wall.

I couldn't help but wonder, what were the strange signs being projected onto the walls? How was the crystal projecting them? I had to shake my head, trying to clear my thoughts. There was an opening and cool air was coming from that direction. We had to get out of here before anything else could happen. We barely had the energy left in us to even try to get to the door. None of us could get up to run or even walk to the door and our escape. We pretty much crawled and dragged each other out. Even Bach had used most of his energy to move the crystal and open the way out.

I prayed that it wouldn't close before we could all get there and make our escape from this crystal oven we had found ourselves locked in. Only trouble was I couldn't find an ounce of energy to move. We were all drained and looking death in the face from all this extreme heat. Who would have thought that heat could kill you so fast? I felt like I had one foot stepping over the astral plane into the spiritual but I kept hearing this voice, trying to call me back.

"We have to hurry. There's no way of knowing how long the way out might stay open." Shi called to us. "I know it's not easy but try harder girls. You have to move. It's your choice, use your free will to decide right now whether you live or die. We can't do it for you, find your strength and use it now."

I could feel the cooler air whispering to me. It kept saying, "Come on, lets go out to play. Come play with me." I tried. I tried as hard as I could to roll over and start to crawl out toward the opening. Becka was only a little to my right and I whispered in her ear to come and go outside to play with me. She slowly opened her eyes and blinked like she was trying to understand what I had said and was trying to find some energy of her own to move with. We were all so dehydrated any movement hurt.

I don't know how the two of us managed to start crawling but with each other's help we did it. The cooler air was bringing my mind back from the brink I turned and looked back before we made our exit from the crystal chamber to look at the signs that were projected onto the crystal walls. I couldn't memorize them, there were too many of them. What could they mean? What were they saying? Was it a seed crystal and was this the history of Lemuria, the encoded written proof of its existence?

I couldn't look any longer, Shi was urging us to move and get out now. Becka and I both managed to find some inner strength and together we made it through the exit and onto solid ground. Finally we were under the sky of the Universe we were familiar with. At least it looked like we were back in our world even if we were on the other side of it. I could feel the dirt under me again and thanked the powers that be for getting us out of that death trap.

As we were resting, trying to find the energy that was all but drained from our bodies, I looked to the sky once again. I was breathing in and trying to revive myself. Becka was doing the same.

Bach said,

"They are the Pleiades, the stars you are gazing upon."

"They're beautiful tonight. I feel like I could reach out and grab them from here. I don't think I've ever seen the stars look so large and bright back home." I answered him. Seeing the night sky was the first sign of time passing that I had really noticed since we started this journey.

There was a slow, grinding noise from behind us. We all turned our heads to see what was making the ghastly sound. The exit from the hidden chamber was closing. We had managed to get out with maybe two minutes to spare. The final closing resealed the chamber and all it's buried secrets and truths. It was with a feeling of relief and freedom that I took another deep breath of crisp cool air, glad to still be alive.

Shi seemed to be recovering already from our ordeal, he was getting up, looking around, trying to survey the surroundings. Bach joined him and started pointing to the distance as they talked. We were going to have to try and find the way back to the top of the mountain and the ruins again. I could hear many things as I was trying to find the strength to stand up again. I could hear some birds in the night air, a couple bugs or frogs I wasn't sure which. I could hear something else too. I could hear what I thought sounded like a babbling brook or at least some kind of moving water. It was getting my attention because none of us had any water left. During our imprisonment we had drank it all, right down to the last drops. We needed water and we would need it soon if we were to continue on this search.

"We should all have a little fruit, there will be moisture and some strength in it. Soon we will have to leave. There is so much to do just to get back to the ruins. Hiking back up the trail will be hard, eat now and we'll try to leave shortly." Shi told us all.

"I think I hear water Shi. Can you hear it too?" I asked. "I think it's over this way behind us."

I could almost feel the water on my parched throat. Hearing it was almost enough to make my mouth water but I was too dehydrated for that to happen. Shi started to walk back over to where the three of us girls were sitting. He stopped. We were all quiet, listening, trying to hear the sounds of water moving.

"I think I hear it too, maybe a small creek or brook. Just the sound of it awakens and speaks to the soul, doesn't it? You know the sound of moving water is music to the soul because it's like a small child listening to their mothers' heartbeat? It helps to relax you and set your vibration back to nature's rhythm. You're right Kat, I hear the water too. You girls wait here. Bach and I will check it out. Give us your pouches; we'll bring enough water back for everyone."

We handed over our water pouches and hoped they found the water quickly. I was already imagining having my first drink, feeling the cool water bringing life back to my poor dried out throat and body. Who would have ever thought I would be dreaming with so much anticipation about having a simple drink of water? Wouldn't Gram be pleased to hear me thinking such thoughts? She always told us never take the simple things for granted.

Mu watched the boys disappear behind us and started to talk,

"Your world doesn't seem to understand or appreciate the true value of water on this planet. You treat it as if it's not a living thing, as if it could never run out or die, much the same way you treat many other things, like the animals and forests of the world. Soon there will be nothing left and the Guardians will need to begin a new, to create man in another spiritual realm or dimension on some other world, all because we have destroyed this one with our greed and abuse. Your world is repeating the same mistakes ours did and our mistakes all but finished the people of Atlantis. I don't know ii it's too late to save your world. When you go home, you must work to make people understand they can't keep poisoning and polluting the oceans and rivers. You have to get them to start somewhere to save what we have left."

We both promised to do what we could.

The boys returned with full pouches and handed each of us girls one. Shi cautioned us to drink slowly and take our time. It wasn't easy to heed his words of warning. I wanted to drink it all down and ask for another pouch full. We did as he suggested and tried to slowly savor the water in our mouths before we swallowed or took another drink. The water was doing it's magic. Life was returning to all of us. Everyone's color looked better and we were all sitting a little straighter now. I felt like soon I'd be able to get up and stand on my own two feet again.

As the two boys stood there Bach started speaking,

"Water is a miracle of life, without it no energy can manage to keep the human body alive. Did you know that water displays different invisible patterns, based on the positive or negative energy, words or thoughts that it is exposed to? When you expose water to positive words and thoughts it displays beautifully balanced patterns. When it is negative, the patterns are deformed and out of balance, lacking beauty. Think how negative words and thoughts would affect your body, as it is mostly water. Many things in this world are not visible to the human eye but that doesn't make them any less real. Think good things and give thanks for the miracle of the water you drink so it may do the most good for your person. It works much like saying blessings over your food before you eat. Be thankful for this little miracle of life."

Bach was so full of knowledge, so all knowing. I would have to remember his words. I wondered if there was any research I could check on to see if what he said was true. I was sure it must be. Bach was not a story maker. He seemed wiser than anyone I knew so far in my life.

It was dark and I wasn't sure if the boys would want to leave before day light or not. I would have voted to sleep and rest awhile even if it was only a couple hours. I had no way of knowing how long we had been up since the last time we slept. Maybe the kids were used to going more hours without sleep. I didn't know what their daily habits were but I was really hoping right now that they too were as tired as Becka and me.

Bach must have been reading my thoughts again because he spoke up and said,

"We should probably rest here for a few hours. The way will be a lot easier when the sun is up and we can see where we are climbing. I think we all need some rest to be our best for the search we have ahead of us."

"I vote for that." Becka said.

"I agree, lets all get some rest. We'll leave when the sun rises." Shi added. Then he and Bach both sat back down and tried to find a flat place to lie down. Becka and I curled up close to each other and Mu curled the opposite way behind Becka. We were all asleep in less than 30 seconds.

The sun came up over the ridge of the mountain next to us. The first rays seemed to shoot right down into my eyes. I squinted and rubbed my eyes with both hands. Could it be morning already? I did feel rested even if I had slept on the hard ground. It felt as cozy as my bed back home. I don't think I had ever needed a place to sleep as much as I needed this one the night before. As I moved my hands away from my eyes I turned my head to look around and see who else was awake. Mu was sitting there behind Becka in the lotus position and she looked like she was meditating. All the others were still asleep. I slowly moved into a sitting position myself. I stretched a little and started to really wake up.

I couldn't help but wonder if I'd had a dream last night. Had any of the things I saw and felt really happened? Here with the cold fresh mountain air all around me, the sunrays starting to pour down over us, it was hard to know for sure. It could have been a dream. Or maybe it had all happened. Otherwise, why were we here, in the middle of nowhere? It seemed more plausible that it had all happened, and that's how we ended up here, on this knoll this morning.

A little panic started to set in. How much more time would we have before the head count back home would show we weren't there? Becka would have a cow if she thought I had gotten us in over our heads. Maybe I should wake the others and we should get going. I had no sense of time and it did seem as if a day had passed. I prayed that Shi was good at time bending and could keep us from getting in trouble with our parents.

Becka started to stir, almost as if she could hear the panic going through my brain.

"Morning Becka. How do you feel this morning?" I asked

"What time is it Kat? Is it still morning?" she asked as she sat up and did the same kind of eye rub I had done before.

"I think it's morning Becka. The sun just came up over to the east." I answered her.

"I feel like I just slept for days. I don't know what made me feel so tired." The words were hardly out of her mouth when she opened her eyes and looked a little surprised to be out in the open, surrounded by me and three other kids.

"Oh! I forgot. I thought all this was just some wild and crazy dream. I felt so rested and comfortable I was sure I was home in my own bed."

"After yesterday, I bet we both will think about staying a lot closer to home from now on. I don't know if I'm cut out for all this adventure and excitement."

Shi and Bach were starting to move around and it looked like they had a plan.

"Let's all eat something, have a little water then refill our pouches and get started. It's a long walk back to Machu Picchu. We have much to accomplish today." Shi suggested as he dug into his own food pouch to retrieve an apple.

We ate in silence and in just a couple minutes we were all standing and ready to go fill the water pouches again. We followed the boys towards the stream they found the night before and each of us filled our water pouches back up. I took a good long drink and refilled my pouch a second time. After yesterday being in the pressure cooker I didn't feel like I had recovered yet. The taste of this spring water was sweet. With the sun up and the hike ahead of us I wanted to start with plenty of water in my system. After all, who knew what might be ahead of us today?

Shi and Bach started us on our way with Bach taking the lead. We'd only been walking about twenty minutes when Bach said not too far up ahead of us was the old Inca trail and it would get us back where we needed to go. Just hearing him say the words Inca Trail brought so many images into my mind. I could picture the Incas walking these same trails where I walked now. I guess I was day dreaming too much because I tripped and started to fall. I screamed and tried to grab a hold of anything. Becka, Mu, some tall grasses, a boulder, anything but I didn't seem to do anything except keep falling. I slipped again, this time falling totally to the ground and in my struggles I rolled and tumbled down at least twenty feet off the trail. The others were calling my name and coming after me.

By the time my body finally came to a complete stop I was a little shook up. I landed face first, downhill and skinned up my chin on the way. Almost as if it was a miracle I had stopped just before a long drop off. Had I gone over that edge I don't think I would have been going anywhere else today. My eyes almost popped out of my head. I was so close to the edge and it was so far down and lots of rough rocks along the way to break your bones on. I just stayed there a minute or two while the others worked their way down to me and saw what a dangerous spot I had found myself in.

"Wow Kat, I was so afraid when you lost your balance and I saw you falling to this little ledge. You could have gone over!" Becka said breathlessly.

I rolled over very carefully and looked back towards her voice. Once again I couldn't believe my eyes and just stared for a full minute before I could find my words and said,

"Oh my word Becka! Look at what I see." I pointed just behind her. From up above you would have never seen them. There within arms reach was the exact plant we came all this way searching for.

They all turned to see what I was pointing to. Immediately they all recognized the plant. Bach told Shi,

"You all help get Kat back up on the trail. I'll get the plant and follow you as soon as I can."

Mu looked back to me and said,

"What luck you have Kat. I'll have to remember to keep you close by. First you don't fall to your death and then you find the very plant we have been searching for. Your near catastrophes turn out pretty good, far better than mine."

The three of us all laughed at her statement. The boys didn't seem to see the humor we did. Mu extended her hand for me to use to get back up off the ground. I took it and Becka joined in helping me keep my footing and get away from the edge. While the four of us made our way back up to the trail Bach dug up and packed the plant to take back with us to Atlantis.

The girls helped me get back up to the trail and Shi followed behind us making sure if anyone lost their footing, he'd be there to block their fall. My chin was bleeding a little and Becka seemed hell bent on cleaning the dirt off my face before she'd be happy that I was okay. I did feel a little shaken from the fall and the realization of how close I had come to going over the ledge. That was twice in just a few hours that I had come close to what could have been the end of this lifetime. After nurse Becka finished working on her patient I was allowed to stand and move around a little.

There was joy in our steps as we paced on the trail, waiting for Bach. . Bach was almost a full five minutes behind us. He took special care to pack and prepare the plant for its journey back. We talked while we waited and discussed the possibility of where we might find the next plant. Because find it, we would. We were sure of it now.

By the time Bach was back on the trail with us, we all had found new reserves of energy we hadn't had earlier. We felt like conquering heroes returning home. All we had to do now was get back to the parking lot at the ruins and find our bus to get back to the coastline. Then a swim back to Easter Island and a sinkhole swim back to Atlantis. We hoped by the time we got back to our beach that we'd see Shi had done all he said he could. If we weren't on lock down for the rest of our lives, we'd have to work hard to help the merkids find the remainder of the plants they needed. This was only the beginning and we still had a long ways to go.

Adventure #2
Australia

We were treated like royalty again as we reentered Atlantis with the first of the sacred plants from our trip to Machu Picchu and Easter Island. The kids were enthused and you could tell they felt triumphant with the quest to save their population and ultimately the Guardians on their return to Atlantis. We stayed only long enough to see Bach safely deliver the first plants to Chou and the others.

Becka and I were both worried if Shi had been able to keep time at bay while we had been gone. If not, Becka and I were going to be in deep do-do with our parents and would probably never see the light of day again. We both knew we'd be on total lock down if something had screwed up with Shi's ability to bend time enough to cover things at home for us.

The swim back to our Florida beach was just as beautiful as all the other times. I think both Becka and I were a little concerned, hoping with all our hearts that time had been on our side and we wouldn't get home and find ourselves in trouble. We told Shi and Mu we would get back with them in three days, just as we had done before to give them a report on what we might be able to find out next.

It was Mu, who spoke up,

"This time we have another plan. Here." She handed each of us a large, flat opal disc about two inches long, over an inch wide and about a fourth of an inch thick. They were beautiful pale creamy colors with pastel pink and green fire dancing through them. We each took a stone from her and looked to see what she would say next.

"With these stones, if you lie down, place them over the third eye and meditate your findings Bach will be able to hear you and read your message. This will save time and if you are able to discover anything before the three days we won't have to wait or lose any valuable time."

I had to ask her,

"How will these opals let Bach read our thoughts?"

Mu patiently explained to us,

"The Opal is a stone of creative intuition and psychic awareness. Many shamans throughout history have used them to invoke visions and stimulate the higher powers. One of which would be mental telepathy. Bach will hear you, as he will be tuned into both of you and will be waiting to hear your thoughts. The opal crystals will amplify your thoughts and meditations, which will enable you to be a sender. Trust me, it will work and you will find it an interesting process. Just focus your thoughts on him and let him know you have a new location and have discovered another plant to tell us about. Bach will let you know when we will meet with you again."

Becka was the next to question her,

"Are you sure we'll hear Bach? I've never done anything like this. What if we don't understand what ever he says back to us? I'm just not sure I can do this."

"Trust me Becka, you will be able to hear and understand Bach. I have no doubt and you shouldn't either. Have we failed you yet with anything we have said we could do?" Mu answered her.

"I know but this is us doing something we've never done before. I'm just worried we might not be as good at all this as you seem to think we might be."

Shi stepped closer and told us both, "Trust us we know the power of the stones. We have used them many times and they are very powerful. Both of you are more open and receptive than you realize. Having been with us your energy has risen and you are vibrating at a high enough level, we know you will be able to work with us this way. Believe us." With those last words Shi and Mu dipped back into the water and headed home.

Well that was that I guess. We'd try to do what they asked. As we looked at each other trying to digest everything we both suddenly snapped out of the daze we had been hit by. Time to get home. We'd know soon enough if all had gone as hoped.

We both went to Becka's house first. As we entered the door into the kitchen Becka's grandmother called out.

"You girls finally back? How was your day? Where are your bags? I thought you were going to the mall to do a little shopping?"

We both stopped and sort of looked at each other. I thought maybe it was better for me to say something.

"Oh we went to the beach and we ran into some friends of ours. They had a few things they wanted to do so we went with them for a while and decided to save shopping for another time. Sorry we didn't call and tell you all we changed our plans. We're not late are we? We sort of lost track of time while we were with them."

Gram kept stirring the pot on the stove as see looked back over her shoulder at us.

"No you're not late. In fact you're just in time to set the table for me. Oh by the way Bunny's been by a couple times looking for the two of you. You might want to call her. She seemed to think something was really important and was very disappointed you weren't home."

"Thanks Gram, I'll call her after we get the table set. Come on Kat lets get this done so we can see what's up with Bunny."

We sat the table and went to Becka's room to call Bunny.

The minute she answered she laid into us. "Where have you two been? I've been looking everywhere for you all afternoon."

Becka told her,

"We ran into some friends at the beach and got tied up with them for a while. What's up? What are you so excited about? Did you find one of the plants?"

"Yes. I found one I think grows in Australia. I've been checking and double-checking. It used to grow in Australia anyway. It was a plant the Aborigines used in their medicines. It's very rare and could be extinct already. Let's get together after dinner and I'll show you what I have."

"Sounds like a plan. Do you want us to come over to your place or do you want to come here?" Becka asked.

"You should both come over here. I'll see you after dinner."

"Okay, we'll see you later."

Becka hung up the phone then we both washed and got ready for dinner. I was spending the night at Becka's so I didn't have to check in at my house tonight. I think we were both so elated that everything went the way Shi said it would. No one was aware of where we had been or what we had done. Heck, I still couldn't believe what we had done or where we had been. We almost had to wonder if we had been dreaming again or not.

As we sat in her room waiting for dinner to be ready we just sat and looked at each other. Could it all have been real? Could those kids bend time, read minds, swim like fish? It was really hard to believe but we both knew it was. It was a little mind bending to say the least. It all made us think so much more now, about everything. The kids talked about the mistakes the earlier peoples made on our poor little planet. They almost lectured us about the importance of water and other resources that we didn't seem to be taking as good a care as we should be. Becka and I would have to think of ways to try to make a difference. Was there some way that either of us could affect how other people treated this planet and the resources on it like water?

Just then Gram called us to dinner so we had to shake off the meditative state that had come over us. Dinner was a blur. Everything was good. All of Gram and Mrs. Bakers dinners were great and you never wanted to miss one if you had an invitation. Becka and I both seemed starved. Like we hadn't eaten in a week. Mr. Mac and Gram both commented about how much we were eating. I just kept smiling and eating. I hadn't realized until we sat down to eat, just how hungry I was. Becka must have felt the same way. We both over ate and still stuffed desert down on top of the giant meal we had just consumed. We'd have to waddle over to Bunny's house.

We helped clean up after dinner before we walked over to Bunny's house.

We didn't even get to the first step when Bunny had the door open calling out to us. "It's about time. Were you having some kind of medieval feast at your house tonight? It took you so long I didn't think you were coming. Come on, let's go to my room." She just turned and headed down the hall towards her room.

"Hi Mrs. Christian." We both called out to Bunny's mom as Becka shut the front door and we turned to follow Bunny to her room.

"Hello girls, nice to see you."

Bunny was already at her desk when we walked in.

"Look at this." She said and pointed to her laptop screen with one hand and held the drawing up next to it with her other hand.

We both hurried over to her side. Looking at the two pictures I'd say she had a match. Wow, the merkids were going to be so excited. The second plant found and we just got back. I had to wonder if any of the other kids had found the plants they were looking and searching for. Wouldn't that be something! We'd have to check with the other kids later or in the morning.

Bunny was so excited, she was close to bubbling over.

"I have to tell you, this has all been the strangest experience. I felt like the more I read about Australia the more I knew but it was also like I already knew most of this stuff."

I so wanted to tell Bunny about what we had just done. We promised the kids we wouldn't tell anyone but it wasn't easy. I really wanted to tell her. It would just blow her away if we could. Heck it was still blowing my mind and I'd had some time to get use to the idea of all this. ATLANTIS!!!! OMG!!! MERKIDS!!! It really wasn't something you could tell someone and probably even have them believe you. I think it's one of those things you'd have to see to believe. Then you still wonder a little. Still feels like it could have been a dream. I reached in my pocket and rubbed the opal Mu had given me. I knew it was real.

"Oh, good job Bunny. How did you figure it all out?" Becka asked.

"I took your led from Mr. Mac. I started looking up sacred plants, checking all the original cultures around the world. With the Aborigines being the oldest culture I decided to dig there first. If there were sacred plants it seemed like they would be a people to check into. I stayed up almost all night. I was so tired I almost couldn't keep going. Something told me to just try one more site. Then boom, there it was. After the excitement of finding it I was so tired I had to go to bed.

Then the dream I had, WOW, it was so amazing. The dream was so real to me. There were strange wooden horns or giant flutes, called Didgeridoos they played and it was the strangest, vibrational sound. I felt like the sounds were communicating with spirit or something. I sure felt like they were communicating with me.

I just kept having one dream after another and they were all about Australia and the time they call the Dreamtime or the Dreaming. Which if you don't know is their story of creation. It's so amazing all the things I was reading and learning. The Aborigines are such incredibly spiritual people. I almost can't remember half of what was in my dreams. Then when I finally woke up I find out, you guys were up and gone long before I crawled out of bed. It was such a let down. I thought I'd explode before I finally got your call."

"Sorry Bunny, we didn't think about much when we headed to the beach. We would have come home sooner if we had known." Becka tried to apologize.

"Wow how cool you found the second plant. I wonder if anybody else found anything yet?" I added.

"Nobody called me if they did." Bunny threw in.

We all talked a little longer before Becka and I told Bunny we were pretty tired ourselves and wanted to head back over to her house and bed. We were stuffed and tired. Neither of us had anyway of knowing how long we had actually been gone on our little adventure with the kids but it seemed like days to me. Before we could go to sleep we'd have to try to let Bach know what we'd found out so far from Bunny.

On the walk back over to Becka's we talked about using the opals Mu had given us. We'd see if we could communicate with Bach. We were sure the kids would go ballistic when they heard we found another plant location. We decided we'd clean up and get ready for bed before we tried using the opals. Becka and I had both used stones to meditate with before but this seemed like an entirely different thing all together. Neither of us had ever done or tried mental telepathy with some merkid hundreds of miles away. We just hoped we'd get it right.

Once we finally lay down on the beds and placed the opals on our foreheads over the third eye, we just tried to breathe deeply and focus our thoughts. If Bach were out there waiting for a signal from us, hopefully he'd read our thoughts and know what Bunny had done. We did try to add that we hadn't talked with any of the other kids but would in the morning and then try to get back with him.

Becka and I both thought we heard the words, "Okay I will wait until tomorrow." If I hadn't been so tired I think hearing his words would have been too much for me. I would have been up all night chattering away to Becka about how insane all of this was. Maybe we were both losing our minds and just didn't realize it. All of this was freaking me out a little. That was one opal I'd want to hang onto forever if Mu would let me. You'd think by now I'd be getting used to all this strange stuff the kids could do and the things they had been able to enable us to do. This was just as cool as the crystal earplugs that allowed us to communicate under water with each other. I never knew rocks could hold so much power and psychic abilities.

We both tucked our opals away in the stone pouch bags Ronnie had given us as gifts. We couldn't think of a safer place for now. Sleep was taking us into its arms and we slept the sleep of two weary travelers. My last thoughts were 'could water travel cause something like jet lag?' 'How did I get this tired?'

The next morning when we woke up, it was with a strong sense of what we had to do. We needed to eat and get chores done so we could talk to the rest of the kids. Maybe someone else had gotten lucky and just hadn't called us yet. With a good nights sleep behind us, I think we were both feeling a little more like our old selves. After we ate we hurried to call and check with the others to see if there were any more finds.

No one had come up with anything yet but they all promised to keeping working on the project. Once we told them it was super important they each pledged to dig deeper and spend more time on it. We decided to call Bach again before we did our chores. So we got the opals out and did our meditation once again.

After we sent our thoughts to Bach we waited to see if we'd hear or recognize any response back from him. It surprisingly didn't take but a couple seconds and we got our return message. Bach wanted to meet with Becka and me again today at the beach. In fact he wanted to meet us in less than an hour. We'd have to hurry and do a few chores so we'd be able to get out of the house.

Just as we were finishing our list of chores Gram came into the room.

"Don't forget you have a doctors appt. today Becka, we'll have to leave in just a couple hours. You'll have to stay home. No running around with Kat today for you."

We looked at each other. Now what? How could we meet Bach and Mu at the beach if Becka had to go to a doctor's appt.?

Becka looked at me and said,

"I can't believe I forgot about this appt. Kat. Let's go to my room and visit before you leave." As soon as we got in her room where no one could hear us she shut the door and turned back to me. "I think we should call Bach again. Maybe if I can't go you could take Bunny with you. After all, she's the one who found this plant. Maybe they'll let us bring Bunny into our little adventures. Grab your opal and lets do this."

I listened and we both lay back down with the opals in position over the third eye chakra once again. After Becka and I explained what was going on and how it was Bunny who actually made the discovery, Bach said he and Mu would meet Bunny and me on the beach and we'd talk. I think he wanted to get the promise from Bunny's lips if he was going to let her know about them or get involved.

Now the big question was what would Bunny think or say when she found out? Even I had to chuckle to myself, just thinking how Bunny would handle some of what we had already been through with the kids. It would be so cool for her to see and be part of this hunt with and for the kids. Bunny was going to get her mind blown away.

If Bach thought I had a lot going through my mind, wait until Bunny was there to ask all her questions. I even considered she might be able to tell Bach a thing or two. Bunny was close to being a walking encyclopedia. I would just hope now that Bunny would want to go and be involved. It would be so great to share all this with her. She would never believe us about the first adventure unless she went on one. Nobody who didn't see it all for them selves would ever believe us, they'd just think we were kids with very vivid imaginations.

Before I left Becka's I called Bunny and asked if she could leave for the day to do a little running around with me. She said sure and promised to be ready in 15 minutes. When I got to Bunny's, Mrs. Christian answered the door. I told her Bunny and me were going to the beach to meet with some friends of mine. I asked if it would be okay for Bunny to go with us to do a little running around. My friends were looking for some plants and I had promised to help them. I promised her we wouldn't be too late and should be home before dinnertime. Unless of course, Bunny decided she didn't want to go after she met my friends.

"Sure, you girls have fun. Where's Becka today? Why isn't she going with you?" she asked.

"Doctor's appt." was all I said then both Bunny and I turned to head out the front door.

After we were down the steps and out of earshot of Mrs. Christian I started to talk to Bunny about what I thought I could say without really spilling the beans about what was coming.

"The friends I'm taking you to meet are a little different and I want to tell you, they are different but they are real. I feel like I know them really well and can trust them. Becka and I both trust them. In fact we'd trust them with our lives. Mostly I just want you to kind of prepare yourself for some rather shocking and surprising things. But like I already said, you can trust me and you can trust and believe them." I kept trying to find the words to prepare her for a shock but I couldn't say too much.

So mostly I think I was just sounding like an idiot to her, rambling and saying nothing. Just talking in circles.

"So what is it you're trying to say to me Kat? Are your friends Vampires or something?" she inquired.

"Well no they're not vampires but they're different and it'll take a little adjusting for you to get used to them when you meet. Just do me a favor and stay open and don't go ballistic on me. Promise me you'll be cool and not flip out."

"Wow, now I'm really curious. What sort of freaks are you taking me to meet?" she asked

"You'll see." We had finally gotten down to the beach and as I walked towards our meeting place I could see Bach and Mu out in the water about 20 feet off the shoreline. "That's them over there. Come on, lets go out to talk with them."

She stopped and said, "Why can't they come in?"

"Don't be that way Bunny. Just get wet and come on. You won't melt. We need to go out to them. Trust me, this is really, really important."

She wasn't too happy with having to get wet and wade out so far. The kids were in water chest high so Bunny couldn't see their tails. As we got up close to them I introduced them.

"Bunny this is our friend Bach and this is Mu. Mu and Bach, this is our friend Bunny who found the plant we talked about. Becka and I have both known Bunny for years and years. We know you can trust her. Becka couldn't be here and I think Bunny could take her place. So what do you think? Will you invite her to come?"

It was Bach who spoke first.

"Hello Bunny, I am pleased to meet you. Mu and I are here on a mission of extreme importance. We do need your help and appreciate the help you have already given us by finding tone of the plants we need. We must ask you to swear never to speak to anyone other than Kat and Becka about what you see or learn while you are with us. There are things I will explain to you if you swear to help us and keep our secrets."

Mu started to talk as soon as Bach stopped,

"We wish you no harm and if you swear to help us and keep our secrets, we will do everything in our power to keep you safe. Do you swear?"

Bunny looked at me like these people were aliens from some other Universe. She looked a little bewildered but she looked back to Bach and Mu and promised.

"I swear I will never mention to anyone other than Becka and Kat anything about either of you. No matter what it is I'm going to learn about you."

I let out my breath. It was over and now I could say anything to Bunny about the kids and what we had already done with them. I figured I better explain a few things pretty fast so Bunny could decide if she was up for this next adventure of ours. If she wasn't I guessed I'd be going with them by myself this time.

"Bunny I know you're first reaction is going to be that it's not possible but hear me out before you interrupt and the kids will show you something that might convince you. This is Bach and Mu, they are merkids and they're from the lost continent of Atlantis."

"Yeah Right." was her first reaction.

"No, it's true." Mu told her. "Look down and you will see our tails. We only have tails when we are in the water, other wise we have legs and function just as you do. We are from Atlantis and we are on a mission to find seven sacred plants needed to save what's left of our people. Both Kat and Becka have been to the city and seen Atlantis for them selves. We are not joking." with those last words Mu flipped her tail fins out of the water and I thought Bunny's eyes would pop out of her head. I could totally understand her reaction. I had the same one when I saw their tails the first time too.

"It's true Bunny. I know it's a lot to take in and there's a lot more to tell you. So listen up. We need to go with the kids to Australia and help them find the plant you searched for and found. Bach and the others are able to bend time. We can be gone for what will seem like days or even weeks and no one here at home notices. That's where Becka and I were yesterday. We went with the kids to Atlantis, then onto Chichen Itza and Peru to Machu Picchu. I can't explain how they do it but they did everything they told us they could do. It's going to blow your mind all the things these kids can do. They read minds, bend time and have psychic abilities that we've never known anything about."

"Holy cow, you guys aren't pulling my leg are you? If this is all really real, I'll have faith and believe you Kat. I'll go. I've been a lot of places with my Mom and Dad but Atlantis isn't one they've ever gone to. If we're going to do this, how does it work? How do we get there?" Bunny asked as she looked back over at Mu and Bach.

Mu explained things for Bunny while handing her a food pouch of her own, the crystal earplugs and her breathing mask. Each time she explained everything to her and how it all worked. Bunny kept shaking her head like she couldn't believe it all. Actually I thought she was taking it rather well. Bunny wasn't big on getting wet or going to the beach so I thought it was going really well so far.

Bach said,

"Today we plan to go directly to Australia. We'll have to use the sinkholes and the under world passageways again. It's the fastest way to get there. Are you ready?"

I told Bunny,

"You're going to be amazed Bunny. Everything under the water is so beautiful and there are so many exotic things down there that we've never seen before. I can't wait until we get to Easter Island. You're in for the adventure and thrills of your life. It's easy, just hang on and enjoy the ride. We'll be able to hear your every thought and you'll be able to hear ours. This is one trip you're going never forget!! Are you ready?"

She didn't verbally answer me. She already had the mask on and just nodded her head in the affirmative. The kids slowly worked their way into the water and took us down gradually. Bunny took to everything pretty well. She snorkeled with her Dad several times in Hawaii and other places they traveled to. So this wasn't as big a deal for her as I was worried it might be. I was surprised she didn't ask anything about what they meant when that talked about the under world passageways. Maybe in the excitement of everything she didn't pick that one up. I was sure that would be the part where we'd lose her and she's back out.

"I'm amazed that this breathing gear works off of crystals and algae. I wonder what things our scientists would be able to do that could ever work this well. It's so utterly simple and yet so unbelievable. What a combo, crystals and algae." Bunny was thinking in her normal everyday manner and I expected nothing less from her on this trip.

"I hear you Bunny and you're right...it's totally unbelievable, all of it. Wait until you get to see Atlantis." I told her. "Wow, I wasn't thinking you'd all hear every thought I had."

"Don't worry," I told her. "If you chatter too much, you'll hear about it! I couldn't stop myself the two times we've been with them and I got a little lesson in the value of silence and meditation."

We swam as we had before, down around the southern tip of Florida past the keys. Near Key West we swam in with a whole school of string rays. That was pretty intense and something I'll never forget. I ran my hand over the backs of a couple of the string rays. They were so smooth and soft to the touch. They actually didn't seem to mind me touching them. It felt like it was their way of saying hello back to me. This time we continued on, past the keys into the Caribbean where the water became such an incredible azure blue. It was a color I had never seen before. I just loved all the different colors and hues the water had. There were so many I had never seen or witnessed before, it was like a water rainbow of blues, greens and every color in between.

As we swam past the entrance to Atlantis we saw a lot of small sharks and a couple bigger ones too, once we even saw several swordfish swimming together. I kept looking towards Bunny, watching to see how she was doing. I had heard so many of her thoughts and she was having a great time. Finally my thoughts got away from me and Bunny answered me back,

"I'm incredibly terrific Kat. You were right. There's nothing that'll be able to compare to this. I've already seen so many shipwrecks and the stingrays, oh my word, can you believe we've been swimming with stingrays!! Now the sharks, that was a little scarier. I can't wait to see the rest of this adventure. What do you think we'll see when we get to Australia?"

"Who knows Bunny, when I'm with the merkids I never know what to expect or what'll be around the next corner. I can't wait to see Australia either. I fell in love with everything I saw during the last trip. I just wish we had a camera for pictures." I answered back.

As we entered the underworld water passages Bunny was taking every angle in. I couldn't pick up any of her thoughts so I wasn't sure what she was feeling or thinking, she seemed to be holding onto her thoughts. My first trip I was a little panicky wondering and worrying where they would end and if we'd get lost forever. Bunny didn't seem to be experiencing any of those kinds of thoughts.

I was feeling stunned again, I couldn't help it. I found it hard to believe we were traveling half way around the world to an island that had probably been part of the lost continent of Lemuria. At least I hoped we were headed towards Easter Island and the kids hadn't made any wrong turns.

To make things even more amazing, we made it and nothing creepy tried to grab us while we were in the under worlds. I looked up to see the blue sky again. I wanted to kiss the ground as soon as I could get my feet planted firmed on it again. It was only about 25 feet overhead to the rim of earth at ground level. Next we would have to climb out of here. I couldn't believe my eyes when I saw Mu swim to the far side where I could see what looked like earth steps circling the wall of the hole. It made you wonder how many people came and went through this sinkhole that there were steps to make it easier access? Once we climbed up out of the sinkhole and made our way to the surface I couldn't stop myself. I grabbed Bunny gave her a big hug asking her at the same time,

"Can you believe we just did what we did? I'm vibrating and tingling just thinking about where we are."

"I know Kat. Me too. I've been thinking maybe we're dreaming all this just couldn't be true could it? I'm so happy to have that swim over with."

"Yeah I don't know Bunny. Could we both be dreaming the same dream? Could our minds have dreamed all this up? It's pretty amazing. Holy cow, Bunny, look at that!" I pointed to what looked like one of the monoliths off in the distance.

Mu spoke up then,

"I can tell you without a doubt, this is part of Lemuria. My vibration has been rising ever since I stepped on this ground. I feel a knowing of having come home, back to my beginnings and my roots. It's like your salmon that swim upstream to return to the place of their birth. I feel a peace that I never felt back in Atlantis. This is definitely my original birthplace. My earthly vibrational beginning."

Mu seemed lost in her own thoughts as she talked. She was experiencing something new and yet from what she said, maybe a feeling that all of us feel as we return home after being away for a very long time. Somehow as she spoke about it, I thought this is something Bunny and I wouldn't feel the same way. I wanted to ask about the vibrational thing she had mentioned but she seemed like she was somewhere else and it didn't seem like the right time to interrupt her. Was this tingling thing I felt something like what she was feeling?? Bunny said she felt it too. Bach gave her a couple minutes to experience her feelings while he tried to get his bearings and find our direction. He looked to the sky and all around us and then he said,

"This is the way to the Ocean. We need to head out now. There is ground to cover and we must walk."

Mu seemed to shake off the hypnotic, trance-like feelings she had started to experience when we first arrived.

"I'm ready. Did you feel it too Bach?" she asked.

"I feel nothing different. It must be a trigger for you. Maybe later we will explore what it means. Perhaps it's a female thing. The other two said they were tingling. Maybe they don't know their own vibrations. Maybe you should talk with them."

Mu sort of looked at us like she was considering the idea and then looked like she didn't think it a good idea to consult with us. She looked like she didn't think we could be feeling anything like what she was feeling just now.

It didn't matter to us if Mu didn't want to talk to us; Bunny and I were mesmerized with the view in front of us. I could see several of the monoliths in the distance. We were really here. It was really Easter Island in the middle of the Pacific Ocean. Now it was only another 6600 miles to Australia. Wow. I was tired just thinking about getting there but all I could think of was, I want to touch them, no matter how far I have to walk. I didn't want to keep going if I don't get to touch one and experience it up close and personal.

"Bach I have to ask if we can walk by the monoliths. I have to be able to touch one. Please. I can't have come this far and be this close and not be allowed to touch one. I have to feel the rock and know it's really real."

"We have come this far because of your help. How could we refuse your request? We will pass by the Moia you see shortly and we will give you some time to get acquainted with them." Bach answered. He didn't seem at all upset with my request.

"Oh thank you Bach." I was almost dancing I was so excited. "Did you hear that Bunny? We're going to get a chance to meet the monoliths of Easter Island!" Now I was literally dancing around Bunny. She just smiled at me and said,

"Behave yourself Kat, they'll think you're nuts."

I tried to contain my enthusiasm but it wasn't easy. I fell back to walk next to Mu and asked her,

"Would you tell me about what you were feeling when we first got here and you talked about your vibrations rising? If you'd rather not talk about it I'll understand and apologize for asking a personal question."

She looked at me and I think she could see the desire to understand in my eyes.

"I think you know that vibrations are the energy that we all come from: it's what makes us and everything around us. Each place also has it's own energy and vibration. When you come from one local you share it's energy and you will always resonate to it when you are there. I believe that as my greatest ancestors came from Lemuria and because I have reincarnated to Atlantis, this would be my true home and beginning. I feel the rising of my energy and vibration. It's opening me up and I feel very balanced and serine, more so than I have ever felt before. It's almost as if I am floating above the ground at a finer, more spiritual level than I have ever experienced in Atlantis. I have traveled many places and never felt this change or level of vibrational perfection. I feel as if I am out of my body and not feeling the physical at all. It's like I am floating here next to you. It's the strangest sensation. It's like being in two places at one time. Even during meditation I have never felt this kind of coming home vibration."

"Wow. That sounds so incredible. I can't imagine it. I mean I'm tingling and I'm so excited I almost can't keep from dancing. What you described sounds more like some very special spiritual bliss. I wish I could feel what you're feeling just to know what it's like. I envy you this new discovery about yourself." I fell silent and just walked with her until we reached the monoliths.

I raced up to the giant who stood before us. I was in the presence of a Lemurian God. Maybe it was a God of some special spiritual vibration, standing watch all these thousands of years. Guarding the heart and soul of Lemuria. I especially liked that idea.

"Can you believe this Bunny? I'm touching something someone made and carved thousands of years ago. Feel it. The stone is cold and so rough to the touch. I wonder how many men it took to make this one? I wonder how long it took. What kind of tools do you think they had to have used? Oh man where's my camera when I really need it? Wouldn't Mr. Mac be blown away with a picture of us here with this monolith? I wish I had my camera."

"I wish we could have a picture too Kat. It is one of the most amazing things I have ever seen too." Bunny was standing looking up at the monolith and we were both feeling very small in comparison. She placed her hand on the stone and closed her eyes. I followed her lead and did the same thing.

I didn't feel anything or get any pictures popping into my minds eye either. I hoped Bunny was feeling something and she'd be able to tell me about it.

Bach had been quiet most of the trip but he finally spoke up and got our attention.

"This land was once called the center or Navel of the World by the people who lived here. There was also an earlier culture that walked this land long before much of it became submerged with the water levels rising during the destruction of Mu. They called it Eyes looking to Heaven.

These Moai were raised with the use of the vortex energy and the anti gravity affects that can be created at any of Earth's vortexes. One has only to apply the knowledge of the ancients. How do you suppose man could build any of the great wonders he has created around the world?"

WOW!!! Bach was a young man of few words but when he said something, you should be listening. He continued to explain.

"Many scholars from your world have speculated that this was once part of a larger island. The truth is, the volcano here is a natural vortex and part of a Pacific Rise that is an important node in a global grid. We call the two most important lines of the grid Dragon lines. There are hundreds of vortexes around the globe where these lines meet or cross each other. There is a sacred geography of the planet and this place is a geodetic marker of sacred value. In the time of Lemuria it was the site of an astronomical observatory.

The Moai were placed around the island to help create a second circular vortex of energy. This was a spiritual, ritually prepared site, which then helped to charge the area with a magical essence or spirit they called Mana.

Mana is the magic you would call the soul. It is the energy that makes all things and the magical energy of life. It is your energy and vibration. Many people call it by other names but it is all the same. Some call it Chi but it is still considered the natural energy of the Universe."

We were mesmerized listening to Bach, explain so much about Easter Island and the vortex energy. It made me think about the visit we made to the Coral Caste in Homestead Florida. I still wondered how one man had made something of such gigantic proportions, all by him self. This vortex, anti gravity energy might explain it all. The builder of the Coral Castle would only say that Electricity was the answer to everything. But wasn't electricity just another vibration of energy? Before I could come back from my memory of the Coral Castle Bach was saying it was time to move on. I turned and looked once more upon the Moai I still had my hand on. What an incredible memory this was going to be. I was trying to lock the image forever in my mind.

"We're coming Bach." Bunny called out to him. He and the others had already turned back towards the ocean and were walking away from the giant we all just met. Bunny grabbed my free hand and started leading me away from the Moai I still touched. "Come on Kat, we got

The balance of the hike across Easter Island was made in silence. I think Bunny and me were still reeling from the surreal feeling of what we were doing. Mu still seemed to be lost in the feelings of her semi-out of body experience. Occasionally I'd see Bach point towards the sky and nod to himself. I was content to walk in silence saying a little prayer, hoping that my parents weren't going to ground me for life if this didn't go the way it's suppose to.

I had never been on a volcanic island before. It was surprising how barren the land was. There were no trees in sight, only grasses and rocks to trip over. I think I must have tripped over at least a dozen of them. We walked in fairly low rolling landscape until we reached the beach. Luckily for Bunny and me it was mostly all down hill. I had seen in the distance higher land and what I thought looked like the volcanic craters. I stayed busy the entire time looking in every direction, which is probably why I kept stumbling over the rocks that seemed to be everywhere. I wanted to take in everything. And make a memory of it all in my mind. I saw so many of the Moai statues in the distance. I would have paid a kings ransom to have my camera with me for this adventure.

As we reached the beach it was decided we'd eat a small snack from our pouch before we started the swim to Australia. It was here at the beach that I saw the first trees on the island. They were beautiful graceful palm trees reaching towards the sky. The beach was a beautiful white sand expanse, of slightly sloping shoreline. Even here at the beach the rocks were scattered through the sand down to the waters edge. It was nothing like the cliffs I could see in the far distance going around the island to the north of us.

Bach told us girls,

"I think it best if you only eat three of your dried figs, we need to conserve our supplies and they will be a great source of energy for the swim. Also better try to limit how much water you drink it'll be awhile before we'll be able to refill that supply too."

We sat on the grass close to the sand and ate our small energy snack while we mentally prepared for the long swim ahead on us. I think Bunny and I were both excited and anxious. We would be in Australia soon and neither of us had any idea what would happen next. This was the wildest thing the two of us had ever done. We asked Mu how she was feeling and tried to make a little small talk to help cover up our nervousness. Mu definitely wasn't a small talk kind of girl. She was a kind person but you could tell she was feeling things she hadn't felt before and she was trying to sort her feelings out. She didn't seem in the mood to be bothered by anyone right now. Maybe she'd be better and back to her old self once we were off the island. I hoped so anyway.

"Time to go. Are we all ready? "Bach asked.

Bunny stood and brushed the sand off of her shorts saying,

"I'm ready. How about you Kat?"

"Me too. I still wish I had my camera. What pictures I could be taking." I couldn't help myself. I was always saying what I thought and all I could think about was two things. All the really cool stuff I was seeing and wishing I could be taking photos of and the wild craziness of what we were doing. If I thought about the photos it might take away some of the butterflies I was feeling in my stomach about what we were doing. I couldn't imagine what Bunny was probably thinking about or how nervous she might be. Bunny was always such a careful, cautious person. Right now I couldn't read her and had no idea what she was thinking.

The four of us walked down the short distance to the waters edge. We got out our breathing gear put it on and adjusted things getting ready to go. The water was warm and clear as we walked out into the gentle waves and dipped into the Pacific.

The ocean on this side of the world was just as full of wonderful things to see as the Atlantic. We passed by a pod of whales and swam in a school of dolphins. These new friends of ours are the most amazing people we've ever met.

We were passing so many wondrous sights, tall waving grasses, fishes and string rays, plus stones that looked like ancient city ruins. There had been at least a dozen old shipwrecks we saw just off the coast of Easter Island. There were seals in the water and penguins: two things I never expected to see. I had no way of knowing how long it was but it didn't seem like any time at all and we were working our way back up to the waters surface. The water was warmer and the smaller fishes were darting all around us. The trip had been full of so many creatures from the southern hemisphere. We saw whales, penguins and seals. The underwater adventure was it's own thing with shipwrecks and occasionally what looked like an old ruin of some kind.

We seemed to swim forever before the ocean bottom started to rise up towards us again. Bach said we were in the Coral Sea and the Great Barrier Reef was just ahead of us. The water was changing colors again. The coast was just up ahead of us. The merkids swam upward until we all broke the water's surface and Bach started to look around. It was nighttime. I hadn't expected that since we left home during the early morning. Even in the moonlight I could see the water all around us was ranging from a beautiful royal blue to turquoise. The coast was spotted with sandy beaches. Bach pointed towards one of the beaches right in front of us.

"Lets head in that way then we'll decide what we do next." He directed us towards the moon lit sand straight ahead of us.

As we swam by the reef, even in the moonlight we saw all the beautiful corals. There were so many kinds and there were dozens of different colors and textures. Some looked like giant gray and white brains and others were bright red with hundreds of fingers. Some were like fans and others looked like little trees. I never knew there could be so many different colored and shaped corals in one place. This was the most beautiful living piece of nature I had ever seen or been witness to. I would have loved to have stayed and looked at everything there on the reef. Forever. This was a magical place to be sure. The fishes were pretty marvelous too. Some were tiny, neon green and swam together by the thousands. Others were larger with stripes in yellow, white and blue. I even saw a few that were mostly red and a little black near their fins. There was one that was huge with brown and white spots. It was like being part of the largest seawater fish tank I ever saw.

Bunny and I were both busy with all our mindless chatter. Wooing and awing about everything we saw.

"Even in Hawaii the fishes and coral aren't as beautiful as these. My dad would be jealous if he knew what he was missing here." Bunny finished with before Bach interrupted our chatter.

Bach decided to head into a cave just off the reef before we actually made it all the way into the beach.

"This way, this is the cave I've been looking for. We'll go in and rest until the sun comes up. It'll keep us out of sight and protected while we rest."

We all followed him up to and into the cave's entrance. I hadn't seen it and was surprised to realize what it was there, as we followed him in. It hardly seemed big enough at first glance for even a fish to enter. We all made it without a problem it must have been some kind of optical illusion. Mu heard my thoughts and answered back on them as we swam in.

"It is not an illusion Kat, it is how the Earth keeps her sacred places secreted away from unwanted eyes. We see the aura or energy of the gateway. Sometimes we can feel it before we can see it. Apparently you cannot. You are either too closed and need to learn to get back to the knowledge of the ancients to open yourselves back up or you have lost that ability all together. When Bach talked to you about you having too much mental chatter. He told you then, to hear your soul speak, you much learn to be silent and listen. Once you can hear your soul speak, your third eye with open as well and your soul will be able to see again." With her last thought she flipped her tail and swam in a little faster.

We didn't swim in too far when we lifted up to let our heads break the waters surface inside the cave. Bach and Mu already had their beam crystals on their foreheads. It was enough to light up the interior of the cave. The four of us were looking round to take in the new environment we found ourselves in. As we turned to inspect the other side of the cave behind us, we were all shocked and surprised to see someone there.

"Oh, who are you? What are you doing here?" I asked.

The young aborigine was just sitting there, looking back at us.

"Who am I? What am I doing here? This is my home. I was told to wait here, to meet you and to guide you on your journey. The spirits of the Dreamtime spoke to me during a dream days ago. I heard their voices in the sounds of the didgeridoos coming from the south. I was beginning to think you weren't coming."

"Whoa" It was the only thing I could think of to say.

"My name is Cobar. What name do all of you go by?" He asked.

Mu and Bach both spoke introducing them selves then introduced Bunny and me. He laughed a little when he heard Bunny's name.

"You must be a spirit dreamer too. You have the name of a totem. We will have to talk. I think you and I will have a lot in common."

I thought I saw Bunny blush from his words.

We all started to work our way out of the water and up into the cave to join Cobar on dry land.

This time, it was Bunny who asked him, "Cobar is an interesting name. Do you mind me asking what it means?"

"It means 'burnt earth'. I guess that makes me, and most of Australia, one and the same." He smiled like he enjoyed what he had said and found some humor in it.

"What did you mean when you said you were told to come and meet us? What exactly did you hear when you heard the didgeridoos? I've been reading a lot about Australia lately and I'm very curious. Is it an energy thing or do you hear words?" Bunny was just being Bunny. She had a thirst for knowledge and always asked lots of questions, where I asked questions more from curiosity with a little quest for knowledge mixed in with it.

We had worked our way out of the water and onto dry land inside the cave. Cobar was just what you would have expected of an Aborigine boy, he was dressed in some sort of loincloth, tied with rope at the waist. He was barefooted and looked like he had some kind of white dirt on his skin. He did look a little dusty and I wondered how he could have swum in and still look dusty. So I had to ask.

"Did you swim in the same way we did?"

"No I didn't. I came in another way." Was all Cobar said, he didn't volunteer any additional information.

Bach and Mu both decided it was time to ask their own questions.

"Do you know who we are Cobar?" Bach asked.

"Yep, you two are the ones from the sunken city. You need the meme plant. They're here to help. Now you've got me too."

Mu asked him, "You know where we can find the meme plant? Are they easy to find? Will we have far to go in our search?"

"What's with you women? Nothing but questions, questions, questions. I do know of the meme plant. It's rare and not easy to find but I have a good idea where we might find one. Will we have to go far? Well, that depends on your definition of far. Nothing comes easy in this land and nothing is right around the corner."

"What is your plan then? When do you want to get started?" Bach asked him.

"We can start now if you want. We have to go this way." Cobar said as he pointed deeper into the cave. "There are many caves and under ground passageways we can use. There's less heat by using this route."

"We're ready if you are. Will we be going far?" Mu asked.

"It'll be a bit of a walk about, we will follow this dreaming track to Uluru. It's near the top of the rock I was told we'd find your meme plant."

It was Bunny who popped up next with another question.

"Is a dream track the same thing as a song line Cobar?" she asked.

"Yes I believe they are. In other places they are called dragon lines or ley lines. They are the nerves and energy flow of this land. The energy is sacred and has been since the time of the first Dreaming. Each of these lines or tracks, follow the path of our creator-beings. They left their footprints for us to follow. Are you all ready?" He asked.

We were, and all followed him into the belly of the cave. I only had one other experience with being inside a cave and I didn't like that one too well. I was hoping this trip would be a lot less scary with no unpleasant surprises for us. I have to admit I was feeling a little closed in. I like seeing the big blue, sky overhead and I hoped this wasn't bothering Bunny. I thought I was breathing a little faster than I needed to and my heart was beating a little faster too. I hoped I would settle down and adjust to this cave before anyone else noticed.

Bunny fell back a step to walk beside me.

"This is so far out Kat. I can't wait for this to happen and to get back to see Atlantis. How could anything else be better than seeing the lost city? What did it look like Kat? Tell me what you saw."

So for the next hour or so I told her all about what we saw during our two trips in Atlantis. Even down to the giant cigar sized cockroach. It was so cool to be able to tell someone about it all. Bunny was all-eyes and ears and full of questions like always. We hardly noticed our current surroundings. The cave was just a nice simple smooth walled cave. Looked like it was sandstone or something related to it. At least so far we weren't going deeper, down into the earth like we had done in Peru when we found the lost city of gold.

It was strange hearing our voices and nothing else. The others were all quiet and putting up with our jabbering. Which is what I knew Bach and Mu considered most of our conversations. I did appreciate the beam crystals we were all wearing except Cobar. I hated darkness. It made me wonder, if Cobar had walked in the darkness when he came to meet us. Who knew, maybe the Aborigines didn't need lights to see in the dark. I had seen a lot of strange and wondrous things about them in movies and television. Sometime later, maybe I'd have to ask him.

We reached a point in the cave where it was starting to twist and turn and weave like a snake. We had to pay more attention while we were walking not to bump into the walls and we could only walk single file now. Bunny was excited and thrilled with this new adventure. She told me she was tingling with the thrill of it, even had goose bumps running up her arms.

We noticed on the walls of the cave the rock colors were changing and I could see layers of textural changes too. I ran my hand over them, knowing I was I touching layers of history. They were varying from dark almost black and gray to reds and sand colors. It had to be layers of ash, volcanic lava and magma. I could almost picture the changes the world had gone through. I don't think I ever thought about how the world had actually formed until seeing this hidden, inner world Cobar was taking us into.

As we came around the next corner I was surprised with what my eyes fell on. There were very primitive paintings on the wall. I had heard of the Aborigine art that was in sacred places around Australia. Seeing something someone painted hundreds, maybe thousands or even millions of years ago. It was pretty awe-inspiring. While I was busy just wondering what it all meant Bunny was already asking Cobra what it meant or represented.

"Cobra, I'm fascinated with this cave art. Can you tell us what is means or what it's saying. Do you know if there are more paintings in here? Are they sign posts for you to follow?" she asked him.

"You might call them something like sign posts. They are from and about the Dreamtime, when the world began. I know from these three symbols that I am on the song track and if I follow there direction I will reach my final destination. This is a very spiritual place that I am taking you to. If the Dreamtime didn't tell me to bring you, it's a place you would never see or even know existed. Even in my years of studies, I have never been here or known about the way. Only a few of the most sacred people have ever been here or used this track. That much was given to me in my dream. I have studied for years in the ways of the Dreamtime and my people. I want very much to carry our ways into the future and to later pass it all on to the next generations," he explained.

Bach stepped up and started to inspect the artwork on the wall then a couple seconds later he said.

"Cobra is right. This painting was done in the earliest beginning of

Earth's people. It's millions of years old. I sense it as a clue or a puzzle piece. This is the first piece and clue to finding the jumping off point between dimensions. That is the sacred end to this song track we're on."

I knew Bunny would be popping out of her skin with what they were saying. I was getting a little used to all this wild stuff but she immediately jumped in to ask,

"What do you mean jumping off point between dimensions? What dimensions to where? Are you talking other worlds or Universes? How can you know that?" She was all over Bach with her questions.

Bach gave her a look. Then he looked towards me and back to her. He told her, "We are a people who had used and improved our psychic abilities over many, many generations. I am able to read almost anything. I can read the energy of people, places and things. These paintings were placed here as a directional guide, for those who know how to read them to travel to a sacred place. That place was a gateway to the other astral planes or dimensions. Once you can cross over through dimensions you are able to travel anywhere in the Universe or even into other galaxies and Universes. There are millions of them out there."

"WOW!!" was the only word Bunny could utter. She almost fell backwards a little. Like the power of his words had pushed her back against the cave wall. Definitely when they all spoke and said something, it was a mind blowing conversation for us to digest and try to absorb. Their powers were so polished and they were able to do so many things that we could not. It was hard to believe it all.

Cobra turned and started to walk off in the direction ahead of us. So we stopped with the questions and followed him in silence. I was sure Bunny was mulling over all that both Bach and Cobra had just said. She would cross-examine every word they had said, in her mind until it all gelled and settled into place for her.

I walked behind them all and sudden started thinking about being the last person in line. It made me think about those scary movies where some creature picks off the last person in line in a group and then the next and the next until they're all gone. I found myself looking back behind myself more than I was looking forward.

It seemed like we walked and walked, hour after hour. The passageway would veer to the right and then a little to the left and back and sometimes climb a little up or down but nothing too steep. Bunny and I were getting a little tired and bored. Cobra kept a speedy pace and we weren't used to such long distance walks. It was surprising that it wasn't hot in the cave and there seemed to be plenty of fresh air to breath. Those two facts and the beam crystals made it a little easier to follow them deeper into the core of this place.

I didn't want to say out loud any of the things I was thinking. I wondered what Bunny was thinking, caves weren't my kind of place and I wasn't sure how she felt about them. As we rounded the last turn the others stopped and we couldn't see why yet. I hoped it was nothing bad.

Finally Mu and Bach stepped to the side a little and let us get closer to what had their attention. I could hear the running water before I saw it. The cave opened into a cavern space with water trickling down the side of the cavern wall into a pool of water. Cobra was already kneeling by the edge of the pool getting a drink. He used his cupped hands to scoop up water and raised them to his mouth to drink. Then he turned and told us,

"You all should have a drink, there won't be much more water for us to share while we're inside." He didn't have to tell us a second time. We all joined him at the waters edge. The four of us filled our water pouches, drank and refilled the pouches.

Bunny spoke next,

"Isn't this a beautiful spot? Who would have ever dreamed it would be here inside where it can't be seen. Did you know it would be here Cobra?"

"It was all there in my dream. I told you, I've never been here before. It's all been here forever though and there was a time when others saw it. It was a much more sacred time then. It's a very special energy that fuels this water. The benefits from it will heal what ails you. You might even say its something like holy water."

Mu and Bach were both nodding at Cobra's words.

"I can feel the spiritual power of it." Mu announced.

It was Bach who clarified things even more. "I can tell you this was a cleansing and healing area. People who came here were working towards ascension into the higher dimensions. This cavern was just the first phrase of their journey."

Bunny looked at me and asked,

"Is he always right? How does he know so much about everything?"

I told her,

"I think Bach is maybe a psychic's kind of psychic if that makes any sense. He can tell you everything about anything. He's pretty amazing isn't he! Mu told us he reads the energy of things, people and places. So I guess there's nothing he can't read and explain."

Bunny's mind was spinning and I could almost see the wheels in her mind moving. She looked at me and smiled with a twinkle in her eyes.

"Maybe we should be asking him all our unanswered questions and take notes. You know, things like how did they build the pyramids? Are there really ET's? Is there a heaven and hell or just astral planes when you die?" She rattled off a few questions we've always wondered about before Mu started to chuckle to herself.

"You haven't told your friend Bunny the second reason why we need the plants for the cure yet? Maybe you should enlighten her or would you rather we did?" Mu asked.

Bunny started looking around to see who would say something next. She had that look on her face like somebody better tell her soon what was up? We had told her about the search for the sacred plants and the kids needing them to cure what was killing them all as they reached adulthood. We hadn't told her the part about the Guardians coming and they couldn't risk infecting them with what ever this disease was. I had thought it best to tell her only what she needed to know for the beginning of our trip with the merkids. Maybe it was time to blow her mind and tell her the rest of the story.

Bach spoke before I could decide the best way to explain it all to her.

"You don't have to wonder about the answers to all your questions anymore. I will tell you all I know about anything you wish to ask. The pyramids were built with the use of anti gravity and levitation, as well as a lot of manpower. It was the Guardians who gave them the blueprints for the construction and purpose of the pyramids. I know your next question will be, who are the Guardians. They are the source of life on this planet. You call them ET's. They are the Beings of Light who came from many constellations and Galaxies, who started life here on Lemuria."

Bunny looked pretty dumb-founded and a little disbelieving.

"Whoa," was all she said in answer to Bach's words.

"It's true Bunny. I haven't seen them but the merkids have. I didn't know if you'd believe me if I was the one to tell you that part."

"Holy crap Kat, this is getting to be a pretty wild adventure. Will we be seeing any Beings of Light while we're with you?" she asked.

Mu answered her,

"We don't know the answer to that question. We don't control them they come and go as they please. They are the Guardians and we are just their children. Anything is possible. They are often in the sky. Haven't you all seen them before?"

"No," Bunny told her "We've never seen any. We've read stories about them and other people sighting them. What are they like? What do they look like? How many times have you seen them? How do they communicate with you? I want to know everything you can tell me about them."

Mu chuckled a little more before she answered,

"We have seen them many times but not so much since the adults all started to die. They are kind and gentle people. Different in appearance from us as their bodies are less dense for their world. They don't have the vanity of beings on Earth and they are far more intelligent than any of us."

Cobra looked towards Bunny and said,

"They are here often. Maybe we'll listen for the sound of their call and if they choose, you might get to meet them at Uluru, once we leave the under world."

"HOLY CANOLIE" I can hardly believe this. You've all seen them. Did you talk with them? Can you understand them, do they speak English?"

Mu looked at Bunny like she was some kind of bug and told her,

"They are just like anyone else they just look, a little different. In your world there are Japanese, Chinese, Europeans, Africans, Spanish, Mexicans and you. In our world there's us, you from the upper world and the Guardians. Do you see any difference? To us there is none. We all look a little different on the outside that's all."

Bach stepped closer to Bunny and said,

"We are all Beings of Light. We all started from the same source and we will all return to the same source. It's in our fragile bodies that we become vane or stupid, successful or barbaric. On your world you have a saying don't you that says, "sister or brother from a different Mother? Try to think of it a little like that, we are all related and connected to each other on levels you may not understand yet."

Bunny looked at me and asked,

"Am I dreaming Kat? If I not, pinch me so I know this is really happening."

"Okay, but remember you asked me to do it." With those words I gave her a good strong pinch on the arm.

She responded with a loud "OUGH!!"

Cobra stood and walked away from the pools edge and said,

"If you all are done with your conference we better head out again. It's still a long way to Uluru."

So we began the journey once again, following Cobra even deeper into the cave and the underworld of Australia. After seeing the Barrier Reef with all it's colored corals and fishes it seemed strange to be in such a darkened inner world of rock and sand stone. As we walked on we started to come across more and more stalactites and stalagmites. It was quickly becoming a stranger and more wondrous world inside the cave. Once again I wished I had my camera to be taking pictures. How could anyone explain the detail and beauty of such wonders if you couldn't see them for yourself without a picture?

Bunny and I were taking in the exotic, strangeness of the cave. These were things we had never seen before. Some of the stalactites and stalagmites were small and some were incredibly large. It was becoming a little maze to walk around and through them. I couldn't help but think about some of them falling and what damage it would do if they hit one of us. I walked a lot more carefully after having that thought. It was right in the middle of all the sand stone and rock ice cycles that we came to a very narrow and scary looking pass over. There was another primitive art piece on the wall at this point. I tried to figure out what it could possibly mean. We were all trying to study the design when Cobra just started to walk out onto the narrow stone bridge towards the other side.

It was so narrow, I thought it was insane for anyone to try and cross over it. As I looked down it appeared to be bottomless. The idea of falling off into the abyss was one you couldn't help but think about as you were looking down. Cobra looked back at us. I think he could see the fear, on Bunny's face and mine. He had walked, turned and talked as if he was on flat ground. He casually called back to us,

"Just don't look down. You'll be all right. It's like a walk in the park, no big deal unless you make it one."

Easy for him to say this seemed to be his kind of environment. He was one of those all nature and easy as pie kind of guys. Gram and Mr. Mac would have called him a natural curtain climber. For him it just seemed to be a natural instinct and came with no real effort. For Bunny or me this would be a major ordeal to over come. I wasn't so sure I could pull this one off and Bunny was a little less athletic than me, I could just image what she must be thinking.

It was Mu who started to give out the instructions,

"Here we'll put one of you in between each of us and we'll all go together. You'll be okay, just do like Cobra said and don't look down."

Cobra turned and came back over to our side. What ever they did, they better not ask us to turn around once we got out there. I wasn't so sure this was going to end up the way we all wanted it to. Bunny and me might have to stay here and wait for them to all come back. They might have to go the rest of the way without us.

"I'm not so sure I can do that," was all, Bunny said as she looked down into that bottomless pit and then back up to the tiny little bridge of stone.

"Me either." I managed to spit out. The bridge seemed to go on forever. If I had to guess I would have said it was at least 30 feet across to the other side. I remembered all the movies where someone has to cross something like this. Usually they always made it but this wasn't the movies this was real life with at least two, really scared kids. Plus usually in those stories the people almost fall to their death or one or two people other than the main character fall and meet their end. So many scenes were playing out in my head.

"Plus, how do you know that narrow little bridge will hold all of us at the same time? It's pretty old and I'm not so sure it's that strong." I added. "You got any special tricks you can do to get us to the other side without having to walk across?"

Cobra was back on our side and he took my hand.

"Don't even think about it. You know where the stone is, just walk across feeling with your foot for the center of the bridge before you put your foot down completely to put your weight on. Don't look down and just follow me." He took off, pulling me slightly. I didn't budge.

"Oh come on Kat. This is easy. I'll even go backwards so you can look at me while we're crossing." He looked into my eyes and it was like something happened. I felt safe and all the worry seemed to melt away. This time when he pulled me to go with him I did. I didn't look down. I just did what he said and kept eye contact with him and with each step I found my balance before I put my full weight on my foot.

It seemed like it only took seconds and we were both on the other side. I made it and I was safe. Nothing bad or traumatic happened to either of us. As I looked back I could see the look of shock and disbelief on Bunny's face. I hoped that gave her more courage to make the trip over because she was next. Cobra went back and did the same with her. For him it must have been like herding sheep because somehow he got us to do just what he wanted with no more resistance. Maybe it was his hypnotic eyes. Had he mesmerized us somehow? Clearly one of us would have to ask him how he did that.

After Bach and Mu came across we continued on into another cave. I thought to myself, I hope there's another way out and we don't have to do that again. We walked for a long time before it started to open up again into another cavern area. I noticed the walls seemed a little lighter in color and as I was walking and looking up, I almost fell on my face. As I tried to catch my balance I looked down and back to see what I had tripped over. It looked like a branch or something sticking up out of the floor of the cavern. As my light shined that way and lighted a little more of the space I could tell it wasn't a stick or log.

Holy cow, it looked like some kind of skeleton. It was kind of half in the rock and half sticking up out of the rock. I could see a strange looking skull and what looked like a short arm and an extra long leg and maybe even part of a tail. The others had stopped to see what happened. When I started to trip and felt like I was falling, I let out a blood-curling scream. They probably all thought I had been attacked and in some way I sort of had been but it was, apparently by an old fossil.

Bach and Mu stood still as Cobra came to see what was going on.

"Oh, it's just the fossil remains of one of the first, big old roos. In the beginning they were much larger creatures. This one looks like he was at least 10-11 feet tall. You just tripped over his rib. Better watch your step a little better. There could be more here in this area."

"You mean Kangaroo?" Bunny asked. I thought they were more like 5 or 6 feet tall."

"In the beginning many things were larger than they are today. Many creatures didn't survive. The giant roos are all gone. This is one of them. This fossil and remains could easily be millions of years old."

As we turned and started to walk on we did see several more giant

Roo skeletons and fossilized bones. What a creature they must have been, I just couldn't imagine standing next to a ten-foot kangaroo. Bunny wondered out loud,

"I wonder if it was over crowding that forced their size down? What do you think Bach?"

"I believe it was one of the factors. The bigger the creature the more they had to eat and the larger supply of food it would take to keep them all alive. Smaller creatures of any species could survive on a lot less. These particular animals were victims of volcanic eruptions. They died unable to breath the toxic air. Australia was once part of Lemuria. It has the oldest fossils of walking vertebrates to leave the sea and be able to forage above the tide line on solid ground. It's also the place of the oldest dated rocks on earth. Even in your world they often say 'Australia is the land where time began.' Most don't realize that it was all part of Lemuria, there for they are correct.

Cobra was nodding in agreement with each new fact Bach talked about.

"In the Dreamtime, this world was all one land, just as we are all one. It was the Motherland of man and over millions and millions and millions and millions of years it torn apart and became the seven continents of today's world. The spirits have come and gone in many forms of land, plant and animal. For right now, we need to more on, there will be time later for more history lessons."

So we stopped all discussion and followed him once again deeper into the cavern and on to another smaller cave. It was a smaller cave but there was plenty of room to walk without having to duck or weave around things. We were seeing more fossils and some even had the skeleton remains still there imbedded in the rock. What a fascinating lesson in world history and evolution this place was proving to be. I had no idea how long we had been walking but it seemed like days to Bunny and me. Finally as we reached another small opening the others decided we should stop and eat a little fruit and have some water again.

Bunny and me ate in silence listening to Bach and Mu talk about what was happening back in Atlantis while we were gone. Bach and Sheba had mentally communicated. She told him the kids already had more of the first plant we returned with produced from the single original plant and they were anxious for us to return with the next plant. They had the botanical reproduction hydroponic dome set up and ready to go.

Bunny was almost humming she was so happy and excited.

"I feel like I'm vibrating. It's like a few times when I had too much caffeine from my soda. Was it this exciting for you when you made your first trip with them? Do you feel like that, this trip, or is it just me?"

I smiled when I answered her.

"I did feel like I was vibrating that first trip with them and its just as cool this time. It's pretty hard to separate the excitement from the vibrating. I think the hair on my arm is standing up most of the time but maybe that's a little fear. Mu said before that she felt a coming home vibration on Easter Island that she had never felt in Atlantis. Maybe you should ask her about how you're feeling. Maybe she could relate or talk to you more about it."

"I'm wondering how long we can be gone and not get in trouble when we get back home. How can you tell what time it is? How can you tell how long we've been gone? I feel like we've been walking for days. How long do you think it's been?" she asked me.

"I don't know the answer to any of those questions." I told her. "This is the third time I've gone with them and so far no one back home is aware of us being gone."

When it was time to move on again Bunny slipped up next to Mu to talk with her about how she was feeling. There I was bringing up the rear again. I'd have to see if there was any particular reason why I kept being the last person in line. I have to admit, it wasn't a position I really enjoyed or liked.

Again it seemed like we were walking for hours and hours, the cave stayed wide and easy to travel through. I appreciated that we didn't have to crawl or squeeze into any tight places and hoped it stayed that way. While I was thinking about my boredom with the all the walking I spotted what looked like a big patch or vein of fire opal in the wall of the cave.

"Did anybody else see this?" I asked out loud. They all stopped and looked back towards me.

"Oh wow." Bunny said as she stepped closer to me to inspect the opal.

We both put our hands on it and ran them over the stone. It was so beautiful. The colors were intense, blues, greens, reds and orange. Even in the light we had the fire of the opal blazed brightly. Never in my life had I seen anything like it. The vein or stone I saw embedded in the cave wall was at least 2 by 8 feet in size. It was so big I wasn't sure at first that it really was an opal. After we walked away from it, we saw other pieces even bigger. Now I was wishing I had a hammer and chisel so I could take a nice big piece home with me.

I could have stayed there and played with the opal for hours, just feeling and trying to experience it's energy and power. Once again I was wishing I had a camera. So many great things to be taking pictures of and me always without my camera. All this walking without Bunny to talk with almost had me talking to myself. My thoughts were all over the place.

I wanted to ask how much farther we had to go but I didn't want to seem like a whiner or some little kid. Clearly there were no buses here in the cave so there wouldn't be any way to get out of walking the rest of the way this time. Now was the time to give myself the pep talk about why we were here. How could I be part of such a noble search and journey and be bored or tired? With all the things we had already seen in the cave, how could I even think I was bored now?

I was thinking, maybe it was time to catch up with Bunny and Mu. Maybe Bach could bring up the rear. The idea alone made good sense to me. There should always be a guy in the back to take care of things. What ever those things might be.

Besides it wasn't my way to be quiet and I had walked in silence for a long time now and I needed to talk to somebody. I was sure it would help make the time and all this walking go by a lot faster. I just scurried by Bach and caught up with the girls and fell in right behind them.

"Hi." I said to let them know I was there. "How's it going up here?"

"Hey Kat." Bunny responded. "I'm glad you said I should talk with Mu. She totally understands how the vibrations feel and I think she sees even more things than you or I realize."

"I'm glad you could talk to her, especially if it makes you feel better about everything. I told you this was going to be an historical journey and adventure all at the same time. Don't you feel like some kind of astronaut exploring new worlds?" I asked her. "Until Mu told us about the under worlds and all the passageways that existed, we had no idea such places were here. Isn't this the most mind blowing experience ever?"

We made a shape turn as the cave almost did a 90-degree turn to the right. As we passed the shape turn and walked another mile or so, I could feel the temperature start to climb. My first thought was, "Oh

No!" I didn't want to end up in another pressure cooker like the one in Machu Picchu. As the first beads of sweat started to collect on my forehead I asked,

"Is anybody else starting to get hot?"

It was Cobra who answered my question.

"I think we're all feeling it Kat. There's some old volcanic activity in this area. Maybe that's where the heat is coming from. I don't think there's anything to worry about. In my dream we didn't have any problems getting to the end of our walk about. There's still plenty of fresh air so no worries."

I muttered to myself, "NO WORRIES!," easy for him to say. He wasn't there with us when we all just about died from the heat in the crystal chamber. It wasn't a memory you'd soon forget, or the triggers that started it. Being confined in a small area under ground and suddenly being hot and things getting hotter still, was a fear that I couldn't shake away right now. "What next?" was all I could think right now.

We probably hadn't walked another half mile when we entered another, opened cavernous area. There was a large hole up ahead of us and it didn't look like any way around it. The one little ledge I could see to the left didn't look 8 to 10 inches wide. Now what were we going to do? It looked like we'd have to turn back or try to find another way. This certainly looked impassable.

"No worries, we can get around." Cobra said to the group of us standing beside him.

"No worries?" I said, "how do you figure, we're going to get around that?" as I pointed to the open pit with the red glow coming up out of it.

Even Bunny spoke up,

"I can't see how we could get by on that tiny little ledge."

"Oh, so much drama girls. You don't see Mu and Bach worried do you? They know it's just a little mind over matter. There's plenty of room to work your way around, heck there's even a wall to lean against. This isn't like tight rope walking. You have to stop being afraid of everything and open your mind to all the things you can do. Don't limit yourselves so much. Calm down. I'm sure you'll start to see how easily it can be done. Do I have to demonstrate again?"

Both Bunny and me stepped a little closer so we could actually look over the side and down to the bubbling, boiling orange glowing lava, far below. It was a long way down. It had to be thousands of feet to the molten hot bottom. So if we tried this and slipped, not only would we fall to our death, we'd burn to a crisp as well. Heck maybe if we were lucky we'd die from the heat before the actual impact. This dying from the heat had a familiar ring to it. How was this happening again?

"All you have to do is but your back to the wall and without looking down just place your feet on the rim. Feel your way and move at your own speed. We won't rush you. We'll put one of you between each of us. This is no big deal girls so don't try to make it more than it is." Cobra made it all sound so easy like a walk in the park.

Mu was the first to actually move. She took me with one hand and Bunny with her other hand.

"Come on girls, we've got important business to get to."

The boys each took their place in the front and rear. They had us lined up and started to head towards the rim of the volcano chimney. Bunny looked over at me and said,

"I can't believe all the craziness you've dragged me into Kat. This better turn out okay or I'm going to haunt you on the other side and my Mom is never going to forgive you if this doesn't work out." She looked towards the rim as we moved in a little closer." I think I'm going have to close my eyes so tell me when it's over."

I felt the same way. Why did wanting to help our new friends have to turn into so many scary trials? I was beginning to think I was a coward at heart. Never in my young, short life have I had to do so many hair-raising, heart-stopping dangerous, physical challenges. Before this, the scariest thing I'd ever had to do was jump off the high diving board at the swimming pool at the local Fun Splash Park. Maybe I'd close my eyes too.

"It's okay if you want to close your eyes. That might make you feel safer. You'll be able to use your other sense of touch to feel your way with a lot less stress. Good idea." was Mu's reply to Bunny's remarks.

They kept to their word and didn't push us. We went slow and easy and I made sure to keep the heels of my feet tight again the wall of the cave. Mu held my wrist, which left my hand free to touch and feel the wall. I have to admit that made me feel a little safer I might have felt even safer if my hands had suction cups on them. I was leaning so hard into the wall with my whole body I thought you'd be able to see an impression I would leave behind me. We literally inched our way across and around the rim. I could feel the heat coming up from the chimney and the sweat was starting to drip and run down my forehead into my eyes. There was no way I was going to try and wipe the sweat away it could just sting my eyes when I opened them again on the other side. Right now I couldn't think about anything but getting to the other side without falling.

It was a good thing we weren't under water where everyone could hear all of our thoughts. I'm sure Bunny and me both thought a lot of things we'd rather keep to ourselves. Your fears really aren't something you want everybody to know about especially not all the gory little details of them.

It seemed like an eternity of feeling our way along the rock wall and ledge. I felt the rough sandstone under my hands and the smooth rippling form it seemed to have. I dragged my heels against the wall as I molded my butt, shoulders and head against it. I could feel the sweat dripping down my face and worried I might pee my pants from the fear of falling. Finally I heard Cobra say,

"See, that wasn't so bad, was it?"

I hadn't even realized we were off the rim of the chimney and back on more solid footing. After hearing his words I very cautiously opened my eyes to see if his words were true and we were safely on the other side. Now that it was over and we didn't fall to our deaths, maybe it wasn't that bad. Definitely didn't want to do it again and certainly hoped we wouldn't have to. I was half afraid to ask,

"Is there another way out after we get where we're going? We don't have to do that again do we?"

Cobra just looked our way and replied,

"What did I tell you girls? Don't be so afraid of everything. You're capable of so many things and you 're limiting yourselves too much."

I didn't consider that an answer to my question but it looked like it was all I was getting for now. Because Cobra turned and headed back into the cave away from the volcanic chimney we just passed.

"Come on. Lets go girls." Mu said as she turned to follow him. Bach stayed behind us as we turned and followed her. On we marched for hour after hour, nothing too exciting to look at. More sandstone and a few places of opal in matrix but nothing as large as what we had seen earlier. Then suddenly as I was thinking again how boring all this walking was getting we came to what looked like man made steps and stairs leading up. The lines were straight and at a perfect 90 degrees on the cuts. This definitely wasn't natural to the cave.

My first thoughts were would it be another city or town like in Peru? I was excited to see what we would find next but we just seemed to climb and climb the stairs just kept weaving around, then up and down again. It was beginning to remind me of a time when I got to climb up inside the Statue of Liberty in New York. I didn't think those stairs were ever going to end either.

There was a mist of falling water. I don't know if I would have called it rain or not but it seemed odd to be underground like this and have water pouring down like rain. Finally at one point, as we climbed even higher up the stairs I looked to the open side away from the wall, I could see what I thought was a waterfall cascading down into a giant open hole.

I haven't noticed the hole before. The water from the falls had been making something of a shower over there hiding the hole from sight. Otherwise I would have been more careful climbing. I had the thought, I've never seen it rain underground before. Now the waterfall explained it but I had also never seen a waterfall underground before either. Heck, before our trip to Peru, I had never been underground to know what was normal or unusual. Bunny and me were talking about all the water making it feel a little cooler as we climbed all the stairs. After the heat from the volcanic chimney and all these stairs the mist was really sort of refreshing. An escalator would have been nice but I guess that was too advanced for the guys who made these stairs..

I noticed high above what looked like tiny stars in the sky and asked,

"What's that? It looks like the stars shinning in the night sky?"

Cobar was the one who answered.

"Those are glow worms. They do sort of look like stars in the sky don't they. They are just part of cave life in this part of the world."

As suddenly as the stairs appeared, they disappeared. We were back in what seemed like the old cave once more. I found myself wondering again where in the world could we be? Were we half way there? Oh I really hoped it was more than half way. My feet were starting to hurt. Next time I go somewhere with the kids I'm wearing better shoes. Maybe next time there would be a bus again. Knowing them, I sort of doubted it they had all these under world passageways and sinkholes they liked to use. Not too many bus depots there.

Cobra and Bach decided it was time to stop, have something to eat, a little rest and water then we'd push on again. As I looked down at my watch, the waterproof one I had worn this time, only an hour had passed since we left home. Holy cow that created thoughts that really played with my brain. An hour, I felt like I had been swimming and walking, for at least a week. No wonder we weren't sleepy yet. I was sore and tired. It made me wonder if bending time affected your muscles.

The fruit and water tasted so good. We had apples this time for our snack. They were crisp and juicy, only thing missing was the saltshaker I liked to use with a fresh apple. The three best things to put salt on for me were apples, tomatoes and cucumbers and they were the best right off the tree or plant. You didn't even care if the juices ran down your chin. It was good and that's all that mattered. It was a living in the moment kind of thing, enjoying food. A lot of people had lost the art of enjoying taste and smell but not me.

Break time was over too fast and they were saying we had to move on. Bunny had been talking a mile a minute. She had asked Cobra a couple dozen questions about the volcanic activity in the area, the chimney we had just passed by, the artwork we had seen and the way he mesmerized us into crossing the narrow, stone bridge beam earlier. Cobra seemed entertained by Bunny's questions and was busy answering each one. He told her he hadn't mesmerized us he'd just made a visional soul connection with us. He told her it was an Aborigine thing. It was always fun for me to be around Bunny because she was the one person who asked more questions than I did. It made me seem a little less chatty which didn't happen often for me.

So we were walking again. The fruit had been good and I thought I was ready for whatever walking was left to do but I didn't say anything about it out loud. I didn't want to put my foot in my mouth, just in case they had more surprises up ahead of us. This was one of those times I was taking Bach's advice and just being quiet.

We'd only been walking a few hours again when we started seeing amethyst in matrix along the walls of the cave. It had started with small clutters of spikes and they started getting larger and closer together. Some of it was very dark and some was very light in color. I love amethyst it's my birthstone. So I was very drawn to it each time I saw more of it. I was touching at least half of everything I was seeing especially the bigger pieces. Bunny, was a few steps ahead of me when I heard her say,

"WHOA!! Look at this Kat."

I hurried to her side to see what had grabbed her attention. It was like looking into the world's largest geode. The amethyst was everywhere, up over our heads, to the left, the right and in front of us. There was no path or walkway between the spikes and spears of the huge amethyst. Everyone was looking ahead, trying to assess how to maneuver the purple, crystal maze of spears. It looked as slick as glass and some of the spears and spikes looked pretty shape as well. This could be a very dangerous crossing and this didn't look like one we could hold hands to get through. At first thought, it made me think about going to a Mc Donald's and working my way through the play land jungle gym. Maybe it wouldn't so dangerous. For a change I had the idea to attack it just like the play land equipment. Start here, slide down over there, climb around this then that, try to craw over this and then scoot over that.

"Here, I think this time I have the right idea." I said as I worked my way past them all and started to climb into the amethyst wonderland.

'Where do you think the exit is at Bach? What's the right direction to aim for?"

As soon as I saw the direction and destination he was pointing to I headed that way.

"Come on Bunny, let's show them how it's done. It'll be just like the old days at Mc Donald's. Follow me. Let's go."

Bunny was right behind me and the others followed her. We zig-zagged this way and that. Now I was glad I had rubber shoe soles, they didn't slip or slide on the amethyst surface. It was like polished glass the spears were so big I could actually hug them as I tried to work around some of the bigger pieces. No body knew if there would be a way out on the other side. We were going by what Bach had read on the area. He'd always been right so far so I was trusting he knew what he was saying now.

I just kept looking for the easiest way and if I had to go back a little to get ahead again, it didn't matter. It was like playing a game. We were making progress and would reach our goal soon. The amethyst was so beautiful I would have given anything to be able to take some of it home with me. This was a reoccurring theme for me. I wished I could have some of everything we were seeing and exploring.

I was very excited being the leader for a change. I wondered how that had actually happened? What had I been thinking to take the lead away from Cobra and Bach? No one seemed at the time to be coming up with a plan. My brain just clicked and I was taking over. I wondered maybe there had been something in the water we drank during our break because something kind of took over inside me. It was thrilling to be leading the way and knowing what to do next. It took a little time to work our way across the enormous geode. A picture of this would be worth a million words. I wasn't sure a million words could even begin to describe this to anyone who hadn't seen it!

I loved the leadership role I had and didn't want it to end. We were reaching the other side and a little of my joy was slipping away. First I loved this amethyst and second I finally was able to show our new friends I wasn't a worthless member of the team and third I wasn't afraid of everything. It was like the stone, this high, energy crystal amethyst was calming me and guiding me in ways I could have never guessed were possible. I always heard the amethyst had the ability to build inner strength as well as open the third eye and enhance intuition. Maybe that's what happened. I didn't really want to leave this place but I could see the opening on the other side now. My fun was quickly coming to an end but that was a good thing for all of us. We had mastered another obstacle and could continue on our search.

"WOW was that as cool for you as it was for me Kat?" Bunny asked as we exited the monster geode.

"Oh yeah. Could you imagine having a headboard for your bed made from some of those Amethyst spears and spikes? I'd sleep and be so calm all the time. That was actually very relaxing for me nothing like the stress from having to cross the volcanic chimney. I can say I feel like I've gotten a new lease on relaxed energy. I'm feeling very calm and relaxed. How about you? Did the rest of you feel the energy of the amethyst?"

Mu was the first to answer,

"Of course we felt the power of the purple crystals. Why are you two so amazed to feel it? There are no elements of earth and this universe that don't have a power and energy that can influence us. We've talked about vibrations and the energy that everything has. Amethyst is a healing, calming vibration of a high psychic level. That is why you see the purple color; the crystal is reflecting the light, turning the vibration into a color."

Bach joined in and gave us his reading of the geode,

"Earth started from a spark, an egg of sorts. We just passed through that egg. It was Earths origin the energy and vibration of it's beginning. Consider it like the gut, the place where your intuition comes from. The planet has grown around it, protecting it and hiding it from harm. What a privilege to experience the power of the Mother seed."

"Can you believe that, the Mother seed of Earth? I would imagine the energy and power of something like that could change you for the rest of your life." I felt the words leave my mouth but I hadn't thought about it before I said it.

"You have been on a journey. It's one many have made in the distance past. You didn't recognize you were retracing your steps from that long ago time?" Cobar asked us.

"Are you talking to me or Bunny?" I asked him "Or are you talking to Mu and Bach?" I was so stunned by his words. He must be talking to Mu and Bach. They were the ones with so much history and the ones who had roots back to the beginning of time.

"I'm talking to all of you. Don't you recognize your brothers and sisters?" He answered me.

Was he talking in riddles now? Maybe he smoked too much waiting for us in the cave last night. He was definitely on something because he was talking pretty wacky.

"Are you saying that the five of us have all made this journey before? Some other lifetime back in the beginning of the world?" Bunny asked.

"Yes, you didn't know that's why you are the ones here at this time? I didn't understand that you were all lost to the truth and true purpose of this journey. The didgeridoo's didn't tell me you were unaware of your true mission and the reason for your walkabout. I didn't know I was to be more than just your guide for this search."

"Wait a minute," Bunny said "You're saying we're not here so much to find the plant the merkids need as to make some special journey we've made before?"

"Yeah, you got it." Cobra answered her.

"So fill us in, what's the purpose of this special journey or walkabout you're taking us on?" she threw back at him.

"Hey, don't get your shorts in an uproar at me. I'm just saying there's more to your walkabout than you seem to realize yet. This is a cleansing, soul awakening, Dreamtime, Australian walkabout. You're repeating the ritual. There was an accession from the physical back into the spirit through the dimensions of heaven. I only know what the didgeridoos told me. They didn't fill me in on all the facts."

Mu spoke up,

"I've felt it. I don't understand it yet but I've known since we were on Easter Island that something was happening. I feel different. I can't exactly explain it all yet but I know I have a purpose and it's a soul search. I guess I thought it was our search to find the sacred plants and save the rest of the kids and ultimately the Guardians. I just keep thinking it's a coming home vibration that I'm feeling. Does that have something to do with it Cobra?" She asked him.

"Hey, I told you, I don't have all the answers. I just know you've been together before and you have an even bigger journey you're on as you hunt down the plants you need for your people. It's more of a family or tribal gathering. They said there's power in your numbers."

Bunny looked at me and asked,

"Are you hearing all this? What do you think about what they're saying Kat?"

"I don't know what to make of it Bunny. They're blowing my mind again. Which has happened a lot since I met these guys. I just know one thing. I believe anything they say is possible."

"So you think it was fate that had Becka going to the doctors so I'd come this time? What would be the purpose of me being here in Australia? What past life or metaphysical things could need me and you here now, doing what ever it is we're doing?" she asked me.

"I don't know Bunny. Maybe we should ask Bach if he can figure it out."

"It's not that easy Kat." Bach said, "I can read energy and I can read a place but I can't read things about myself and the past."

"Come on, we can talk later. There's still a distance to go and we need to move on." Cobra prodded us. So we tabled the discussion for now and followed him once again further into the cave and the heart of Australia. We knew we were headed to Uluru but had no idea if we were there or even close yet. We did know what the plant was we were looking for. Now we would wonder as we walked, what was this other search for? Were we looking to find our souls? Would we uncover the truth about the beginning of time? Or would this be a coming home of our souls? I was totally lost in thoughts of what ifs.

As I walked I was racking my brain, what could be the bigger picture here? What was Cobar talking about? Was there some strange destiny that I had, not just with the merkids but with the kids back home too? Was Cobar part of it too? How was it going to come together and for what ultimate purpose? I was never good with games. How was I going to figure out this mystery? Maybe Bunny was thinking and would come up with something.

We must have walked another few miles when we entered a large chamber. I wouldn't have called this a cavern. It did look natural but it wasn't like any other place we'd been in so far. Cobar stood in the center of the chamber and looked around. There were three large cavities in the wall with ancient artwork. Some of the figures looked like space men or ET's. Other than the artwork, all I could see was stone. There were several rays of light coming in from over head: we must be close to the top of Uluru. I could smell the fresher air coming through the holes and was able to take off my beam crystal because of the sunrays pouring in. I could also feel a little more of the outside temperature.

"The spirits told me this was the place." were the only words out of his mouth as he looked around the chamber again.

"There's nothing here Cobar. Are you sure they said here? Maybe they meant on the top of the mountain and you misunderstood. There's nothing growing here. Its just sandstone nothing could grow here." Bunny said to him as she sat down and leaned back against the wall of the chamber.

It was Mu who started to look at the walls a little more closely and said,

"There must be something here. If this is where the spirits said the plant would be then it must be here we just have to find it. Everyone should be looking."

Bach stood next to Cobra in the center of the chamber and said,

"Give me a couple minutes to read the area. Maybe I can pick up which direction is right. We'll find the plant if it's here. Spirit is never wrong but it can be a little off from time to time. They're in another dimension and their time and space is different than ours."

We all stood or sat still to give Bach some time and silence to do his magic except Cobra. He kept looking around, covering every inch of the chamber with his eyes. Mu watched him as he moved slowly across the wall then she started to run her hands across the floor of the area around her feet.

Bunny looked at me and asked,

"Could the plants be so small that we'd have to search with a magnifying glass?"

"I suppose it could be something really small like mosses but I didn't think from the picture it looked any different than a regular sized plant. Nobody said all the pictures were the same size so I guess its possible." I answered her.

"Nothing I read when I found the plant said it was small or an unusual size. Maybe this just isn't the right place." she added.

Bach spoke next,

"The plant has changed with the changing world it's been growing in. Millions of years can make a big difference in a species. The plant we seek is here. I suggest we look in the holes overhead. There is probably more moisture there and it's the best source of the sunshine it needs to keep growing."

We all looked up. Now how were we supposed to get that high to be able to look for anything? I saw Mu look from the holes overhead to each of us and then back to Cobra.

"Cobar, you and Bach are the tallest of us. Maybe if one of you helps to lift the other. Maybe if one of you could stand on the others shoulders, you would have enough height to see into the openings of the holes."

Cobar looked up and then looked at Bach and back to the holes.

"You might be right Mu. Here Bach, I'll lift you to my shoulders and you see what you can see."

For a couple minutes it was almost comical to watch the two of them trying to get Bach upright on Cobar's shoulders and stay balanced long enough to even get close to the ceiling and the first hole. Eventually they managed to do it and Bach was inspecting the first hole. Nothing was there but sandstone and dust. They were getting better with the balancing act and managed to check a second and third hole.

They took a short break as Bach had lost his balance. Once he was back up on Cobar's shoulders they made it to the fourth, fifth, sixth and finally the seventh hole.

Bach said something I couldn't understand but it made us all look up. He had found something. It was a good thing the ceiling wasn't any higher or Bach wouldn't have been able to see anything.

He had found a small patch of the mossy little lichen we were looking for. This one hadn't been so hard and I didn't have to risk my life finding it either. I was enjoying this. It made me think about the next five plants we still needed to find. I was hoping the kids were having some luck with their searching while we were here.

While Bach gathered the small little plant and got it ready to take back with us we were exploring the chamber we were in and the artwork on the walls. I was trying to make a mental picture of all of it. Maybe I could go home and make a copy of it from memory. I really wanted to remember this and add it to my journal.

I decided when I wrote in my regular journal about that first day at the beach when we met the kids that I should have a second journal of just my time and experiences with them. If only I had my camera. The thought went through my head, 'maybe I could get a water proof camera to bring with me and try to keep it tucked away in my food pouch for extra protection.' Pictures of the things I was seeing would be incredible to have even if I could only share them with a couple people or just to keep for myself. It just wasn't fair seeing so much history and not being able to record or preserve it in pictures. No photo nut would think otherwise.

As Bach was finishing up his final preparations for the return trip with the little specimen he had collected. We started to think and talk about the way out.

"Cobra, did the spirits tell you another way out or do we have to go back the way we came?' Bunny asked. "I see other caves or tunnels leaving here. I'm hoping we don't have to do the chimney and stone bridge walks again. Please tell me there's another way out that's easier."

"You two are very entertaining just listening to you gives me a good laugh. You will be happy to know, there is another way out that we're taking. It should prove to be less weary for you and a lot faster. If Bach is ready, lets go."

"Ready" Bach said as we stood and placed his treasured package around his body. The pouch he carried the plant in was something like a money belt. And apparently water tight like our food pouches.

"It's this way." Cobar said as he headed down another cave away from the chamber. The rest of us followed and as we left Bunny reached down to pick up something off the cave floor. She gave it a quick look and tucked it on her pocket.

I didn't really see what it was but it looked like a long cord or string maybe.

"What did ya pick up Bunny?" I asked.

"I'm not sure but I thought I'd take it and check it out later. Maybe it's some old artifact. When we get back out in the day light we'll see what it looks like."

We hadn't walked very far when we came to a slightly enlarged area and Cobar stopped.

"Okay mates, here's where the fun begins. This should be something like a water slide and it's the quickest way out. Might get your butts wet but it beats walking and climbing out. Just follow me." With those last words he just slipped into an opening where the water seemed to be running down and was gone.

I looked at Bunny and then the others. Just like that he left us and took off. I thought I'd want to have a closer look at what was ahead of us. Who wants to just hop into a hole and trust everything would be okay? Not me. I wanted a closer look but before I could get closer Mu jumped in just the way Cobar had and yelled back at us,

"You better huurrrrrrrrrry!" as she slipped out of sight.

"Come on girls, don't be afraid. I can tell it will be okay. Trust us. Wait just a minute and then one of you follow Mu and then another minute the other will have to go and I'll wait and be the last to come down."

"You go next Bunny. It's a leap of faith but you've got to do it and then I'll come after you." I told her.

"It's okay Kat, I'm not afraid. This is getting exciting. Makes you wonder what's going to be around the next corner doesn't it?"

Bach motioned for her to go and she did. Then it was just the two of us. I guessed I could handle it. I hadn't heard any blood curdling screams coming back at us. It did sort of make me think and feel like Alice in the story of Alice in Wonderland, going down the rabbit hole. Who knew what we would find next. I was really hoping it wouldn't be the Queen of Hearts and the rest of that group. I mean I'd already been down another hole with these people and it had a few ups and downs but turned out okay. I would just have to hope for the best.

"Your turn Kat." was all he said. I was already to go and just pushed myself away from the opening and the top of the tunnel opening. My butt did get wet. That was the first thing as I watched the walls whizzing by. It was just like a slide at one of those water fun places we'd visit in the summer, nothing to be afraid of here. Now I'd just pray it didn't get me going too fast. I wanted to scream as I got going faster instead I tried to tell myself this was easier than all those stairs again. Plus it was a lot more refreshing with the water to keep you cool. It seemed like the cave tunnel went around and around but not so fast as to get dizzy from it. I kept wondering when it was going to end, the ride just seemed to keep going and going and going. Heck by now we should be back down to sea level. Suddenly I was back in an open cavern and I could see the others waiting off to the side for us. I slowed down as the rock leveled off and the water didn't run as deep. Wow, that was some ride. Bach seemed to come out almost right behind me and we joined the others.

"That was some ride, wasn't it? Still a little ways to go so follow me." Cobra said and turned to work his way through some stalagmites to our right.

It didn't take long to dry off. Bunny and me walked and talked a little about the ride down as we followed the others. Soon you could see more daylight up ahead. We must be close to the end of the cave. The only sad thing, as we got closer to the light and the opening, it started to get a lot hotter.

As we stepped out into the opening we had to shield our eyes from the intense sunlight and the feeling of heat was so heavy it could almost knock you down.

"Welcome to Australia mates!" was all Cobar said as Bunny and I started to complain about the heat.

"Holy cow, is it hot like this all the time?" Bunny asked.

He chuckled to himself as he said,

"You'll get use to it. It's really not that bad. Besides the heat will help keep you mind off the salties and freshies"

"Salties and freshies? What do you mean? You mean crocodiles?" Bunny asked. "I read all about them when I was searching for the plant. I thought they were more around the rivers and low lands. We don't have to worry about them here near Uluru do we?"

"It won't be long and we'll be in the low lands. We'll be going through the Northern territory maybe even a little of the Kimberly but we'll be going through crock country. There's no other way to get back to the coast."

As we stepped totally out into the open the heat started to make us swizzle. We put our hands up to help block the sun from our eyes as we surveyed the country in front of us. OMG this was going to be next to impossible. At least in Peru we didn't have to walk through the dessert. I wasn't sure how we would all survive this walkabout. Before there was too much time to thin about it Cobar took off and we all just followed once again.

There wasn't too much to look at. This land was dry and didn't have a lot growing on it. I watched Cobar as he walked bare footed. I don't know how he was able to do it, as the ground was rocky and rough. I'm also sure it probably carried a lot of heat from the sun just baking down on it. I know I couldn't have done it without my shoes. It certainly said something about the toughness of these people and the environment they had to deal with everyday. I also noticed he wasn't wearing sunscreen. Or maybe that's what all that white dirt and dust was all over his body, sort of a natural sunscreen. I couldn't tell you if he is dark from having a tan or not but Bunny and me would be as red as a lobsters if we had to be out here very long. Nobody suggested we bring any sunscreen for the trip. I guess it's not something kids think about until it's too late. If Bunny and me go home today with sunburns, they might start asking us a lot of questions.

It was almost as if Cobar could read my thoughts because he stopped and suggested,

"I think we best be covering you all up a little so you don't end up with a bad sunbake. Here, watch me and do the same." He reached down and took hands full of dirt and started to pour it over his exposed skin. The sand and dirt was creating a cloud of dust all around him. We each did the same thing hopping it would prove to be worthwhile in the end. It probably would have been funny to have watched us as we coughed and chocked but kept on pouring more dirt and dust all over ourselves.

We walked and walked and walked some more. The sun beating down so unmercifully didn't make it easy. The sweat was running down from my forehead, my back my arms and my legs. In fact I don't think there was an inch of me that wasn't sweating. The water was dripping out of me way too fast. Our water pouches would be empty again soon. None of us was exempt except Cobar who seemed to not sweat or need water at all. What a tough individual he was.

Finally the sun began to set and Cobar said we should stop and camp for the night. We'd need our rest tomorrow would be another long day of hiking through the outback. There wasn't any shelter to find in this country for the night. We'd have to sleep out in the open and I wasn't too sure how that was going to go. What creatures might there be hunting and looking for a warm place to sleep as well? I could just imagine waking in the morning to find some snake or crock curled up next to us. That was a scary thought. Maybe I should ask what sort of animals we could expect to be seeing while in this area. Or maybe it would be better not to know. I decided to trust Cobar and let him take care of our well being for the night.

He made a small campfire after collecting a few twigs and branches, from where I don't know. I didn't see any of it as we were walking earlier. As the darkness over took the sky we laid on the ground, tired and weary from the day of hiking in all the heat and baking sun. Off in the distance we could hear a strange sound. I asked,

"Cobar is that a didgeridoo?"

"Aye, that's what it is." He answered.

"Do you understand what they are saying?" Bunny asked.

"They're speaking to the spirits asking for the rain to come."

"It's such an interesting sound." Bunny added.

For a few minutes we were all lost in though, listening to the didgeridoos in the distance. As we listened, we had a little fruit from our pouches and shared some with our new friend. Each of us was careful to only drink a little of our water. We were lying quietly around our little campfire I believe we were too tired for anything more. Soon the heat and work out of the day pushed us all into a deep sleep.

Cobar was waking us while it was still dark. The first rays of the sun hadn't come over the horizon yet.

"Better we get our start while the sun sleeps. It'll be easier for the four of you if we start now. It's going to be a long day and there is a long distance to go. Wake up and take care of your needs so we can leave soon."

"Is it still night?" Bunny asked as she opened her eyes and started to look around the camp.

I stretched and tried to wake up. My eyes still felt heavy from sleep. I was surprised after having slept on the hard ground how rested my body felt. It would only take my eyes a minute to catch up with the rest of me. Once they were open and focused the first thing I did was check for any sleeping partners near me. Luckily there were none. I hadn't heard a sound or woken even once during our rest. I had slept very well.

We had a quick snack of fruit, dates this time and a little water before we were off. The walking before sunrise was a lot easier than it was later as the sun rose high in the sky overhead. We talked a little but tried not to use any more energy than necessary. Today we had to make our water last and talking would use more energy and would take more water. The scenery was beautiful and different from what we were use to seeing back home. What a wild and wonderful country Australia is.

Cobar was always up ahead of us leading the way. He seemed to know exactly where we were and where he wanted to take us.

"How do you know the way so well Cobar?" Bunny asked him.

"I follow the song lines. There's an energy there and it makes a trail that's easy to read when you know the words to the songs." He answered her.

"Where do the song lines come from?" I asked.

"They are from the Dreamtime like rivers of spirit. They have been here from the beginning of time. If you open yourself you should be able to feel them too. Think of nothing else and feel the energy direct you." He answered.

Bunny and I both started to look around and try to feel the lines sing. It didn't take long and we both decided it wasn't working for us. Maybe we were too tired or too hot and sweaty to read or feel anything. It was hard to keep putting your feet in front of each other, this walking and trekking across Australia wasn't easy. It seemed like days of walking and we still hadn't gone that far. I kept hoping to see the coastline up ahead of us.

Finally we started to see a few trees. They were every strange looking and different from our trees back home. Cobar explained they were called Boabs and were a member of the bottle tree family. They had huge tall, fat trunks or bodies and some branches at the top growing in a small cluster. Once again I wish I had a camera for pictures. They were interesting and made me think of trees with their hands in the air with their fingers all separated or maybe a giant cucumber with a feather head piece on like the Indians use to wear. The branches looked more like tentacles or maybe some kind of ameba from a science class I took last year.

Cobar told us the when the trees were young they had very tasty, edible roots, something like sweet carrots. Also in the old days some of the trees had even been used as prisons and had iron gates on them. That seemed a really strange idea but he said they were handy and kept the people from having to build a structure to put the prisoners in. He said the trees could hold up to 100,000 liters of water during rainy season. Also there was a nut that grew on the tree as well as flowers that bloomed on them too. I felt better just seeing trees again. I was hopeful it meant we were closer to the shoreline.

It felt like days were passing and all we were doing was walking. Cobar never seemed to grow tired. He ate and drank very little. Bunny asked him once if he did so in order to be more spiritual and clear in his energy. He told her he ate when he needed food and did the same with water that neither men nor women really didn't need too much. He believed it was good not to over do with either food or drink, it was the Aborigine's way.

"It's how I keep my sexy, muscular physic." He told her and chuckled to him self a little.

The landscape started to change finally and there was something besides just arid scenery. The land started to have a little roll to it and we saw a few more trees. Some of the sloping areas looked as if water had been there at sometime. Cobar explained they were called Billabongs. There were areas where water collected in rainy season or parts of rivers and streams that created dead ends and small lakes. He said they would be full of freshies if it were rainy season. The salties would be closer to the coast where the salt water and origin of their names came from. They were all crocks just different by the fresh or salt water they lived in.

That wasn't too fun to hear about now I'd have to have both eyes open and be on the look out for crocks. What would be next? I could remember the movie Crocodile Dundee and the narrow escape the lady news reporter made when a crock lunged out of the water and almost got her. She had to be saved from the jaws of death by the hero of the story, the famous Crocodile Dundee. Hopefully nothing like that would happen to any of us. Cobar didn't have any knife or gun to save us with if it did happen and although he talked and joked about his muscular physic he didn't look strong enough to me, to tame a crock with just his bare hands.

We did finally stop to take a break. Cobar said usually he'd travel by night but figured with us along he's have to change his ways and switch to a routine that would work for us. Rest and breaks wasn't something he was use to doing. If you traveled by night you could use the stars to find your way and beat a lot of the heat. Aboriginal people understood that in the darkness the mind and eyes worked together in a different way. He added that modern man depends too much on his physical senses.

We didn't break for long before he was up and ready to go again. Bunny and me looked like worn out, wet rag dolls. Bunny even wondered out loud if this was ever going to come to an end. The endless walking and the heat, not to mention the flies and other little swarming bugs that constantly were attaching us, was almost more than we could bare. I will admit the dirt we put all over our exposed skin did seem to help with sunburn. With the sweating we did have to keep reapplying and soon we looked like Cobar with a layer of mud caked on us. Now I understood why the natives always looked so dusty in Australia.

Surprisingly as we came up over a little rise we saw water. Not the Ocean unfortunately but I guess it was some sort of pond or small lake. I didn't know if it qualified as a billabong as it wasn't rainy season yet. My first thought was to look for crocks and be on the alert. Cobar said it was fresh water and we could drink and fill our water pouches back up. He walked ahead of us and checked things out before the rest of us approached the waters edge. Bach checked on the plant specimen he was carrying and added some water to it as well while we enjoyed the water. It felt great to splash it up onto our faces and arms. No one cared about being wet or dirty because for a few minutes we felt a little cooled off and slightly refreshed. It definitely wasn't cold water but it wasn't hot and it was wet and our skin soaked it up like we were sponges.

After relaxing there for just a short while when we all had our fill of water to drink and filled our pouches, Cobar was up and ready to go again. Where did this guy find his energy? We all felt baked and roasted even the merkids weren't use to the climate or elements we found ourselves in. We could only hope we were getting closer to the coastline and the swim back to Atlantis. I was getting dazed just thinking about the water and the cooling affects it would have on my skin and the end of all this walking and trekking through such an arid place. Just thinking of it helped to take me away from the heat for just a few minutes.

This place seemed endless. No matter how far we walked it was like we were walking in circles never getting anywhere. I wondered to myself if that was what was happening? Maybe Cobar didn't know where he was going and we would never get back to the coast. Maybe he was following the wrong dream or song line because this was beginning to feel like some kind of nightmare. I wondered if the heat didn't end soon if the four of us would make it.

After going for what seemed like days again the sun finally started to come down towards the horizon and it was cooling down a couple degrees. Soon it would be dark and we would rest again for a few hours. There was hope we would survive the day. I could see an end in sight and it gave me a little renewed energy. Cobar seemed to be watching for a place to make camp. He finally said,

"Just a little farther ahead. I see a good place where we can get water again."

I liked the sound of that. Maybe we could drink and get more water for tomorrow. Then if we were lucky actually take a dip, soak and float for a while. Even if it was only 10 or 12 inches deep I could really use a chance to cool down. I hoped it was enough water we could do that even if we had to take turns. As we got a little closer we could all see what Cobar was talking about, to me it looked like a regular oasis just like in the movies, when the half dead travelers can't go on any further there it is, the oasis that saves them.

It turned out to be deeper than the 10-12 inches I was dreaming about. The oasis or billabong which ever it was had a good three to four feet of depth to it. This was a regular paradise after all that desolated countryside we had been trekking through. I was ready to dive in and never get back out.

First we all drank and filled our water pouches then we talked about how we would enjoy this little pond. It would feel so good to get all the sand, grit and dirt off my body and feel clean again. We decided the girls would all go first and we'd bathe as best we could under the circumstances, relax and maybe even wash our clothes off a little before the boys got their turn. It sort of reminded me of when I was little at my grandmother's house. She'd bathe all the youngest kids first and add water to the tub as they got out and the older kids got in. There was at least five or six of us at her house sometimes and she usually popped two or three of us at a time into the tub. She was definitely a water conservationist.

I can't even begin to describe how good the water felt against my skin as I submerged my entire body under the surface. The three of us girls had stripped down to our underwear and slowly walked into the pond. Once we were in to the deepest part I just went under head and all. I didn't realize how gritty my hair and scalp had gotten. It felt like I hadn't washed my head in months as I ran my finger through my hair trying to loosen the dirt. We laughed and splashed each other and actually had a little fun. It was the best I had felt since we left the coast and started this little adventure.

Bunny and I finally grew tired of all the splashing and stepped back out of the pond. We sat near the edge to try to dry off before we put our clothes back on. Surprisingly they were barely damp now. Once we had washed and laid them out to dry the heat had done a good job of drying them. It wouldn't be the same as putting on clean clothes but they were cleaner than they had been and that was great for now. I wondered what it would really matter because tomorrow we'd be pouring the dirt back on trying not to get "sunbaked" as Cobar called it. But for tonight it would feel good to sleep in clothes that felt a little cleaner and softer without all the dirt encrusted on them.

Mu was still in the water. Her tail was back and she seemed to be relaxing and soaking in the water almost as if she needed it more than we did. The boys didn't seem too anxious to get their turn in the water so we just took our time and decided to wait for Mu. Wanting to stay more refreshed we sat at the waters edge with our legs stretched out into it while we talked. Bunny reached into her pocket and pulled out the thing she had picked up in the cave chamber where we found our plant.

"Look, I almost forgot about this. Lets see what we think it is." She said as she pulled it out of her pants pocket and dangled the thing off her right hand. It was some kind of leather cord I think and it had some small shells knotted on the ends. There were some beads or something else there too. Bunny dripped it into the water to wash the dirt off of it.

"Wow, look at these. Don't they look like rubies and emeralds? These might even be opal." She said as we both inspected it.

"I think you might be right Bunny. The beads definitely look like gem stones. I wonder how old this thing is? I wonder if Bach could read it for you and tell us what it is or was." I said.

"Yeah, lets go ask him what he can read off of it. I wonder how old it is and who it belonged to."

The boys were only sitting about 20 feet away from us so we gathered our things and walked over to see what Bach could tell us. Bunny was holding her treasure in her hand as we walked up to them and she dangled it in front of Bach asking him if he could read it for her. He took it in his hand and closed his palm over it as he closed his eyes and tried to get a reading on it.

"This was a head strap of some sort worn by one of the sisters. She lived during the time of the Dreamtime and beginning of man on earth. She lived a very simple spiritual life and visited the chamber often. This strap was her personal jewelry and was made by her own hands. It has been there in the ascension chamber since her departure millions of years ago." He opened his eyes and lifted his hand to give her back the piece. "You should be happy to get this back."

"No, no, no let me go!! HELP SOMEBODY PLEASE HELP ME!"

It was Mu screaming for help. Bunny and me turned and ran towards the water as the boys both rose and followed us. We got there first. We stopped at the waters edge but I couldn't tell what was happening. I didn't even see Mu. The water was splashing and churning but we didn't see her.

Then suddenly there she was. She was trying to get away from something or someone. Then I saw it. It was a crock and it was a big one. It had Mu by her tail and was trying to take her under again. Both the boys ran into the water to help her. They were able to grab her arms and began to pull her and the crock towards land. It looked like they were making progress and then they'd slip back into the deeper water. It was a battle that kept going forward and then back. It looked like a game of tug of war and the crock seemed to be winning.

Mu was still yelling and screaming. The crock wasn't letting go or giving up the fight either. That old crock flipped and twisted its body thrashing around making the water look like a boiling pot. The boys were having a hard time trying to hold onto Mu. She almost slipped from their hands a couple times. They were slipping and falling into the water but they never let go of her.

It seemed like the battle raged on for a long time before Bunny and I finally found the courage to jump in to help. It wasn't easy to make that move. We were both scared to death but we were afraid our friend Mu was going to die if we didn't get in and at least try to help the boys save her. With the little extra help we were able to give, we got her closer to dry ground and out of the water where the old crock couldn't flip and twist so much. Just as we had Mu about half way on land she let out a blood curdling scream and suddenly we were all falling backwards to the ground.

The fall backwards knocked the breath out of all of us. We looked to see what had happened. The crock was gone and out of sight. The water was still and motionless again. Mu was crying and as we pulled her the rest of the way out of the water we could she her tail had a big piece missing. Some of her scales were gone and the flesh underneath looked all torn and mangled. Once she was totally out of the water her tail and scales disappeared and her legs were exposed again. It was one big nasty bite that old crock got. Her leg just above her ankle was torn up and bloody. It looked like there was a big chuck of muscle missing too. Cobar jumped in and started to use one of the straps he had around his thigh as a turn kit to stop the bleeding. We looked on dazed, wondering how any of this had happened.

Mu was crying a little more quietly now but you could tell she was in great pain. I couldn't imagine if that were my leg, I probably would have died of a heart attack before they got me away from the crock. The adrenaline was still pumping through my veins. I was too shocked to begin to think how we were going to deal with this new dilemma but I realized we needed to cover her bite and try to keep it from getting infected. We were going to need to get her some real help or she could die. I don't know why but suddenly I was tearing the bottom of my shirt so we'd have something to wrap around her leg. It would keep the dirt out and that would be some help for right now.

Bach started talking softly to Mu. She began to breathe a little deeper and she stopped crying. They were using meditation to help her deal with the pain. That was a great start but how were we going to get her some real medical help? The though hardly ran through my mind before I saw Cobar look up and say,

"Hey Mates."

Without hearing one sound from them, three other guys had walked up behind us. They were aborigines and apparently Cobar knew them. They looked at all of us and then back at Cobar saying they heard all the screaming and figured to come see if there was anything they could do to help. Cobar explained our situation and they said they'd help get Mu and the rest of us back to their main camp which wasn't too far from there. We all agreed it was the best thing to do. There would be a medicine person there who could do more to help Mu than we could.

The other guys were carrying spears of some sort. It only took them a couple minutes to put them together and tie them to make a carry all for Mu who couldn't walk. It wasn't until we began to walk away from the pond that I started to shake. I think the reality that it could have been either of us was just starting to set in and the shock was something I would have to try to walk off. I would never be able to enjoy water again in the same way because the memory of this night would be with me for a very long time to come. That old crock could have killed us and it was a very sobering thought.

I don't know if I was just lost in my own thoughts or not but it didn't seem like it was very long before we were coming up on a large group of aborigines all sitting around a campfire. They exchanged a few comments about who we were and what had happened. They sat Mu close to the fire so the elders could look at her injury. The first thing they did was to give Mu something to drink. They had mixed some powers in it before they handed it to her. It wasn't long and she seemed to relax and almost fall asleep. Bunny, Bach and I watched on as Cobar and his friends took care of Mu. They packed her wound with more powers and then covered it with mud and wrapped it all in some big leaves. I looked at Bunny and wondered where they got all these things so quickly. I was a little concerned that they were putting mud on her open wound but remembered many people in older times had used mud to help heal. Bunny looked just as amazed as I did. Would the wonders of this night ever end?

I was feeling suddenly very tired myself. It wasn't like I had drank any of the drink they gave Mu but I was almost falling asleep on my feet. I had to sit down and I told Bunny,

"I'm so tired I don't think I can stay awake anymore." I just lay down and curled into a ball at her feet and fell asleep almost instantly.

"It's okay Kat, I'll wake you if I need to. Sleep tight." Bunny sounded excited and not at all tired.

I woke up a few hours later. Bunny was there at the campfire with Bach and all the locals and they seemed deep into some conversation. I couldn't help myself it put a smile on my face seeing her there with them because I knew she was questioning them about something. As I got up and went over to join them I could hear what they were saying. One of the older men was talking. He said,

"The Dreamtime history has been handled down through all the times to each generation of Aborigine people. The spirits came here in the beginning and they became all, the mountains, the sky, the rivers, the animals the rocks and man. The Dreamtime is never ending and it goes into what we call the future. It knows no end. We experience the Dreamtime every day and live our lives in accord with the laws of the Dreamtime. We have no written histories. Our oral history is the oldest in the world. The earth has been here for billions of years, the Dreamtime has been forever."

"So," Bunny asked" would you say the Dreamtime is anything like meditation or channeling like psychics do? Or is it more like what some people call the cosmic consciousness?"

"I don't know this thing you call the cosmic consciousness. Meditation may be one way to connect to the Dreaming. I'm not sure if I have ever done it, as I am not a man who meditates.

There is Jiva that is the seed power that resides in everything. It is a vibration that echoes out explaining all of its creation and it resides in everything here on earth and above. It is through vibrations that we can communicate with spirit. The vibrations that are the residue of creation echo out of everything and tell its history of creation that is the Dreaming. Dreamtime was the creation. We believe the beings who created the earth and all on it have left their footprints here on Earth through the seed power or Jiva." He answered her.

Another elder added to the lesson,

"All the oral history we have from the Dreaming and the Dreamtime has been written down and proven by the modern worlds scientist to be true and accurate. No other people have as much history of the world and it's beginning. The Dreaming was a time when the spirits who created all bequest the land to humans. If you are quiet, if you listen and you believe, you will know and can experience the Dreamtime. It never goes away and it has always been."

Cobar said it was time to get some rest. We would have to wait and see how Mu was in the morning. He hoped the powers and poultice would do the work it was expected to do. She wouldn't be as good as new but hopefully she'd be able to walk on her own. The Aborigines were all going hunting and they needed to get going.

Bunny was a little reluctant to give up her conversation with the elders but she knew we all needed our rest and they had things to do. I don't think her adrenaline rush ran out the way mine did. She was psyched and didn't look like she even understood the word sleep right now. We both found a spot close to the fire and talked a few minutes before we wound down again. Sleep wasn't too far behind the last words we shared.

The first illuminations of the morning to come were in the sky as Cobar woke us. The Aborigines were all back from their hunting. They handed each of us a stick with some meant on it. It was the first protein we'd had in a while. It was tasty and warm. I ate it and enjoyed it down to the last bite.

"That was delicious, what was it?" I asked.

"That was from the tail of the crock that bit your friend," they told me. I thought I might choke when I heard what they said. It was a funny thing, to have enjoyed the meat so much and yet to want to throw it back up when I knew what it was. The creature that almost killed one of us, you'd think I'd consider it like a conquest. It seemed ironic that the crock had taken a bit out of Mu's tail and now we had just eaten some of its tail. I wasn't exactly sure how I felt about eating part of our enemy. I wondered if Mu knew what she was eating. Maybe she'd enjoy it more if she knew.

I was surprised to see Mu was able to stand this morning. She didn't seem to be in pain and as I looked at her leg it didn't even look swollen. The night before when I saw the torn flesh I couldn't imagine her doing so well today. I was sure she'd be in big trouble unless we could get her to a hospital. The walking we still had ahead of us wasn't going to be easy for her.

The elder gave her a small packet of some of the same power he gave her the night before. He told her to only use it when she had to and to use it sparingly. He said one small pinch inside her cheek would help with discomfort. They had her wound repacked this morning before we ate. The elder who had packed her wound the night before also had done it again this morning. He held his hand around the packing and said some words we didn't understand. I wondered if he might be a healer, how else was she doing so well? Cobar knew what to do if it needed to be repacked before we got back to the coast. When we left the camp that morning they gave Cobar one of their spears. They also gave Mu a stick to use as a cane if she needed it.

It was another day of endless walking. The country was just as arid and hot again today, that hadn't changed. Starting out before the sun came up was great and the only part of our day with out sweat dripping down our faces and bodies. I was surprised how well Mu was doing. She hadn't complained once about her injury or pain. She wasn't even walking with a limp. That really surprised both Bunny and me. I hated to admit it to myself but even if I had meds for the pain and someone was able to hypnosis me, I don't think I could have done as well as Mu was doing. I'm more of a drama queen and a whiner.

When we finally reached the low lands near the coast Cobar warned us to be on the look out for more crocks. He said the salties weren't any less dangerous than the freshies. Often they were even larger than their cousins. Hearing that, made the hair on the back of my neck, stand up on end. I think I saw Mu get a little closer to Bach and winch when she heard the word crock. From that moment on we were all looking, scanning the area in front of us, to our sides and occasionally behind us. After having been in the struggle and fight the night before none of us wanted to run into another crock.

At one point we could finally see the ocean in the distance. It was re-energizing to see our goal ahead of us. It would still be a long hot walk getting there but now we could see the end of the heat and it was straight ahead of us. Some breezes were starting to reach us and you could smell the salt air. I think all of us were feeling like cattle in the old westerns that when they could smell water they just wanted to run to it. I wanted to run. I loved helping the kids but I wanted this adventure to come to an end. I was so tired of the heat of being this hot and uncomfortable. Right now I just wanted to have all the crocks, the heat and the adventure behind us. I didn't want to have to worry about another encounter with any of them.

It seemed like hours and I didn't feel that we were getting any closer to the coast, then we were down a little hill and I couldn't see the coastline any more. We were beginning to run into ponds and billabongs now. I was totally alert and a little freaked out watching for the crocks and worried about what would happen if we ran into one. Cobar was still out in front leading us so I could only hope he'd keep us safe and away from any dangerous creatures. The landscape was getting a little greener and less arid as we got closer to the coast. It was an encouraging change of scenery that lifted all our spirits a little.

I think it was out of boredom that Bunny started another conversation with Cobar about the Aborigines beliefs and history. Cobar told her they wanted to keep the old ways but with the younger people it was getting harder to do. They all wanted Internet, cell phones and TV and it seemed they were more interested in getting cars and being cool than carrying on the ways of the Dreamtime.

He was a strong believer of the Dreamtime ways otherwise he wouldn't have been there to meet us and been part of this journey. Understanding their beliefs and how they saw the world made me see Cobar in a new, deeper way. We were all on the same side of the fence wanting to see a better world for everyone. Cobar and his people felt it was crucial that we all started to act now to save the world and everything on it. He said if man didn't start to listen to the Jiva and adjust how he used the Earth the spirits would cleanse the world and start over again. He said that everything was constantly changing and we were just ignoring it all: that it would come back to bite us in the tail just as surely as that crock bit Mu.

As soon as he said that about the Croc biting Mu we topped the little knoll in front of us and there they were and there were hundreds of them. The crocs were laying everywhere. For as far as I could see, all I could see was crocs by the water and in the water. Everyone stopped. At first not one of us said a word. It was almost as if we were afraid if they heard us speak they'd be on us. The three of us girls stepped a little closer together. Safety in numbers, who knows what each of us was thinking when we did that. Maybe we thought we'd look bigger and be a little frightening to them? Probably if it did anything it just made up look like a bigger meal. Suddenly I wanted to turn and go back the way we'd come. Going underground had been so much less heat and there had been no creatures of any kind to deal with. The only animals we had seen had been long dead ones. I'd rather deal with tiny narrow stone bridges and volcanic chimneys than these beasts.

Bunny started talking about what she'd read on line about Crocs.

"I read on line that saltwater crocks were mostly 7 to 11 feet long. Most of these look longer than that to me. Some of those have to be more like12-18 feet long. I never thought the Internet would be wrong about stuff like this. Thank goodness the one last night was nowhere near these sizes. They must weight at least 600 pounds or more. It looks like there are hundreds of them. What are we going to do? How are we going to get past them?"

"Yeah, crocs have a pretty mean character. They're not one who even needs to be provoked to attach. Many consider him a sacred animal. The truth is crocks are our brothers they have been here forever and are part of the dreaming. I think it best we give our brothers a wide path and we look to find away around this marsh. If one of these buggers gets a hold of ya, that'll be the end of ya mate."

As we turned and headed to the west trying to find a place we could travel pass the marsh I made sure I wasn't the last one bringing up the rear. It was surprising that I didn't pull all the muscles in my neck: I couldn't help myself, first I'd be looking to the right, them I'd whip my head around and check all the area to my left. I was so scared that one of those giant crocs would pop out of nowhere and grab one of us and I didn't want it to be me. I don't know when I'd very been more nervous or afraid. Cobar said they could strike with lightening speed and if you saw one very close to you, you could be gone before you got to say, "Oh is that a cro....".

For most of the next several hours I was a nervous wreck and so were Bunny and Mu. I couldn't tell how Bach was doing boys never show their feelings the way us girls do. Nothing ever seemed to really bother Cobar. You would have thought he was taking a walk in the park and just encountered some mud or a puddle he wanted to miss. There was no fear in his eyes like there was in ours. After seeing what that little croc did to Mu I didn't want to even think what kind of damage a big croc could do. I think the four of us just wanted out of there and couldn't wait to get away from all these dangerous creatures. I couldn't wait to get home to my nice warm, comfortable bed and I was thinking I might sleep for the next week I was so stressed and worn out.

As we were trying to shirt around what looked like a giant croc convention we saw a couple big ones having a go at each other. They looked like they were fighting to me. I was surprised by the sounds they were making because they sounded like lions roaring and it was amazing how big their teeth looked from where we were. A few of the others were moving into or out of the water but most of them were just taking in the late afternoon sun and looked motionless for the most part. The farther away we got from them the better I liked it.

It was a long time before we were able to get beyond the swamp area where we encountered all those crocs. It felt like we would never see the end of them. Cobar said as long as we were near water, we'd be around the crocs. So I was all for leaving the river area. I'd take heat, dust and arid scenery over crocs any day. Mu looked a little more relaxed too now that the crocs were behind us. It was unreal how well Mu had done all day with the hiking we were doing. Her leg didn't seem to bother her at all. It didn't look like there was any swelling and she wasn't limping or even favoring her injured left leg. She had used the powers the elders gave her earlier in the day but not since.

The walking seemed endless but we were getting closer to the coastline the air smelled fresher and seemed a little cooler as it blew onto us now. I was hopeful we'd see the ocean again soon. When we had found the plant, I had hoped the hardest part of this journey would have been over but this trek through croc country and the hot arid Northern Territory was so easy feat. After going through the dessert in Peru I hadn't thought to find myself anywhere that hot again.

These outings with the merkids were proving to be full of danger and adventure. I had seen so much interesting scenery here in Australia. Some of the boulders and rock structures were so different, it was easy to see why the Aborigines thought them to be spirits they had such different personalities and looks. There were times we saw palm trees growing in rock canyons, even a few areas that looked more like rain forest with cascading waterfalls. I saw kangaroos, Kola bears and more crocs than I care to think about.

I found myself counting the minutes until we could be headed home again. I needed some reassurance that the world I had left behind was still there waiting for me. I wasn't too sure I hadn't fallen down the rabbit hole with Alice.

Things were going pretty good after we left the crocs behind and felt the cooler ocean breezes. Then the scenery started to change. Things were getting greener with more trees and grasses. In a few places now we could see water with Mangrove trees. Suddenly I was alert again there would be more crocs now. I hadn't seen one yet but we knew they'd be there. Getting up to and away from the coast could prove more dangerous than I had considered.

We came up to an area where it looked like nothing but mangrove trees and waterways. It would be too dangerous to try and go through the waterways, they'd be full of crocs and the water was murky enough we wouldn't be able to see them coming. Cobar said we'd have to work our way through the mangroves, the roots of the trees would keep the crocs back and we'd be able to go through safely. Sounded like a good Aborigine trick to me but I'd still be a nervous wreck doing it.

It wasn't easy trying to walk in between the mangrove roots. The mud was deep and it was hard trying to keep our balance. We tried to follow each other in a single file line and still be watching all around us just in case some smaller croc or snake decided to join us. There were times that we tried to walk on top of the roots and a few times we even sat and half crawled over them. That was a long and grueling trek. I slipped and scrapped my knees a couple times as well as getting my butt wet more than once. It was a nasty business traveling between all those mangroves there were spider webs and spiders every few feet not to mention all the other creepy crawly things that lived there.

There were a lot of places that were almost impassable if we hadn't been following Cobar I think we would have all been lost. Holding onto the upper trunk and trying to walk on downward roots was next to impossible. I was so busy trying to keep a forward motion and not fall on Bunny who was right behind me that I couldn't have told you if we were going in circles or not. I was surprised that Cobar could keep his direction on track but he never seemed to question himself and always seemed to be right. Not once in all our trekking together had he made a mistake. If he had screwed up anywhere none of us had noticed.

He told us more than once that the dream or song lines were the energy or imprint that he followed and they were never wrong. He said they don't change and anyone could tune into them. Try as I might I couldn't tell what he was talking about. I tried to feel something different but couldn't I tried to hear the song he said was there but I couldn't hear anything either.

When we finally got out of the mangroves and back to the coastline I couldn't have been more relieved. I had felt like a retarded monkey trying to climb through those mangroves. I never realized I was so clumsy when it came to physical tasks, I had always been good in gymnastics at school but this had been nothing like that. It also felt good not to feel like the hairs on my neck were standing up from the fear of another croc encounter. I think the fear and stress made it even more difficult to focus on the climbing and maneuvering we had to do, all the spider webs and bugs didn't help either.

Once we were standing on the beach the breezes were so refreshing I felt like I could have stayed there and camped out for the next week, I didn't want to budge another step I was so worn out.

"Well, we've made it." Cobar said as the five of us looked out over the Timor Sea. The water was so beautiful it was the brightest turquoise blue and so clear. I think all of us just wanted to take in the brilliance of it. For me it was like seeing a miracle because there were times I wondered if I would make it this far.

What a wonder of nature this land was. How could anyplace go from such red orange dry arid colors to such intensely clear blues and turquoise? There were places we passed that looked like something you might see on the moon and others that reminded me of home. It had been a torturous journey across the world's largest island. Now as we finally stood on the sand and looked at the water in front of us, that's what it totally felt like, the world's largest island with a totally tropical setting. What a contrast of scenery and beauty this land held.

Each of us was feeling relief to have arrived at this part of the journey and after several minutes of total silence, Cobar spoke again.

"Well Mates, this is it, time for me to head back. It's been my pleasure. If you decide to ever come back, I'll look forward to you looking me up and stopping by. I think you know the way from here. Hope the rest of your journey is a safe one. Take care." He didn't shake our hands or hug us goodbye. With his last words he just turned and headed back the way we had come. What a strange guy he was. After all that we had been through I would have like to say thank you and have given him a big hug.

"Hey Cobar, wait up a minute." I called out to him. He stopped and looked back so I ran up to catch him and deliver that hug. After I hugged and thanked him, the others were behind me, waiting to do the same. He was blushing I think, I couldn't tell for sure. He didn't seem too comfortable with us expressing our thanks and gratitude but he accepted the hugs and handshakes he got. He seemed in a hurry to get away from our show of emotions, so off he went again after he received the last hugs from Bunny.

As Cobar disappeared into the mangroves the four of us were left just standing there. It took a minute for us to start to function on our own again. Bach took back control of our little group and suggested,

"I think we should check on Mu's injury and make a decision about how soon we can head back to Atlantis. Lets just take a break, eat something and see how Mu is doing."

He wouldn't get any argument from Bunny and me. I was ready to just sit, eat, drink and do nothing else. Especially since it didn't involve watching out for crocs. We walked back a little closer to the sand bar that reached out several hundred feet into the turquoise sea in front of us. The breeze was good out there away from the tree line. We decided to eat and relax before we unwrapped Mu's leg. I really hadn't given it much thought what we would do if Mu couldn't travel right away. This could be a real problem for us. I had no idea how long we had actually been gone and was worried it might be too long if we had to wait here for Mu's leg to get better.

Mu commented during the little meal we had that her leg hadn't hurt at all since earlier in the morning. Well that was good and sounded hopeful on her part that she'd be able to travel but we had all seen how torn that wound had been. They didn't try to sew her back together. It was just some powder, some mud all wrapped with leaves and a little laying on of hands by two of the elders. I would hope that the laying on of hands could work miracles but wasn't expecting it. That sort of thing didn't happen in real life.

Mu slowly unwrapped the leaves and tried to wash the mud away so we could better access her injury.

"Holy shit!" The words just slipped out of my mouth. I hadn't thought about cussing but when she washed her leg I was expecting to see torn flesh. Instead I saw what looked like a new, red, somewhat inflamed scar where the torn, jagged croc bite had ripped her flesh apart. How could it be? I always said I believed in healing powers but I had never seen it work like this before. I was stunned and so amazed.

"OMG, that is incredible. Do you see what I see Kat?' Bunny blurted out.

We were all shaking our heads, it was hard to believe that much healing could have taken place is so short a time. There was no problem here, Mu would be able to travel and as long as they felt up to the swim we wouldn't have to wait here much longer. I honestly don't know who was the most stunned with the miraculous healing that had taken place with Mu's leg injury. We were all happy and ready to continue on with the next leg of the journey.

We all got ready and walked into the crystal clear water of the Timor Sea. As the merkids got deep enough for their tails to form Bunny and me grabbed their waist straps and with our breathing gear on, joined them under the water for the trip home. There wasn't as much to see as there had been along the Barrier reef when we came to Australia but there was a lot of beautiful undersea life to keep our interest. The water was the perfect temperature and such a welcome change from the heat we had endured for so long. This was the easy part of the trip for us. We were just along for the ride, the merkids had to do all the work. Mu seemed as strong and able as before, her injury didn't slow her down any.

We were swimming through a lot more shallow waters in the seas between the Timor and the Ocean. Indonesian waters were full of beautiful fishes and exotic corals. As we were actually passing by

Indonesia there was one scary moment for me. A giant eel darted out from the rocks and I thought it was coming straight for us. After the episode with the crocs, it was a heart stopping moment for me. I was afraid it was going to be me who got attacked this time. I wouldn't have proved to be as good an injured person as Mu had been. Luckily it turned out the eel only headed towards us, not at us.

Mu and Bach were at their best in the water. On the land unless it was in Atlantis, it was as if they were just fish out of water in regards to their joy. I could feel it in the water with them. They swam like they felt joyous and moved with the waters currents as if they were one with the water and it just wasn't the same for them on land. It was like they could hear the song of the waves and moved along what Cobar had called the dream lines. They seemed so much a part of the oceans and seas they swam through. I think it was their time of oneness, they were one with the moment and one with the currents.

We got back to Easter Island and it was raining. So it was a wet walk back across the island to our sinkhole. The monoliths were no less impressive when they were wet. I admired them all as we marched by wishing they could tell me their stories. If Cobar was right, they each had a footprint that echoed out from them with the history of their creation in those echoes. If only I could hear them. I would have paid a kings ransom to be able to do just that, if I had a king's ransom that is.

We ate a little fruit and drank more water before starting the swim back to Atlantis. Bunny asked a few questions of Bach about the sinkholes and the other under world passageways while we ate our fruit. He explained everything as best he could. Bunny was relentless with her questions and never stopped asking until she was satisfied with her understanding of his answers.

It turns out most of today's modern world thinks the stories of the under worlds are just stories and superstition. Bach told Bunny there was the time before the floods that the world had much lower water levels and that's when the passageways were made. Once the floods came they were all still there but now they were in the under worlds or beneath the waters surface and used only by a few. So in the upper world as time passed talk of the underworlds evoked fears of demons and devils becoming myths and legends.

I was beginning to see and realize the merkids were so in tune with this world, they knew it's ways and it's past so much better than the rest of us. How was it we had forgotten so much and they were able to refine and keep the ways of the spirit? I wish I could know the answer to that question without having to ask Bach. They talked about being silent and going within. Were they talking about the percentage of the brain that our teachers said we didn't use? Or was this something outside of the brain? When we got back to Atlantis I wanted to ask many more questions myself.

After passing through the amethyst mother seed back in Australia I had to wonder if our intuition was affected at all. Was I starting to open up and pick up on the things around me? Certainly something like that could change you it and could have a new positive affect on you. I wondered what Cobar meant when he said something about the real mission we were on and why we were there. I wondered what it could have to do with us kids? Or even with me? Were we here to learn how to open up and remember the gifts of spirit? I wish he would have told us what he knew but he said it wasn't for him to say what our journey was. We were meant to discover and experience it for ourselves, in our time and place and at our own pace.

Bach was going to get so sick of us, and all our questions now that Cobar wasn't here to answer half of them. We couldn't help ourselves, we just wanted to know everything and find the answers to all these new questions. If they weren't exposing us to so many new things we probably wouldn't have so many questions either.

As we were getting closer to the entrance to Atlantis I started wondering about our time and how long we'd really been gone.

"You don't need to worry Kat, it's only early afternoon back home, for your families. There's plenty of time to see the others in our city and show Bunny around Atlantis a little. We promised to get you home on time and keep you out of trouble." That was the first time reference I'd had in what seemed to me to have been weeks trekking around Australia. I looked at my watch and she was right, it said it was only 2:05.

"I can't wait to see Atlantis. How much time do you think we'll have before we have to head home?" Bunny mentally asked.

"Plenty of time for you to see most of the city center. Maybe another time you can see the rest." Mu answered. Bunny's eyes lit up when she heard the words another time. It would be a close contest between my friend Bunny and me as to which of us was the most inquisitive. Putting the two of us together and having to deal with both could prove a little stressful at times for our companions.

Going through the under world passageways was beginning to feel like walking a winding path back home in the woods near our house. I knew where I was and I was very comfortable with it. I was beginning to know my way around. Not that I thought I could maneuver the way back and forth on my own but it wasn't frightening or intimidating to me any more. Being in the water, with the merkids was becoming second nature to me and I felt like I was part of them when we swam together like this. It was like when two people ride a bike together they pedal together, lean together and feel the wind in their faces the same way.

We were headed back up I could see the light from above in the entry or arrival chamber. As our heads broke through the surface and we headed to the stairs out of the water, I didn't notice as many kids coming to greet us this time.

Bunny was looking all around and taking everything in. The area was nothing but smooth rock walls, maybe it was even sandstone. I had never asked what kind of stone it was. I remember feeling the same way the first time I arrived. I wanted to remember every square inch of Atlantis from this water entry to the top of the ceremonial pyramid in its center.

Before we were even out of the water Bunny said,

"Wow, I can't believe this is really happening. How did you feel the first time you came in Kat?"

"Same as you Bunny, it just blew us both away. This is nothing wait until you get to see the city. That's when it'll really blow your mind."

We gave Mu and Bach a minute to move out of the way and then Bunny and me walked up the steps and entered Atlantis. We stayed only long enough to dry off and gather our things back up before we headed into the heart of the city looking for Shi and his brothers.

Bunny was turning and looking in every direction just the way I had the first time. Not that I wasn't also looking and taking things in again myself. Each time I walked in the city I noticed something I hadn't seen before. Sometimes it was just smaller details of things I had quickly scanned over before. Each time I could allow myself a little more time to see the details of everything. Atlantis was amazing!

Walking from the arrival area we took a path that lead directly to the hydroponics building with the sacred plant Bach carried at his waist. We were feeling pretty triumphant returning with the second plant. Lord knew we'd been through a lot to get it and get back. None of the other kids here would be able to understand the effort it took. Now that it was all over and we were safely back here, it didn't seen as deadly or life threatening an adventure.

Bunny started to interrupt the wandering of my thoughts with her questions.

"Oh Kat, did you ever see anything so ancient or so splendid in your whole life? Look at the terraces and all the flowers. It's like what you'd think the gardens of Babylon must have looked like. I didn't expect to see lush, tropical trees and flowers. Where is that sunshine coming from? How does it get down here? Are all the kids, merkids? They look so normal except for the way they're dressed."

I tried to interrupt her before she spit out another string of questions.

"Maybe you should ask Mu so she can explain it all. It's such an incredible place isn't it?"

Mu started to explain how the crystals supplied almost everything they needed. She told her about the protective shield and her family's part in designing it all. With Mu busy trying to answer all of Bunny's questions I was free to think and let my own attention go back to viewing all the creatures and things around us again. I noticed the color in the sky it was such a clear blue shade without any clouds to contrast again it. The walls of the building were varied depending on what they were made from. Some were a sandy color and others were vivid with things like green malachite, blue lapis and white to black marble. It definitely made you wonder about its original construction and how it all came together.

I had seen drawings and pictures of what people said Atlantis the city had looked like in books but I never expected any of them to be so accurate. There was a center with outer rings or channels of water. We were in the center where most of the important buildings were. From here you could also see all a lot of the giant crystals that also created semi circles around the heart of Atlantis. They were beautiful and with the light reflecting through them you could see many rainbows as well.

Shi and his brothers were waiting for us at the hydroponics building. They told us before this was more of the lab and research part of the operations the true production of their food supply was done away from the city where there was more room. That was where they were moving some of the first plant that we brought back from Peru now that they had produced more of it to work with. It looked like they had the secret to Miracle Grow and had supped it up somehow with crystal power. I couldn't believe how much more of the original plant they had now.

They immediately took the new specimen from Bach and started to place it in the mini dome they had set up on a long table to the right. I thought Bunny was going to explode she was so excited and trying to take so much in. She was looking towards the back of the room where it looked like a tropical rain forest the only things missing were the rain forest animals. It would have been another whole adventure getting back in there and checking out all the different plants they had growing.

Once they got the new plant all settled in they suggested we could take a walk and see more of the inner city. Bunny and me were more than ready for that. Once we left the building and were out in the open one of those big magenta-colored birds flew by and landed near us. Bunny and me were ducking for cover it came so close to us. I couldn't get over the exotic look and the wild colors some of the birds had.

We walked by a building that had panels and inlayed pieces of Malachite. What a beautiful building it was and so different from anything in any history books I had ever seen. Mu told us it was a healing center. I guess that explained why it had the green Malachite. She told us the Malachite was,

"The stone most related to the crown chakra. If you needed help receiving information that would help you to attain spiritual evolution you would select Malachite. It will release all of your negative energy and can be especially helpful if you need to release quilt from your past.

You'll notice they have surrounded the malachite pieces with copper. The copper will enhance the power of the stone. The two together will help you to gain insights into any reasons or the conditions behind you having resentments or anxiety in this lifetime. That makes it an excellent stone for a healing center. In Atlantis, every stone laid or metal used has a reason and a purpose. We selected all the elements to create the best vibrational energy possible for each building or room."

"Wow, who would have thought that so much planning went into the construction of the buildings from so far back in time?" Bunny commented and then asked Mu,

"What is this building and what is it used for? This one with the blue stones."

"This building is one that is used to promote total awareness in the spiritual. The blue stone is Lapis Lazuli and it has much power that stimulates the consciousness towards the awakening of the true self. It's a stone that opens your mind or consciousness. The part that already knows that you are part of the "all that is," will awaken when you wear it close to your body. Perhaps it is not accurate to say your mind because it is a word you often link to the brain, which is a physical organ. We do not have a word for the part of your essence that I speak of but it is more real than your brain is. Mind seems to be a word that we can try to relate our meaning with. It is a beautiful structure, is it not?"

Bunny never ran out of questions.

"Why don't all the buildings have stone inlays? Why are some so much plainer on the outside?" she asked.

"What makes some buildings of more importance are their special stones. There must be some spaces between these stones of power or we would be too charged with their energies. Some buildings need to be more grounding to the earth. One cannot work at super vibrational levels all the time or we would become unable to deal with issues of this earthy existence. We have to remain grounded to this world or we would perish completely from it." Mu answered.

"Wow. Some things here are so similar and so many are so different. I never thought that ancient people would have given so much care to what things they put on or into a building." Bunny added.

"The placement of elements is an art long used and studied in this world. There has always been a reason for the specific arrangement of things in the home and work place. Has your world forgotten this too?" Mu asked.

Bunny answered,

"No we have the ancient art of placement the Chinese started, it's called Feng Shui. That is what you're talking about right?"

"We have not given this name or any other name for that matter. It is just a knowing or understand we all have. You must surround yourself with things that up lift you and have a purpose for your wellbeing. That is why we dress in the colors and elements we do. Whether it's close to your body or just in your general area, color and all elements of the earth have energy and a power to help you. You need to respond to those powers when you select what you wear or have around you. Just as Cobar said the things of this world all have an echo of their original footprints left behind from spirit that created it. You must listen and reach out to feel these things.

There is this and the astronomical bearing that many buildings and temples have. They have often carried the secrets of the constellations from above to the placement of things here on Earth's surface. There is a reason for all things being done this way or that way."

Just as I was starting to feel as if I was getting one of Mu's lectures, she laughed and walked over to a strange looking creature that had just landed on the stonewall next to us. It looked like a butterfly to me but also something like a bat with butterfly wings or maybe not wings but fins I though they looked like the fins of a beta fighting fish. They had moved with a grace and flow of movement that butterfly wings don't have. It was like no butterfly or bat that I had ever seen before. Mu reached her hand out towards the creature and it climbed into her palm. She turned and lifted her hand out towards us and showed off the little what ever it was.

"Isn't it just the most beautiful creature you have ever seen?' she asked as she showed us her treasure. "This is Baby, she is my Ren."

"Wow and double wow. What is a Ren?" Bunny asked. "I've never seen such a creature, not even in a book. Is it a bat? Or related to a bat?"

Mu pulled her hand with the Ren in it, closer to her body and lightly petted the little thing, on its head. Bunny and I cautiously stepped in closer to her, to get a better look. Resting in her palm the ren had folded or pulled back it's wings, they had to be wings, because it had flown in before landing on the stonewall, next to us.

"A Ren is neither butterfly or bat. It is related to the bat perhaps. She is lovely isn't she? They are very affectionate creatures. She likes to curl up near my neck at night when I sleep. She has missed me while we've been gone, she must have decided to come looking for me when she sensed our return."

Bunny and I just looked at each other. Wow, what a strange, strange creature this little pet of Mu's was. I couldn't help but think about all the vampire bats back home and all the stories attached to bats. It just didn't seem like the kind of animal one would want as a pet, or that they could be affectionate! I just kept waiting to hear the Twilight Zone music start to play in the background.

"Off you go Baby. Fly home and wait for me there." Mu told her as she lifted and kind of thrust the hand holding Baby into the air to help give her flight.

We walked a little more across the city center taking a different route back toward the arrival chamber. We both knew we wouldn't have a lot of time in Atlantis because we needed to get back to our own world soon. Mu continued to explain what some the buildings were for and threw in a few interesting facts about Atlantis along the way. There were statues in some of the gardens around some of the buildings. I saw statues of Centaurs and Mermaids as well as men and women. The gardens were beautiful and well taken care of. Everything seemed so clean and organized there wasn't anything out of place or litter anywhere that we could see.

We all turned as we heard Shi calling out to us.

"Hey girls are you ready to head back home? Sheba's going to meet us in the arrival chamber and then we'll be ready to take off. Everyone thought it best to let Mu rest and try to recover from her injury. This is one trip she doesn't need to make with us."

"Well in that case. I'll leave you here and say goodbye. I hope you find the other plants soon so we can meet again to continue our search. Thank you again for all your help. Take care my friends." As she started to turn and walk back towards her home Bunny said,

"Mu, wait up a minute, you're not getting off that easy. Where I come from when friends say goodbye, they say it with a hug." With those words she threw her arms around Mu and gave her a big old bear hug goodbye and told her, "I hope you're well soon and thank you for all your help. Thank you for everything!"

After Bunny released Mu from her grip I decided to give her a proper goodbye too. I remembered seeing Mu fighting for her life with that old croc and knew we were lucky she was still with us. When the hugging was over and Mu could make her escape, she did and we walked back to the chamber to leave with Shi.

When we arrived in the chamber Sheba was already waiting for us. Shi introduced Bunny to Sheba and we downed our gear to leave. Bunny looked back as we worked our way down the stairs into the water to take off. As soon as our heads were underwater I heard her words, "please let me come back, please let me come back, please let me come back." I knew exactly how she felt.

It was another beautiful swim back through the Caribbean into the Gulf of Mexico. I couldn't wait to get home and share everything with Becka and see if the kids had found any more of the plants we needed. I hoped someone had some luck while we were gone. Sometimes it was easy to forget why we needed to locate the plants so badly. All the merkids looked healthy and death didn't seem like an issue they would be dealing with.

There were times I wished we could tell the adults because I couldn't help but think maybe they could find things faster or be able to get to the cure the kids were looking for sooner. It seemed funny to be tackling such heavy matters without having the help of any adults. This was just all us kids taking matters into our own hands, I could only hope it would all turn out for the best.

Gram had said once that sometimes adults tried to over think things and made things more difficult to figure out. Keep it simple was what she said. So for now it was just we kids trying to keep it simple.

Find the plants; find the cure, save the merkid's world!

Adventure #3
Tibet

When we reached our beach we said all our goodbyes, promising to contact Brach or Sheba as soon as we had any good news. Bunny and I stood there watching the two of them swim away before we turned and headed back up the beach towards home.

"Tell me we weren't dreaming Kat. Were we sleeping on the beach having a joint dream? If that wasn't a dream how am I ever going to be able to put all this into perspective?" Bunny was talking a mile a minute she was so super charged.

I was feeling a little exhausted myself. This was the second time this week and I reminded myself that was our earthly time frame of weeks, not the merkids bent suspended time frame, that I had traveled the globe with them. But I totally knew what Bunny was feeling.

"I know Bunny, it's a little hard even for me to put all this into perspective and I've gone more than once." I answered her.

"I can't wait to see Becka and tell her about this one. Just remember, Becka and me are the only ones you can talk to about any of this. If the rest of the kids are let in by the merkids, then it'll be okay but for now you've got to keep their secret. Don't forget your promise to them." I reminded her.

"Oh you don't have to worry Kat. I can keep a secret. I would love to tell Mom about all this, it would totally knock her over. She'd want to know every little detail too. It won't be as hard for me not telling my mom, as it will be not to tell the rest of the kids. You and Becka haven't told anyone else? I can't believe you didn't tell me before, or that I couldn't see a difference in you. I feel like it's written all over me...."I've been to Atlantis."

"You might look a little flush in the cheeks and a little more tan but other than that, I don't see anything different about you. It's just what you're feeling and thinking that makes you think it'll show on your face. There might be a little more sparkle in your eyes and you do kind of look like the cat that swallowed the canary." I told her. "So wipe that smile off your face before the whole world guesses your secret!" I teased her a little. "I'm heading home to clean up. Maybe we can meet at Becka's after dinner tonight. "Play it cool with your Mom, you don't have to lie, just don't tell the whole truth. You'll find it works better that way sometimes. '

Bunny looked at me and nodded. "Okay, I can do that. I'll call if anything comes up otherwise I'll see you then. Bye."

"Yeah. Later!" I called back as I headed up towards the house.

After I got home I showered and cleaned up. Oh it felt so good to just stand under the running water and feel really clean for the first time since I left home. It felt as if we had been gone for weeks and weeks, how the merkids could bend time and turn one day into weeks of time in the same world was beyond my thinking capabilities. That wasn't so surprising though, most things they did and were capable of, were beyond me. They were such complex beings and yet they were also such simple, natural people. I wasn't even sure that was something you could say about anyone else in the Universe.

Just thinking about them and having the thoughts that were spinning around inside my head made me remember they were trying to keep their disease from spreading to the Guardians when they returned to Atlantis again. That ET thing was another bucket of worms that was hard to wrap my brain around. I had always heard about them and read that a lot of people had said they saw them, including Presidents. But to think I was trying to help someone in order to ultimately save the extraterrestrials. Now that was too much to think about right now. It would totally knock my dad over if he could know all this. He was a believer in ET's and he was always saying he was ready if they wanted to come and take him for a ride.

I was a little quiet at dinner, mostly because I was still so tired from the big adventure with the merkids but my dad was the only one who really noticed and he didn't say much. After dinner I asked to go over to Becka's house and my dad said, "Sure. Tell your sister hello for me when you get there. Maybe you could tell Mr. Mac, I said if they're in the mood come on over for a game of cards."

"Sure, I'll tell them. Bye see you later." I called back to him as I left the house headed for Beckas.

When I knocked on their door, it was Mr. Mac who came over to answer it. When he opened the screen door to let me in I told him what my dad said about a card game at our house.

"Hey, that doesn't sound like a bad idea. I feel lucky tonight too. Maybe I'll see what Ellen wants to do and I'll give your dad a call. Becka's in her room." He let me pass by and shut the door behind me. I could hear him as he walked to the kitchen calling out her name and saying something about a card game at Eddie's house.

"Hey Kat, how did it go? Did you find the plant?" Becka asked.

"Oh yeah, we finally found it. You aren't going to believe what we went through to get it and get back though. I'm exhausted. Between battling the heat, the endless hiking and the crocs, Bunny and I are both lucky to be back here. Mu almost didn't make it. A fresh water croc got her one night and I didn't think we were going to be able to save her. Lucky for us we ran into some of Cobar's friends and they helped." I told her.

"Wait a minute, who is Cobar? What do you mean Mu almost didn't make it? What happened? You better tell me the whole story from the very beginning."

"Maybe I better wait until Bunny gets here, she'll want to share it all with you too. She promised to call if she couldn't make it." Just as I finished saying the words Bunny popped up in the doorway.

"I'm here." She said as she walked in and sat on the bed next to Becka.

So there we sat for the next hour or so, telling her every detail and move that we made. We told her about all the strange and unusual things we had seen the Boab trees, the kangaroos, the crocs and Koala bears, the Aborigines. We told her all about the Mother seed and the volcanic chimney. We didn't leave anything out.

"Look what I found in the accession chamber. Bach said it belonged to one of the original sisters, who ever they were. I forgot to ask because things got a little wild and crazy right after he read it for me. I'm sort of surprised that I still had it in my pocket after what happened. Once we heard Mu screaming for help I didn't remember even putting it in my pocket. Then I forgot it again until I changed clothes at home today." As Bunny tied it around her forehead she said, "What do you think? Does it do anything for me?"

"As old as Bach said it was, do you think you should be wearing it Bunny? Maybe you should put it away someplace safe." Before all the words were out of my mouth Bunny was shaking her head no.

"I think Bach might be wrong this time. This is in such great shape, how could it possibly be more than a few years old? Maybe it fell into the chamber through one of the holes up above it. I think it looks more like a headband from some old hippie type who climbed Ayers Rock and lost it. I rather like it. I think I'll start wearing it. Besides it's the only proof I have of the trip we made. I think it's the coolest souvenir," she said.

Becka was admiring the beads on the headband and said,

"You know Bunny, these sure are beautiful beads what do you think they are? Did Bach say anything about them?"

"No we didn't ask and he didn't say," she answered her.

"They sure sparkle like real gemstones. These other two are beautiful opals aren't they? If one were the real thing, you'd think they all would be. You should get this checked by a jeweler it could be worth a small fortune." Becka told her.

"I never thought about it being worth money. Maybe I'll do that just to see what they say." Bunny answered her.

Finally I told the girls I was tired and needed to go home to get some real sleep.

"Hey before I go," I had to ask," Did anybody find anymore of the plants?"

Becka looked up from the bed and told me,

"Amy thinks she might have found the one she was looking for. She said she just wanted to check a few more things to confirm it. Cookie said she thought she was getting closer but hasn't called me to say for sure. Ronnie and me, we're still working on it."

"Okay then, I'll see you both tomorrow. I just can't stay up any longer. I don't know how you're doing it Bunny. I'm just exhausted. Good night"

I left the two of them talking away, mostly Bunny talking and Becka listening. I could totally understand Bunny's excitement but I was just too tired right then to be part of it.

I barely remember getting undressed and climbing into bed that night. I was so tired all I wanted to do was sleep for the next 10 to 12 hours. I'm not sure how well I slept because I spent the whole night dreaming. I was dreaming wild and crazy things. I saw myself in Egypt.

I was some kind of priestess in charge of the tablets from Atlantis. I had a special temple built under the sphinx and then when the tablets were safely tucked away I had the whole place buried under sand. I hid the secrets of Atlantis with the entire Sahara Dessert.

When I woke up the next morning I didn't feel rested at all it had been a busy, busy night. I wondered where such dreams would come from. I liked things about Egypt but I didn't know where those ideas came from. Maybe Mu had said something yesterday in Atlantis to trigger my night of dreaming.

Maybe later today I could talk to Bunny and Becka about the dream and see if Bunny remembered something Mu said that might have sparked something in my mind. Something caused me to have the most vivid dream I'd ever had. I could remember every detail so I decided to write the dream down and keep it in my journal. I had a feeling I'd want to explore this again sometime and I wanted to be sure I remembered it all. My journal would be the way to insure I would never forget all the little details.

By the time I finally got dressed and got going it was after 10:00 in the morning. I had a little breakfast, did a few chores and headed back over to see Becka. When I arrived Amy was already there. I could tell by the smile and excitement on her face that she must have found what see was looking for. They turned as I entered Becka's room. Amy who was always so calm and reserved jumped up and started explaining everything to me.

"Hey Kat, I'm so excited I found my plant. I spent so many hours researching and it all paid off. Look I printed it all off to show you. The only problem is, the site on the Internet didn't say if the plant still existed. All the information came from ancient history and legend. I couldn't find any record of it in modern day. Do you think that means it's extinct? That would be a bummer wouldn't it?"

"Yeah Amy, that would really be a bummer. Where did you find it? What country?" I asked.

"Tibet. I read it grew high in the mountains near Shambhala. Only problem, Shambhala is a mystical kingdom that's suppose to be hidden in inner Asia it's not a real place on the map. Some people say it's near the sacred Mount Kailash. There were a few conflicting theories or stories. Tibet is the best answer I have for you, exactly where in Tibet is anybody's guess unless you know the way to Shambhala."

"Isn't that great Kat? We're making progress, this is the third plant and Cookie thinks she's getting close to finding her plant too." Becka chimed in.

"Yeah, that's more than great. It's fantastic. Now we'll have to try and figure out how to narrow down this Shambhala place." I told them as I sat down on the bed next to Amy.

The three of us talked for a few hours before Amy said she had to head home. After she left Becka and I talked about letting Bach and Sheba know we had located another plant but without any true location to aim for. We had no idea what they would want to do about this one. According to everything Amy had read Shambhala was a hidden kingdom, possibly not of this Earthy plane.

Many accounts said the place didn't exist here on Earth but in some other mystical location or dimension. But Mount Kailash was an exact location and a place we could find. My head started spinning just thinking about this one. Tibet, the high snow topped mountains wasn't a place I would want to go hunting around looking for some plant that might not exist any longer. I had walked and hiked all over Easter Island twice now, into the mountains of Peru and across the arid heat of Australia. I didn't want to think about what it would take to travel to Tibet and freeze in the cold of that desolate locale. Becka and I googled Mount Kailash and it has an elevation of over 21.000 feet. How could any plant still grow there?

I knew one thing for sure I wouldn't be climbing anything that high, not anything anywhere near that high. I'd probably get a nosebleed if I even thought about it. I looked at Becka and said,

"Maybe I'll have a doctors appt. to go to and you can go to Tibet while I sit this one out!" I couldn't help but smile at her when I said it.

"I didn't plan that and you know it. Besides, it gave Bunny a chance to see Atlantis with you and have her own little adventure. I would have gone if I could have." She threw back at me.

"Yeah I know, I was just trying to give you a hard time. You would have melted in all that heat anyway." I threw back at her.

Becka just smiled at me it was one of her, the cat that swallowed the canary smiles, it meant no matter how hard I tried, I wouldn't get the best of her. She turned and flipped open her laptop and turned it on. We spent the next hour checking things on line about Shambhala hoping we'd have a better knowledge before we tried to communicate with Bach and Sheba. Amy was right about everything she had told us.

When we finally lay down to communicate with the merkids I just fell asleep. It must have been all the stress and timebending, the adventures had put me through. I was totally lost to everything that Becka and the merkids said and it wasn't until she woke me up a little while later, that she filled me in.

They were going to get back with us the next day and let us know what they thought we should do. In the meantime Becka, Amy and I were supposed to keep checking and see if we could narrow things down any more. Personally I loved the idea of a Hidden Kingdom in another dimension, the big question being if you could find it, how would you get in? I wondered if someone had Heaven and Shambhala mixed up? Maybe it was just another one of those old legends and never existed. We decided we should focus on Mount Kailash that at least was something we could find so we googled it on Google Earth. Of course being China it had to be on the other side of the world I just loved these long distance trips. All we saw was snow and it didn't look like much of anything anywhere around Mount Kailash. How could we pack warm clothes when we didn't get to take any luggage? Even though it was summer time, the snow on Mount Kailash was always there at the higher elevations. Hopefully we wouldn't have to go anywhere near the snow line if we had to climb it in search of the plants we needed.

Bach told Becka to try to get back with him the next day at the same time and he'd let us know what the merkids wanted to do regarding the Tibetan plant. When I went home that afternoon I started looking for the plant I was suppose to find. Becka and I hadn't had as much time to look for the plant drawings we'd taken. So it seemed like I better apply myself or it wasn't going to get done by me. I wanted to have the thrill of the search and the pleasure of finding the plants location myself.

I started checking for sacred plants and then went to religious groups around the world trying to find anything that would be my first clue. I came across something about Alexander the Great that sparked my interest. In perusing that story I came across something about Cleopatra from Egypt. The Cleopatra story really interested me and I was off on some wild search of plants and herbs she used and came across a couple things of interest that I would check into the next time I had a chance to get on the computer. Dinnertime came and I had to leave the pyramids of Egypt and return to my little house and the dinner table.

I didn't get a chance to get back on the computer after dinner because we had company and I had to stay in the living room to visit. I did finally get a good night of sleep that night. I was starting to feel like my system was getting back to normal. Traveling with the merkids was a little like getting or having jet lag. Last time I didn't get much time to recoup before I had to leave again. We had no idea how this next adventure was going to come together so I was glad to get to rest for now.

When we got together to communicate with Bach and Sheba the second afternoon, I was able to stay awake. I was surprised when we got their message and request. They wanted to know if we could get two of the kids to come with us. They wanted to take a bigger group to possibly divide up once we'd get there and cover more territory in the same amount of time. Even they couldn't make time stop long enough for us to explore all the possibilities once we got there unless we separated into groups. Bach suggested we ask Bunny and Amy since she found this new location. They would have Shi and Chen come as well so there would be eight of us.

If anyone wondered what we were doing it would look like a school outing.

So the next thing Becka and I had to do was talk with Bunny and Amy. This would be the first time the merkids left it up to us to explain and ask Amy for her sworn oath. We were sure she would give it. It was more an issue about if she'd believe us. Seeing the kids made it easier to believe, I mean if there could be merkids then why not Atlantis? Oh we would be able to convince her. I was pretty sure about that, after all there were three of us who had seen Atlantis now. She would see the truth and the joy of the adventures in our eyes and she would believe.

It was exciting to think about an adventure with the four of us going together. I always wanted to see China so how could I not be excited? I wasn't so sure about all the walking and climbing we might have to do. I also wasn't sure that Tibet would be the most exciting part of China either. From classes in school, I thought that Tibet was the most mountainous area of China and also the least populated and remote. We wouldn't be seeing the Great Wall or anything super like that. Too bad, it was a dream of mine to walk on the Great Wall and take thousands of pictures.

There was eight of this time and we were headed towards Angkor Wat in Cambodia, to the ruins there and then onto Tibet, via a second under world waterway. Amy had given her sworn oath to keep the merkids secret, as we knew she would. So this trip it was Becka, Amy, Bunny and I, we were all excited to be heading out again. This was going to be the best trip yet because the four of us were together this time. Sharing with our best friends would make it a true adventure that would be beyond any of the other trips so far.

The sun was just starting to rise as we reached the ruins at Angkor Wat. We had started at a cave entrance back in the Gulf of Mexico off the coast of Texas and managed to get this far without coming out of the under world. Now as our heads broke the surface of the water we all looked around to take in our surroundings. No one was sure where we would end up when we arrived. I had removed my breathing piece and my mouth was just above the water as I took in the beauty that was in front of me. The water dripped from my hair as I started to admire the building and ruins I saw before me. The beautiful temple right beside us was aglow in several shades of gold, amber and pink rays of light.

I felt, the most inspiring sensation, as I saw the temple building and ruins for the first time. The glow of the rising sun made everything seem magical and almost unreal. Times like this I needed someone to pinch me so I'd know I wasn't dreaming. It was so beautiful it just about took your breath away. I don't know if the others thought or felt the same way, just our heads were out of the water and I couldn't hear any ones' thoughts. Because no one had started to speak, I could only imagine they were thinking and feeling some of the same things as me.

I didn't want to be the first to break the silence. It felt as if the sound of my voice would shatter the incredible magic of this moment and I didn't want to do that. It was a few moments of magic, like I had never known anything like before. We had emerged in what looked to be to be a pool or man made structure right up next to some ornately carved temple. There were lily pads all around us floating on the water's surface and a few lotus flowers were opening with the morning sun.

Without saying a word we all slowly swan the couple feet to the edge of the pool and started to climb out of the water. Everything was sand stone and the colors were alive with the first rays of the morning sun. There aren't words to describe the mystery and beauty of this place. The temples rose with such simple majesty and intricate lines and design.

Some of the walls looked as if the waters of time had rubbed them smooth and others had fabulous carvings with minute detail. The color rose in alternating layers from golden sand to burnt brown with rusty orange in between. You could only wonder at the magic and artistry of the people who designed and built this place.

Bach was the first to speak,

"This place was called Banteay Srei which means 'The Citadel of Women" we will have to walk a short distance to the actual Angkor Wat temples and our next water passageway."

As I looked in the direction Bach was pointing toward I could see majestic palm trees growing at least 30-40 feet into the air. What an adventure this was going to be. We were once again walking through a piece of man's history that had been both magnificent and magical. Who had carved all this sand stone and recorded so much of their history? I would have loved to have met the artists who did this work and taken lessons from them.

As we walked across the semi jungle and forest area to the temples ahead we passed more temple ruins and structures. Some were under restoration and some had trees growing over them, hugging and trying to hide them from view. Some looked more gray and green with mosses growing on them. The jungle was alive with its fight to take over the ruins once again and it looked like man was fighting against them to preserve and save it for all to see.

The four of us from home were pretty quiet considering where we were. Each of us were looking at everything trying to seer the details into our brains and capture the images forever inside us. Bunny had made a few comments and Amy just nodded as an answer to her. I believed that Amy was over whelmed just as we each had been before. When she did finally say something I was surprised and sort of shocked by her words.

"I've been here before. Some other lifetime, I can feel it in my soul."

HOLY COW!

Here was Amy who was usually the most quiet of all of us and she was speaking up, saying pretty definite things she was feeling and feeling very strongly. "Ever since we came up through that pool I've been vibrating on the inside and I know I am headed home," she added.

"Wow" I told her, "that's how Mu felt when we were on Easter Island and at Machu Picchu."

Bunny spoke up and told us,

"That's kind of how I felt when we got to Australia but it wasn't like I knew I was going back home. I was just vibrating but really felt balanced out but also relaxed with the place. When we talked with the Aborigines I felt like I was with them about what they believed and how they felt the world came into being. It was like I was one of them. I'm not vibrating like that now either."

Bach and the boys were just listening and not making any comments. They always thought we talked more than we needed to. I knew Amy and she wasn't usually so out spoken around people she didn't know. I could only assume she was feeling very strongly about what she was saying. She had blown me away with her words. I didn't feel that way any place we had been to so it was hard for me to relate. I mean I was excited, that's for sure but I never felt like I was going back someplace I had lived before in some other time. I think I loved too many places to pin point only one as my home.

One of the structures we walked by was being covered and taken over by a tree that Bach told us was a strangler fig. What a fascinating tree, it wrapped itself around and over itself literally trying to strangle the building it was trying to capture with it's legs and roots. I had never seen a tree like this one before. It was like a sculpture that had a grace and smooth movement to it's over lapping roots and base. It looked like if given enough time, it would totally cover and hide the structure it was climbing around and over. There were a couple places where it looked like the trees had done just that for centuries and only a couple carved faces peeped out letting you know there was something more behind the trees.

This place was more like a town with all the temple estates or compounds spaced apart with Jungle and forest in between them all. I'm not sure what I thought it would be like but this wasn't it. Some of the ruins were totally falling into complete decay. Others were restored and back to most of their original beauty and elegance. The architectural design was so different from anything I had ever seen, there was definitely nothing like this back home. Once again I thought to myself they must have been smaller people back them. Some of the doorways and buildings looked like they were built for children. Indonesians are smaller people even today but some of these places looked like I'd even have a hard time getting in and having room to move around. The only other place on Earth I had seen anything that came close to having a similar look were some of the structures in India from our history books. I even remember seeing a show about world travelers' way back before Columbus who traveled from India to this area of the world maybe that explained the similarities.

The jungle was alive with birdcalls and bug sounds. A few monkeys were screeching in the distance. I hadn't thought about what kinds of animals we might run into here, I was hoping no crocs. I thought I could handle almost anything else.

Shi spoke up and said we should watch our steps as the jungle would have many different snakes even Tigers and elephants still ran wild and free here. Oh great, just as soon as I thought I was safe he had to talk about tigers, man eating tigers no less. I mean they are beautiful creatures and I had seen more than one or two at the zoos but to be in the cage with them, it wasn't something I'd want to do and although this wasn't a cage, it was their home ground. I think his words affected all of us as you could watch everyone looking more to the ground and around them, checking the space close enough for things like snakes to strike in.

The sun was coming a little further over the horizon and the jungle was coming to life even more as we trekked our way towards the larger compound called Angkor Wat. Things were going to get a little tricky today as this was also a tourist attraction and there would be other people around and we would have preferred not to attract too much attention to what we were doing and where we were going.

There were monkeys climbing in the trees around us out searching for their morning meal I supposed. What a trip to be in the jungle with the monkeys so close and not paying any mind to us at all with their morning antics. They apparently were use to the hundreds of tourist who came to see their ruins everyday. They were definitely in a world of their own but very entertaining to watch as they climbed and swung from tree to tree.

Mu started to tell us girls a little about our surroundings,

"The name Angkor Wat means Temple City. It was built as a model home for the gods, meant to represent the true home of the Gods. The towers symbolize the Mountain peaks of Mount Meru. The walls and the moats represent the mountain ranges that encircle the cosmos and the ocean or waters of the cosmos. The builders were a people who considered the center of all physical, metaphysical and spiritual Universes to be Mount Meru. As with all sacred locations around the world, the measurements and placement of the temples in relation to one another have a strong cosmological significance. There are vortexes here and the crossing of dragon lines, which made it a very high-energy location. Take into consideration the under world entrance and it was the perfect location for man to build his temples."

As we got closer to the main compound called Angkor Wat it was easy to see what an incredible place it must have been in it's own day. What a grandiose temple it had been and it was pretty spectacular even now. There were five towers of the temple, four towards the outer corners and one larger center tower, all together they created a silhouette once seen, could never be forgotten. It was surrounded by a squared water moat it was a wide channel that circled around the entire compound with a long impressive roadway into the property's entrance. It reminded me of the channels around Atlantis except they were round and this was square. As I surveyed the area again, I wondered where we would have to go to reenter the under world from here.

I felt so much awe looking at the carving and reliefs of the walls and buildings. There were so many elephants in their designs clearly they were a big part of their lives here in Cambodia. Definitely they had a good working relationship, it appeared they did every chore with the help of their elephant friends.

By the time my daydreaming stopped our little group had also stopped. The boys were talking about the way to move through the crowd to get to our under world entrance. No one was exactly sure where it was. Bach was reading the temple compound. He knew it was here but no one had drawn him a map. It was up to him to read the area and lead us to our entrance. We were standing at the beginning of the main entrance roadway or bridge onto the compound. It was so simple in it's stunning beauty. I heard a tourist near by say this temple was the largest religious structure on Earth. I was surprised by that statement and wondered if he was right.

As we approached the causeway to head in, I heard a tour guide say to his group that over 2,000,000 people a year come to see the temples and visit Angkor Wat. There were a lot of people here and we were blending in, no problems. At least I didn't think we looked like people who should be watched or followed. Chichen Itza had tourist when we were there but not as many as I saw here today. I hoped this didn't keep us from doing what we needed to do.

I was totally enjoying the scenery as we walked towards the main temple grounds ahead of us. Amy was pretty quiet, Bunny was busy talking to Shi, Becka was walking with Mu and it looked like Mu was telling her more about our surroundings. The other two boys were walking ahead of us all talking with each other. Bach seemed to be leading the way again so I assumed he had his reading and knew where we were going.

I decided I could easily picture myself living here in some other time but I didn't feel the way Amy did. I mean, I was excited as all get out to be here and see these things but I wasn't vibrating and getting all these deep spiritual feelings like the others had. I could picture myself living in many exotic countries and places, I could have been one of those women in the reliefs we saw on all the temples. I would have been a dancer I was sure of that. I loved seeing all the different designs of the woman and the things they were doing in the reliefs, especially the dancers.

Bach pulled me back to this world when he stopped the group and told us,

"We'll have to wait until dark when the others leave to be able to enter the temple and enter the gateway to the under world. It's not an area where they allow the tourist to go and there are people watching the temple entrance until then."

"Maybe they'll take a lunch break or something and if we watch, we could get in a little sooner." Amy suggested.

"It's possible that could happen. We'll have to stay close and see if the opportunity opens up for us." Bach answered back.

"Wow, does that mean we could really play tourist and take turns checking out the grounds and the temple here?" I asked. I couldn't help myself, I wanted to see it all and there was so much of the temple we hadn't seen yet.

"I suppose we could all check it out for awhile and then come back in a couple hours to see if they leave their post." Bach looked like he might like to see more of this place too. So that's what we did. We turned and as a group started to explore the temple grounds and take in the wonder of it all with Bach being our tour guide.

"Angkor Wat was built as the residence for the god or gods of the time. That is why you have the water surrounding the grounds to represent the cosmic oceans as Mu already said. This sacred territory was chosen and the structure built to reflect the sacred mountain with its five peaks. Their religious beliefs changed over the centuries. You will see many reliefs of Vishnu, Shiva and Brahma, these were the Gods of the time and they also represented the great Buddha in their reliefs. It also served as their capital city for a while it was later the structures became temples."

We over heard another tour guide talking to his group saying the temples were built around the 1400's.

Bach turned and looked back at our group and said,

"I sense this date isn't accurate. I'm reading a much earlier date, maybe closer to 600BC. The Guardians had their hand in the design and construction of this and many other structures that man takes credit for."

One of the structures had a scene of what looked like crocs and fish to me. Suddenly I was worried that maybe there were crocs here too and no body warned us. As I moved to view the next scene it was easy to forget the crocs. I was really impressed with one of the other buildings we had seen on the way to the main temple, it had so many elephants carved and one of the walls had three elephant heads on each side. Their trunks turned down to become pillars resting on the base of lotus flowers. I wondered when I saw it if there was special meaning to the way this wall was designed. Many of the Elephants were done to full life size in their designs so it was more than just impressive. It was over powering to stand in its presence. Every time I viewed a new piece I was once again taken with the craftsmanship of the artist who did the work.

Before we knew it, it was time to head back and check on the men posted at the doorway where we needed to gain entry. We worked our way through the crowds again and wove our way to the inner temple. Luck was with us. There was no one there so we quickly slipped inside. Bach had his reading of the area and made every turn until suddenly he stopped. The way was too crowded for me to see what had made him stop. Then I heard someone up closer to Bach, say the words "King Cobras".

Oh no, one thing I really didn't like was snakes and I wasn't expecting us to run into any snakes inside. Out in the jungle forest maybe but not here in the inner temple building. Now what? I wasn't going anywhere near, those King Cobras and no one could mesmerize me into doing it either. Shi had been in front of me and he started to move to the front of the group where Bach stood waiting. Amy, Bunny and Becka all started backing up toward where I was standing.

I could see what was happening after the others got out of the way. Chen and Shi both walked a little closer to the Cobras. I was holding my breath and wanted to yell at them not to get any closer. What on Earth were they planning to do? Surely they wouldn't try to capture them?

Before I could think another thought, the two of them started to cautiously work their way in closer to the two coiled Cobras. Still moving very slowly each one of the boys reached out slowly with their arms, almost mimicking the movements of the snakes. The boys separated and got the snakes turned away from each other with their little snake charmers dance. With perfect precision they both reached out at the same time and took a Cobra by the back of the neck. How in the world did they do that without the Cobras striking them both? You couldn't have paid me any amount of money to get me to try that! They each walked passed us carrying the snakes, headed to another secluded area to leave them and return to our hallway. As they passed by me I couldn't help but wonder if those two cobras weren't the true guardians of the entryway. The boys weren't gone very long and they were back ready to continue on with us. Bach pushed a panel and we all followed him in.

We were down a few steps and there in front of us was a small waterway. Bach gave us all instructions and got ready to drop inside first. The opening was only large enough for one of us at a time to go in. The rest of us lined up, girl, boy, girl, boy. I moved a little closer when I saw what they were doing and this time Mu would be the last to drop in. Being last wasn't my favorite place.

There was no way of knowing how long we'd be in this under world passageway this time. I hoped we were getting close to Tibet. This passageway was a little darker than the first ones we'd been in and I hoped it didn't stay this dark for the rest of the trip. I heard Bunny and Amy both agree with me. It was a little scary for all of us mere mortals. The merkids were never afraid of any of the under world. I never did ask them if they could see in the dark.

"No Kat we don't see any differently than you but we use our other senses far better than you. We can sense the walls and sides of the passageways a little like radar. We feel our own energy bouncing back into our main aura body. We can sense the direction of the currents and we get into the flow. It helps to carry us and keep us on course." Shi was the one who answered my last thought.

Never did a single thought get by any of our merkid friends when we were in the water wearing the crystal earplugs. We tried not to think about the darkness and just enjoy the ride. Sort of like one time when I was on an airplane and the turbulence was so bad it felt like we were on a roller coaster ride, only worse because most of the people on board were getting sick and throwing up. I closed my eyes that time and tried to imagine that I was riding a ride at the amusement park. It helped me then and it was helping me now. If you tried not to think about it and just went for the ride it wasn't near as bad. Plus I closed my eyes so it wasn't so obliviously dark and scary. It was my way of trying to have control over my fears and myself.

When the other girls heard me thinking about it, they decided to do the same thing. So it was my little trick to survive a turbulent plane ride that helped us all make the long swim into Tibet. I'm sure the merkids were happy we were quiet for most of the swim into our next adventure with them. They didn't appreciate mindless chatter and so I had been told before.

We started to head to the surface again and I opened my eyes to see what was coming. I finally saw light coming from the water up above us and we were already there. We came up in a lake near Mt. Kailash called Manasarowar. As we broke the surface of the cold lake water we walked to the edge and walked out, happy to be back on land again. This was the coldest water we had encountered so far. I wasn't freezing but I had the shivers and figured our clothes would be wet and cold a lot longer here in this climate.

Surprisingly for all of us, once we were out of the cold water, moving around the sun started to dry us off and the shivers went away a lot faster than I would have thought. As we looked around at our new surroundings it was a pretty desolate and uninviting place. All I could see for miles in every direction was rock, more rock and more mountains. Mt. Kailash was pretty impressive, standing in front of us at over 22,000 feet. It was snow capped which made it look as if it was some white haired old sentential standing guard over all this nothingness. I couldn't see a tree anywhere.

It was decided that we would stay together until we got closer to the base of the mountain and then we'd split up and start our search. Bunny was already busy shooting up next to Bach to walk and talk with him. Poor guy, I knew he was going to be in for a lot of questioning by her. Amy was staying pretty quiet again as if she was lost in her own thoughts and feelings. Becka dropped back in the group to walk with me while the other three pulled up the rear.

What a rocky place this part of the world is. We had read on the Internet while we were doing our search for the plants that the mountain name meant 'crystal' and 'precious one'. I could see no reason or justification for either name. It didn't look like a crystal or a precious anything. It would have to be something you felt with some other sense other than seeing, I guess. I would wait to pass my final judgment of the place until we were ready to leave. Maybe somewhere there would be some redeeming quality I couldn't see at this point in time.

I heard Mu telling the others that the mountain was considered by the Buddhists to be the home of the God Shiva. We already knew it was considered to be one of Earths Chakras. In fact she said it was considered to be the crown chakra. I could see the height of Mt Kailash making it the crown chakra it had to be one of the tallest peaks on earth. But it was the dragon lines that really gave Mt. Kailash its special distinction of being the crown chakra of the planet not its height.

Mu told the others the Hindus consider it to be Paradise and the spiritual center of the world. She added they believed that it was the destination of all souls to end up at Mount Kailash. The mountain was considered to have four faces each one made of a different material one each made of crystal, gold, ruby and lapis lazuli. The four rivers that flowed from the mountain divided the world into four regions and spread its spiritual waters to the four corners of the globe. This all made for a very strong spiritual place, which made it all the more surprising that it was so desolate and barren.

If all those things were true, you would think the home of Shambhala or Paradise would we tropical and lush, flowers and vegetation growing everywhere, not this rocky almost colorless place. Or maybe I was missing something?

The last thing I heard Mu say was,

"Mount Kailash was also considered to be Mount Meru which was the sacred mountain the temples at Angkor Wat were built to represent."

Apparently different sects of religions called the same things by different names, possible because their languages were different. So even though they were all saying similar stories about the same things, they called them by different names. Hindus said Tibet was the magical land of the Gods and that you could find the fabled Shangri La here. So were Shangri La, Paradise and Shambhala all the same place, just with different names?

As I looked ahead at Mount Kailash I could see the domed like temple of the mountain's peak. It was still covered in ice and snow. Mu had said the people here would never think of setting foot on the mountain to climb it. This was a sacred place and considered the home of the Gods. They would circle the base of the mountain to pay homage but never try to climb it.

"Many come here from all corners of the globe to meditate and look for enlightenment. Since ancient times there are many great teachers who have come to find perfection here." Mu told us as the group finally stopped to rest and make plans to begin our search.

"I think we all should stay here at the lower levels and search first. We can all take different areas and meet back here later. No one should climb any higher than this base level for now." Bach informed us. He divided us up onto four pairs. Amy was with Chen, Mu was with Becka, Shi was with me and Bunny was with Bach.

After Bach's directions were handed out, we split up, four going towards the right and the other four going to the left. We'd walk awhile before we split into smaller groups, it was going to be a long walk getting around the base of this mountain so it was nice to have a little more company for now. Amy and Chen were walking with Shi and me. Amy was almost glowing she looked so happy, or maybe it was the brisk cooler air and elevation here that had her cheeks so rosy.

The weather here was so nice compared to Australia where we thought we'd cook before we got out. The breezes were blowing and the sun was shinning. It wasn't too hot and it wasn't too cold, definitely cooler than back home though. I couldn't imagine what our plant would be doing growing here. How could anything grow in all this rock? How could anyone think this place could be paradise?

After walking for what seemed like hours we finally got where there was some vegetation, so we separated and started to study every plant. Mostly it was all some kind of scrub brush, none of it looked like the plant we were searching for. The boys decided it was time to move on plus we heard something up ahead of us, maybe someone coming from the other direction. The sounds were like hoofs possibly horses or some other larger animals. We heard the sound of their hoofs against the rock and shale long before we saw them. There were two riders on ponies.

The way they were dressed Shi said they must be monks. They were wearing red robes tied simply at the waist. Their heads were shaved and they were riding the ponies towards us in silence. They lowered their heads as they got closer but never said a word as they passed us by. Shi said it was a show of respect for the people here doing pilgrimages around the sacred mountain.

We were walking on and on around the mountains base, this walking part was feeling familiar. The terrain was rocky, sometimes the rocks were larger and sometimes they were smaller it wasn't easy at this altitude to keep going with all the loose rock under foot. I could tell we weren't at sea level anymore even my breathing was a little labored, I couldn't imagine having to climb any higher up Kailash even if it was allowed. It seemed like forever before we heard anything besides our feet making the rocks slip and slide making a crunching sound under our feet.

When we finally saw what the noise up ahead of us was, it turned out to be a couple young boys with three Yaks in tow. The boys were very colorfully dressed and they were smiling as they walked by us. I couldn't help but turn and watch them as they passed beyond us on the trail. I called out to them as they were leading the Yaks away.

"Hey, you don't happen to know the way to Shambhala do you?" It seemed a silly thing to do and I guess I was bored enough to try to be humorous with our little group. Heck, the two boys probably didn't even understand English. Everyone had been so quiet as we walked for all those hours, so I guess you could say it was me being me, doing something, trying to start a conversation. To mine and everyone else's shock and surprise, one of the boys yelled back to me,

"My great grandfather says, it's right there in front of you. Just open your heart, that's where you'll find the key. Then don't be afraid to use it and take the first step when you see the gateway." They laughed a little and kept walking away from us.

That was all he said. Like it would be so easy. At least he knew what we were talking about. I thought about yelling one more time to ask if we were in the right neighborhood or not. I didn't, they were moving further away and it really didn't seem like anyone in my little group was amused with my craziness or me at the moment.

We had walked forever when we finally heard sounds of something or someone coming up ahead of us again. When we finally saw what was making the noise it was Bunny Becka, Mu and Bach. We had hit the half waypoint and met up with them. Well now what were we going to do? If they didn't find anything on their side of the mountain, and we hadn't found anything on our side, where would we go from here? Oh please don't let it be up, I thought to myself.

Shi and Bach were having a little conference while the rest of us chatted about the barren surrounds we were gathered in. It had a few advantages over the last place I visited, it wasn't anywhere near as hot and there weren't any crocs here either. So maybe I could start to appreciate rocks a lot more. Maybe there was some new angle I hadn't tried yet but they weren't diamonds and rubies just what looked like granite and plain old gray rocks.

Something made me reach down, pick up a medium, small sized rock near my foot and put it in my pocket. Maybe a little souvenir to take home, I even thought I should have started this the first trip. One rock from each place I got to visit with the merkids, including Atlantis the next time I got to go. I liked the idea, I could get a special container to put them all in and have a real collection.

As I was thinking all my silliness about the new rock collection, I was a little surprised the sound of Bach's voice broke through my thoughts and got my attention.

"We have to rethink what we're doing. How we're looking at things. I can sense we're close, I just can't read it completely yet. It's like I can almost reach out and touch it but it's just escaping me. This doesn't usually happen to me. I need time to think for a few minutes I'm sure it'll come to me."

Shi looked at the rest of us and as Bach turned and walked about twenty feet away, Shi said,

"I don't see how the plant could possibly be anywhere near the base of this mountain. Plants don't grow in rock. There has to be some other place where the plant can be found. Maybe we should be looking for Shambhala. It would probably be a more productive hunt."

So that's how it started, the real hunt for Shambhala. We started right there, the seven of us while Bach was focusing on his reading of the mountain. We looked, touched and tried to see things in the formation of the rocks. Yes, we were literally looking for the proverbial gateway to Shambhala. We were starting to feel as if the area we were in couldn't hold the gateway and we were ready to move on when Bach came over and joined us again.

"Nothing yet" was all he said as he joined us again.

We moved on, continuing in a counter clockwise direction around the mountain, retracting the steps the other four had just made. Now instead of the sacred plant we were looking for the fabled city of Shambhala or more correctly, a gateway into the city.

I thought it was a good time to explain to everyone my theory about being able to get into the flow of the mountain's energy.

"We're going counter clockwise that's the direction all energy flows, I personally don't think you can get into the flow if you aren't going in the right direction. So this is the first step in the right direction. Anybody else got any ideas for the second step?" I asked.

Shi said,

"Bending time is a little like going into another dimension so maybe we need to raise our vibrations with some meditation. That might get us closer to the gateway."

Becka said,

"I think, we should try anything, you all think will work."

So there we were in the middle of nowhere, eight kids sitting lotus style meditating in the middle of a river of rock. I would have loved to have a picture of that. All things considered, it probably wasn't anything too unusual for the place we were. People traveled from all over the world to come here to find cleansing and purification, to circumvent the mountain and be empowered by it. This was a very religious and sacred place with tremendous energy or chi flowing around it. I felt certain if anyone could find the gateway, it would be Bach, Shi, Chen or Mu the merkids were incredible people to be sure.

After the meditation we all stood up, stretched and started to try and see our surroundings with new eyes. We split up into the pairs as we started out and began the new search. Shi and I were walking and looking over the short ledge and drop off to our right.

"It's here somewhere close." I heard Bach call out. We all froze in place and looked more closely at everything around us.

"Look could this be a gateway?" Amy asked and pointed to an outcropping of rock that looked like the ruins of some sort of gate way or pass through. If you used your imagination it could look close to some ancient kind of gateway, I thought so anyway.

When Shi came closer and looked from my perspective he agreed. He took a couple steps closer to it and put his hands out to feel the energy near the rocks. As Bach looked our way and gave the area his full attention, he called out,

"That's it, I'm sure of it."

"Okay, I'll try this first and we'll see if I can find the way through." Shi told the group as the others gathered closer to us.

"It's okay, I'll go. I've been here before and I'm not afraid." Amy said as she stepped by Shi and across the pile of rocks.

One minute she was there with us, the next she vanished into thin air. HOLY COW. Where in the world did she go? I mean I had seen magic shows and seen people supposedly disappear but this was no magic show. On this side of the pile of the rocks I had seen her and then as she stepped across them, poof she just disappeared. I was stunned. I think my mouth even dropped open from the shock of it. Becka and Bunny both rushed up next to me for a better look.

"Holy crap!!!" Bunny said, "Where did she go?"

"She made it. She's in the next dimension." Becka stated. The three of us were just staring into space where she had been.

How was it even possible? Maybe the merkids understood it but I sure didn't. If we all followed her now, where would we end up? Could we even follow her? I didn't know how I could. Suddenly Shi stepped into the same void where Amy disappeared and came back. Holy cow... he did it too and he was back with us.

"Wow, what was that like?" Bunny asked.

"It's easy." Shi told her. "Here Kat you grab my hand, you can make it as long as you're with me. Don't be afraid. Don't even think about it. Come on lets go." And with those last words he led me into the gateway right behind him.

He didn't have to worry about me thinking about it. Heck, I didn't have time to begin to think about anything before he just took me with him to the other side.

"WHAT THE........."

There was the strangest swooshing sound as Shi pulled me in. I didn't feel bad but there was a minor sensation that was hard to define or describe. It was as if Shi pulled me against a strong force field of some kind and I could feel something like a G force against my body as it entered into the other side. Was this Shambhala? If it is, all the writings of it pale in comparison to the real thing. Man didn't make words that could describe the beauty and wonder of this place, where ever or what ever it was called.

I couldn't believe my eyes. Suddenly my surrounds went from barren wasteland and rock to the most tropical, lush paradise anyone could ever imagine.

I've never seen so many flowering trees and lush greenery in one place. The trees were every color, some were white, pink or yellow others were purple, orange or red. It definitely felt like were we in some unbelievable oriental garden. Everything in every direction was beautiful and gracefully laid out. By the time I managed to look back behind me I could see the rest of the kids were here too.

Wow, what would we be doing next? The merkids had not only taken us half way around the world now they had taken us out of this world into a different dimension in time. I couldn't even begin to wrap my brain around this one. It was even slowing down the merkids while they looked at everything and tried to take it in. Amy was the only one of us who seemed to know exactly where she was. She said she had been here before and knew the way. So I guess our next question should be to her.

"So Amy, if you've been here before, tell me, where are we? Is this Shambhala?" I asked.

She was just beaming and glowing. Apparently she was extremely happy and experiencing some special bliss. Her face looked like she had found peace. Just a few minutes before she had seemed anxious and uneasy, what a difference a few steps had made in her demeanor. I do think all of us were experiencing different feelings and whether it was shock or awe we were still stunned a little from that giant leap of faith we all just took.

"We should go this way." Amy said as she pointed to her right. It was decided we would follow her directions because Bach agreed with her. We all realized we stood a much better chance of finding the plant we needed here. The big question would be if we found it could we find our way back home and would the plant make it out with us if we did? Somehow I couldn't help but think about the trip Dorothy made when she left Kansas and I hoped we would all make it back just like she had. This didn't look like Oz to me but it was probably as close to it as we could get.

Everyone was looking and inspecting the plants as we worked our way through the garden behind Amy and Bach, who had the lead. We saw a couple men up ahead of us. For some reason it was surprising to me seeing other people. I don't know what I was expecting but I think it was spirits or ghosts, not men like us. What was this place and how could we just jump in? I mean, why didn't everyone just hop in for a visit? If it were this easy you'd think more people would be doing it.

The two men were older, a lot older; they both had long white beards and looked like they were from some other time in the long distant past. They were wearing what I would have called ceremonial robes of very high-ranking men. The closer we got the more details I could see of them and their clothing. They walked with the slow gait of the elderly. Their hands were fragile and ancient looking. The skin was weathered and aged. It actually looked like the skin was just holding their bones together without much muscle to give them strength. If some one had asked me, I would have said they looked like they were thousands of years old.

As they got closer it was easier to see the features of their faces. They had warm smiling eyes set in an equally ancient face. The wrinkles and lines looked like they had been carved into their faces for centuries. One of them had the most spectacular power blue eyes and the other had pale emerald green ones. The last thing I ever expected to see was colored eyes. Except for the merkids I had never seen any oriental people with anything but brown eyes. The first thought I had was, are they related?

I shook my head and tried to clear my thoughts as the one ancient with the hypnotic blue eyes started to talk.

"Welcome to Shambhala." Was all he said as he put his hands together as if to pray and bowed his head as a sign of greeting. The second old man did the same gesture without speaking.

It was Bach who spoke next,

"Thank you, thank you both very much. We are here for a very important reason and if you could help us, it would be greatly appreciated."

Blue eyes looked straight at Bach and then towards the rest of us and said,

"It will be our pleasure. How can we best assist you?" he asked.

Shi stepped forward and showed the two men the drawing of the plants we were looking for while Bach explained the true cause for our mission.

Blue eyes looked at the drawing and started to speak,

"You have only a little farther to go. The plant you seek grows in abundance to the northeast, of us. It hugs the sunny side of the hills, as you get to the valleys of Shambhala you will be able to see it. Don't worry you won't be able to miss it. Just continue on as you are and you will be there in no time."

It was so strange standing there watching these men talk to us as if we were any other travelers and it was no different than if we had been back home and asked someone for directions. I know I had a million questions I would have loved to have asked them and I was sure Bunny would have had even more. But there wasn't time for socializing. We had a lot to do and a long ways to go just to get back home.

As the two passed by the rest of our group, they both stopped and looked Amy right in the eyes and said,

"Welcome home Suchandra. You are a most welcome sight. We sensed your return and have been waiting for you. We wanted to return this to you, I believe you dropped it during your last departure." Old green eyes handed Amy some sort of bracelet. They bowed their heads again and slowly moved away. Amy just smiled at them with the sweetest look on her face, she bowed her head in return as she slipped the bracelet onto her wrist and said,

"Thank you, you have my deepest appreciation."

"Wow, so what was that all about?" Bunny asked as she shook Amy's arm trying to get her attention.

"They're just old friends I haven't seen for awhile." Amy answered.

"What do you mean, just old friends you haven't seen for awhile? What are you suddenly remembering and what's triggered all this? How could they recognize you? You're a teenage girl and look nothing like the Suchandra person they called you."

"I don't know for sure Bunny but it seems like the minute, we started heading towards Tibet, I've had memories reawakening inside me and they just don't seem to want to stop. I have memories, of being the first King of Shambhala and studying with the Buddha. Isn't that incredible, I knew Buddha. As for how they recognize me, the soul or spirit, has only one face or look, it never changes and that is what they see when they look at me, not the girl that I am today. The eyes are the window to the soul and when you look into the eyes of a person you can touch and feel and see their soul." Amy explained.

"Yeah, I'd say that's all more than just incredible. Are you sure you didn't hit your head or something like that?" Bunny asked.

"Stop badgering her Bunny. She said she's remembering another lifetime. We all believe in reincarnation. Just because we haven't remembered our other life times, doesn't mean she can't remember hers." Becka told her, "Besides there has to be some pretty heavy sacred energy here with Kailash being the crown chakra, who knows what it might be doing to any of us, just by being in it's flow of energy."

After Becka got Bunny settled down, we all decided to just head to the valleys, that old blue eyes told us about. It would save a lot of time if we didn't have to keep searching along the way. We were sure they would know what they were talking about. When we were doing our research for the plants and Tibet, we read that Shambhala was an enlightened society where all lived in bliss and contentment. We couldn't see where anyone in the state of Bliss would misdirect you or supply you with false information.

We hadn't walked but a few minutes when Bunny started talking to Amy again.

"So Amy, if you've been here before and were a king and knew Buddha, please explain to me, how it is we were able to get here? Is this like Heaven? How is it we're here in our bodies and not just here in spirit form? Is this Astral Projection?"

Amy looked at Bunny and smiled before she tried to explain.

"The world is a multi dimensional place and we are all multi dimensional beings. There are times our spirits can leave our bodies but we don't have to, in order for us to take our physical bodies with us into other dimensions you need only to open your spiritual mind and heart to the same desire, your physical body will follow your spirit where ever it wants to go.

It's not exactly what you would call time traveling but something like it. Sometimes you hear people say the phrase "mind over matter," in this case I would say it's fourth and fifth dimensional travel over third dimensional but it is a matter of the spiritual mind believing or knowing. All you have to do is lift your vibrations to match the next dimension you wish to enter, if you are able to do that, you will find yourself there in the twinkling of an eye."

"But how would we know if our vibrations are high enough that we could go? Or how to get there, if we haven't been before?" Bunny asked almost before the last word left Amy's lips.

"You have been there many times, the second you have the desire, your spirit mind and heart will lead you back. It's like going home after being gone a long time. You recognize the path because it is familiar and comfortable it's like returning to the arms of the ones you love."

Bunny hit her with another question,

"Tell me why is all this happening now? I don't feel any different. I haven't had any great cosmic awakening or change that I am aware of."

Amy seemed so peaceful and was beginning to sound a lot like Bach, as she told Bunny,

"The changes you have experienced have been subtle ones, things that you often didn't notice. You drank water from the purest source on the Earth to cleanse and heal your body and spirit. Your soul sang with joy as you entered the Mother seed and the Amethyst there refined and balanced your soul's energy. When we came up through lake Manasarovar we all cleansed our souls of the sins of all our previous life times. You have walked through sacred energy and vortexes in several places, each time, raising and fine tuning your spiritual energy as well as opening your own chakras and giving life to the kundalini energy within you. You have been preparing for this and much more for some time now. You are aware on a spiritual and soul level but aren't remembering when you are in the physical body. It will come to you when the time is right for you to remember. Have no fear, there is a plan and a purpose for all of this."

Before Bunny could throw more questions at Amy we heard Bach and Shi call out.

"Look, we can see the valleys. We're almost there."

We all looked up and towards to the valleys in the distance. How beautiful this place was, the mountains and valleys ahead of us were grand to gaze upon. I wondered if any artist could paint the view before us and do it justice.

I wasn't sure if Bunny was too puzzled over Amy's statements to ask her any more questions or if she was just lost in her own thoughts. Even I had to think a little about what she said. Did the same things apply to Becka and me? Were we all here for some other purpose or reason that we didn't understand yet? Did her words sound familiar because Cobar had said something similar when we were in the under world with him in Australia?

If that was the case, what did they know that we didn't? I might have to start asking Amy some of my own questions. Just how much did she know that she wasn't telling us? I wondered if Becka was wondering the same things? Some of this seemed too personal to talk about in a group.

Especially with the merkids always thinking we chattered too much. I'd rather wait until it was just the girls and I back home and then I'd have a list of my own questions for all of them.

I wondered if Amy would have the same enlightened intuition when we got back home or if it was this place that made her remember and seem so wise and all knowing. I mean, WOW she had known the great Buddha.

I don't know why but I reached down and picked up a small oval white stone I saw on the ground in front of me. I wondered if this one would make it home with me or remain in Shambhala when we left. Would this be a multi dimensional test or what? It sure felt like a real rock, it felt smooth and flat to my touch just like any rock at home might feel. It felt solid and warm to the touch as I placed it in my front pocket.

The merkids were starting to talk a little among them selves. As we got closer to the valleys, Bach said he felt certain that we'd be able to find the way back out but wanted to talk more to Amy about where she thought would be the best place to try. Shi agreed with him. Mu suggested we find and gather the plants we needed and then have something to eat and drink before we moved on, whatever direction that might be. She seemed concerned more for us, and our needs. Maybe that was because she could hear my stomach growling. I hadn't been thinking about food but apparently my stomach was. I wondered if that might be another multi dimensional thing, not thinking about food?

As we got closer to the Valleys we could see a couple different groups of people. They were small groups sitting together in the grass. It looked like Yogis, or Guru's teaching or lecturing students. No one seemed to care that we were there. They saw us and slightly bowed their heads as a greeting or acknowledgment and then paid us no mind.

The whole group stopped as we listened for a couple minutes to the words the teacher was telling the group.

"It is through meditation that individuals first begin to experience the Seven Rays. They are the seven energies of the cosmos that filter down through the Universe, each as a different color and level of energy. Each colored ray going through a different planet in the galaxy, then through Earth and her chakras into each man and woman and filtering down through their chakras and bringing to them the enlightenment their souls seek. Man must learn that we are all as one. Each soul is as, the end of a nerve, on the skin or surface of the Mother Earth. All nerves are connected through the Universe to a single God mind. When the nerve endings fight against each other, as man does with his pollutions, wars, and crusades, Mother Earth has a reaction. When the reaction is violent there are earthquakes, floods and worse. Man must learn that every thought and word uttered will have an affect on every living thing, which includes Mother Earth, mankind and the rest of the Universe. Thus the saying, for every action, there is a reaction.

Man needs to understand it is the Seven Rays that cleanse and nourish not only his soul but also that of the Earth and the rest of the Universe. Each man, planet and star is an individual living and breathing entity and without the Seven Rays, all would parish. Just like the nerves and veins in man connect all the arms, legs and organs to a human brain, the Rays are the connecting veins and nerves of the Universe, they filter down and connect each of us to our beginnings and the Creator."

Wow, I was impressed with how easily he made me think about being connected to everything else. I had never heard about the Seven Rays he spoke of but I knew all things had energy or an aura that was a life force. It made me wonder about rainbows and their colors. My Mom really believed in reading her horoscope, I wondered if the Seven Rays might explain how the planets could affect a person on a daily basis and if horoscopes and astrology, might not have more importance than a lot of people gave them any credit for?

We all seemed a little lost in our own thoughts as Bach led us away from the group and back towards our journey. It wasn't long and we saw another group sitting and talking. They were speaking about energy and sacred geometric shapes: about the seven levels of the astral planes and dimensions of the spirit. Man apparently didn't begin to understand the multi-dimensional world, the shapes, sounds and levels of energy and what they could do, that he lived in. Their conversations were a little more over my head, in fact they sounded like genius's talking in ten-dollar words that I couldn't understand. The group didn't stay with them too long.

There were more groups but Bach said we had our mission and couldn't stop to listen to them all. As I looked at the different groups, I couldn't help but wonder what they were saying. One man looked like a Druid Monk, another like Einstein, and one even looked like he could have been Jesus. I could hear a few words coming from the one, who looked like a Druid Monk,

"The stars and moons are just as responsible for building the Cosmic Kundalini Energy."

They were all different and the people sitting and listening to them were all very different looking too. The people or spirits here, what ever they were, were from all countries and nations, from all times in history by the look of their clothes. It was hard to follow Bach and leave this area where it seemed so many were learning so much.

We walked into the heart of the valleys before we saw what looked like the plant we came in search of. There were hundreds of them. They were all along the sunny side of the valleys, on the foothills, just as old blue eyes said they would be. This was a first for us, there were more plants than we could possibly need or take. All the different kinds of plants here seemed to be in abundance. We had seen fruit trees, berry bushes, every kind of plant and flower imaginable. Now here was the sacred plant we needed so desperately and it was growing wild like a weed, taking over the hillsides.

Bach and Shi gathered what they could and packed it carefully for the trip home. Mu suggested we all eat a little something and have some water. We'd rest until the boys finished what they were doing. So we had our snacks, later we'd make our plans for going home.

This was the first time we didn't have to walk halfway across a country or continent. It was refreshing to me to not be sweating and cooking half to death or being terrified by crocs. We hadn't really talked about leaving and going back another way so I had no idea what plans they had up their sleeves this time. Going back the way we came didn't make as much sense, as just getting out here as soon as possible but we didn't know where here was.

When the boys were ready they talked with Amy and asked her what she thought. "Leaving from here will be fine. We'll be much farther to the north, maybe closer to Beijing. That would bring us very close to the coast and the Yellow Sea. Will that mess things up for the return in the under world passageways?" she asked.

"If we make it to Beijing and then the Yellow Sea we'll swim to Hawaii and from Hana we can enter the Seven Sacred pools and locate our return passageway to Atlantis." Shi told her.

Bach agreed with the path,

"If you can help us pin point the way back through, the rest will be easy and we can reroute through Hawaii as Shi just said. That seems like the most direct route from here."

"The only thing is, I don't know if I want to go back with you, "Amy said to no one in particular."

"What the...." Bunny blurted out as she shot over to Amy's side. "Now I know you must have hit your head cause you're not thinking or talking straight. What do you mean you want to stay here?"

"This is where I found peace and happiness in the past. I want to stay. I can do more to help the world from here than I can going back with you now." She answered.

"Oh I don't know about this Amy," Becka told her, "You may not have thought this all out. Would you want to hurt your parents like this by not going back? Would you really want to leave everything and everyone you know and love?"

"My love would always be there, that wouldn't change and I would always feel the love from all of you. This is where my mind and heart have known the greatest joy and peace. This is my home."

The four of us stood and talked, we argued and tried to persuade her that she had to come home with us. Her parents would kill us and there's no way we'd be able to explain what happened to her. They would never believe us, not even in a million years.

Mu suggested that we continue on our path to leave Shambhala and talk with Amy along the way. She obviously didn't think we were going to get anything decided standing here debating each other. This was not an easy issue for us to deal with. How could we leave Amy here? How could she think we would leave her? I don't care who she was before or how much peace and tranquility she found here before this was not her home this life time and we couldn't go home without her. Didn't she know that?

Bunny was going at Amy while Becka and I listened, trying to think of our own points to change her mind and make her understand she had to return with us.

I think it was right then and there, I thought to myself, I'll drag her through if I have to. Bunny would help me, I'm sure the two of us could over power her if we had to. There was just no way we could let Amy stay here, no matter how much she thought she wanted to stay. We had read where they said many of the people who found their way into Shambhala were never seen again. Either they perished trying to find it or they found the way in and preferred to stay and never leave. It never crossed my mind that any of us would feel that way. I mean this was a great, really great place but stay and not go home?

We walked only a little longer when Amy said she thought we had reached the best spot to go back through. She said we'd be close to Beijing and could easily work our way to the east and the Yellow Sea and out to the Pacific. Bunny and I had talked briefly after her arguing with Amy we decided we'd drag Amy through if we had to. Surely she'd understand and forgive us later. We would have to hope she'd think differently on the other side and that she would forgive us. We decided we'd let a couple of the others go through and then we'd grab her and take her with us. We'd just have to make sure she was close to the gateway so we wouldn't have to fight or struggle too much to get her close enough to get through.

Once Bach was certain he had the right spot he went through. We all watched as Mu got ready said goodbye to Amy and she went next. Amy started saying goodbye to the three of us. As Shi went through he told Becka to come next. As soon as he was out of the way Amy gave Becka a hug and told her goodbye. Becka turned with tears in her eyes and stepped through the gateway. She was barely out of the way when Bunny looked at me and as Amy started to give her a hug and kiss goodbye, we both grabbed her by her arms and dragged her through the gateway with us. Without us realizing it, Chen tried to grab Amy when he saw what we were doing. So it was the four of us who went through the gateway together.

BIG MISTAKE!!!! One thing we didn't know was, how safe or unsafe it was for more than one person to go through the dimensions of the gateway all at one time. Didn't even think about it until we dove through the gateway and felt the pain begin. If I thought I had a time bending jet lag from the other trips. That would prove to be nothing, compared to what happens when you force too much physical matter through the gateway of one, energy dimension to the next.

The four of us were twisting and turning as we dove through the gateway. Bunny and I never let go of Amy's arms and we didn't know until later that Chen had a hold of Amy, from behind by her shoulders. The pressure I felt coming in was nothing to the pressure we felt going out through the gateway. I felt as if all my muscles twisted, ripped, and then froze tight leaving me feeling almost totally paralyzed. I landed hard with Amy and Chen falling on top of me and Bunny fell to my side. The four of us all let out a cry of pain as we landed in a pile on the cut stones of the walkway, right in the middle of one section of the Great Wall of China.

We were where Amy said we would be but the big question now, was would we ever be able to move again? It was apparent that none of us could move on our own right now. Mu, Becka, Shi and Bach all raced over to where we landed in our pile of dimensionally warped bodies.

Oh no, I couldn't move and apparently the other three couldn't either. We could only hope and pray this didn't last. What had we done to ourselves? The others tried to help Chen and Amy get up off of me but they just cried out in pain when the others touched them. I could hardly breathe and they couldn't get them off of me. Maybe I was going to die right here in the middle of the Great Wall. If somebody didn't get them off of me soon I was sure I would stop breathing altogether.

"You have to get them off of me. I can't breathe. Please do something and get them off of me." I cried out to Bach and Shi.

Bunny was the first of the four of us who could move and she tried to get out of the way. I could tell it was hard for her and she was in pain. She wasn't moving normally at all. She looked like she had some terrible disease and none of her body seemed to be functioning correctly. She managed to sit up and turn her body a little. Becka was trying to help her but Bunny couldn't get up yet.

"What in the heck happened? "Bunny asked. "I feel like someone ran over me with a stream roller and I can't make anything work right yet. My body isn't responding to my desire to move. I feel like every muscle is twisted or torn. It feels like I must look like Frankenstein. Tell me the truth Becka, do I look the way I feel?"

Becka sounded like she was trying to be kind,

"It's not that bad Bunny, I'm sure it will go away and maybe you just need to move a little to work it out. Maybe you just cramped your muscles. Here let me try to massage your leg muscles and see if it helps any." Becka suggested.

"No, No stop. Don't do that. It hurts too much." Bunny spit out through gritted teeth. I could tell she was experiencing pain but she had been able to move a little. At least she was sitting up. I felt bad for Amy and Chen but if somebody didn't move them off of me soon I was going to croak.

"Some body has to get them off of me." I repeated.

Mu and Bach were talking and as they walked around me to get closer to Chen and Amy, I was really hoping they would do something to help me. The tears were running down my face and very muscle in my body was screaming bloody murder.

Bach talked to Chen. I couldn't hear what he said to him but it was only a few words and then, the two of them tried to move Chen. He moaned and tried hard not to cry out. They stopped and he was still there on top of me.

"It's okay, Bach. Just do it and get it over with Kats being crushed. I'll survive. Just do it." Chen told them.

I knew this was hurting him but I couldn't feel too badly about it. As soon as they lifted him to the walkway and he was off of me I started to feel some relief. I could breathe a little easier. Amy hadn't said a word since we came through the gateway. As I looked to see if I could see her face, I saw her tears. I didn't know if her pain was worse than mine or if she was upset that we forced her to come back. I was afraid to ask too.

"I'm so sorry Amy. We didn't mean to hurt you. I hope some day you'll forgive us for bringing you back. We just couldn't leave you there. We couldn't go home without you. Are you ever going to speak to us again? Or are you in too much pain?" I asked her.

"I understand Kat, I might have done the same thing, I don't know. Right now I hurt too much to talk about it. I'm sorry I landed on top of you but I can't move either, none of my muscles will do what I want them to do. Talking seems to be all I can do at the moment."

Bach and Shi told Amy to get ready, they were going to move her and they would try not to hurt her too much. Then before she really had time to think about it they picked her up and gentle moved her off me onto the stone pathway. Amy only cried out a little before they sat her down again.

It felt so great to be able to breathe again. I realized as I took in a deep breath it was mostly my arms, legs and neck that hurt so much. Maybe my back muscles too but not as much pain was talking to me from my back right now. What in the world were we going to do? This was making it impossible to get up, much less walk and then swim home. As I was there, twisted and unable to move or even sit up I thought what am I going to do if this doesn't go away? Then panic started to set in.

"Bach, please tell me this is only temporary and it'll wear off." I begged him.

"What I'm reading is, it will go away but we need to get you some help because it won't go away right away without it. When you all came through the gateway at the same time it messed up your individual molecular structure in all your muscles that were struggling on the way through. If you hadn't been pulling and trying to drag Amy through it wouldn't have happened at all."

"You might say that was instant karma." Mu said matter of fact.

I didn't like the way that sounded but Bach said he didn't think it was permanent and I was sure if we all recovered, Amy would forgive us.

"So where can we go to get help? What do we need? I'm not sure if we can go anywhere the way we feel right now." I told them. The others agreed. We were in pretty tough shape and we didn't think they could carry us even if the pain didn't do us in first.

Bach, Shi and Mu started looking over the sides of the walls, scanning the area for anything they could use to help get us out of here. I didn't think we'd be able to even get off the Great Wall, How far would we have to travel to get down. Did we have to maneuver stairs or was there ramp ways?

I felt so strange, my neck seemed to be twisted and my head felt like it was almost leaning on my left shoulder, which felt like it was Charlie horsed up in the air as far as it could go. My hips seemed twisted as well and I was sure all my toes were curled under on both feet. What in the heck happened? I mean I heard what Bach said about coming through from the other dimension but how was anything like this possible? It didn't feel like this was something that could easily go away and I thanked God that it wasn't going to be permanent.

It was Becka I hear call out,

"Look, there's a boy with a cart. Maybe we can get him to help us. How far do you think we'll have to go to get help?"

"If we can just get into the next town I think we'll be able to find someone who can help us." Bach answered her.

It was Shi who ran down and talked with the boy. It turned out he was headed into Beijing and if we could get to the cart, he would give us all a ride. This would be a feat not easily accomplished. The four of us waited our turns as the others tried to carry us, one at a time down the stairway to the cart. The young boy was very patient and friendly. He spoke very good English and seemed amused with how strange the four of us looked. He said he thought we looked like twisted human pretzels. Sadly I didn't find it as amusing as he did. I was however very grateful for the ride he was giving us even though each rut in the way made the ride full of painful jolts. If he hadn't come along, no telling how long we would have been laying there in our misery.

I had been to the Great Wall of China and it was something I had often dreamed about but now I hardly even noticed it. What a waste. I tried to look back as the cart started to roll forward and take in the majesty of the greatest building project even made in China. It turned out to be a very long and uncomfortable trip into Beijing but I did have a lasting imprint inside my minds eye of the Great Wall and I would cherish that forever.

As we approached the out skirts of the city Bach asked the young boy if he knew of any acupuncturists in Beijing. So now we knew whom Bach was taking us to for help. I thought for sure he would have been taking us to a hospital to some doctor who could hopefully give us a shot of something to relax our muscles and let us move normally again.

I definitely didn't care who did it, what ever they needed to do to make us feel normal again but an acupuncturist? This felt like a very big problem to me and I wasn't sure that someone sticking a few needles in us could correct it all.

She was taking the words right out of my mouth when Becka asked,

"Are you sure we shouldn't be taking them to a hospital?"

It was Mu who answered her.

"Trust us Becka, we know what we're doing. We need to get the energy flowing correctly again in their bodies. Acupuncture will relieve the stress that has them all twisted up. Mostly we need to correct the molecular structure and acupuncture is the best and safest way to do that with the quickest results. If we took them to your hospital a doctor would give them a shot of something and we wouldn't make it half way home before they would be in trouble again."

Bach tried to reassure us all when he said,

"Acupuncture is one of the oldest practices and it is proven to work with the most natural use of healing energies. We have to get the energy flowing in balance again. The Ying and Yang are out of balance and this is the result. Acupuncture will get the energy back in balance and they will be like new again. If we are to get back on time, we can't delay on getting this done. We know of no other way to help them."

I wasn't looking forward to having needles stuck into me but if it fixed what was wrong with us, it would be more than worth it. I could endure almost anything I think right now if it fixed me. There was no way we could get home in the shape we were in and if we didn't get home.

Man I didn't want to think about what that would mean. For sure we couldn't go home looking like this either. Our parents would die if they could see us now.

The cart seemed to hit every pothole and dip in the road as we worked our way towards Beijing. As we talked with our new friend Joe we learned that we was 15 and we was headed into pick up supplies for his grandfathers farm. He was a bright and witty fellow entertaining us with his stories of life in China today. He liked to get on the Internet just like us and was a member of Face book. We all promised to send him a friend request when we got back home.

Finally Joe slowed the cart outside of a small structure with the sign hanging above the door that had a couple Chinese characters on it that Joe said read Acupuncture/ Herbalist. Shi went inside with Bach and we all waited for them to come back out.

When they returned they said the gentleman said he could see us all and to come in. We each thanked Joe before they started to carry us in. While Becka held the door open the two boys tried to carry us in, without causing too much pain in the process. Mu thanked our friend Joe and once we were all inside he took off.

The man who said he could help us didn't look too old or ancient for an acupuncturist. I was expecting someone like old blue eyes to be the one doing his magic on us. In clear, perfect English he asked what happened to us, to cause such a problem. He asked for the truth so he could better perform his services.

So it was Bach who explained what happened. I fully expected him not to believe a word Bach said but he seemed to believe him and not be too shocked by what he was told. So there were no secrets here between us, and our new friends. Inside now, I was only able to look around a little but just enough to notice there were three partitioned areas or little offices where there were tables and just enough room for someone to walk around the tables. The gentleman who had been talking with Bach called out some girls names and suddenly five girls came out of nowhere and each started to help one of us into one of the rooms. The fourth girl started to set up another table there in the open area for Chen and the fifth girl started to make tea or at least that's what it looked like she was doing. Perhaps she would be in charge of entertaining the others while we got our treatments.

It wasn't easy getting moved onto the tables. They turned me face down on the table and the young girl who was helping tried to massage some of my muscles so they could place me with the least amount of pain and discomfort. I tried to just grit my teeth and not cry out from the pain it caused. I didn't cry but the tears came and ran down my face anyway. I could hear the others and I guess they were trying to do the same thing.

Our acupuncturist said,

"You can all call me Eddie. I will have my daughters work with us today. They will begin to massage some of the stress out of the muscles to get you started. Ling will make you some tea that you will have to drink and then we will place the needles to try and balance the ying and yang energies you scrambled when you came through from the other dimension. I believe what you did was to short-circuit yourselves and this can be corrected. It will be at least a two-hour treatment and then we will see how you are doing. If there is not enough correction we will have to do another treatment a few hours after that. Let us hope that you have not done any permanent damage."

Wow, I hoped he was really good at what he was doing because I thought the worry of any permanent damage was not something we had to worry about. Now I could see this picture of Amy, Bunny and me always looking like some kind of freaks back home because we got screwed up coming back through the gateway forcing Amy to come home. Not a pretty picture I can guarantee you.

The massage felt good and bad. It did hurt some but it also felt a little better after she worked her fingers over the rigid twisted muscles of my arms and legs. It certainly would have been a lot more relaxing if we hadn't been in so much discomfort at the same time. They had some soft Chinese music playing in the background somewhere and it smelled like there was incense burning. The only light in the little partitioned areas was from candles and there were a lot of them on the little shelves along the walls.

It was so nice to be still after our ride in Joe's cart. Getting knocked around and bumped was very uncomfortable; it was a lot easier to try to relax as I felt Ming's gentle touch and the soft music in the background. It was peaceful here for right now. Ling showed up with my cup of tea. Apparently it was some herbal treatment to go with the massage, and acupuncture. She held a straw so I could more easily drink the concoction. It didn't taste very good at all. In fact, it kind of tasted like what I think dishwater would taste like.

"You must drink every drop," she told me as I pulled my head away from the straw and made a face that showed how awful I thought it was. It wasn't easy to pull away from the straw either, because that hurt almost as much as that tea tasted BAD. It was totally unpleasant but I did as I was told. I didn't want to look like this by the end of the day. Heck if they told me it would help I probably would have drank anything they put in front of me.

I finished my tea then Becka and Mu came in to help to get me undressed. That wasn't an easy task. It would have been kind of comical if it hadn't been so painful. I was placed back on my stomach and Ming placed a towel over my butt. I'm sure my face was beet red. I couldn't imagine having some strange Chinese man see me naked. Eddie came it into my little cubical just as the girls left.

He must have seen how red my face was and said only,

"There is no need to be embarrassed. I am only here to work with your energies and return balance to your flow of Chi. I will be placing many needles into the special power points along the dragon lines of your physical body. You should feel nothing and you will need to just relax and think about your recovery. Let the tea do its work and use this time to meditate if you know how. If not, just try to relax and float along to the sounds of the music you hear. See yourself as you were before."

Eddie was right it didn't hurt. Of course so many other things did hurt who would have felt the little needles he gently inserted to the surface of my skin. It seemed like he was there a very long time, using way more needles than I would have thought he'd have to. He must have used hundreds of them but he talked while he worked, explaining everything to me.

"The art of acupuncture is more than 5,000 years old." He told me while he worked. "The art of it has been handed down through my family for many generations. I learned it from my father and he learned it from his father and so on. I am teaching all of my girls, they are my students along with three others. Acupuncture is very simple. The meridian lines or dragon lines as we call them are an invisible circuit of energy networking that runs through the body. It allows the chi energy to flow something like the veins and arteries of the physical body. This is where you get the Ying and Yang energies. Yang energy has the sun as its source where as Ying energy comes from the Earth. Because of their source they both have definite patterns that they flow in. Many people do not realize that every tooth has a connection to a specific part of the body, somewhat like reflexology connects certain areas of the body to each of its organs.

Chi is the energy that creates all movement throughout the Universe. Just as the Earth and the human body have many similarities the same kind of similarities can be found with the Universe. There are wormholes that conduct the energy of the Universe much the same as the dragon lines of man's spiritual body or the Ley lines of Earth conduct the Chi energy through our bodies and the planet. One must have faith because they cannot be seen or felt by most people. We are a microcosm of the Universe. All miracles work in the same manner with the same energy whether with man, the planet or the Universe."

That had something of a familiar ring to it. What had I just heard back in Shambhala? Seemed energy, the Meridian lines and all those things of the astral and human body had a balancing counter part in Earth and the Universe and they were all connected somehow.

"Now you will have to be still and let the needles and the Chi do their work. I will be back to check on you soon. We will check on your progress and if needed apply some electros to a few of the pressure points. It's nothing to be alarmed about. Electro acupuncture helps to stimulate the power point just a little more than the needles can do on their own. Because you and your friends have put your bodies and the body's Chi in extreme distress, this may not be an easy turn around. As I said before, you may need more than one treatment. Relax and I will return shortly."

I'm not sure who was next to get Eddie's treatment. I couldn't see anything right now. There must have been some special drug in that tea they made me drink, or the needles did strange things to you because I couldn't lift my eyelids. For a split second I was panicked that I was getting worse, my eyelids worked fine when I came in here. In fact it was one of the few muscles I could move besides my mouth to talk.

I must have fallen asleep because I don't remember anything else until Eddie was gently shaking my shoulder to try and wake me up. It didn't hurt when he touched me. In fact for a minute I forgot where I was and what I was here for.

"Good, you're awake. Lets try a couple things and see how you're progressing. Can you wiggle your toes for me?" he asked.

I tried to concentrate and do as he asked.

"Yes. Very good, you are making progress. I can see the distress in your neck is still quite apparent. I think I should help that Chi along with just a little electro charge added to the needles there. Relax and try to just breath even breathes. This won't hurt. You may feel a little buzz but it won't hurt you, I promise.

Becka and Mu stepped in to watch Eddie hook me up to the electric current he used for this treatment.

"You're looking a lot better Kat. All of you are. Does your body still hurt? Are you feeling better yet?" she asked me.

"You know, now that you're asking. I don't hurt like before. I thought they must have put drugs in the tea because it tasted so awful and then shortly after I drank it I couldn't keep my eyes open and I fell asleep. How long have I been in here?"

"Only about an hour so far." Mu answered.

"We just talked to Amy a couple minutes ago and she said to tell you she forgives you and Bunny for bringing her back. She's doing a lot better too." Becka added.

I could feel some fuzzy little buzzing feelings where Eddie was doing the electric boost to the needles. He shooed the girls away and told me to rest and meditate again. In less than ten minutes I could feel my neck finally start to relax. I had been saying a little prayer, hoping the needles would do the job and I could be normal again.

When Eddie returned to remove the needles he told me not to try to get up or move yet. Ming would be back to work some of my muscles and then I would have to drink a different tea before I could try to sit up. He would come back then to see if the treatment had worked and determine if I needed another one or not. I was feeling pretty optimistic that the treatment had worked. I could tell my arms and legs were relaxed and the pain was gone from my back as well. My neck muscles had been the last to give in and relax.

I could hear a couple of the others getting up and moving around just a little. Eddie told them not to do too much too soon. They had to sit and rest again. Finally he came back just as I finished my second cup of tea. I was hoping I'd be allowed to move soon. Three cups of tea was making me a little uncomfortable, wondering where the nearest rest room was and hoping it was somewhere close.

Eddie gave me the okay to try and sit up. What a difference a few hours and some acupuncture can make. I could sit up with almost no help.

It was only because I was trying to keep the towel wrapped all around me that I couldn't sit up completely by myself. A bigger towel would have been helpful and made sitting up a lot easier. I was so thankful to be able to sit up and actually move again.

"How can I repay you for what you've done for me?" I asked him. "I don't have much money with me but I could send you more from home when I get back there."

"I am honored to treat you and your friends. Most people live their entire life never knowing Shambhala even exists. I have had the honor of treating and meeting eight who have been there and come back. That is payment enough for my daughters and me. We are honored to serve you. Sit for a little longer before you try to stand and get dressed." He answered me before he left and pulled the curtain across the opening to give me privacy.

I sat and slowly moved my feet, then my arms I didn't want to tempt fate but I wanted to be sure I was okay before I tried to stand again. Everything seemed to be working and I thought I could do it. So I slipped off the table and felt strong again as my feet touched the floor. I hurried to get dressed and sat down again as I put my shoes back on. Yes I told myself, I was feeling 100 % again. What was in that tea? Maybe I should ask before we left, it just might be something good to know but maybe first I'd ask about the restroom.

There were hugs all around as we saw each other well and normal looking again. We sat and had tea one more time with Eddie and his daughters. This time we talked and told him what we saw and thought of Shambhala. I remembered the flat white rock I had picked up while we were there and reached into my pocket to see if it came through the gateway with me or not.

"I know it's not much Eddie but I picked this up while I was in Shambhala, in the valleys where we found our plants. I would like to give it to you for all that you and your daughters have done for us." I extended my hand with the stone in it towards Eddie. He reached out and took it saying,

"Thank you. I will honor this above all my other property."

Bach stood and said,

"Perhaps I could leave you one of the plants we brought back with us. I took more than I actually needed just because they were so abundant."

"I would be deeply honored to accept your gift." Eddie just beamed as he watched Bach unwrap and remove one of the plants he had packed away so carefully.

As we finished our tea and said our goodbyes Eddie gave us the general directions we needed to work our way around Beijing to the bay, then the Yellow sea and out towards the Pacific and Hawaii, our next stop.

I was surprised to be thinking it but walking felt good. There was a time at the Great Wall and after when I was afraid I might never be able to walk normally again. So I was enjoying this little hike around the city.

The lights of Beijing were beautiful at night. It looked like a very magical place to be sure. It had certainly held a lot of magic for us already thanks to Eddie and his daughters. What a gigantic miracle his little acupuncture needles had delivered for us. Never in this life did I ever want to feel like that again. You could bet if I were going dimension jumping again, that was one mistake I would never repeat. Lesson learned.

Eddie gave Bach some tea to pack for when we got to Hawaii. He told us to have another serving of tea before we started home from there. He thought that should be all we needed to get us safely home.

We walked and enjoyed the sights of the city always working our way towards the east and the bay. There were doorways we passed that smelled so good you had to wonder what delightful dishes they were making inside. Music rolled out from some of them and always there were people everywhere. What a city. Millions of people lived here and it was alive with the energy of them.

Once we made our way around the main city and got near the harbor we passed the boats and found a quiet, deserted wharf where we walked to the end, slowly and silently entering the water. The eight of us were happy and excited to be heading home, the last hours had been trying and emotional for all of us. Bunny and me both felt so bad for all the trouble we caused and the pain and suffering to Chen and Amy, as well as ourselves. I was ready to go home and do nothing for at least a week. I was already thinking about being home in my own bed, sleeping late and just enjoying my big fluffy mattress and pillows.

The water in the Bay was a little murky and polluted, I was anxious to get out to cleaner water and away from the city. I remembered when the Olympics were held here and some of the events had to be cancelled because of the algae that took over the bay. No matter what, we just wanted to be away from this Bay and get home soon.

When we finally reached the Pacific the colors were beautiful and intense again. The whales were singing and fishes of all colors and sizes were swimming in giant schools. The Oceans were wonderful places and full of something new every time we were in them. It was like every National Geographic and Discovery Channel special you've ever seen all rolled into one special and the real thing was better than any movie special ever.

We swam for a long time. I was feeling okay but it was probably a lot easier for us girls than it was for Chen. He had to swim and tow one of us, we just had to hold on and go with the flow.

You could tell as we got close to the Hawaiian Islands, the water got more of a rainbow design in the layers of blues and greens in it's color. The sand below us was reflecting the sunlight and you could feel the warmth of it radiating back up towards the surface. I always wanted to see Hawaii so this was very exciting for me. I hoped we got to see some of the island before we had to enter the under world again I knew we'd stop long enough to have our tea. That wasn't going to be simple since we didn't have a teapot. I wondered if anyone had thought about that when Eddie gave us the tea maybe Bach or Shi would have some special trick for making tea without a pot.

As we neared the island of Maui on the northern shore we got a dolphin escort leading the way in. It made me feel a little like a mermaid with the dolphins swimming along beside us. When our heads finally broke the surface of the water it was to see the most beautiful shoreline and Tropical Island in front of us. Maui had majestic palm trees soaring towards the sun, an impressive display of waves crashing into the black lava cliffs to one side and creamy sandy beach to the other. The farther you looked up from the beach, the more you could take in of the worn down volcano mountaintop: so this was the famous Haleakala, one of the dormant volcanoes of the Hawaiian Islands.

From where we were the water looked royal to powder blue in color and the Island was black and green in comparison. We were just floating and bobbing around in the water, admiring the island while we waited a minute for Bach to set our direction for going ashore. First we would figure out the tea situation and then we'd find the Seven Sacred Pools and our way home.

Bach pointed to the beach on our right and headed that way. I'm sure if anyone noticed us we just looked like a group of tourist out snorkeling this morning. The sand was warm under our feet as we walked onto the beach. We stopped and Bach started to read the area. He suggested we head up away from the beach to find a place where we might be able to order hot teas without the tea. He thought he sensed a beachside food stand just up around the corner. I was looking forward to seeing the look on the clerks face when Bach asked for four teas without the tea. That might make us stand out a little from the rest of the crowd.

He was right as usual and there was a small stand where one could buy things like coffee and tea, soda, hot dogs and snow cones just up off the beach a few yards. There were a couple other people there, getting coffee to start their day so we just got in line. Becka told Bach she would order and pay and asked the others what they would like to have. There were a few concrete picnic tables with benches back on the grassy area where you could sit and eat or drink what you had. So we all sat together at one of those tables.

At the table next to us was a Hawaiian gentleman in swim trunks and flip -flops drinking a cup of pineapple and mango juice he had just purchased ahead of us. He turned on his bench and asked us,

"How was the snorkeling this morning? See anything good?"

Bunny answered him,

"Oh yeah, we swam with a pod of dolphins or rather they swam with us. That was pretty sweet."

"We're having a luau later this afternoon down by the park. You all should come. I'm sure you would enjoy it. There's no better way to experience Hawaii than to eat and dance with her people." He said as he offered us his invitation.

"Oh I don't know if we could make it or not, we planned to be at the Seven Sacred Pools this afternoon. I don't think we'd have time to come." Mu said, "But thank you for the generous invitation. We've never been to or seen a luau before."

"Then you should change your plans. Get on Hana time. That way you could do the Luau and hit the pools later. They're much more enchanting in the moon light anyway." He answered back.

"Well, maybe we could talk about it. I'm not sure right now. Thank you for the invitation." Mu added.

"Well if you can make it, it starts around noon and goes until every one too full or too tired to keep going. If you can make it, tell them Moa invited you." With those last words he rose from the bench and walked away from saying," Aloha." as he left.

The tea was making me feel sleepy again. It appeared Amy, Bunny and Chen were having the same problem as me. Looked like we might have to find a shady safe spot to take a little nap before we'd be able to continue on.

"Sorry guys but I think I'm going to have to find a soft spot somewhere to take a little nap." I told them as I sat the empty cup of tea down on the table in front of me.

"I think I might have to join her too." Bunny said.

"Us too I'm afraid to say. I know this will mess up our departure time but it just can't be helped. I can hardly keep my eyes open. I think we better find that safe place pretty soon." Chen announced in the middle of a big yawn.

Bach started to look around and finally said.

"I think this might have to do. Let's go over there where the trees are shading the ground a little more. We'll stay here and watch over you while you all sleep."

He didn't have to say it twice, I was trying to get up and get there before I ended up curled up in a ball at their feet right here in the sitting area. So the four of us semi dragged ourselves to the more shady area and just curled up on the ground to sleep. The ocean breezes were blowing in across the stretch of land there just above the beach and it was very comfortable. I could almost imagine I was home in my nice big comfortable bed. It's the last thought I remember and I was gone.

When the four of us started to finally wake up, hours had passed. The breezes were cool and refreshing. I sat up first and started to look around to take in my surroundings. Oh yeah, with the merkids in Hawaii this morning. I hadn't been home in my own bed this time. Becka, Mu, Bach and Shi were all just sitting and talking.

Bach had figured the route to get out to the Seven Sacred Pools and they were just waiting for the four of us to wake up.

"Oh good you're all waking up," he said as he watched us starting to move and knock the sand off of our bodies.

"Yeah, I don't know about the rest of you but I'm feeling kind of hungry. Think we could go to the Luau that Moa talked about before we head to the Pools?" Bunny asked.

"It may be possible. It will be on the way and we are, all in need of some nourishment. If we go, we can't stay any longer than we need to eat and thank our hosts." Bach answered.

So with those last words we all got up, gathered our things and headed in the direction Moa had pointed towards. It didn't take too much walking before we could smell the most delicious aroma in the breeze. It wasn't the wonderful smell of the Hawaiian flowers that smelled so great. That smell was there too but it was the mouthwatering aroma of roasted pig and other yummy foods. As we got a little closer we could see a group of about 35 people and Moa was there at the fire where the pig was roasting over an open pit. When he saw us he waved for us to come over.

Bunny and I weren't being bashful; we wanted to be first in line if he was handing out food already. As we got closer we picked up our pace, it was like the aroma of that roasted pig was pulling us in. I hadn't realized how hungry I was until I got the first whiff of the roasted pork back down the beach. Moa waved his arm in greeting and said,

"Aloha, Glad to see you changed your plans and could make it. Everything is ready. How about all of you? You hungry and ready for the best food you ever had?" he asked us.

"You bet ya." Bunny told him. "Where are the plates?"

Moa laughed and pointed towards a table just behind us,

"Grab what you need over there and come back. I'll fix you up."

Several of us all called out,

"Thanks again Moa." Then we headed to the table to get a plate and check out what goodies were over there.

Every one was laughing and smiling. Most everyone had a plate loaded down with all the Luau foods. I couldn't wait to get mine. Everything looked and smelled so good.

"Remember we have to do a long swim after this. Be careful not to eat too much. It's important we have as much energy for the trip as possible. No matter how hungry you might think you are, try to eat with your head." Bach warned us.

Well he had a good point. I think if he hadn't said something I probably would have over eaten and been unprepared for the long swim back to Atlantis: I would have been whining and wanting another nap. So when Moa started to shovel the roasted pork onto our plates we all said thank you and pulled our plates away before he could over load them.

Once we all had our plates full Moa walked with us over to a small group of older people. He introduced both his parents and his grandparents to us.

When we walked up to the small group they were telling some stories about the Menehunes and laughing. After the introductions Bunny had to ask,

"What are Menehunes?"

Moa's grandfather was the first to speak up.

"The Menehunes were the small race of people who first lived in Hawaii. They are similar to what the Irish call the little people, they are considered to be like tolls and fairies. They roam the forests at night and work their magic. They have been said to build an entire building over night. We believe they live inside the mountains and volcanoes of our islands. History tells of a whole race of smaller people who ruled over our islands in the beginning of time. There are some who say the Menehunes were ET's, they believe we all came form the stars."

"Wow" Bunny said as she tried to chew the piece of pork in her mouth. "That's very interesting. Recently I saw a show called "Ancient Aliens" and they said things very similar. They were talking more about Egyptians and American Indians but this could connect it all."

"Yes" he told her in return," We watch that show too. Love it. It's about time they tried to bring the truth to the public. It's our favorite show."

I thought Bunny would choke on the pork she was trying to swallow. I guess you could say his answer totally surprised her. Maybe she thought they were too old to be up on such shows or consider a show about ET's as one of their favorites. It was a little eye opening for all of us.

Moa's grandfather started telling Bunny,

"The Hawaiian people have long been keepers of the planet and our little piece of it. Kumulipo is our name for the source of life or creation. The story of Kumulipo is told in a chant, called an oli, known by the Kahunas or priests of our people. Some call the oli of Kumulipo the song of creation. We are a people who believe all life came from the cosmos as do all true believers."

"Wow that's cool." She finally said when she was able to finish swallowing.

"Did you see the Ancient Alien show where they talked about the ancient cities they've discovered that were thought until now to be myths?

There was one in India called Dwarka? I really enjoyed that episode." He added.

"I know. I'm always amazed with the stories they report and the new things I learn from the show."

Just then Mu and the other merkids walked up.

"We all wanted to thank you for inviting us to your Luau the food was wonderful. Regrettably we need to move on so we can visit the Seven Sacred Pools before we head home. We can't thank you enough for your hospitality."

"Yes we loved it all." Bunny chimed in.

When Moa's grandfather heard we were heading up to the Seven Sacred pools he told us,

"Hawaiians believe all fresh water is sacred. That's why we call them sacred pools. We have simple beliefs and put great value on the natural things in this world, all the important things like water, wind, the sun and everything that grows because of it. Have fun while you're there but keep an eye to the mountaintops, if it's raining be cautious; flash floods will carry you away if you are in the pools when they come. Aloha."

Everyone shook hands and our hosts wished us a safe journey as we made our departure.

Bunny was still chuckling to herself as we walked away from the Luau and hiked up the hill.

"What's so amusing Rabbit?" I asked.

"I'm just cracking up inside. Who would have ever thought I'd be introduced to a family of Hawaiian people I'd meet at a Luau and their favorite television show would be 'Ancient Aliens'? I mean, what are the odds on that?"

"Yeah, I thought I saw some little pieces of pork almost fly out of your nose when he said that. You're probably lucky you didn't choke." I countered back to her.

We had fun chatting on the hike up to the Sacred Pools. It helped to make the time fly by because before we knew it, we were close enough to see them up ahead of us. The pools terraced down the hillside, each one just a little higher up the hill from the other. A couple of the pools were larger than the others and they all looked very inviting. Sometimes when we got to places like this I tried to feel the energy that made them different or special. Usually it was something too fine and I couldn't tell the difference. Sometimes I could feel a very fine little vibration like when we were on Easter Island.

As we finally approached the bottom pool Mu turned to Bach and asked,

"Which one is the way back? Can you tell yet?"

"I haven't been able to read the entire area yet. You'll have to give me a few quiet minutes to figure this one out. I'm not picking up anything down here."

As Bach started to work his way up towards the next pool, Shi and Chen followed him and us girls sat down putting our feet into the first pool to cool off. It wasn't especially hot but after hiking up the hill it was refreshing to just stick our feet into the cool water and relax. It was a good thing we hadn't eaten any more than we did or I'd need another nap.

As I sat there with my feet dangling in the water I couldn't help but contemplate how amazingly good I felt, especially compared to when we arrived at Eddie's acupuncture offices, after the fall through from the higher dimensions in China. I'd still like to know what was in that tea, it and the acupuncture sure worked wonders on the four of us. While we sat mostly in silence, each of us lost in our own thoughts we watched as the boys climbed farther up to the third and fourth pools. Finally they yelled down to us and waved their arms in the air motioning us to come up.

We hiked up to the fifth pool the guys were there, waiting on us.

"This is it, but we may have to wait a little while until that group up above us takes off. It might be too odd for a group of eight to disappear right in front of their eyes. Besides we need to safe guard the secret of the passageway. Why don't the four of you get in the pool and act like tourist until they come down and leave the area. We'll lay back like we're working on our tans." Bach suggested. I guess he didn't think it would be too smart for them to get in the water yet. It might be really hard to explain their tails if that other group stopped by this pool to talk or visit with us. Yes it was better for now, for the merkids to stay out of the water.

The four of us, did as told, we climbed into the pool and started to enjoy the setting while playing tourist. The sky was blue, the sun was shining and the breeze like the pool's water was so refreshing. The view from up here in the pools was incredible. Hawaii was one of the best slices of paradise on Earth I'd ever seen. The rocky cliffs along the coast were this coal black color in most of the places we had seen them just like the rock here at the pools. I guess they said it was old lava rock. The palm trees and plants were the most lush and healthy, the water was a lot like what I saw in Australia with such beautiful shades of blues and greens. Unlike Australia, Hawaii had a wonderfully moderate temperature and this great ocean breeze. From the moment me came onto the beach until now, I had continuously felt this gentle breeze. It couldn't have been more perfect. This was a memory I would lock in my mind, to keep and treasure for the rest of my life.

The group up above us in the next pool didn't seem to be in any hurry to leave. I was enjoying myself immensely and didn't mind at all. I wasn't as worried about getting home on time like I had been on the other two trips. I just didn't worry about it anymore. For now I was enjoying the sheer joy of doing nothing and just floating here in this sacred pool.

A few of the things Moa's grandfather told us about what the Hawaiians held sacred came back to float between my own thoughts. How wonderful that they lived such simple ideals and believed that the water, the wind and all life are sacred. Too bad more people didn't think the same way. The cool thing about what Moa and his family believed was that they also lived in accord with their beliefs. So I guess you could say just like Cobra, his friends, and the merkids, Moa and his family talked the talk, and walked the walk as well. I really admired them all for that.

It seemed like hours had passed when it started to rain. It rained from almost out of nowhere. One minute it was sunny and no clouds in the sky and then, boom the sky was falling down on us in a torrential vengeance. The other group finally moved on. They hurried down from the pools and passed by us, never looking back. They were hardly out of view when Bach took action and had everyone in the pool gearing up for the swim back to Atlantis. Just before he dove under the surface of the pool he told us all,

"Follow me to the right, the opening is just large enough to swim through one at a time, we'll be in a wider channel soon. For now, just stay close together."

As Bach dove under, I tried taking one last look around, at the piece of paradise we spent the last few hours admiring but the rain was so thick I couldn't see any of it.. Goodbye Hawaii, hope to see you again some day.

We were off and away. The way back from Hawaii was fast and easy. The passageways weren't as dark as the ones going to Tibet. I enjoyed seeing the walls of the caves and passages, there were a couple places when we first left, I could have sworn I saw and felt the heat of hot lava in the distance. I never gave a thought to being cooked by one of Hawaii's killer volcanoes. It suddenly occurred to me that the volcanoes could have blocked off our way home or worse yet, trapped us in the middle with neither way out. I didn't want to think in that direction at all.

Having heard my thoughts Mu chimed in, "Often the world has events that change and close off some of the passageways. Sometimes new ones open up. It's an ever changing under world. Nothing is the way it used to be. You can trust Bach, he never would have taken us into this passage if he sensed it was closed or had a problem."

Once again I was reminded that the merkids were capable of so many wonderful things. Being with them was like going to some other planet, I could have never done any of the things I'd done in the last week if I wasn't with them. It was like when I was with them I could fly, even if it was in water in the under world.

Each time we entered the under world it seemed to be shorter and shorter trips getting back to Atlantic. Before we knew it, we were in the final passageway headed back up into the hidden city. This was Amy's first trip so I couldn't wait to watch her reaction to seeing everything for the first time. It was still magic to me so it was easy for me to imagine what she would be thinking and feeling.

Sheba and a large group of the kids were there in the arrival room waiting for us as we all broke the surface of the water together. This was getting to be a warm and welcome sight to me. Atlantis the hidden city of the lost continent, I loved saying it almost as much as I loved seeing it. This was my fourth trip in and this trip was just as thrilling as the first time.

Amy was looking around while Bunny was pointing and saying something to her. The merkids were headed to the stairs and the landing while we were still gawking and talking about being in Atlantis. The other merkids were excited to greet Bach and take the plants from him. This was the first time we were able to bring back more than one plant for reproduction.

The four of us were still treading water and gawking when Sheba and Mu called out to us.

"Come on girls."

"There's much to talk about this time and I want to show you all something in my home." It was Sheba who was inviting us to her place.

Cool, this would be the first time to really have much time with Sheba and getting to see her home would prove interesting. Usually our time here was limited and we were busy with more important things so we had never seen any ones actual home. Thoughts would run through my head sometimes, things like, would they have books or nick-nacks on shelves? Would there be pictures on their walls? Did they sleep on beds like us? Now I'd get to find out.

The four of us worked our way over to the stairs up from the arrival passage and joined the others to dry off on the main landing. The other kids were more excited about the plants we brought back than they were about us. Once they had all the plants from Bach they were off and it was just the eight of us left standing there.

"If you're ready, let's go girls." Sheba said as she turned and headed to the city.

We all followed and as we walked onto the first terrace where you could finally see the city for the first time we stopped. Amy's eye's glowed with the joy and excitement of seeing Atlantis for the first time. Actually I think all of us were showing the amazement of seeing Atlantis again, how could you not? What a wondrous place this was and it was alive and teaming with activity in every direction. Bunny was pointing, showing Amy the largest pyramid to the left of us and all the buildings of interest in between.

It was funny to think of us as tour guides for this place but each time I saw it, it felt more like home than the last time had. The place was so lush and beautiful it was a piece of Shambhala or vise versa. I wasn't sure which was the right way to say that one after all I didn't know, which came first?

We passed a lot of new interesting buildings as we followed Sheba to her home. It turned out to be another one of the buildings that was built back into the hillside much like our underground geo-thermal homes in the United States. I wondered if they did it in order to use the cooler temps inside the hillside to help keep the temperatures even and comfortable inside? Maybe I'd have to ask Sheba or one of the other kids about that sometime.

Sheba's place was on the top level. This particular building had seven homes to it, each one was on top of the other like our condos or apartment buildings, and so it was sort of like home. They each had the same open terraces we had seen on so many of the buildings when we first entered Atlantis. When she opened the front door I was sort of holding my breath, waiting to see what her home looked like. It was simple and clean with a little beachie, Zen feel to it.

Instead of doors on the inside there were cascading chains of tiny little shells that reminded me of the beaded curtains the hippies used to hang in their doorways. They made an exotic sound as you pushed them aside to walk through. The walls were mostly smooth they looked more like rock than concrete. I didn't see any pictures hanging but there was one wall that was painted like it was part of some temple or ancient cave. The furniture, if you could call it that, looked like it was built from and stone or concrete, with cushions to make it a little more comfortable to sit on. There were cushions on the floor as well. It felt like a cross between modern oriental and hippy pad with a little ancient art thrown in.

Seeing her home was an interesting avenue into Sheba's personality. I wondered what she would think of our homes? Sheba went to the center room which had a circular set up of cushions on the floor with a round low table in the center she asked everyone to sit down and get comfortable. Sheba sat facing the five of us and we waited to see what she wanted to say.

"I think the best way to explain this is to show you with the help of my hologram." She picked up what looked like a nook reader and touched it a few times and abracadabra; there was a large hologram in the air space between Sheba and the rest of us. It was a round globe like image that looked something like the earth only it didn't have continents, just one large land mass.

"This," she said "was Earth when the Seven Sisters of the Pleiades came to start their settlements and begin life here." As she was telling us her story the hologram was moving and as she said things, it changed and things happened that helped to explain and illustrate her story. It was mesmerizing trying to watch the hologram and listen to what she was saying.

Your scholars called this Pangaea when the world had only one land mass. The people who populated it called it Lemuria. Later they started other colonies. This was the time that Atlantis came into being. When the first destructions came the land mass separated and there were areas that went under the waters, while others rose up. New continents were forming and Earth was changing. It was volcanic action and the earthquakes that resulted because of the volcanoes and earth shifts, as well as floods and ice ages that helped to change the world as the earlier settlers discovered it."

Her hologram showed the shifts and how the world had changed over millions of years. This was amazing to watch on the hologram. I had heard some of this before. The Aborigines, the Hawaiians, American Indians, the Muslims, Christians and every other religion and race had a story with similar events that followed Earths history.

"The Seven Sisters left a prophecy of reuniting when they were needed. Bach has picked up the signal that the time is approaching for them to come together again." Sheba touched the pad once more and the hologram disappeared just as fast as it had appeared.

Bunny spoke up first,

"I've heard about a lot of different prophecies but I don't think I've ever read anything called the Seven Sister prophecy. What culture did that prophecy come from?"

Sheba looked at Bunny like she was a bug and told her,

"The prophecy comes from the days of Lemuria and the beginning of time. There are no written records found yet for you to read about in your history books or on your Internet. If we weren't able to tap into the energy of the cosmic consciousness we wouldn't know what we know now. It is quickly coming to the time for the prophecy to be fulfilled. The planet is suffering and being destroyed by man's miss use and abuse. It will take the love and ancient knowledge of the Sisters to begin to balance the world back out. Their mission will not be easy and it will require their united forces to bring it together in time to save Earth."

"Sheba, why are you telling us about this prophecy today? Is there something you think we can do to help in someway?" Amy asked.

Sheba looked Amy straight in the eye and said,

"Bach asked me to tell you all the story of the Seven Sisters and the prophecy because the five of you sitting here with me are five of the Seven Sisters."

"What in the heck do you mean we're five of the seven? You've got to be joking. Right??" Bunny asked.

"I couldn't be more serious Bunny. We're only telling you all this now because we believe you need to know what will be expected of you in the near future. Bach said it was time to open your eyes to the future so you can make your decisions accordingly. There is much weight that will be on your shoulders the future of the world may very well be in your hands." Sheba answered back.

"Now I know you've got to be joking. Who in their right mind would put the fate of Earth in our hands?" Bunny simply stated.

"It's not a joke and I am totally serious. This is more important than the mission we're on now to save the rest of our population. Now we are out to try and save the rest of the world. I would never joke about that." Sheba clearly declared.

"Who are the other two sisters? Do we know them now?' Becka asked.

Becka asked her question as if she believed everything Sheba was saying and just needed a few more answers. This had to be a joke or a dream maybe I'd wake up soon. Heck, I was still reeling from the reality of the mission we were on with the merkids. Now to hear one of them say there was something even more important we would have to do. Who did they really think we were? When I looked in the mirror I saw a kid not some savior of the world. Just what exactly did they think we were going to have to save it from? How did they think we'd know what to do? Heck, how did they think we'd even be able to figure out how the other two were suppose to be?

"We don't know who they are. We're not sure if you already know them or not. That is why we needed to tell you about the prophecy. You may meet them at any time and we don't want you to pass them by. You need to make contact, recognize them so you can start to work together with them." she answered.

"How in the heck are we supposed to recognize them? We've all been friends forever but meeting Mu isn't something I would have recognized as meeting a sister from some lifetime in Lemuria." Bunny threw back at her. "How will we know when we finally meet them, how are we going to recognize them? You got any ideas?"

"We want you all to try to tune yourselves into the idea of looking for them. There has to be some way you will know. If your vibrations have risen as much as we think they have, you'll all be more open and should be able to tell when you're with them." Sheba replied. "If Bach knew all the answers he would tell you. He hasn't been able to see or read all of the prophecy or the future you all have together."

"Where in the world are we supposed to be looking for them? Could they be anyone like Eddie's daughters in China? I didn't sense anything special around them. I mean I appreciated how they helped us but I don't think we're going to know how to know them if and when we meet them. If you could at least tell us where they live. I'm still having trouble believing we are five of the seven. How is any of this even possible?" I asked.

Bunny spoke up,

"I want to know more about the seven sisters and what you can tell us about them. Maybe there's something that could help us to figure out who the other two are. Could our friend Cookie be another one of the sisters? We're really close with her. Do you think she could be one of them?"

"The Seven Sisters are stars from the Pleiades. They were the first beings of light that came to Earth to begin life here. There have been others who have come from other stars. They have come from many of the galaxies from all over the Universe.

When Lemuria suffered destructions the sisters each traveled to different corners of the globe. One went to China, one to Peru, one to England, one to Australia, one to Egypt, one to Bali and one to the United States to Mount Shasta. They took with them the records and proof of Earths true history, the records of Lemuria and Atlantis. Beyond that we know only that they were advanced beings and had many of the skills of the soul that they used to advance their people and settlements. That is all we know."

We were all just sitting there shaking our heads in disbelief. I felt so bewildered by all this information. I still couldn't conceive that any of it could be real. Surely the kids were playing a joke on us. Maybe they were punking us and we should be watching for someone with a camera to come around the corner laughing because we started to believe them. Sheba wasn't laughing and she looked as serious as I had ever seen her look. I felt stunned and wondered if the others felt the same. Even Mu looked dumb founded by what Sheba had said. I never thought I'd see her looking bewildered. Clearly we were all blind sided by the story we had been told and I wasn't sure I could ever believe this one hook, line and sinker.

My mind was buzzing around from all the things Sheba had told us and I almost don't remember walking back through Atlantis when it was time to head home. I hoped that Amy was able to take it all in because it would be sad to think of her not having as many memories as possible: Atlantis is such an unbelievable place.

The swim home was just another big blur in a day filled with mindboggling events. That was actually the norm for days with the kids but this time so much more had happened. We were lucky we could move after the fall back through the time dimension from Shambhala, little did I know when I prayed to be able to return to my old normal life what that would include. Was it possible that we could be some of the original beings to populate the Earth and have lived through so much of the earliest history including Lemuria and Atlantis as places we called home? I dreamed dreams of living in other times and places but I never saw myself as being someone of such importance, not in a past life or in this lifetime.

Where would we begin? What was expected of us? I couldn't think this was just way too much to try and digest right now. I tried to block all the thoughts out of my mind as we neared the beach back home. Before we got too far in the kids took us to the surface. We all said our goodbyes, they turned and headed back while we finished the swim into the beach.

We had barely begun to leave the water when everyone started talking at once.

"Can you believe what happened? Is it like that every time you go somewhere with the merkids?" Amy asked.

"Depends which part are you asking about?" I asked.

"Well, really I guess all of it? The under water passageways, the beautiful exotic places, the wild dive into the higher dimension. The people you meet while you're gone. It was all so cool. I still can't believe I almost stayed there. I don't know what I was thinking. My parents would have died if I disappeared like that. So I guess I owe you two a big thank you. I am just sorry my stubbornness caused us so much trouble and pain." Amy replied.

"Well, you are welcome." Bunny told her, "Just don't ever try to do something like that again!"

"Yeah, I'll be having nightmares about that for awhile. "I told them.

"I'm still reeling from the stuff about the seven sisters and some prophecy we're suppose to be part of." Becka spoke up.

"Yeah, that blew my mind too. You should have been there when the croc nailed poor Mu by the tail. I thought I'd die and the adrenaline rush was pretty equal to the one we got when we grabbed you and dragged you back with us." Bunny told Amy.

"Well, one thing about your little adventure Amy, you didn't have to do half the walking and hiking we did the other two trips and you didn't have to just about cook going through the desert heat in Australia or Peru. You got lucky. Other than the pain of coming back from Shambhala this was the easiest trip yet." I told her.

We all just dropped down onto the sand after we got on the beach. That is where we were now having this conversation. I think we all just needed to talk to reassure ourselves that we were back to the real world, our old regular lives and yes, it had all really happened. None of us was too sure how real the seven sister thing could be. Not one of us felt like the kids could be right about this one. Besides what was the prophecy exactly? What were the sisters suppose to do? This was just too much to try and figure out right now. We decided to head home, have dinner and sleep on it. We'd get together again the next day to talk again.

So we headed home and when we finally got to our street we split up and headed towards our individual homes.

I yelled back to everyone,

"See ya tomorrow at Becka's."

I wasn't as tired as I had been the last two times when I got back from my adventures with the merkids. I wondered for a second as I entered the house if the acupuncture could have had anything to do with me feeling better this time? Obviously this was my first experience with acupuncture not to mention my first experience with dimension jumping. But I felt good and I decided to get on the Internet and do some more checking for the plant I was suppose to find. All my adventures hadn't left me much time to do my own research.

I was so totally absorbed with my Internet hunt I didn't hear my folks come home from work. I felt like I was making some real progress and then finally, there it was. Eureka!!! I found my plant. Egypt. Yeah, the Egypt of my dreams, home of the Great Pyramid at Giza. It made me relive for a couple seconds the wild crazy dream I had about being under the Sphinx and hiding something. Wow, now I wondered where had that come from? Didn't Sheba say one of the seven sisters took her records to Egypt for safekeeping? I was so excited with my discovery I had to call Becka and tell her everything.

"I'm so ready to go to Egypt." I told her, "The only bad part is, its another dessert! Oh man, I don't know if I'm ready for another dessert and the journey through it. Do you think it could be another easy one and maybe not end up in the middle of the Sahara?" I asked her.

Becka laughed at me and kidded me a little,

"Maybe this is the one you should sit out and just let one of us go in your place."

"Yeah like I'd do that. Egypt has always been the main place I always said I wanted to go to. Does it make you wonder? Could Sheba and Bach really know something about our past? Could I be the sister who went to Egypt? This is starting to make me think about a lot of things. Are you questioning yourself like that too?" I asked.

"It did give us all something to think about didn't it?" she answered before she said she had to go because they were calling her to the dinner table.

I had a lot to think about that night. I was so up about finding the plant I had been researching. Then on top of that there was all the stuff Sheba said about the seven sisters and how Bach said it involved all of us. How was I supposed to digest all this? I still didn't feel like I could be someone who had a giant role to play in the history of the world. They had to be joking, I don't know why they would do that but it just couldn't be true. Could it?

I decided it was more than my poor little pea brain could deal with right now. So I decided to put it all on a back burner and said I'd get back to it another time. Maybe the next time I got together with the girls we could all talk about it and deal with it together.

When I did finally make it to bed that night, I slept like a baby. No dreams that I could remember when I woke up and I was rested and ready to go, no merkids jet lag to deal with this trip. Becka and I would need to get together and let Bach know we had been successful in tracking down another plant location and see what they wanted to do next.

When we got together using our opals to contact Bach, he said he had been expecting us, if we could meet them on the beach tomorrow, early in the morning, they'd be ready to go. He suggested this time it should just be him, Shi, Becka and me. I didn't need any coaching for this one. I was really looking forward to this next adventure and going to Egypt. The Great Pyramid, the Sphinx, the sands of the Sahara, it was going to be a dream come true for me. Waiting was going to be the hardest part. A day in this world stretched out longer than a couple weeks with the kids in their time.

Adventure #4
Egypt

We were on the beach, anxiously waiting before sunrise: not just because I was so excited but also because it was the best part of the day. Being able to watch the first rays of the sun peek over the horizon, starting to illuminate the sky was a very magical time of the day. It always felt like you were part of something special when you got to witness a sunrise or a great sunset. Plus we had no idea what time the kids would show up but we wanted to be ready.

Maybe I should say, I was ready, because Becka was still yawning and trying to wake up and we'd already been waiting for 20 minutes. Usually it was me who was the sleepy head and Becka was the one waiting for me to wake up. Not today though, we were headed to Egypt and I was more than ready to go. I couldn't say it enough, it was a dream of mine to see the Pyramids and experience Egypt someday. Today was going to be my someday!

Because Becka hadn't had much time to do her research we talked a little about the last three plants we still needed to find. Maybe we'd have to ask the others to help her or maybe we'd all double up on the last ones we still needed to find. We were lost in our conversation when we finally saw the boys break the surface about 20 feet out in front of us. Both of us stood, brushed the sand off our shorts and waved to them before we headed in. The water was a little cool yet this morning but it probably helped to finally wake Becka up.

We said our hellos. The boys handed us our pouches and breathing gear. Then we were off. Once under the water I asked Bach which way he planned to travel today. Was there an under world passageway that we would take or would we go via the ocean?

"The Ocean into the Mediterranean is how we've charted this journey. After we get in the Mediterranean we'll work our way to the Nile River. Once we're in the Nile we'll be making landfall probably somewhere near Cairo." He answered my thoughts.

Just hearing the name Cairo brought so many pictures into my mind. Ancient Aliens and the History channel always did shows about Egypt with great shots of all the temples and pyramids. Seeing Egypt's monuments from the past, in person was going to be better than all the other places and things, all put together that I had seen so far with the merkids. I wasn't sure when we saw Angkor Wat that anything could be more beautiful and exotic but I was starting to think Egypt would surpass all those feelings and thoughts. Did I mention, seeing Egypt was a dream of mine?

"Your energy levels seem high today Kat. Your aura is a wonderful purple color." Shi told me. "Are you excited today about something?"

"I think we're both happy to have found the fourth plant but I'll be honest, I'm really excited about going to Egypt. I've always wanted to see the Great Pyramid and everything else. I'm just about vibrating from the excitement. Can you hear my electrical hum through the water?" I jokingly asked him.

"No, but I can see it in your aura." He answered back.

We were swimming through the Bermuda Triangle today on the way towards Africa. So I couldn't help but wonder if we would be safe. I don't know if the color of my aura changed or not as we entered the triangle but the boys definitely picked up on my thoughts again.

"There's no need to worry Kat. We are aware of the dimensional gateway that exists in the triangle but we won't be going into it during our trip. We'll skirt around north of it up past Miami. You're both perfectly safe and there is no need to worry that anything negative is going to happen to you.

The Triangle's energy comes from the original Atlantis power plants, they were very similar to your nuclear plants today only ours were run by giant crystals from both Earth and other sources. It was the malfunction of the energy plants that helped to destroy our world. It is the energy of those three plants that created the Bermuda Triangle and helps to explain why the Triangle is so erratic in it's strange and unusual phenomena. The crystals are not receiving solar energy at the same time in equal amounts most of the time. When they are the potential for phenomena increases and it is very unstable. The uncontrolled vortex energy created by it and all the disappearances have haunted us ever since. It's something we don't know how to fix and when we have tried in the past it didn't turn out very well, so over the years we just stopped trying and the world gets to live with our mistake.

It was us who gave it the name 'Devil's Triangle' because we have no control over the vortex energy it created. There are times it acts as a wormhole into the Universe. It's possible the Guardians know how to work with the energy and control it but I have never had the chance to ask them." Bach told us

The waters off Miami were crystal clear and a rainbow of blues and greens that were a delight to see. No wonder Miami and South Beach were such popular places. The trip across the Atlantic Ocean was pretty uneventful. We saw an assortment of shipwrecks and even a few crashed airplanes when we were in the more shallow areas. The oceans were full and alive with more kinds of sea life than I ever realized.

We didn't do much mental chatting. I think Becka must have been on autopilot or maybe she was napping, I wasn't sure which. I had learned a little when it came to keeping my focus and not letting so many random thoughts escape. I just focused on trying to see the images of all the wonders of Egypt that I hoped to see while we would be there in my mind as we swam. I considered it a practice in the power of positive thinking and mind control. The boys never said much, in or out of the water.

When we entered the Straits of Gibraltar the water became several degrees warmer and the color changed drastically. We were getting closer, I could tell by the goose bumps I was getting. We were swimming along the coastline as we headed for Egypt. I was amazed with all the ruins and relics we were swimming past.

Definitely looked like some other time the world had a lot less water and the shoreline had been a lot farther into the current water line than it was now. It was the only thing that could explain so many cities and towns now under water. Seeing all this really made me think about the ruins I saw they discovered off the coast of India. It was believed to be the famous city called Dwaraka. Up until this discovery, it was considered just another myth. Like the city of Troy, it too was always considered a myth until they finally unearthed it back in the late 1800's.

Seeing the world like this, made all those history channel shows even more significant. I could stay here and swim the entire shoreline of the Mediterranean, I'm sure the ruins of Turkey, Greece, Italy and the rest of the European countries would prove just as interesting. What a real taste of history this time with the merkids was proving to be. From now on my History classes in school would always be more interesting.

When we finally were nearing Egypt Bach let us know he planned to enter the Nile at Rashid, which was a port city east of Alexandria. The Nile had several tributaries and this was just one. He felt it was the safest for us to travel so we headed in, our next destination would be Cairo which I understood, wasn't too much farther.

Cairo was a huge city. According to Bach the total population on the inner city and surrounding area was over 16 million and that made Cairo the second largest city in the Muslim world. Wow. I wondered how we'd find our way around a place so big to even begin our search for the plant we were here to find. Becka and I both came with a little stash of cash, after that first trip to Peru we decided never to leave home without it. Buses and admissions into places weren't free and the merkids didn't have money that worked in our world.

The Nile was alive and simmering with people along its' banks as well as boats everywhere. Finding a safe place to make land was a little challenging. We tried several times to carefully check out an area only to find women washing clothes, men huddled around a little campfire having tea or tourist all watching and taking pictures. Finally Bach found a storm drain and we went in through it. By the time we found our way out of the drain on the other end we were dry and easily fit into the crowd of people on the street above.

I was getting my famous 'new adventure whiplash' again. I couldn't help myself, there was so much to look at and take in. On the surface the city was like any other large city but when you looked closer that's when you noticed what made it Cairo. There were Mosques everywhere sprinkled in between the modern hotels and skyscrapers. There were street vendors here and there, some trying to sell tourist things from Egypt like papyrus prints or small artifacts. The one thing I saw that really surprised me were the soldiers with machine guns standing on the street corner. It looked like they were standing guard, definitely not something I expected to see on a street corner in Cairo or anywhere else right now.

Sometimes it was hard to absorb the reality of being in another part of the world. I mean, things looked different, especially the people but living in the United States we don't tend to think about the trouble and unrest in so many places around the world today. It made us love being Americans all the more because we knew a lot of Americans never see all the poverty and problems first hand to realize how great we have it. Seeing all these different people I couldn't take my eyes off of them. There were dozens of Muslim women dressed in their traditional black garments everything covered but their eyes some of them carrying large baskets or bundles of things on their heads. I'm sure that was easier on the arms but I would think not so good for the neck and spine. Never was there a time I missed my camera more than right now.

The city was one of the busiest I had ever seen. Up on the street level things were even more hectic. The traffic was buzzing by and people were everywhere. I saw a herdsman under an over pass of the highway, with a flock of sheep. A man driving a donkey cart was in the middle of all the traffic, with car horns honking at him, to get out of their way. A bus drove by and there must have been over a hundred people on it. They were everywhere, hanging out the windows and door, it looked like a giant over stuffed can of sardines! My head was whirling from so much happening and so much to see. I had no idea where we would go or what we would do next.

When we finally found the plant on the Internet it said it could be found around the Nile Delta area, near Giza. Could it be any sweeter? Giza was the home of the Great Pyramid. I wondered how close we'd have to be, to be able to actually see the pyramids? I had no idea how far out into the desert they would be but when we googled it, back home when we were doing our research, it didn't look far, only a few miles. The Delta area was some of the most fertile land in Egypt everything lived along the banks of the Great Nile River, the source of all life in Egypt.

Bach and Shi wanted us to work our way towards Giza because we had no other clues to help us get started with this search so he read the area and we started off through the city. It was uncanny how Bach could make all the right twists and turns in a place he had never been to before. Becka and I both were always amazed with his accuracy; it was like he had some built in radar or GPS system.

Along one of the streets we passed a Bazaar. It was impossible not to look through the shop doorways and openings. Some of them were filled with metal trays and bowls of beautiful designs and craftsmanship others were clothes and clothe in ever color. I passed a basket of pig legs with the hoofs sticking up out of the top of the basket, right there in the middle of the sidewalk. While I was looking back at the basket, in wonder at food like that just sitting out in the open on the sidewalk. A couple men walked by each carrying a couple white-feathered geese. The geese were honking and screeching as if they knew they were going to market and ultimately someone's dinner table. What a wild world of color, smells and sights. More than once, Becka grabbed me by the arm, to remind me to keep moving when something had caught my eye and I stopped to look closer.

"Come on Kat, we don't have time for this right now." She muttered as she tugged on my arm trying to get me to move again.

Seeing the people on the streets in the garments of the area was fascinating to watch. Men in caftans with Keffiyeh's on their heads and woman wearing Hijabs it was all so mesmerizing to me. Seeing these people in their native dress made it impossible to think you were back home, I didn't need to pinch myself this time, I knew for sure I was in the exotic area of the world known as Egypt.

I found everything so interesting and exciting. I couldn't wait to get out near the pyramids. I had no idea if Giza was as large a place as Cairo but I was hoping once there I could at least see them in the distance or if I got lucky, maybe even up close. What I wouldn't give to have a little time here to play tourist like we did in Angkor Wat. I'd say a few prayers to be able to get close enough to touch them and burn the image of them into my brain.

After seeing the loaded buses pass by I wasn't sure we'd ever want to try and travel on one of them, heck a person would probably be crushed to death if they tried squeezing into any of the ones we had seen pass by. I wasn't sure how far it was from this part of Cairo to Giza but Bach said it wasn't far and walking would at least let us see more of the city. I tried to keep up with them but for some reason they didn't seem as inspired by our surrounding as I was.

"Did you see that Becka?" I asked as I passed another shop doorway. Inside I could see a bunch of kids sitting at weaving looms. There must have been more than a dozen of them and it looked like they were weaving rugs or some kind of tapestries. They were young, a lot younger than us. Apparently they didn't have child labor laws here because those kids looked like they were maybe 7 to 8 years old. The one girl closest to the doorway had turned and smiled at me, she had a scarf with beautiful colors covering her head and was wearing eyeliner. She looked very exotically Egyptian for such a young girl.

"I thought there were laws against stuff like that." I said to no one in particular and everyone at the same time.

"Come along Kat, this is normal in Egypt and countries on this side of the world. Most children don't get to go to school and get educations like you and your friends. These children are orphans and they feel fortunate to be taken in and taught a trade. They get fed and clothed and have a place to live while they learn to make a living. It's a good trade to learn and they don't have to try to live on the streets which believe me would be far worse." Bach informed us.

After walking a while longer, we had worked our way to the out skirts of the city where the land looked like small farming parcels. We saw mud huts and oxen working to plow the land in a few places. There were beautiful palm trees spotted here and there along the road and between the land parcels. The dirt was a dark rich brown, almost black color. I was sure it must produce good crops, it looked too rich and dark a color not to.

The walking became a little easier for me because there weren't so many sights for me to get distracted by. After walking for what seemed like hours it even became somewhat boring. Seeing the same basic countryside mile after mile, after mile. It was still Egypt but it wasn't the city or the pyramids. This was the sad part of the country, the poor people trying to live in little mud huts and shacks on the sides of the road. Sometime there were up to five or six children sitting there next to a hut that didn't look more than 6 by 8 feet wide. I couldn't imagine what it must have looked like inside those huts. Hopefully they had enough food to eat because it didn't look like they had much else.

Shi said,

"We'll work our way out to the edge of the desert, that might put us somewhere near the Pyramids. Once there, we'll start looking for the next specimen. If need be, we'll speak with the locals and see if any of them recognize the picture or know where we might locate them."

"Well, it's as good a plan as any I could think up." Becka answered him.

All I heard was the word Pyramids. Man oh man we were going to get to see the pyramids. I could have danced a jig I was so ecstatic. There was a lot of traffic on the roads away from the heart of the city or I might have started dancing or turning cartwheels but I was afraid if I did, I'd get run over.

"What's up with you today Kat? I don't think I've ever seen you this excited?" Becka asked.

"I don't know I just can't wait to see the rest of Egypt. I can't explain the goose bumps or the excitement but ever since I knew we were coming here, it's all I can think about. I'm feeling obsessed about Egypt and everything about it. I never would have thought I'd feel this way but I do." I answered her.

"Well," she said, "Get over it, we need to focus on the task at hand and you're acting too much like a spaz'."

Well, what was I doing that she thought I was acting like a spaz'? I was just looking and taking in the sights. I hadn't done anything to embarrass her or the boys. Maybe I should warn her, if she thought I had already spazed out she better watch out, when I got to see the pyramids there was no telling what I might do.

"Well Becka maybe we better ask Bach how much farther he thinks it is until we get to the pyramids cause I think I'm really going to spaz out when we get there." I jokingly told her.

"I'm sorry, I don't mean to interrupt but did I hear you say you were going out to the pyramids?"

The four of us turned and looked to see who was talking to us. There next to us on the roadway was a young Egyptian boy on a cart being pulled by a donkey.

"Were you talking to us?" Shi asked him.

"Yes, I couldn't help but hear the girl say she wanted to know how much farther it was to get to the pyramids. I'm headed that way and I could give you a ride. My name is Nuri and I live near the entrance to the attraction so it wouldn't be any trouble for me."

The four of us looked at each other and all kind of said, why not.

"Sure, we'd appreciate a ride. We could pay you a little something if you'd like." Becka informed him.

"No pay is required. I would enjoy the company. I make this trip several times a week and it's rather boring most of the time. Hop on board and we'll get going." Nuri answered.

We climbed on the cart behind Nuri and Bach took the seat next to him on the front of the cart.

"You disguise your blindness very well Nuri." Bach said as Nuri started the donkey moving again.

Blind? What did he mean Nuri disguised his blindness well?

"Yes, I am blind my new friend but I don't try to disguise it. I have been blind all my life and I am very used to living in my shadows of darkness here in Cairo. How about you, where are you from and what are you all called?" he asked

Bach introduced us all and told him we were from the United States. Here now to see the pyramids and explore Egypt.

"If I can be of any assistance, I am free from my work several times during the week. Should you need a guide, I would love to be of help. I like to work on my English and find it easier to do so when I speak with others. I love the slang and it is easier to get the newest lingo when I get a chance to visit and converse with Americans. I live in Giza with my Grandmother and would be close by. Do you know the name of your Hotel? I could drop you there if you'd like." Nuri offered.

"Oh no we're going to the pyramids today and then we'll decide where we'll stay. We like to play it loose and easy, kind of like gypsies. Sometimes we like to sleep under the stars." Shi told him.

"My name means Gypsy in the Egyptian language. So maybe we'll find we're a lot alike. I too like to sleep under the stars." Nuri informed us.

We talked and visited about dozens of things. Nuri was very curious and had more questions than even Bunny would have asked. He was very happy to learn a few newer slang words from us. When we finally got as close to the Pyramids as he could go, without missing his turn, he dropped us off.

"Don't forget my offer. Should you find yourself in need of a great tour guide just tell anyone here that you are looking for Nuri the blind boy. They'll get your message to me and I'll come. Or come looking for me, I live behind the Desert Camel Café anyone there can point my home out to you. I hope you have a wonderful time and enjoy your visit with the pyramids. Goodbye my new friends. Safe journey." He waved to us as he rode away. We all called out to him our goodbyes and thanked him one more time for the ride.

As we turned back around, there they were the three main pyramids of Giza. What majestic fellows they were too. All of us were impressed and just stood and admired them for a couple minutes. I was busy trying to burn the image of it all into my memory banks. This was something I would never forget for as long as I lived. My biggest dream had just come true. That is unless we got to go inside and visit the King's Chamber. That I was afraid was just too much to hope for because I had read the public wasn't allowed inside anymore because of reconstruction and repairs being made.

Wow, the place was alive with people and tourist everywhere. It was like watching ants at a picnic. So much was happening. Cars were everywhere parked along side the road way, buses were coming and going, people were gathered in groups everywhere I looked. The energy was very electric and left me feeling like we were all on an adrenaline rush of some kind. I wasn't sure how Bach could get a true reading of what to do next or how to find our way to the plant we were here to search for. It would have been like a radio trying to tune into a very small frequency with tons of static all around to interfere.

"You said you read about the plant being near or in the desert didn't you Kat?" Bach asked me.

"Yes, that's what it said. The plant could be found in the Delta region near the desert at Giza." I answered.

"I just can't read anything very clearly right now. There's just too much activity around here. Lets go out that way and get away from some of these people." He said as he pointed out to the other side of the pyramids towards the desert."

Hey, this was good, really good, I was getting closer to the pyramids and I would be close enough soon to touch or even sit on one. There were a lot of people doing just that, climbing a little on the lower levels of the great pyramid. It was the one with all the psychic power linked to it and the stories told about it. Some said it was an ancient generator or nuclear reactor of some sort, others said it was the initiation temple or a gateway to the other dimensions. Now, after having been to Tibet and Shambhala I could really relate to the gateway theory.

It was just a short hike over to the other side of the pyramids. I was vibrating with the excitement of the giants in front of me. Over to the far side I could even see the Sphinx. I felt like I must be dragging my feet as I walked with my head turned back toward the mighty Sphinx, what a thrill to see this all in person. WOW and double WOW! Becka seemed almost as excited as me because she too was looking back at the Sphinx and it slowed her pace as well.

As we finally turned to watch where we were going, the boys were only a short distance ahead of us, near the great Pyramid. The closer we got, the bigger the blocks and the Pyramids looked. The blocks were unbelievably large. Noticing their size made me start to wonder how they did all this. They must have had help. Levitation could explain it but why hadn't others today, figured it out if that was the answer?

"Holy cow Becka, can you believe this? We're not only looking at but in a minute we'll be touching the pyramids of Egypt. Think how long they've been here and we'll be standing right next to them. We'll be able to touch one of the biggest pieces of history in just a few more seconds." I chattered away at her.

"It's pretty awesome Kat. I almost can't believe it's true either. What a trip this is and we just got here. Let's hope it only gets better!" she answered back.

"I don't know if it could get any better than this for me." I stated.

The boys had stopped right next to the west corner of the Great Pyramid. For the first time I could see there were even smaller pyramids off to the side of the third and smallest pyramid of the main group.

Bach looked at me looking at the smaller pyramids and said,

"Those were the Queens of Khufu. Most people know little about these smaller pyramids in the group."

"Thanks Bach, I was wondering." I wondered sometimes if he wasn't reading my mind. It was a scary thought because sometimes I had little control over what was racing through my head. It could prove embarrassing if he was reading my thoughts but I didn't waste too much time worrying about it. I was in front of the Pyramid! I was in seventh heaven and I could touch it. I had my hand on one of the megalithic stones.

I would have loved to have some kind of vibration hit me like a bolt of lightening, not the pain part of that but the metaphysical enlightenment part. I would have hoped to have some magical, wild and significant knowledge delivered from the touch. But it didn't happen. I wished and I prayed while my hand was on the cornerstone but try as I might, nothing happened.

"You're trying too hard Kat. You have to be able to clear your mind and heart. Otherwise you've got too much emotion getting in the way."

Shi informed me. "It's like you're blocking any signals from coming in because you want something and the desire blocks it all."

"Thanks Shi, I'll try to remember that. I guess I'm just too excited to settle down right now." I told him.

"Yeah, I don't know if I've ever seen you so excited and hyper." Becka chuckled.

She and I started to walk along the side of the pyramid, to check it out but also to give Bach some quiet time so he could try to read the place. It would have been easier for him if he had a plant to hold and focus on, that would give off an energy that he could read. Trying to pull something out of thin air was a lot harder, I was told.

Becka and I walked along the side of the largest pyramid. I ran my hand along the wall, touching the limestone the entire time.

"It's magnificent isn't it?" I asked but actually I was telling her.

"I totally agree." She answered.

"Can you imagine living here when it was Cleopatra's Egypt? Or when these were being built?" I was day dreaming a little with my questions.

"I think you must have been here way back then Kat. You live and breathe this Egyptian stuff, you always have. Maybe Bach and Sheba are right about the sisters, if they are, you must have been the one who came to Egypt." Becka stated kind of matter a fact.

"Wow, do you see this? Look at the little pieces of shell and mini fossils of sea shells in the limestone." I called her attention back to the giant block I was touching.

"I never would have imagined that I'd see something like that in the blocks of limestone at the Great Pyramid of Egypt. I guess that's what made up limestone when the world was first being formed but I never thought we'd ever be able to see the design of some of those ancient mini shells in the pyramids. Wow it's a strange and interesting world isn't it!" Becka answered back as we started to move on again. I still ran my hand along the side of the blocks as we walked and talked. Since getting here I couldn't stop thinking about being able to touch so much of history.

Since meeting and traveling with the merkids, we talked and thought a lot differently these days, we didn't take anything for granted but now we believed a lot more things to be real or possible. We were just walking and talking, occasionally looking back towards Shi and Bach, nothing going on there right now.

"Hey Becka, I think we're doing this the wrong way." I stopped so she stopped too and we both looked back toward the boys. "Lets get going counter clock wise, if there's anything special to pick up by being here I think it has to be in the counter clockwise direction. If there's anything to Pyramid power I'm sure it has something to do with a natural vortex direction." So we turned and headed back towards the guys.

It was warm here on the edge of the desert but there was also a breeze that kept whipping around us. It was just enough to cool things down a little without whipping the sand up to blast against your skin. This was Egypt and I expected nothing less than to cook and roast a little while walking the Sahara. I could see people on camels getting their pictures taken. Oh how I wished silently to myself that I had my camera. This was a once in a lifetime chance and I didn't know if I'd ever get back here again. As we got back to where the guys were standing Shi said to keep going Bach needed more time.

"We'll just make one quick trip around and be right back," I told him. He nodded his head in the affirmative and we kept going. After we turned the next corner I saw a piece of limestone and picked it up. It was rather small and fit just into the palm of my right hand.' This one's going home with me,' I thought to myself and deposited it into my pocket.

There was so much activity, all around, everywhere you looked there were tourist and guides. Maybe not as many people right here near the pyramids base as in line other places to get to special picture spots or to hear special information about the pyramids and the Sphinx. I was still feeling so excited, it was hard not to just run or turn cartwheels. I wanted to celebrate the feelings I was feeling for this place but walking, staying near the boys was all we could do for now.

By the time we reached the third corner we saw two very old Egyptian looking gentlemen sitting near the corner, one stone level up above us. They were talking to each other and watching everything around them, including us. As we got within a couple feet I looked up and said,

"Hello" to them.

"Good afternoon ladies. How are you this fine day?" the one on the left asked us.

"We're great, how could anyone be here and not be great?" I asked as my answer back to him.

"Many people come for many reasons. What is your reason?" he bantered back.

Becka spoke up,

"Actually we were looking for a special plant today, maybe you know of it? We were told it was growing here in the Giza region near the pyramids. If I could show you a picture could you tell us if you know of this plant?" she asked.

"I'm not much of a plant man but I know what I know, so yes. Let me see the picture of the plant you are looking for and I will see if I can help you." He said as he reached out his hand to see our picture.

Becka took the artwork from her pouch and handed it up to the man. He opened the drawing and looked at it for just a couple moments. Then he folded it back up and handed it back to her.

"Yes, I have seen this plant many times. It doesn't grow here in Giza any longer. In recent years I've only seen it in the Luxor region. There is a large Oasis near the Valley of the Kings on the West Bank across from Luxor. You would be able to find it there. When we were there two weeks ago it was in bloom near the waters edge."

"Thank you. We appreciate your help very much." Becka told them as she folded and put the artwork back into her pouch.

As we turned the corner to continue on our way we both just smiled at each other and started to run back to where we left the boys.

"We know where we can find the plant." Becka called out to the guys, as we got closer to them.

Shi looked at us and asked,

"Where did you get your information?"

"We just talked with two men who were around the other side of the pyramid. We showed them the drawing and they said we'd have to go to Luxor that the plant didn't grow in this area anymore. He said there's an Oasis there near the Valley of the Kings and we can find it on the banks at the water's edge." Becka told them.

"Well, I haven't been able to pick up anything here. Maybe that's why. If it doesn't grow in this area any longer we'll need to move on."

So without much more being said, it was decided we'd have to go up the Nile to the city of Luxor and then find our way to the Valley of the Kings and hope Bach would be able to find the Oasis they talked about. Suddenly I thought, wait a minute there are hippopotamus in the Nile River, even worse there's crocodiles. There's no way I'm swimming where there's so many dangerous animals, I learned my lesson in Australia. Maybe I should remind Bach because there were buses and other means of travel, we didn't have to try and swim the Nile. Surely he didn't mean he wanted to swim there. Definitely we'd have to talk about this before I'd get back in the river.

When we brought it up Bach said we needed to talk, he wanted to try the swim. He believed if we tried to stay in the middle and deepest part of the river we'd be safe and it would be much faster. Well, I wasn't so sure about that. I was thinking there was no way I'd be willing to get in where I knew there were crocodiles. I'm surprised I hadn't thought of it when we came here and first entered the Nile. I guess that was just an example of how excited I was. I must not have been thinking at all. But I was thinking now.

Becka and I both felt very strongly about not swimming to Luxor. Bach and Shi tried very vigorously to convince us we'd be safe. Bach kept saying the incident with Mu and the croc in Australia wasn't the same thing. He wasn't trying to read the water then. He absolutely guaranteed us he could read ahead and all around us while we swam and he could get us out if it looked like any danger was near.

"Besides" he told us, "since they built the Aswan Dam and many years before that as the climate changed the hippos and crocodiles migrated south to the lower levels of Africa and the Nile. They aren't suppose to be in this part of the Nile anymore it's just not something I think we'll have to worry about."

I just kept saying 'no way.' Becka backed me up on this one. So there we were, hiking back towards the Nile arguing back and forth about how we were going to get to Luxor. The boys were certain we could go via the Nile and Becka and me were certain we couldn't. Or maybe we should have just told them, we wouldn't. They kept coming up with one argument after another about why and how we could do it and be safe. I just kept shaking my head no. No. No. No.

By the time we got back to the Nile and stood looking at the water flow by, Becka and I stood together, holding hands, united in our refusal to get back into the river to go south. Each of the boys stood to our sides, as if they were trying to surround us and maybe give us their last argument for the swim. It took a few minutes but it was finally decided what we were going to do.

Don't ask me how they did it but there we were, the four of us dropping back into the Nile getting ready to head up river to the ancient city of Luxor and the Valley of the Kings. They must have hypnotized us. Or used some other form of trickery. There's just no other way we would have agreed to get into that river to go deeper into Egypt. I clearly remembered saying no and saying it more than once.

Shi heard my thoughts as we were back in the water.

"We didn't hypnosis you Kat, we just helped to raise your vibrational level a little. In raising your vibration it opened you both to the higher good and the vibration of trust. It helped to wipe your fears away and opened you up to believing more in the forces of good then the negative ones of fear. No real trickery there.

It was the same or similar to jumping into the gateway in Tibet. You didn't need to be with me, you actually did that all on your own. I told you, that you could do it if you were with me, but all I really did was make you believe you could. When you believed it, you made it happen. I had no power over you. At the time, it was just faster than trying to talk you through your fears of what you thought you could and couldn't do."

"Well you tricky little devil you." was all I could think to say back. He certainly blew me away with what he had just said to me.

There were a lot of boats on the river, some smaller ones and a lot of larger ones. I noticed several ferries and cargo barges. I noticed everything, the trash and debris in the river. The pollution was bad in the Nile. I wasn't sure it was safe to be in the water for that reason only, not counting the beasts that still might be up ahead of us, no matter what Bach said I was still worried. I had my eyes scanning the water ahead and behind us, looking for any trouble coming our way. This was not going to be one of my more favorite trips by any means. I was thinking I should have been scared to death but wasn't and I was still wondering a little how had the boys pulled this one off?

We swam for a long distance and Bach started to head to the surface again. I was hoping and praying this meant we were there. No such luck. There was a very large group of hippopotamus up ahead of us in the river. What the heck?

I could heard Bunny's voice in my head as I relived a conversation the three of us had back home when we knew we were going to Egypt. She said a lot of things about the crocodiles and the hippos. She told us she read that the hippos were a very vicious group, especially when they were in the water. She said they were fast swimmers and could be very territorial in the water as well.

Bach said only a couple things,

"Obliviously nature decides where she wants her beasts to be. There aren't any fences or pens to keep them in one place. The best way to handle this situation is try to think about how majestic and beautiful the animals are, don't let your fears surround you. The hippos are just another creature of the Universe and they are willing to share the river with us." and he started swimming again. Easy for him to say, apparently he could turn his fears off at will that is if he had any fears.

The animals were mostly towards the banks of the river so we might be able to slip by, out here in the middle without too much danger. We moved very slowly and kept our eyes on the big beasts. My heart was beating fast and I could feel it as clearly as I could feel my fear. I hoped that didn't draw their attention to us as we tried to sneak by. One of those big boys could crush any of us in one fast bite, have you ever seen the giant teeth on one of them? The guys didn't seem too worried and when it looked like we were clear of the group of more than 8-10 hippos they took us back under, into the depth of the river again.

After we left the hippos behind us we started to make good progress again. I started to relax, maybe just a little. I was just hoping we'd get there soon, I could hear Becka's thoughts; she and I were on the same wavelength that way. Neither of us had figured out yet just how the boys ever got us in the water again back in Giza, raised vibrations or not. It was very puzzling to us because we hadn't felt anything different. One minute we were saying no, no, n and the next we were going in to the water.

Just when I thought things were going pretty well and they were right, we would be safe as long as Bach was reading the water around us. Bach headed towards the bank of the river and we were heading up the riverbank out of the water. I instantly started to look behind and all around us. What was wrong? I didn't see anything to be worried about. Bach headed up to a point where we could see around the bend in the river up ahead.

"Oh good Lord!" Becka uttered. "Now what?"

"We'll have to hike for awhile until we get around them." Bach answered her. "Don't worry, we're almost there."

When I saw what they were looking at, I thought I would faint. There were more giant Crocodiles than the big ones we had seen in Australia. They were the most enormous animals I had ever seen or believed possible. They had to be 20 feet long or longer and easily 2 to 3 times the weight of the ones in Australia. After seeing these guys, I wasn't sure anyone could raise my vibration high enough to get me back in the water again.

Those were some pretty real hippos and the crocs were giant ones: so much for no hippos and crocodiles in this end of the Nile River. Surely people saw them and knew they were here in the local waters. Some one needed to rewrite the information on the Internet and reference materials.

We walked and skirted around all the crocs along the riverbanks, I couldn't help but keep looking back towards them, I didn't want any of then sneaking up on us. Here I was again, pulling up the rear. I had to do something to change that so I scurried by Shi and fell instep with Becka who was right behind Bach. We walked for hours before we could start to see something up ahead. Off in the distance I thought I could see some buildings and a road. Hopefully this was Luxor and the end of our travels for the moment. At least it would mean no more crocs for now.

As we entered the smaller city there were horse drawn carriages on the roads, also cars, trucks and buses. This was a much more rural town, nothing like the activity of Cairo and Giza. I saw plenty of people but this didn't feel like the millions who lived in Cairo. Turned out the city or town was called Karnak and Luxor was just up beyond it, no more river for me today. I can honestly say I was happy to be walking and hiking around in the Egyptian heat, rather than swimming with the crocs and hippos.

The people were all around us as we entered the town. They were taking things towards Luxor and they were busy working. Everyone we saw looked like they were going somewhere or doing something. We pretty much went unnoticed. There were other tourists around so we didn't stand out or draw any attention to ourselves. Bach seemed to know exactly where he wanted to go. It was great when our human compass was on tract and working 100%. I had total faith in Bach on the ground and pretty much in the water but not so much when there was man-eating crocs in the neighborhood. I had to admit he did get us here safely.

As we finally worked our way into the city of Luxor I was once again amazed with the scenery. The shop doors were open and I couldn't believe what I saw. The baker had his breads all out in the open, pretty much just displayed on the brick and pavement in front of the shop. I kept thinking, doesn't it get dirty and aren't you worried about the bugs getting on it? I couldn't see myself wanting to eat any of it or for that matter any of the meat at the butchers shop. Again the meat was all exposed and there were flies on it and as the people and carts went by the dirt surely was getting on it too. Nothing here was like what we were used to back home. The spice lady had all her spices out in burlap bags with the tops curled down to the level where the spice was. It was all neat and tidy rows of bagged spices with interesting colors and textures to look at. Many of the people just had their goods laid out on the ground. Some used cardboard to keep things a little cleaner maybe?

There were clothes and tapestries and all manner of fabric items hanging across the walkway high up overhead. There were carpets and shops with metal trays and bowls again like the ones we saw in Cairo. So many vendors with jewelry, all the colors and sparkly items it could make you dizzy trying to see it all.

There were some owners who had clothes and shoes and all sorts of interesting baskets and more than one had beautifully colored glass perfume bottles. I had never seen so many beautiful little bottles in every color of the rainbow and in so many sizes. Most of them had extra design detail painted on them making them very exotic and Egyptian. It was tempting to stop and buy something but I wasn't sure I'd be able to get it home with out breaking or maybe losing it along the way. Besides we still might need our money for something much more important before this little adventure was over because I definitely wasn't swimming back to Cairo after seeing what lived in that river. I don't care how much they tried to raise our vibrations, it wouldn't work a second time because I'd be thinking about those monster crocs for a long time to come.

We worked our way through the shopping area and around through the town and there we were, staring at the ruins in Luxor. I wasn't expecting to see ruins right here in the middle of town. What an impressive place this must have been in its time. I was pretty dazzled by it today. The four of us stopped and just took it in for a minute. There were huge columns reaching up to the sky and the walls were at least 40-60 feet high. We started to walk along the roadway and head towards the front of the temple ruins. There an amazing row of statues flanked the walkway into the temple. I heard someone say, they were still excavating in the temple area, discovering more every day. Wow, this was such a huge complex I couldn't imagine how much more they could uncover.

I couldn't believe all the history of Egypt we were passing by as we walked along the roadway. The Nile was there just a few feet away from the road. I could see tour boats, ferries and smaller boats with sails on them all over the river, coming and going. Across the Nile was the West

Bank. Somewhere to the east behind us were the Valleys of the Queens and Kings and the Oasis we were searching for.

The roadway was busy with people walking, carts being pulled by an assortment of different animals, cars and trucks trying to get by without hitting any of the pedestrians. A lot of the people were like me they were mesmerized by the ruins and almost couldn't take their eyes off of them, until suddenly confronted by a vehicle trying to get by them. The sound of the blaring horns got your attention pretty fast.

"You better start paying attention Kat before you get one of us run over." Becka scolded me.

I couldn't help it; the structure in front of me had some kind of pull on me. It was like I was coming home and it was all so familiar right now. I really wanted to go inside but Bach said there was no time. Maybe if I got lucky on the way back we could take a few minutes to slip inside before we headed home. It was like the building or this place was resonating with an energy that spoke to me, it reminded me of the stories in Australia that Cobar told us about the Dreamtime. I could hear the song and it was calling to me almost as if it knew my name.

The pillars were so tall and the hieroglyphs and designs on everything were like a magnet pulling me to them. I wanted to run my hand over everything I saw. As if the touching would tell me the stories of its history. As we passed by the last of the temple compound it was Becka tugging on my hand and arm constantly that finally got my attention back to the group.

After talking with some of the locals we discovered the Valley of the Queens and The Valley of the Kings was on the west side of the Nile. Which made sense as the Egyptians considered it the Land of the Dead. On the East bank of the Nile was the Land of the Living. Bach explained later that the east or sunrise was considered the Land of the Living and the sunset, west side was considered the Land of the Dead in general terms regarding their religious beliefs about life and the hereafter.

So here we were, on the wrong side of the river. Becka suggested that maybe we could ride one of the ferries across and mingle with the tourist to get to the Valley of the Kings. From there we'd have to rely on Bach to find that Oasis we were looking for. Bach and Shi decided it was a good plan and Becka offered to buy the tickets for the ferry and the ride to the Valley of the Kings.

I couldn't believe I was getting so lucky. Here it hadn't been a day in Egypt and I had seen and touched the pyramids at Giza, the Karnak Temple in Luxor and now I would get to see the Valley of the Kings. How much better could it get? We purchased our tickets and got in line to board the ferry, which would be loading and leaving soon. The sun was bright and glaring off the water as we waited.

It was relaxing, even in the heat of the day as we watched the small boats with sails moving up and down the Nile. I could see a small group of about five men huddled around a small fire. It looked like they were making tea or coffee there in the small shelter they had built into the side of the riverbank. It was a very small shelter they had and it looked very crowded with them all in it this afternoon. It did at least give them some shelter from the killer sun beating down on everything. Hardly a spot anywhere along the riverbank and roadway wasn't filled with someone or something happening.

Everything was so different from the states. I had never seen so many people with so little. We over heard a guide with the group we were joining going to the Valley of the Kings and Queens say to one of the tourist that he only made $80.00 a month from his job. He also commented he depends on tips to help him feed his children. That certainly pulled on your heart a little and made you think about trying to give him a tip before the end of the tour.

The ferry ride was just a little cooler from the slight breeze out over the water as we crossed to the other side. The sun was high in the sky and starting to beat down on all who were under it with a vengeance. We left the ferry and piled into vans that would carry us to the Valleys of the Kings and Queens. Bach decided we would leave the group in the Valley of the Kings and start on our search for the Oasis that was to the west.

We traveled just a short distance and rode through a small town on the West Bank, it was really only a few dozen mud and stone structures. We stopped and there were several kids playing with a few baby sheep on the corner where we had to turn to leave their town. A couple of the others in our van wanted to get picture of them. The kids immediately smiled and after the pictures were taken they all reached their hands out, palms up for money. They were all saying" Piastres, Piastres, Piastres". Which was the name of the Egyptian money. Personally I thought they really have a good thing going here, they were all so cute, how could any of the tourists resist taking their pictures and then not feel like giving them a few coins in return?

Our van wound around the road, up and over a few small hills heading west. Luckily we had air conditioning in the van or I might have started thinking about another time in Peru when we rode through the desert, I was thankful we were riding again too. At one point we rode by two ruins of statues they were unbelievably humongous in size. It really did make you wonder how they were able to build these things. The guide said they were the Colossi of Memnon and that each was carved from a single stone. The regular tourists with us wanted pictures so we stopped and I got a chance to play tourist too. The boys couldn't get over my joy at being able to touch so many things.

The rest of the ride to the Valley of the Queens was unremarkable and I was thrilled when we finally got there especially since we went there first which meant I would be able to see it as well as the Valley of the Kings. My luck was sure holding up for me on this little adventure. It was one of those places that the look of it was unmistakable. Once you saw it, you would always recognize it the next time you saw it. The front was half way across the base of the mountains that stood as the guardian of the structure below. The sandstone of the mountains and the temple below could have blended together except for the boldness of the temples design.

Bach spoke up and said,

"This was a sacred place long before this temple was built here. The vortex energy is very strong here. Sandstone is actually about 2/3's crystal and this sand stone has at least five different types of crystal in it, which makes it a very pure as well as a high energy place."

"When the energy is this fine and pure you will have the greatest moments of enlightenment. That's probably why they brought so many dead here, so their spirits were able to use that energy, to move on to the higher planes." Shi added in. "Sandstone is also a natural amplifier of spiritual energy and spiritual communications."

Wow, it never ceased to amaze me the things the merkids could tell us. It was sad that we had forgotten so many of our spiritual talents and abilities. I wanted to hear more but our group was collecting around us and the guide wanted to move up onto the first terrace of Hatshepsut's Temple. We walked to the center staircase, what a grand entrance this made, it had to be easily 20-30 feet wide. We walked the stairs up to the first terrace where two stately lion statues still remained as guardians of the temple on each side of the stairway. Our little group started walking and taking in the sights of the first level.

I was feeling the funniest buzz going all through my body. It was almost a ringing in my ears and then I heard what sounded like a very loud pop inside my head.

I put my hand on the terrace wall trying to balance and anchor myself. Something was happening to me. I wasn't sure what it was but nothing like this had ever happened to me before. I hoped at that moment I wasn't having some kind of stroke or seizure and that it didn't get worse than what I was feeling right now. Becka came over to my side to see what was wrong.

"Are you okay Kat?" she asked with a worried look on her face. "What's wrong? Can you hear me?"

I wasn't able to answer her, I couldn't speak right then so I just shook my head that I was okay as I closed my eyes and tried to get my balance back. When I opened them again I felt fine. But I opened them, feeling like a different Kat.

"I've been here before Becka. It was another time and another life and it was all much more beautiful then. These terraces had trees and exotic plants that I had brought back from the land of Punt. There were fountains and beautiful flowers everywhere. I believe, no I'm quite sure I was Hatshepsut. This was a place I had made beautiful for my final resting place. I had a row of sphinxes here along the terrace too I wonder what ever happened to them?"

"WOW. Are you serious?" Becka asked.

"I know and believe me, this is blowing my mind even more than it is yours. Ever since I put my foot on the first step below, to come up to this level I started feeling strange. I don't know how I suddenly know these things but I do and I'm sure it's because I was Hatshepsut. I feel a pride of seeing that my monument lasted all this time and that it's a place of special meaning and many come to see it's beauty still."

"Holy cow Kat, first Amy and now you remembering something, this isn't easy to take in and you're scaring me just a little." She blurted out.

"I was the best female Pharaoh of Egypt and I was a prolific builder because I wanted to see the glory of Egypt and Hathor live on. How wonderful to see that it has. I dedicated this temple to Hathor. Did you know that? She was the Goddess of Love." I finished telling her. I could feel myself walking with a straighter posture and a little more queenly presence. It was a strange feeling to feel like two people at one time.

"Well could you let Hatshepsut return to her slumber and just leave me with Kat for now?" she asked. "You're making me feel a little nervous myself."

"Okay" I told her and started to walk with the others in our group up to the next level. I felt back to my old self again but with a knowledge I hadn't had before of the other time and place. It wasn't like a spirit taking over my mind or body but my memories coming back.

We finished our tour of the temple and walked back towards our van. I hadn't noticed on the way from the parking lot up to the temple the large row of shops. The Market to our left, as the guide called it had all the same goodies we had been seeing in the markets of both Cairo and Luxor. There were so many people trying to sell things to the tourist. People were everywhere bartering and trying to make deals on their purchases.

It was a fairly short ride from the Valley of the Queens around to the backside of the mountain to the Valley of the Kings. There were no great temples or structures here, only openings into the ground and the side of the mountain into the tombs of the ancient Pharaohs. I couldn't imagine the people trying to find these tombs ever getting lucky enough to find the openings and rediscover them, here out in the middle of nowhere.

Bach had us hang back as the others went into the first tomb. We entered, inspected the paintings on the walls and then followed the others back out. It was when the others entered the next tomb that we stopped when it was our turn to enter and quickly scurried away and up to the top of the hillside away from our group.

There were dozens of trails up over into the higher area of the mountain above the tombs. Bach followed one off to the right and as we climbed higher and back away from the area where you could see the tombs we saw a few other people there hiking around. A few Egyptians were there, trying to sell their special something, each one guaranteed to be a true artifact and taken from a real tomb. They reminded me of the movies where vendors tried to sell watches or jewelry from inside their trench coats while they tried to stay away from the law enforcements eagle eye.

Soon we were hiking and there was no one else in sight. I really hoped that Bach was on target this time because I wasn't in the mood to get lost in the Sahara Dessert and that's exactly where we were headed. Maybe we should have asked a few more questions of the locals about this Oasis we needed to find. Some general directions or an idea of how far into the dessert it might be? I hated not knowing how far and where I was going all the time.

We walked and made it onto more level ground in a short period of time. Now the sun was scorching down, un-relentlessly. I was so glad to have our water with us and was hoping that Oasis wasn't too much farther. Walking with the sweat just pouring down off your face and dripping down into the small of your back was not a comfortable feeling. We all had wet sweat stains on our clothes. At least this trip didn't include us having to throw mud and dirt all over ourselves while we were this hot and sweaty. I think the sand would have just worked like a magnifying glass and heated us up all the more. I tried to roll my sleeves down and not think too much about it as I wiped the salty, stinging sweat from my eyes.

At one point Bach finally said he thought we were getting close and hoped we could wait for a rest stop until we were at the oasis. I couldn't imagine stopping and trying to rest standing up out here in the middle of the desert. The sand was so hot to the touch you sure wouldn't want to try and sit down on it. I could feel the heat almost cooking my feet and lower legs. My water pouch was getting low and I didn't want to think about what I'd do when it was empty. My mouth was feeling dry and parched just thinking about the heat.

I kept thinking, it's not whining unless you say things out loud. I tried to be brave and quiet, so I just kept putting one foot in front of the other. We'd be there soon. Becka looked hopeful too, at least that's the look I thought I saw on her face. It wasn't often I saw Becka perspire so it was hard to tell what the look was on her face. We were both getting sun burned and our faces were getting red. We were both hot and half-baked, I could see that no problem.

Just about the time I thought I would have to give up for the day, that I couldn't walk another 100 feet, I heard Bach clear his throat and said something.

"I see the tops of some trees. I think we're almost there. Look over here," as he pointed almost straight ahead of us. "Can you see them too?" he asked.

It appeared at this point even Bach wasn't sure if he was seeing things or not. We were all cooked and getting very dehydrated, he could have been hallucinating.

"I see them too." Shi answered before Becka and I could zero in on what he was pointing at. It took a couple seconds before the two of us saw the treetops too. I could have danced a jig I was so happy knowing we were so close but I really didn't have enough energy. I needed water then maybe I could do my dance.

It was so much easier walking the last of the distance to the Oasis, my feet even lifted a little higher with each step closer that we got. When we got close enough to really see things, we noticed there were other people there. They had camels and it looked like they were out of some old movie camped there at the waters edge. There were three of them and they had 9-10 camels with them all but three of the camels had large packs on their backs. It looked like a caravan from some old novel my mother would have read, made into a movie.

Amazingly as we approached the oasis and them, they didn't seem surprised to see us. Actually they had very little reaction to seeing us and continued on with their own business. You would have thought that every time they came here they saw kids walking in from the desert, all alone, sun burned and on foot. The four of us nodded hello and knelt down at the edge of the water, filled our pouches with water and then drank our fill before refilling them. The water felt so good going down our poor dehydrated throats even my lips felt like they were coming back to life.

We weren't there very long before the water we drank started to bring our minds back to what we were here for and we started looking around the waters edge. Where was the plant we came so far to find? Other than the palm trees and some grasses I didn't see any other plants or vegetation. This couldn't be happening. Where were the plants?

We had trusted the older Egyptians had known what they were telling us when they told us we could find the plants here at this Oasis. So where were they? How could we go so far and be so wrong to have trusted them? We all got up and started walking all around the Oasis it's wasn't far but we took our time, inspecting every inch of sand along the way. We looked up on the banks of sand away from the waters edge. Finally we started hunting around the palm trees and anyplace we saw anything growing. When we had worked our way back, all around the Oasis to where we had begun, we were all just looking in every direction. How could we have missed it? Where could it be? Now what? I even looked at Bach and Shi and asked them the same question out loud.

"Now what guys? Where do we go from here?"

"Let's ask those men if they have seen the plant. Maybe they know where it grows or if it was ever here." Becka suggested.

"Good thinking Becka, They might know something. Right anything is better than what we have now." I answered her.

So off she went with the three of us not too far behind her. She walked up and asked if they spoke English. One of the men, the one closest to her said he did. She handed him the picture and told him we were searching for this plant and wondered if he had ever seen them explaining we had been told we could find them here at this Oasis.

"What is that American saying, 'a day late and a dollar short'? I'm afraid you are two days, too late. We have been here harvesting the exact plant you have come in search of. We finished this afternoon packing the last bundles of dried plants onto our camels and were having lunch before we leave when you and your friends arrived." He told her.

"You took them all?" she asked.

"Yes." He answered.

"Do you know where we could find anymore?" she asked.

"This is the last place we know of. Maybe you could return next year when the new crop will be growing." He suggested.

I think hearing his words did us all in. They just killed them all two days before we got here. How could this be happening? They didn't know what they had done to us. This was bigger than just not being able to get a plant we wanted. This could mean the difference between saving the merkids and all the rest of them dying. This was no little thing.

"Are you sure there's no other place to look for more of the plants?" I asked.

"It's very important to us and we've come half way around the world looking for it. All we need is one plant, that's all."

"Sorry no. I know no other place." He said again.

We were totally deflated and there was no way to try to put a positive spin on it. How could we go back to Atlantis and tell them we failed and wouldn't be able to make the cure happen? I don't know who was the most depressed. We all just sat down and stared into space, each thinking our own gloomy thoughts.

"If you would like a ride back into Luxor, we would be happy to take you. It would only require a few changes with the loads on the camels and we could help you return to the city." The tallest of the Egyptians asked. "You all look as if you could use a ride" and he grinned as he watched to see our response.

"We would love to accept your generous offer for a ride." Becka said immediately, accepting for all of us. "If we can help you at all to change things let us know. We're truly most grateful for your help."

I was actually a little surprised that Becka accepted without asking Bach or Shi what they thought. Maybe she felt the way I did, too tired to walk ever again through another desert and now also too depressed to even think about having to move again. It only took a few minutes and they rearranged the loads on the camels and were able to open up two camels that we could pair up on to ride.

I had never been on a camel before. What a trip. First they made them lie down on the ground so we could walk over and climb on. Shi and I rode together while Bach and Becka got on the next camel. What an awkward ordeal of getting back up with the camel. It made me think of those mechanical bulls you see and the thing goes at several extreme angles trying to throw you off. It was just what I thought those mechanical bulls would be like. Once we were up it wasn't too bad. The camel had an unusual gait and it was a bit of a herky-jerky ride. I had ridden horses and ponies before and they were a lot less movement to try to swing with.

It was wonderful not having to trek back thorough the dessert but this slow motion movement of the camels walk was almost enough to give me motion sickness. You also couldn't really sleep or try to nap because you might fall if you didn't pay attention; not to mention we were up a lot higher and the fall would be a rude awakening. The sweat still ran down our bodies and our faces but I don't believe we were dehydrating as much as when we had to exert ourselves hiking through the sand. We would have to think of some way to thank our Egyptian friends when we got back to Luxor. Knowing they had killed the last of the plants we were looking for, it was hard to feel grateful towards them right now even though they were taking us back with them.

It seemed like even farther going back than when we hiked out to the Oasis but maybe that was because we were so disappointed and we did ride in the van out to the Valley of the Kings before we started walking. We didn't utter a word during the ride back to the Nile. My own mind wasn't functioning. I just couldn't think about what it would mean to the future of the merkids now that we couldn't find one of the plants we needed. None of us knew if the cure could be complete without all of the plants. There was so much that we didn't know.

I started thinking, maybe there's a higher authority we could talk to regarding the plant we were searching for maybe these guys didn't know everything. I wasn't sure what the others were thinking but suddenly my glass was half full. I was thinking positively and it was a leap of faith that I had to make. We had to have some ray of hope that we could still find it, that there was more here somewhere. Thinking about it in a positive way made me feel better immediately.

I was wondering if Hatshepsut wouldn't have known where the plants had grown, maybe there was some clue I could pull up from the past. I started to think, how could I do this? Maybe if I tried to do some self-hypnosis, travel back into my memories and bring back a little miracle. Sitting behind Shi on the rocky ride on the camels back didn't seem as conducive to self-hypnosis as I would have thought. Maybe I could try when we got back to solid ground in Luxor. Maybe Bach could do something.

Riding a camel with Egyptians in a small caravan from an Oasis in the Sahara desert wasn't something I ever expected to be doing. As I thought about the magic of it I was thrilled to be here. I definitely felt it wasn't something Hatshepsut would have done she rode only on beautiful big barges on the Nile and litters carried by slaves. When I felt her presence I became more confident, more commanding and somehow wiser. She was a strong woman with a purpose in life. I knew she tried very hard to fulfill that purpose here. I could see her as she walked and observed the things happening around here in the place she loved. I could feel her pride and sense of accomplishment. It was a life well lived providing much food for the soul.

I didn't know if it was the rocking motion of the camel ride or the fact that I was here and had started to remember things but I was having so many pictures and images flash through my brain and across my mind's eyes. Maybe I was hypnotized and just didn't realize it. I felt not only the time as Hatshepsut but also something else. Another time when I was here and was part of all that happened in Egypt but as another spirit or personality. I couldn't quite put my finger on this one but it was right there on the tip of my fingers almost close enough to take a hold of. I wasn't sure which images went with which lifetime they danced in the semi shadows of my mind and played with me now as the camel's gait lured me into this hypnotic like sleep.

I could feel the strength of the times I helped to build this world and to establish centers for the spiritual growth and soul advancement of mankind. It was strange to feel these things and at the same time wonder could I really have been anyone who had such a strong part of constructing any of this? I was beginning to feel like someone with multiple personalities and it was sort of freaky. I couldn't wait to be able to talk with Becka alone again.

Finally we could see the Nile ahead of us. It was even a little refreshing to just see water again. I could feel the smallest breeze come up as we neared the river. Our new friends said the ferry should be along shortly and they dropped us off at the wharf. We thanked them and asked them again, if there was any payment we could make to pay them back for going out of their way to give us a ride back. They said they were happy to have been able to help. The one who spoke English said he was sorry to have prevented us from our quest of finding the rare Nile Moon lily we traveled so far to find.

While we stood together at the wharf waiting for the ferry to come back to pick up on our side, we started to talk and discuss the possibilities of still being able to find our plant before we had to leave. I personally was feeling a lot more optimistic. There had to be one more somewhere and we'd find it, I was hoping so anyway. The more we talked the better we all felt. The ferry finally arrived so we were able to get right on and get headed back to the East Bank and Luxor. Or Thebes as Hatshepsut thought of it: Luxor was the new name, in her day it was called Thebes and it was Egypt's capital.

Now that she seemed to have awakened inside me, everything I thought and saw was first through her mind and eyes and then my own. It was hard keeping things straight when it was just the difference of time spent with the merkids and my real life back home. This new thing with Hatshepsut's thoughts and memories was a whole lot more tricky to add into the mix. So far I thought I was handling it pretty well. I hadn't flipped out yet anyway.

Suddenly as the ferry moved into the current of the Nile I could see myself in that other time; I was being rowed up the Nile into Thebes on the royal barge. It was some sort of vision, a memory of that other life when I was Hatshepsut. There were dozens of men, slaves who were at the oars making my ride a swift and smooth one. It was a fairly large barge with beautiful carvings and a private curtained area in the center back end where I was reclining on a cushioned platform lounge. There were cotton curtains instead of walls, for privacy that allowed the breezes to pass through. I was there on the lounge being fanned by two slaves and I was talking with my minister about the completion of my funeral monument in the Valley of the Queens. It was called Deir-el-Bahri. I was so into the moment of the vision I could smell the air and the flowers on the table next to the lounge. I watched as my two new kittens played together near my feet, occasionally feeling their soft fur against my skin. I was eating grapes from a bowl and I could taste the sweetness of the fruit.

As the ferry returned to the East Bank I was seeing Luxor/Thebes with new eyes. Ever since I stepped onto the grand stairway going up to the Temple In the Valley of the Queens I had a new set of eyes I was seeing things with and a new serenity had come over me. I felt wiser and at home with this river, the desert and all the ruins, I was able to remember and see in my minds eye the beauty and majesty that these temples once had.

As the ferry turned into the dock Becka said,

"A Paistre for your thoughts." and she smiled at me.

"I'm so lost Becka and yet I feel at the same time like I've found a part of me I always knew was there but couldn't exactly see. I think the hairs on my arms have been standing up from the electric feelings I've had ever since we stepped onto the Temple Deir-el-Bahri in the Valley of the Queens.

If this is anything like what Amy felt when we were in Tibet in Shambhala I understand her feelings about not wanting to leave. It just feels like I belong here. I know this place and I recognize the beauty it had before. I know I've been happy here and I had a destiny that now has brought me back to my homeland.

The funniest thing is I feel like there was maybe another time, another part of me was someone else. The feelings are similar but also very different. It's all so hard to try to explain. I really don't know if I understand any of it myself. I just know what I'm feeling. It feels pretty freaky too." I confided in her." I saw my own face Becka. I was so classically Egyptian. I was beautiful. My eyes were outlined and done as the eyes of Horus. Do you know what that means?" I asked her. "Doing your right eye in this outline and style represents the sun and to do the left represents the moon. Together, both the eyes done in this manner represent the whole Universe, the right side being masculine energy and reason and the left feminine energy and intuition."

"Wow, that was sure more than I paid for and more than I guess I expected to hear. I'm blown away and don't know what else to say. I wish I understood what's happening, first Amy going over the edge and now you. Bunny didn't get such intense feelings? Did she?" she asked.

"She never said anything that would make me think she felt anything this intense." I told her in reply. We just looked at each other for a few seconds. It was a lot to try and take in from both of our prospective.

The boys motioned to us that we could disembark so the four of joined back up and headed towards the dock and land again. We all had lobster red sunburns but we had rested on the ride back so we didn't think we looked too ragged. A nice cool bath and a fresh set of clothes would have been very welcome right about now, not to mention a little time to really rest and think about what we'd do next.

We decided to walk into the Winter Palace Hotel and enjoy a little air conditioning. We'd get something to drink maybe, sit at a table and try to decide how we would precede in this little adventure of ours. Bach and Shi were both trying to think of whom we could contact to enquire about the plant. Where could we get the help we needed? None of us wanted to go home empty handed but we were at a loss now, as far as, what to do next or whom to ask for help.

We entered the Winter Palace Hotel after climbing one of the semi-circular sets of stairs out front. This building it turned out used to be the winter Palace of the rich Europeans of Noble rank who traveled Egypt. It was a grand building on the outside as well as the inside. The hotel had a sign out front that said it was built in 1886. It had large open lobby and sitting areas with walls that looked at least 40 feet tall up to the ceiling. There were heavy drapes at all the windows, detailed designed rails and banisters leading up to the second level that was open to the first in the lobby area. There was so much decorative trim and molding it was easy to picture the rich and famous of the times coming to stay and enjoy the hotel and ruins of the area.

We asked in the lobby and were shown where the dining area was located. We asked if we could sit and just have something cold to drink.

We all got a nice large glass of orange juice and sat to relax while we enjoyed the cool air-conditioned atmosphere. It was a grand formal setting with dozens of tables all formally set around us. I felt we didn't look like we quite fit in.

It was Bach who finally spoke,

"I don't know if we can give up this easily. There must be at least a few plants that are still growing some place here in Egypt. I'm not sure whom we should ask or what direction to take next. I just feel that we can't give up."

"I think we all agree." I added in. "I think we need to ask some of the locals in the market place. The plants were used for medicinal purposes maybe someone with herbs or medicines would have some ideas. I think we should head for the marketplace again. If nothing else, maybe we can buy seeds."

So it was decided while we sat soaking in the cooler air of the dining room, drinking our orange juice; we would go back to the market place and talk to as many people as necessary to try and find some clue that could help us. There just had to be more of the plants somewhere and we needed to find that somewhere. Too much depended on it and us right now.

We left the hotel after paying for our drinks and headed straight towards the market place. This time however we skipped the main tourist market and skirted around to the locals market. There we talked with everyone who spoke English and tried to enlist his or her help in our mission. We talked with merchants who sold spices, herbs and medicines first. Then when we hadn't been able to find a single source of hope we started talking to anyone who would listen to us. We even asked all the kids who spoke English who would stop and talk with us.

We spent the rest of the day talking with anyone who would give us a couple minutes of their time, we talked with people on the streets, in the markets, the hotels, along the riverbanks we even called out to the boatmen on the river. We weren't getting anywhere. The plants were scarce to begin with and now it was past the harvest time for them. Talk about poor, really poor timing, now what could we do?

We started talking about heading back to Cairo. Becka and I told the boys

"No trying to raise our vibrations to get us in the water again. This time we're going to have to find another way to get there."

The last man we had talked with was loading his boat and over heard us talking. Arguing and debating might have been a more accurate way of saying what we were doing.

"I would be happy to give you a ride down the river to Cairo. I only ask if the breezes are down that you would help me to row the boat. It's not a hard job. The river runs north to Cairo and does most of the hard work. I wouldn't mind the company for a change, since my son passed over into the afterlife, I must make my journey alone." The boys looked towards us and you could almost read Bach's thoughts. He found this a solution to our dilemma about getting back to Cairo without having a mutiny by Becka and me.

It was Becka who said,

"Thank you, we accept your generous offer and we will be happy to help in any way we can. But you must tell us your name so we can be properly introduced."

"I am Hanif, and yours?" he asked as he extended his hand to help Becka climb into his boat. After each of us was on board and the introductions finished Hanif pushed the boat into the Nile and climbed into his seat in the rear of his felucca. We didn't talk much among ourselves but more with Hanif.

Becka asked him,

"Hanif is an interesting name, what does it mean?"

"It is an old name in Egypt and means 'believes'." he answered her.

"My name is Rebekha it's an old Biblical name. In Hebrew it means 'to tie'. I always thought that was a strange meaning and it actually makes no sense to me. My mother liked it and named me after Rebekha in the Bible."

He turned his head towards me and asked what was the meaning of my name.

"My mother always told me Katherine meant 'pure' and my middle name Regina means 'queen'. Wow, now that I think about it, that's actually kind of freaky isn't it Becka?" I answered.

Hanif just smiled and started talking about the Nile and his time working and traveling it. He followed in his father's footsteps and took over the family business when he died. He spent his week transporting goods between Thebes and Cairo. He seemed happy with his life other than losing his son a few years back. Tears came to his eyes when he talked about him.

As we worked our way down the Nile towards Cairo, Hanif gave us a history lesson about each of the towns and palaces we passed by. He knew a lot about Egypt and her past. He knew the names of every temple and ruins along the way. He told us when he was younger he used to stop at a new place each time he traveled back and forth to educate his son and to see it all for himself. His lessons kept our minds busy and the time passed rather quickly.

I could see a lot of what he was talking about in my minds eye. I had helped to build many of the buildings he talked about and I had walked and traveled most of these temples many times when I was Hatshepsut. I could remember. Maybe Hanif actually wakened the memories for me with his discourse on every town we passed. I was floating in a haze of memories and emotions as we sailed down the river.

When we could see the tall high raises of Cairo, Hanif worked his boat into some wharfs on the east bank, on the out shirts of the city.

"This is where we must part ways my friends. I need to unload and get the new goods to take back. I don't go any farther into the city." He told us as he maneuvered the boat up to the wharf before he jumped out to tie it down.

"At least let us help you to unload and get your new load onboard. It's the least we can do for all your help as well as the entertaining and informative ride down the river." Bach told him.

So that's how we thanked our new friend. Once we had the last parcel on board and Hanif was ready to push off to head home again we all personally thanked him again. The boys shook his hand and we hugged him goodbye. It was amazing to me all the wonderful people we were meeting in Egypt. So many helpful, friendly people, I thought it was too bad the whole world couldn't be like that it would make the world such a happier place. It was a lesson I was learning on this adventure. Realizing it, I would try to be as helpful to others as all our new friends had been to us. It could be my little part towards making the world a better place.

As we watched Hanif glide away from the wharf we started to assess our next move, we were on the wrong side of the river if we planned to get back to Giza. Looking around there were many boats and barges in the area but not a ferry in sight. There were so many people along the rivers edge it was almost impossible to get in and out of the water without someone seeing the merkids had tails so it was better for all concerned if we rode across the river. Seeing all the trash and debris along the riverbank didn't make me want to climb down the riverbank much less slip into the polluted waters of the dock area here in Cairo. For some silly reason I was more concerned with the pollution here than worrying about any of the water creatures we had seen up river.

Shi suggested we see if anyone else in the area needed help to load or unload goods, maybe we could barter some work for a ride across the river. So we started walking the wharf and asking if anyone needed help. Many of the people looked at us but didn't speak English. We actually hadn't gone too far when a tall thin man said he'd trade our help for a ride to the other side. He needed to run back to pick up something he had forgotten and if we were loaded when he got back he'd give us the ride we needed before he headed south.

The four of us formed a line and started picking up the boxes and bundles of goods, carrying them onto the boat and piling them in the shelter he had constructed at the back of the boat. His boat was larger than Hanif's had been and he had a lot more goods to load and carry south. We worked the entire time he was gone and finished just as he reappeared on the wharf. It was Bach who asked our latest friend what his name was. When he told him,

"My name is Oba." He pushed passed Bach saying," We have no time to visit. I must hurry and get you to the other side. I have business in Luxor tomorrow." As soon as he sat his package down in the sheltered area he returned and started to give orders to untie the boat and head away from the wharf. We did as he commanded and as soon as we were away from the wharf he started to raise the sail and we were off towards Giza.

It was a short ride and Oba wasn't very sociable. We all did as told and kept quiet so we didn't disturb our benefactor. Personally I was pleased not to have to talk and try to draw Oba out of his dark mood. He seemed upset and nervous to all of us. Suddenly I started to wonder what he had brought on board with him when he returned with his forgotten package. Perhaps it was better not to know, what you didn't know they often said, couldn't hurt you. It started to put strange and dark thoughts into my mind. Maybe he was a smuggler or worse, maybe he was carrying drugs or stolen artifacts. As those crazy thoughts started to work their way into my brain I started to get nervous myself and was looking forward to getting off the boat and away from Oba. I didn't like thinking negative things about someone who was helping us but he seemed so nervous and odd about hurrying away, I couldn't help but wonder about him. I found myself looking back behind us, checking to see if it looked like anyone was trying to follow us.

We reached the West Bank and Oba let us off at a small wharf south of Giza. As he started to push away from the wharf he pointed and said,

"Giza is that way." With just those four words he was turning back to his chores and manning his boat, heading for Luxor. For just a couple seconds we all sort of looked at each other and it was Becka who said,

"Well that was sort of strange. He sure seemed nervous and upset. I hope he isn't doing anything illegal."

"I wouldn't worry about him." Bach said," Oba is an honest man. Today I think he was just nervous about getting back to Luxor on time. I didn't read anything sinister about him or we wouldn't have set foot on his boat."

"It's almost dark," Shi said. "Maybe we should get started it's easier to find ones way in day light and we have no idea what the streets of Cairo or Giza are like at night."

"Yes, you're right." Bach answered and he started off away from the wharf towards the city.

It was a little easier to keep my attention on the trip into the city this time. I wasn't near as distracted as I had been the first time we were here. It was still pretty amazing to see so much activity all around us. Every street had dozens of shops and people everywhere were conducting their business. We walked by a group of five men sitting in front of one store that were all smoking from a water pipe and having tea. Wouldn't see that in America.

At another shop we heard the owner send a young boy to fetch back a tray of refreshments for his customers. Bach said it was like a tradition here, the merchant needed to make his first sale because it would be an omen for the rest of his day, so very often they would provide tea or coffee for their first customers of the day. Sort of like our old saying wine and dine them to help make the deal. A lot of the a shop keepers were dressed in typical Muslim clothing, some in more American style garments and others were dressed in a mixture of the two. On the younger people you saw a lot more t-shirts and jeans.

By the time we worked our way across Giza, it was dark and we could see the Sphinx and Pyramids in the distance, glowing from special colored spotlights. They were giving an evening show. We could hear the speakers as the music played in the background and the narrator spoke about the triumphs of Egypt and the Pharaohs who built the Pyramids. I was ready to sit, relax a little and listen to the program but Bach said we should keep moving.

I wasn't sure yet, what plan he had up his sleeve, we were already off the Delta area and in the Sahara as we walked towards the backside of the Pyramids.

"I want to climb to the top of the Great Pyramid and try to tune into the area. Maybe from up there I can tune into our plant. At least I can send out a searching energy better from up there. I think it's best if you girls stay down here. I don't want to cloud my reception with too much other energy. Shi and I will do this together while you wait here. Try to stay out of sight of the guards as best you can while we're gone." With those last words Bach and Shi both started to climb up the backside of the Pyramid.

"I can't really hear the program from back here." I said to Becka, "This is going to be a boring wait. I wonder how long it'll take them to just climb up there?"

"I don't know but I'm sure it'll be awhile. I don't think you or I could get there any too fast. We'll just have to find something to do so we're not too bored. How about we just sit and relax for awhile?" she answered back.

"You know, Bunny was telling me about a show she saw on the History Channel about how the Pyramids were lined up in a formation that matched one of the constellations. She said in the show, if you super imposed the lines from the constellation pattern onto the pattern of the pyramids, the lines the formation made lead them to a small bird tomb or temple that was suppose to be the entrance to the under world area under the Sphinx and these pyramids." I started trying to explain to her.

"Well that's all very interesting but what does that have to do with us and what we're doing?" she asked.

"Well I was thinking, that bird tomb or temple has to be pretty close to where we are now. Maybe we could go have a look for something to do, instead of just sitting here waiting for the guys." I told her.

"Oh I don't know about that Kat. I think we're better off just staying right here and relaxing. Besides I don't think I want to be walking around inside some tomb in the dark at night. I can just imagine the not so fun things we could run into." She answered.

"Oh don't be a wuss Becka, we have our beam crystals and look, the guys aren't getting very far very fast. They'll probably be gone for hours and hours yet." I told her as I looked to see how far the boys had gotten in their climb.

"I'm pretty happy right here Kat. I've gotten enough adventure on this trip and I don't think I need anymore" she told me as she patted the sand next to where she was sitting. "Why don't you just come over here and we'll have a nice chat while we wait for the boys."

I turned and started to look around. I wanted so much to see that under ground passage way that had been discovered. I wondered if the Hall of Records was hidden there somewhere like Edgar Cayce had said so many years ago. He was one of the most famous psychics who ever lived and I was sure he must have known what he was talking about. I really, really wanted to go exploring. Now I just needed to convince Becka she wanted to go too. What fun would it be, to go alone? Not to mention, I found courage in numbers and I didn't like being alone in dark places.

I was standing there, contemplating how I could talk Becka into going with me to explore that Bird Tomb Bunny had told me so much about. There was a strange popping sound I heard inside my head and then it was all so clear to me.

"You must come with me now sister. I have to retrieve something I left behind a long time ago. I know exactly where it is and it won't take long for us to get there and get back. Hurry we must go now if we are to get back here on time." I held my hand out for Becka to reach up and take and she did. I took her hand and headed off into the night.

Somehow I knew where the Bird Tomb was and I took us right to it. It wasn't far from where we had been sitting, only a few hundred yards at most. They had some barricades up in the area but they didn't stop us from getting by them and up to the entrance.

"Wait a minute, I'm not going in there without the Beam crystals, it's too dark and we'll be stumbling around falling over our own feet." she said as she pulled the crystal from her pouch. I looked at her and started to reach inside the pouch I was carrying to do the same. Yes, she was right, much better with light. She placed the crystals on and started into the tomb.

It was a small structure and it was easy to see why it had been over looked for so many years. Who would have ever thought this could be the key or gateway to finding anything?

"I hope you know what you're doing." was all Becka said as we walked deeper into the small tomb. It looked like it was going to be a dead end when we reached a short wall with a ledge on it about five feet off the floor. I only stopped for a second before I started to climb up onto the ledge.

"Come on sister, give me your hand. This is the way we have to climb beyond this wall to get inside. I have been here many times. Don't worry. Now give me your hand so I can help you get up." Becka didn't look too convinced about giving me her hand and climbing into what looked like another wall. As I helped her to get up she could finally see the opening where we needed to go. We both jumped down into the cave area to the side of the wall and ledge.

"This way. Just follow me." I told her. I was walking and talking but it was all like being in a dream. It didn't feel like it was really me. I could hear what I was saying and I recognized Becka but it somehow just didn't seem real to me.

The cave was eerie and there was a strong smell of bat poop. We both pulled the front of our shirts up to cover our noses, to make the smell a little easier to stand. It looked like centuries ago the water must have worn it's way through this cave like some under ground currents had carved their way through. The walls were mostly smooth but at odd angles as if a snake of water had slithered through weaving it's winding trail as it went. There were several places where we had to make changes in the direction we were walking. I knew them all, at each new turn I knew without thinking where we needed to go. I was totally confident about what I was doing and where I was going. Becka didn't look so sure but she followed me and said very little.

We must have traveled four or five hundred yards when I took us to the right again. Soon after we made that turn we made two other quick turns into what looked like a secret entrance of some kind. Then we entered what looked like a large domed temple. There were carvings and hieroglyphs on the walls. To the far end there was a temple altar and several things were still sitting on it.

"Oh my gosh!" Becka exclaimed. I could hear the shock and surprise in her voice.

"You don't remember this place sister?" I asked.

"No why would I?" she asked

"You were here many times in the past. We were here together many times, as were the others." I told her.

"Kat, I followed you here because you sounded like someone else, you were calling me sister and I wasn't sure if you weren't possessed. There was no way I could let you take off by yourself but I have to tell you, I don't remember this place. Are you telling me you lived here? Was this your home down in this smelly place? When did you live here?" she finally asked.

I walked over to the altar and picked up a small object off the top. It was a beautiful small gold Ankh. I wiped off the dirt and dust with my shirttail.

"Isn't it beautiful?" I asked her. "I've missed this for a very long time. It's the key to life as well as the sign of eternal life to all Egyptians. This Ankh has power over Ka. It's a tool to help direct Ka through the pineal gland in the brain. It was the magical powers of this Ankh that made so many Pharaohs try to duplicate it. It's why they all carried Ankhs and used them for all their ceremonies."

"Is that yours? How did you know it would be here?" Becka asked.

"I left it here a very, very long time ago. I'm going to need it again soon so it was important to get back here to retrieve it. Isn't there something you should be looking for too?" I asked.

"Looking for something? Like what? You mean there's something here I should be looking for too? How will I know it when I see it?" she asked.

"No there's nothing of yours here. But you do have something you need to find and you need to find it soon."

I breathed a little Ka onto the Ankh to try and clean it a little better before I slipped it into my pocket.

"Come sister, we need to get back now." I reached for her hand and started to head back out towards the cave. Becka started to go and then she pulled back.

"Wait a minute Kat." She called to me.

When she stopped and pulled back on my arm, I started to look back to see what was the problem and hit my head on an out cropping of the cave wall, in the process.

"Ouch!" I cried out "What did you do that for?"

"I'm not taking another step until you start to explain yourself a little more." she demanded.

"What do you mean explain myself?" I asked as I started to look around and wonder where we were and how we got here. "Where are we and what are you asking me anyway?" I questioned her.

"What the heck are you asking me?" she blurted out with a strong look of indignation on her face. "You're the one who brought us here, you were the one who knew how to get here. It was I following you, not you following me." She took a deep breath and started in on me again. "What was that all about and now you don't know what I'm talking about?"

"I honestly don't know what you are talking about Becka. I remember being at the Great Pyramid and now here. I don't remember how we got here or anything in between. I think I must have been dreaming. It's all a little foggy. You'll have to tell me what happened." I told her.

"Oh Kat. Can this really be happening? You kept calling me sister and you sounded so different. I was worried if I didn't follow you, I didn't know if you'd come back and I was too worried not to go with you. I don't know how we'll ever find our way out of here. It's like a maze and you knew the way so I didn't try to pay any attention to where we were making the turns. We're never going to find our way out of here unless you can figure it out." She said those last words with tears in her eyes.

"Well, don't cry Becka. Let's think about this. If we start back the way we came, maybe you can remember. Just one step at a time, one turn at a time it's the only thing we can do. We have to try it or we'll be doomed if we just sit here. By the way, do you know where here is?" I asked.

"You wanted to check out the stuff Bunny told you about. Some Bird Tomb near the pyramids that has something to do with some constellation. You said you wanted to see if the Hall of Records was really here. But when we got here, you knew the way and you said this had been your home before. You wanted to come back to get your Ankh. What happened that you can't remember any of that?" she asked me.

"I don't know but I've got this big lump on my head, when you pulled my arm I guess I turned and hit my head. I sort of remember that. Maybe it was the pain that made me forget whatever I knew before. I don't know. I don't know any of it for sure." I told her.

"Well what a mess this is." she stated.

"Come on Becka, lets try to work our way back through. Just try to remember one turn at a time. I'm sure you can do it. Just relax and lets try. I don't know what else to do." I told her. I took her hand and waited while she took a deep breath and her first step forward to join me.

We slipped out the same way we had come in. We both stood and looked for just a second or two.

"Okay Becka, which way did you turn when you came up to this intersection of the cave? Try to picture it in your mind and think for a second." I told her.

She looked all around us at the three choices and then back the way we had just come out.

"I don't know Kat. We turned to the right but I couldn't tell you which of the three caves we came out of. I wasn't looking back or to the sides, I was just following you. Even with the crystals it's pretty dark. I never thought I'd have to find the way back. You seemed to know it so well, why can't you remember?" she asked.

"I just don't Becka. I don't remember one single thing about coming here. It's like someone else must have been using me or maybe I was dreaming. I just wasn't really here everything is a little hazy. I wish I knew the way but I don't. Take a deep breath and think for just a minute. Maybe you should try coming out of each one and see which feels like the right amount of turn you had to make." I suggested. "Cause I don't know what else we can do."

So that's what she did. It was almost funny watching her try each cave and make the turn. I could tell by the look on her face she was trying really hard to get this right. As she tried the third cave opening and stepped back towards me, I could see a new look on her face, this time it was sheer panic and fear.

"Don't worry Becka, don't think too hard on it either. Just close your eyes and ask yourself if that was the cave and we'll decide what we'll do next cause we sure as heck can't stay here." I told her.

When she opened her eyes, she had tears falling down her cheeks.

"I'm just not sure Kat. What if I pick wrong and it makes it worse?" she asked.

"How much worse can it get? We don't know and we can only try the way that feels the best to you right now. Pick one and lets just try it." I answered.

So that's what we did. She picked the center cave and we both made a mental note, if this became a dead end and we had to come back, we'd have to pick one of the others. Becka said if it wasn't this cave the other one on the right was probably the next one to try. She was just too confused right now and wasn't sure about this middle one but it was her best guess. So off we went, hoping for the best and praying we were headed back out, not lost forever in the caves under the Great Pyramid and the Sphinx.

I wondered if Hatshepsut had ever been down here in these caves? Had she ever entered this complex of caves or tried to come anywhere down here? Maybe she had known about the temple we just left and the Hall of Records. I wished I could help Becka to figure this all out but I was lost; great time for the memories to stop.

We got to another spot where we had to make another decision about which way to go. This time there were only two other choices. We decided to mark the cave we came out of and tried to scratch an X on the wall. When that didn't work we tried the floor of the cave and succeeded. At least if we had to come back from here we'd know which way we had come from before. That little gold Ankh came in handy scratching the X in the floor of the cave.

So on we walked, it seemed like forever and we just kept going and going and going.

"Do you remember going so far in between turns coming in?" I asked her.

"No I didn't think we walked anywhere near this far without having to make turns into other caves. I think we're lost Kat. Should we turn back now?" she asked.

"Wait a minute, what's that?" I asked out loud.

Becka turned to see what I was talking about. It looked like a doorway had been carved. The cave suddenly didn't have cave walls but carved angles with 90-degree corners on the top of the doorway.

"Wait a minute, that looks interesting, let's check it out." I said as I walked closer to get a better look. I put my hand on the carvings I saw on closer inspection of the area by the doorway. I could feel the receded design of the hieroglyphs on the wall to the right of the carved doorway. I don't know why I did it but I reached into my pocket and I felt the gold ankh I had just retrieved from the other chamber. I pulled it out from my pocket and looked at it for a couple seconds. When I placed the gold Ankh in my hand, into the design on the wall, it was a perfect fit and seemed to work like a key. The door beyond the first doorway just a few feet away opened.

"Oh wow, did you see that?" I asked. "The only thing I did was to place my gold Ankh into the design of the Ankh on the wall." I told her.

"Let's go see what's in there." I suggested.

"I don't think so Kat. What if we go inside and get trapped or locked in? I don't think we should. Things are bad enough now but at least in the cave there's no door locking us in. I've seen too many movies and this is the part where things can turn really bad. Being locked in the crystal room in Peru at Machu Picchu was bad enough and I don't ever want to go through anything like that ever again in my life. Let's just go back and try one of the other caves," she begged.

"Okay, how about you stay here and I go in to check it out. That way, if something bad happens it only happens to me. I really want to see what's in there and what if it's the Hall of Records? I want to see it for myself." I suggested.

"No way are you leaving me here all alone. Being afraid to let you take off on your own before is what got us in this mess but I'm not letting you out of my sight. I don't know what I'd do if I was all alone in this smelly bat cave maze." She spit out and then added," I don't know why I keep letting you get me in deeper and deeper. What are the boys going to think when they come down and we're not there. You know we can't get home without them."

"Well we'll just peek in here and see what's what. Who knows, maybe this has a way out and we'll get back before they even notice we left." I told her.

"You better hope miss, cause you're not hearing the end of this one. Our parents are going to kill us if we don't get home on time. Can you imagine what they'd think if we had to call them from Egypt for the money to get home! That's if we ever find our way out of here and don't die in this bat infested smelly place." She scolded me.

I reached back for her hand and she reluctantly took it. "Okay Kat but this better not get any worse or it'll be me killing you, not what ever horrible fate you've thrown us into." She whispered. Like whispering would keep something bad from happening, like the secret door wouldn't suddenly slam shut if we were quiet.

It wasn't anything like what I would have expected. The walls did have paintings of some strange hieroglyphs but all the lines in the room were plain and simple. No giant columns or statues to make you take special notice of the place. But there were shelves all the way around it with scrolls and tablets piled high on them. Could this be the famous Hall of Records after all? I had never seen so many scrolls or tablets it was like we hit the jackpot. Maybe it was just a library or something else like that. There didn't seem to be any names written on the wall, no signs to say, "Hey this is it, the GREAT HALL OF RECORDS!" I couldn't help but wonder, I mean what else could it be? I had seen pictures of ancient scrolls and the ancient writings of lots of old cultures. They were sort of like that. The tablets were a lot of lines and symbols but not exactly like the Egyptian hieroglyphs but maybe more ancient looking. I wasn't a historian or archeologist, what did I know about such things? They looked really old though. The scrolls were rolled up tight and tied with thin leather straps.

We were both so amazed, I had really been curious about all the things Bunny had told me about the Bird Tomb and the possibilities of the Hall of Records being found some day. Never in a million years did I think we'd stumble into it. It had to be the real deal. As we walked across each wall and looked at all the tablets and scrolls we were feeling a little shock and awe.

"Can you believe it Becka, I think we're in the Hall of Records. The proof that Edgar Cayce said would be found that would prove Atlantis and Lemuria really existed. How can we get some of this out of here to show people?" I asked.

"I think the real trick for us is how do we find our way out of here. If we can, we can always send them back and they can carry it all out of here. I'd be afraid to touch it. What if the scrolls are so old they crumble when you try to pick them up? Better to let exerts do that sort of thing." she said.

"Yeah, you're probably right. Oh my, gosh, look over there." I pointed to two large crystal spears sitting on the shelf on the other wall. "Do you think they could be more seed crystals like the one we saw in Peru?" I asked as I walked over to touch them.

"These won't crumble if I touch them." I said as I wrapped my two hands around one of them. I looked over as Becka did the same thing with the other large crystal sitting next to it.

"If only we could read them and know what they're encoded with. How much do you think they weight? Maybe we could try to carry them out with us. What do think?" I asked, "It would be some kind of proof that we found this place."

"I think we better leave everything right where it's at. Remember the last time someone picked up something they shouldn't have. There could be booby traps and I don't want to get stuck in here." She said back with a stern look etched on her face.

"Oh don't try to scare me with your stern looks. I know you're right but I'd really like to have one of these." I answered as I released my grip on the giant spear of crystal. Becka let go and we both stepped back a step or two.

"Maybe we should be looking for that way out you mentioned might be here some where." Becka suggested.

So that's what we did next. We started searching the walls and the shelves for any buttons or levers, anything that looked like it might help find another way out of this place. After we were convinced we had searched every square inch we decided maybe there was only one door and no other ways in or out. So with defeat in the air we decided to go back the way we came and start over again in the caves.

"Wait a minute Becka. I think I should shut the door don't you? I wouldn't want anything to happen to the scrolls or tablets because we left the door open." I asked as I stopped and turned around at the first doorway we had come up to upon entering. Maybe if I placed the little Ankh in the same design of the Ankh it might just close the door. We figured it was worth a try and just like magic, the door closed again.

"I wonder how many years it was from the last time someone opened that door and today?" Becka said more as a statement than a question.

"Yeah, that would be a cool thing to know wouldn't it" I answered her.

It was almost too much incredible stuff to walk away from, it was very hard to leave it all behind and try to deal with going back into the caves. We were both wondering if we'd ever find our way out again.

Once we were back wondering through the caves it was hard to believe what we had just seem and discovered. We couldn't know for sure if it had been the Great Hall of Records but if I had to bet, I'd bet that it was. There were too many predictions and myths that talked and told the story of the place and where it would be discovered. I could almost feel like a real Indiana Jones. Some of the discoveries we had made with the merkids on these quests to find the rare and sacred plants they needed, were each a trip of a lifetime and here I was making my fourth trip. For me, this had to be the greatest of all of them and here we were, wandering around trying not to step and slip in all this bat poop.

Just as I was thinking about the bat poop I started to hear a noise coming closer to us. I couldn't put my finger on what the sound was. It almost sounded like flocks of birds taking off. Then it hit me. "Look out

Becka I think we better duck!" no more had the last word come out of
my mouth when the largest flock of bats came flying past us. There must
have been hundreds of them, maybe thousands. They almost filled the
entire opening of the cave as they darted by us. I felt like one or two of
them landed on my head and shoulders. I was trying to duck even lower
and avoid having them land on me or bite me. Becka was busy doing the
same thing. We must have looked like two girls doing some wild and
primitive dance. We were howling, yelling and screaming as each of the
bats that touched us made contact with our bodies.

You can't imagine what it's like to have so many tiny creatures of
the night flying into you and catching your hair as they tried to fly away
again. Becka and I were both horrified. When they were finally all gone
and the sound of their beating wings was receding into the background,
we both stood up straight again and checked to make sure none were
still on us.

"Well that was pretty scary wasn't it?" Becka asked.

"Yeah" I answered her as I looked to make sure there wasn't one of
the little buggers still clinging to my shirt. "But the one good thing is,
they were probably all going out so we know the way out is this way." As
I pointed in the direction they all had taken. "I did look up just in time
to know they veered to the left so that's our next turn too." I told her.
"Hey, maybe we'll get lucky and another herd will leave when we have to
decide about the next turn and they can show us the rest of the way out.
That would be sweet wouldn't it!" I finished.

"I don't know that I care to go through that again but if gets us out
of here in one piece, sometime soon, I guess I could deal with it. I just
wouldn't want any more of them landing on my head. That was too
creepy." She told me. "It felt like their little needle claws were puncturing
my scalp. At least I hope that's what I was feeling and they weren't biting
me. I can't imagine what diseases we could have picked up from them
and the all their poop in here. The smell alone is enough to make you
sick and I don't even want to look at my shoes."

We didn't know if we were going out the way we came in or not
but we believed we were making progress and headed out: hopefully
back somewhere close to the pyramids and the boys. I couldn't begin to
imagine what they must be thinking if they came down and couldn't find
us. So far this had really been some adventure but if we lost track of the
boys I wasn't sure what we would do next. We both were really hoping

they were still up on top of the pyramid. Hopefully they would be able to pick up some sign or signal of the plant we needed. We just couldn't go home empty handed. This was the first time ever that we had gotten separated from the kids. Somehow I didn't feel near as confident without them being the ones in control and heading everything up.

Becka and I were used to being together so it wasn't like we were really scared as much as we could have been, we did have each other. It was an everyday thing for us to get in and out of assorted predicaments. Usually they weren't on the scale of this one right now though. The boys were going to be very upset with us for roaming off like this. We just had to hope they hadn't gone off in search of us, if they had I didn't know what we'd do or where we'd have to turn for help. The only other person we knew here was Nuri and we really didn't know him very well.

We came to another fork in the road, inside the cave. Now it seemed I had figured something out. I looked on the cave floor and one cave direction had bat poop and the other didn't.

"I think it's this way out." I told her as I pointed in the new direction "Look Becka there's no poop this way. I figure that means the bats don't fly in and out of that cave. Makes sense doesn't it? I think we should follow the bat poop, maybe that will help us to find our way back out."

Becka looked in the new direction and then back the way we had just come from. "I think you might be right Kat. I never would have thought of that but we have been walking in their poop the whole time we've been in this maze. I think you're right and we should follow the poop."

We laughed and I think for the first time we both thought we'd be out of the cave soon. All we had to do now was follow our noses bat poop was pretty obnoxious stuff not to mention slippery and slimy from the bat pee on top of it.

We couldn't believe our luck. It looked like we finally made it back to the Bird Tomb and our way out. Both of us were gasping for fresh air, as we finally got out into the open with the stars once again overhead.

As soon as we could breath again without that obnoxious smell burning our noses we started to run back towards the Great Pyramid looking for the boys but they weren't there. We looked high and low as well as walking all around the base of the pyramid. The program was over, all the lights were off and it was just dark and quiet. No crowds of people, just Becka and me standing there in the stillness of the night. Suddenly we were feeling pretty small and all alone.

"I'm surprised if the boys came down looking for us that they weren't able to just come find us. Bach can read everything, surely he could have found us." Becka commented. "Where do you suppose they went and what do you think we should do now?" she asked.

"Maybe we should just sit here and try to get his attention with a mental message that we're back and waiting for them to meet up again." I suggested.

"Good thinking Kat. I'm for getting it done and then cleaning this bat poop off my shoes. I still can't get that nasty smell out of my nose either, so maybe cleaner shoes would help me get away from the smell." We both laughed at her last remark.

"Yeah, I think you are right, until we get this crap off our shoes we'll just be taking the smell with us where ever we go." As soon as I finished those words I kicked my shoes off and walked about ten feet away to sit at the base of the pyramid and meditate my thoughts towards Bach and Shi. Becka joined me as soon as she got her feet out of her stinky shoes and walked the few feet to sit next to me.

We were sitting and doing our best to get Bach's attention, wherever he might be. We couldn't imagine where the boys would have gone and why they hadn't returned yet. We were both getting a little concerned. For all we knew the boys could have been arrested and put in jail for being on the pyramid at night. They were still running the evening program when they started their climb and we took off. We were both kicking ourselves for not staying and waiting for them. It was totally our fault that the four of us were now separated: I'm sure if Becka had anything to say about it, she would surely say it was totally my fault, not our fault.

We sat and tried to send our thoughts to Bach wherever he was. It felt good to sit down and relax for a couple minutes. We had been on our feet all day and I was getting a little tired. The stress wasn't helping things either. Between being lost in the caves and now not being able to find the boys, I was feeling pretty stressed out.

After trying to reach Bach for at least ten to fifteen minutes we both decided to stop and try again a little later it would give us a chance to clean up our shoes. The sand was all we had to work it. It was comical watching each of us try to clean our shoes without touching any part with bat poop on them, with our hands. We both knew if we got that nasty stuff on our hands, we'd never get away from the smell. We had no idea where we'd be able to find soap and water to wash up with. So we rubbed them and then scrapped them against the blocks of sandstone the pyramid had been built with.

I couldn't help myself and I started laughing out loud.

"What is so funny?" Becka asked me.

"Never in a million years would I have ever guessed, when I had a chance to be next to the Great Pyramid of Egypt, I'd be scrapping bat poop and pee on it. There's a part of me that feels like I'm almost vandalizing it. Not that I find that funny but it just all seems so ridiculous." I told her.

"I give up, I don't think I'll be able to get these any cleaner without soap and water. Maybe we should try to reach Bach again." Becka suggested as she slipped her shoes back on.

"Okay, I'm ready. Lets do it." I said as we both sat back down near the base of the largest Pyramid. "I just hope he gives us some kind of answer this time."

The two of us were sitting there holding our opals over our third eye when we both heard him loud and clear. He and Shi and been taken down by the security guards and they were in some local jail being held for two days for trespassing. He suggested that Becka and I try to track down our friend Nuri from Giza and see if we could stay with him until they get out and can come find us.

"OMG can you believe that they did get arrested while we were out cave hunting. I guess maybe it's lucky we didn't get arrested with them. "Becka said as soon as Bach stopped with his communication.

"Well see there Becka if you hadn't gone with me, you'd probably be in jail right now. See how lucky you are!" I answered her with a big smile on my face. Earlier I had been in deep poop with Becka in more ways than one. This little bite of news would help to keep me out of the thick of it with her. Turns out, our little side adventure wasn't such a bad thing and everything turned out pretty good for us so far. Now if we could remember where Nuri said he lived with his grandmother.

When he told us where he lived I didn't really think we'd have time to look him up. Now here we were, going to go knocking at his door asking to stay for a couple nights. We both wondered what time it was and if we should wait until morning to go try and find him.

"I think he said he was behind the Camel something café. He did say to just ask anyone in Giza for directions to Nuri the blind boy and they'd be able to tell us where he lived. What do you think Kat, should we go now and end up waking him and his grandmother up in the middle of the night? Or should we at least wait until daylight?" she asked.

"Maybe we better wait until day light. I'm not sure I want to be walking the streets right now, talking to strangers. Let's try to curl up here and get some sleep. I'm kind of tired, how about you?" I asked her

"You're probably right, safer to stay here for right now. At least in the morning we'll be able to see where we're going and there will be more people out to talk to. I am sort of tired too. I hope it doesn't get any colder though. Who would have thought the desert would be so cold at night? You'd think the heat stored in the sand would keep it warm through the night wouldn't you? I mean, how can it be so hot all day and then get cold at night?" Now she was rambling as we both were looking around trying to decide where was the best place to try to get some sleep. Were there guards who would be coming around again before morning? We sure as heck didn't want to end up in jail with the boys.

"How about over here, just the other side of this ridge. Not too far away but hopefully far enough that no guards will come across us." I suggested and she agreed. SO we hiked just a little farther away from the pyramids and after we crested the rise of the sand dune we settled down into the sand.

We both wiggled and squirmed a little to make a nice comfy little nest for us. We curled up next to each other happy for the chance to get some sleep. We were both tired and it had been a long night. Our muscles were happy to settle in for a rest and our eyes didn't take long to close down for the night.

Lucky for both of us, nothing and no one came upon us during the night or disturbed our sleep. I woke up first. It took a couple seconds to remember where I was and what was happening that I was sleeping in the sand, out in the middle of nowhere. As soon as I started to move and try to sit up Becka started to wake up.

"Why am I so hungry? Did we forget to eat last night?" she asked before she even opened her eyes.

"Now that you ask, I don't think we ate at all yesterday. Too much was going on and I didn't even feel hungry or think about food. Now that you're talking about it, I'm starting to wish I had a big stack of pancakes or a plate of scrambled eggs and ham. Where are our pouches? We can have some fruit for now and a little water before we head out looking for Nuri." I said.

"That doesn't sound as good as pancakes or eggs and ham but I guess it'll have to do for now. Here your pouches were with mine." She answered as she handed me both my food and water pouches. We both felt lucky to have what supplies we had brought with us at least we didn't have to go hungry. Our fruit tasted all the more sweet because we were so hungry.

After we sat, ate and drank a little water we tried to comb our hair with our fingers. Note to self, next time bring a comb or brush. I was feeling a little grubby and wished I had some clean clothes to put on. A bath would have been nice too. Maybe if we got lucky and found Nuri, maybe he's let us clean up at his place. We finally stood and brushed the sand off our clothes, looking around to get our bearings. We'd have to head back by the Pyramids and the Sphinx heading towards the road and the way back towards the Giza city. Then we'd start asking directions to the Camel Café that Nuri said he lived behind. We both hoped he's be there and not out working today.

We talked a little about what we'd do when we finally found Nuri's home and if we had to help him with his chores today we'd do it. Otherwise it might be a really long day. We decided it wouldn't be too smart of us to just roam or wander around Giza. Clearly we were two Caucasian girls and we didn't blend in too well with all the Egyptians. I think we both had our fingers crossed that we could find Nuri and that he would be willing to help us out. I was still hoping for a chance to wash up, it had been a long time since we felt clean.

The city was bustling with activity in the early morning. We asked a couple people for directions and managed to find the café in just a short time. It was a small place and as we walked into the open doorway we could see inside where there were a couple small tables with chairs, just like the tables and chairs that had been out front. The café was open and there was a tall slender man behind the counter. We walked over and asked if he could tell us which place was the home of Nuri the blind boy.

"Yes, of course. Everyone knows Nuri. Here, come this way and I will point out his home to you." He said as he stepped to a doorway just behind the counter going out the backside of the café. We followed and as we stepped out the doorway he pointed to a small structure just towards the corner and told us,

"That is Nuri and Abba's home."

We both thanked him and started in that direction.

"Think we should wait and see if he comes out or just knock on the door?" Becka asked.

"Better just be brave and knock. I'm just hoping he's still there and didn't leave hours ago for Cairo." I told her.

"Yeah, I feel sort of strange going to ask someone we only met once to help us out and take us in for the night. What if he doesn't have enough room for us to stay at his place?" Becka asked.

"Well, we'll play it by ear maybe. First let's just see if he's even here." I suggested.

We were at the door and just as I lifted my hand to knock it opened. We were both surprised by the sudden opening of the door and sort of jumped back a half step. It was Nuri and he was laughing.

"I heard you two coming and I recognized your voices. So happy to have you come by. Where are Shi and Bach? They're not with you today?" he asked.

Without thinking, we both looked behind us as if he could see they weren't there. Nuri was a very alert and aware blind person who used all his senses like a fine tuned machine. In the little time we had been around him he amazed us with his awareness.

"We find ourselves in a strange circumstance. We were out by the Pyramids last night and the boys decided to climb to the top. While we were walking and checking things out, they got arrested and have to spend another night in jail. They're supposed to get out tomorrow afternoon." I was explaining.

"Well the two of you must stay with me and my Grandmother until they are released. We can't let you wander the city without the boys to protect you. This is my city but not a safe one for two American girls without a protector." He said before I could finish explaining our dilemma.

"Here," he stepped back to let us in. "Come in and I will introduce you to my grandmother. She is still here. Grandmother, let me introduce you to two of my new friends I told you about the other day."

We entered and turned to see the woman in the back of the first room Nuri was introducing us to. She wasn't much taller than either of us but she was a beautiful woman. She didn't look like a grandmother to me, she of course was very exotic looking but she had the most heartwarming smile I think I had ever seen. Maybe it was partly because we'd been stressed with all the things we were dealing with but her smile immediately made us both feel like the weight of the world had just been lifted from our shoulders. Never had a smile made me feel so safe and suddenly secure again.

In the few seconds it took for that smile to melt us and make us feel like our troubles were over for now, I felt like it wasn't something I had to analyze and decided to just relax and enjoy the feeling. It felt good to let go of all our troubles and just enjoy Nuri and Abba. She hurried over and shook hands with both of us and then hugged us. As she released Becka she said,

"Here you girls sit there, you must join us for breakfast. I was fixing Nuri his favorite and there's plenty. I hope you both like pancakes. I know it's probably not the standard breakfast you would expect for a young Pharaoh like Nuri but it's his birthday today and he acquired a taste for them a few years ago." She said and shot us another one of those smiles that made her entire face radiate. It was almost as if she knew we'd been talking about pancakes earlier and this was her private joke for us.

"Well thank you so much Abba. We would love to join you for breakfast. How wonderful of you to ask us. Is there anything we can do to help?" Becka asked.

"No, I am fine and there is very little room in our cooking area so better I don't have to compete for space with either of you. Sit and talk. I would love to hear about what the two of you have been up to since you arrived in Giza. Where are your other two friends? I was sure Nuri said there were four of you." She said as she started to add to her batter of pancake mix.

"I'm afraid their friends got in a little trouble for climbing the Pyramids and won't be able to rejoin them until tomorrow afternoon. I was thinking we could ask them to spend the night here with us. Would that be alright Grandmother?' Nuri asked.

"Why not?" she said," It will be a party and we can truly celebrate your birthday later tonight over dinner."

"Alright. It's settled then, the two of you will stay here with us until the boys are able to rejoin you tomorrow afternoon." Nuri added in. "What a fantastic birthday this is turning into." He said with a smile that resembled Abba's in its warmth and brilliance.

Both Becka and I were relaxing, enjoying the company of our new friend and his grandmother. What warm and wonderful people they were. Abba hummed a little as she whipped up the pancake batter, reminding me of home and listening to Becka's grandmother in her kitchen; it was a very comforting feeling and made us love Abba all the more for the similarities and the secure feelings it gave us.

Breakfast was delicious, who would have ever thought we'd be in Egypt with new friends eating pancakes? We tried not to act as hungry as we felt. Abba and Nuri kept asking questions about all that we had done so far and were amazed that we had been so many places in so short a time. Abba was curious about the plant we were looking for. She told us she was something of a gardener. She said she had a very small garden out back and promised to show off her favorites later right now she needed to clean up and get ready to leave for her job. Becka and I insisted that they let us clean up and thanked her again for such a wonderful breakfast. We were busy cleaning up the dishes as Abba called out her good byes on her way out the door.

"So what are we going to do today?" Nuri asked as we put the last of the clean dishes away and placed the dishtowels over their drying rack.

"Hey it's your birthday Nuri. What do you want to do? If you have things you'd rather do without us, we can go hang around town for the day." I answered him.

"Oh no, I want to spend the day with the two of you. I just thought since you're visiting here, we should do something you'd like to do. After all, you said you'd be leaving soon and won't have time to do much more in Egypt." He hurried to reassure us and added," I have a friend we could go ride his camels or we could just stroll the market place and take in the sights there. Or I have another friend and maybe I could get him to let us go into the great pyramid and visit the King's chamber."

I thought I would jump right out of my seat when his words finished penetrating my brain.

"You have a friend who could let us go into the great pyramid and visit the King's chamber? Are you kidding me?" by the time those last words were out of my mouth, I was up, across the room and grabbing his arms. "Is this for real Nuri?" I asked.

He was laughing so hard you could tell he really enjoyed my reaction to his suggestion.

"Stop laughing, are you serious or just pulling my leg for a good laugh?" I asked.

He tried to stop laughing while he shook his head in the affirmative.

"Yes I have such a friend and since it's my birthday, maybe he would let us all in. We will have to ask very nicely and see what he says. I can't promise anything you understand?"

Nuri turned his head towards Becka and asked her,

"Well it's obvious that Kat wants to see the inside of the Pyramid but what about you Becka? Would you rather do something else?" he asked her.

I jumped up and turned to look at Becka,

"Of course she wants to go too. Don't you Becka?" I asked as I sent her my most 'pretty please' look. I knew she understood how much a visit like that would mean to me. Surely she wouldn't say no. I'd kill her if she did. She started to laugh out loud.

"Oh if you could see yourself Kat. I wouldn't dare say no, especially to such an incredible offer. Just remember it's not up to me or Nuri, his friend has to say yes. Maybe you should save you're pretty please look for him!" she suggested.

"It's settled then. We will go see my friend." Nuri smiled back in my direction.

I had a thousand thoughts going through my head. I wondered and had to ask,

"Have you been in the pyramid before Nuri? What was it like? What did you think and feel?"

I have been in before, many times. Each time I can say it has been a new experience. Come let's go maybe we can experience and not have to talk about what it felt like for me. We grabbed our things and followed Nuri out the front door. It was amazing to walk through the streets of Giza with Nuri. He made every step and turn as well as a sighted person. He spoke to people as we passed them by. He talked to everyone by name, usually even before they spoke or he could hear their voices.

"How do you do that Nuri?" I asked him.

"How do I do what?" he asked me.

"Speak to everyone by name when you can't see them or haven't heard their voices first?" I responded.

"Oh, that. Well each of us has our own smells, perfumes, foods we've eaten, body odors as well as sounds we make when we move like a small limp or the charm bracelets on their wrist jingling. There are many tells of who is near or approaching. When you don't have your sight, you rely on your other senses all the more. I hear so many sounds that others don't seem to notice, for example. Around the corner I hear a dog scratching the wall of the building. Amazingly as we turned the corner, there was a dog and he was scratching the wall next to a door as if he wanted to get inside. Wow.

"With all the sounds of the city, the people and traffic in the street it's amazing you could hear that dog. But how do you make each turn and step without falling over the curbs and people in front of you?" I asked.

"That one is a little harder to explain. It's a little like, some kind of radar I feel I have. I seem to sense things like there's a part of me that feels things before I bump into them. It's subtle like feeling the breeze when it touches your cheek." He told me.

"Oh, it sounds like your saying your aura senses things and helps you feel what's coming at you. Do you think it's your aura?" I asked.

"I don't know of such things Kat. You tell me? What do you think? ", He asked in return.

The whole time we kept walking and talking as if he was sighted like us. The interesting thing was that he was leading us through the city, not us taking him. We walked the streets as if he could see every corner and curb, like he had walked it millions of times and knew it all by heart. It was nothing like what I thought being with a blind person would be like. Nuri turned and looked at each of us as we talked, he smiled and made expressions, like he was responding to our facial expressions. He was so alive and so happy, never had I met a kinder more alive soul. His happiness radiated from his whole body and I swear he had to be the most open and giant hearted person I ever met.

Becka laughed at something Nuri said and told him,

"God must have put you here on earth to be an example for the rest of us. Where do you find all this love and joy you give away so freely?"

"You can give my grand mother the credit for what ever I am. She taught me to be who I am and to give love and joy where ever I go. Weren't you taught the same thing?" he asked her.

"Yes I was but I don't think I learned the lessons as well as you. I hope you will be my friend for the rest of our lives. Maybe I can learn more from you." She told him.

"I would love that. I keep all my friends in my heart. Maybe before you go we can exchange addresses and we can write to each other. What is it you Americans call that? Pen Pals?" he smiled.

We walked on, Nuri always making the turns and leading us through the city towards the pyramids. As we approached the area is was just as busy as before. The whole place was alive with tourist from all over the world. What a magical thing it was to see each time that we had come. The power and the glory of Egypt's past was alive still in the energy of the Giza pyramids and the Sphinx it was something you could almost feel with your hands; like heavy humidity in the summer heat.

Nuri led us through the crowds in search of his friend. We were working our way towards the Sphinx when we heard someone call out to Nuri. As we turned we saw a tall thin man approaching us with an ear-to-ear grin across his face.

"Happy Birthday my friend. I am so honored to see you on this special day. What brings you here today?" he asked.

"Thank you so much for the salutations. I am honored to visit with you today as always Omar. But I will admit today I have friends and we were hoping if we found you, perhaps we could ask for a special favor." Nuri told him as Omar was embracing him and delivering a birthday hug.

Omar let out a loud belly laugh as he released Nuri.

"So you are here seeking favors are you?" he asked.

"I wouldn't ask with so little notice except my friends are from America, they have been so enthralled by the pyramids and they leave soon to return home and have only today to see whatever we can see. So what do you think my old friend? Is there a chance to take a peek inside the king's chamber?" Nuri asked. "Let me introduce you Omar to my new friends. This is Becka and this is Kat."

"Hello Becka and Kat. If you are friends of Nuri, you are friends of Omar."

Omar smiled and slapped Nuri on the shoulder as he said,

"I think we could work something out. Give me a few minutes and we will go."

I had been holding my breath the whole time the two of them were talking. I could finally start breathing again. WOW, we were going to get to go inside the pyramid and visit the king's chamber. I had read books about people doing this and all of them were looking for something special to happen while there. It didn't seem to happen for most of them but some people said they had very vivid dreams and spiritual experiences while in the King's chamber. I could only wonder and hope that maybe I would feel something special. Just entering the pyramid would have to give anyone pause. Entering a structure that many argued was at least 12,000 years old or older, it would have to make your mind go to magical places for sure. I couldn't wait. This was a dream of mine and I was within minutes of having it all happen and come true. Never in a million years would I have thought this would happen for me, for us. Becka and I had been to some pretty incredible places but this would be the most incredible of all.

Omar was only a few minutes before he reappeared to take us over to and into the Great Pyramid. There was a place just a couple large block levels up from the ground where there was no block but the opening and entrance into the pyramid. I had noticed this opening before when we had been here but I had expected the entrance to the Great Pyramid of Giza to have something grander to mark it I guess. It seemed such a simple entry to someplace so mystic and magical in the history of Egypt and the afterlife.

Once inside, it was a small narrow area, for us to walk in and we had to go single file. Most of the way in from the entrance, until we managed to get to the grand gallery, we actually had to bend over to walk in the short passageway which was poorly lit and probably not much more than three feet high. It was just like in the movies, there wasn't much room or fresh air. It was a little warmer and close feeling inside, on top of having to be bent over the whole time we were trekking in. I was glad I wasn't claustrophobic. Just when I thought I wouldn't be able to stand up straight again from all the crouched over walking, we entered what they said was the grand gallery.

The ceiling was suddenly several stories overhead. Wow we were in the heart of the pyramid and getting very close to the king's chamber. Omar explained everything about the inside passages and the chambers as we reached them. When we actually entered the Kings Chamber it was surprisingly plain. No design to be seen anywhere, no names or pictures carved into the walls. Just tall straight stonewalls and the bottom half of a sarcophagus. It was one dark large single piece of carved granite. I had seen pictures of it before so it wasn't any big surprise to me that it was so plain.

It was something else to actually be here, to know that this was a chamber first walked into at least 12 thousand years ago. I couldn't help but wonder who had been here in the beginning? Had this been a place of spiritual ascension? Or had it been a burial chamber? There was a very big part of me that wanted to believe it had been a place where special people came to get a closer connection to the heavens and the spiritual power of the Universe.

It was as if Nuri could read my mind because right then he spoke up,

"I feel it each time I come here. This had to be more than a burial chamber. The powers of the Universe are here, maybe not as strongly as when it was first built but they're here. I can feel them, can either of you?" he asked.

"I'm too excited to even think much less feel right this minute." I told him.

Becka just smiled and said,

"It is rather inspiring to be here. I'm like Kat I'd have to try to settle down before I could try to feel anything. It's just so exciting for us to be here. We can't tell you how much we appreciate the opportunity. Thank you both." Becka told them.

"Yes, thank you both so much. This is a dream come true for me. Never in a million years would I have thought I would ever be here," adding in "Maybe I shouldn't waste what time we have here, excuse me for a couple minutes while I try to center myself." I put my hands on the granite sarcophagus and closed my eyes.

I don't know what they were doing but everyone was quiet. I could hear my heartbeat and the sound of my breath going in and out. My body felt heavy as I stood there. After some of the things that happened to me already in Egypt, I felt like I was taking a chance looking for something special to happen. I'd have to ask Becka later if she was reading my mind because the next thing I heard were her words,

"Maybe this isn't such a good idea right now Kat." Becka said as she touched my hand to get my attention. "We wouldn't want to take any chances that might upset our friends after they've been so kind to bring us here. Maybe today we should just be happy to be tourists, "she suggested.

"Maybe you're right," was all I said back as I took my hands off the granite. That was twice now in just a few minutes it seemed someone was hearing my thoughts or reading my mind. Becka was right, several strange things had already happened to me when I wasn't trying to direct my energy or thoughts: this probably wasn't the best time to try and make a psychic connection to or with the pyramid. Who knew what character might pop out of me next?

We spent a little more time in the chamber before we decided to head down to check out the queen's chamber. It too was a pain and simple room and smaller than the king's chamber. It was amazing to see so many straight carved stones and blocks of such huge dimensions, soaring so high overhead. You could only wonder at how they had been able to do all this. Omar was so informative about every minor detail along the way as we traveled the inside of the pyramid it felt like we were with the Egyptian head of antiquities.

When our tour was over and we exited the pyramid I gave Omar a hug and thanked him again for our special tour and all his information. He was probably getting tired of hearing how thrilled I was to have been inside and had the chance to see it all for myself. Becka also thanked him again too. After our goodbyes we decide to head back and plan a dinner and go do some shopping. We wanted to surprise Abba with dinner when she returned home from work and to make it something special for Nuri's birthday. Becka and I had money with us and with Nuri along with us we were sure we could convince the merchants to take our American money, after all, money is money and so far we had seen that in Egypt they liked American money better than their own.

The shops were busy as we walked the market looking for all the ingredients for our special dinner. Becka wanted to make a cake but we decided to take Nuri to the bakery and see what he might like for a treat for the evening. We decided to keep it simple and would grill or bake some chicken, fresh vegetables and make a small green salad. When we walked past the spice merchant Nuri suggested we pick up a special spice they liked for chicken, so we did.

We hoped that Abba wouldn't mind that we had taken over her kitchen and made ourselves at home. As soon as we got back with all our supplies we started to get things ready. That's where Abba found us as she entered their home after work. We were talking and joking and she came in with a smile and immediate asked us what smelled so good.

"It's not often that I get a night off from cooking. What delightful company you girls are. We should keep you around for a while longer, one night doesn't seem near enough time to get to know you both." Abba said as she took her seat at the small table. Nuri jumped up and got out the bottle of wine we purchased for her and poured Abba a glass. He was as skilled as a sighted person, it was amazing to watch him move around and do things like pouring a glass of wine for his grandmother.

"For me? You shouldn't have spent your money on something just for me. What a thoughtful gesture. Thank you both." Then she turned towards Nuri and said," Why did you let your new friends waste their money on me?"

"There was no talking them out of it, believe me I tried. I told them you would feel humbled by their gift but you'd enjoy it all the more because it was a gift from the heart." He told her.

Becka and I both smiled as Becka told her,

"You must accept our small gift, it is the least we can do to show you our appreciation for your hospitality. After all we took over your kitchen without asking and now you are stuck with us for the rest of the night. Let us pamper you and Nuri both just a little." With her last words she lifted her glass of water as if to toast her. We all laughed, the three of us tipped our water glasses to her glass of wine and said,

"To friends!"

I still couldn't get over how sighted Nuri appeared. How in the world did he know we were getting ready to clink our glasses together to make a toast? I was so constantly amazed by him. He moved a little like the merkids as if he was sensing some unseen energy that guided him. All through dinner I couldn't help but watch and see how gracefully he ate his meal and functioned without any help of any kind.

We all talked and laughed. Abba was surprisingly funny and told several stories about Nuri that made me laugh so hard I almost rolled on the floor. We were just finishing up dinner when there was a knock at the door and Nuri got up to answer it. Two beautiful girls dressed like harem dancers came in. They were friends of Nuri and Abba who danced at the café in the evening. Real belly dancers, I was totally enthralled and blown away at the same time. The two girls came in all smiles and laughing as they gave Nuri hugs and wished him a happy birthday. They danced around him just a little, laughing and teased with him for just a couple minutes. Then they said hello to us, stopped long enough to give Abba a little hug and off they went, giggling and teasing with Nuri as they went.

"Wow, that was so cool. Are they real belly dancers Nuri?" Becka asked.

"Yes." He said with a sexy little smile, "They are like sisters to me but love to tease and taunt me with their beauty. The three of us have lived on this street all of our lives. They have become very successful dancers didn't you think they were beautiful? If you would like to see them dance we could go inside the back of the café and watch them perform," he suggested, "The owner doesn't mind when we stop in."

Abba started to get up to clear the table as he spoke.

"Oh no you don't." I told her." Tonight we are cleaning up and you are relaxing. But we would allow you to sit and keep visiting with us, I want to hear more stories about you and Nuri when he was younger."

Abba returned to her seat and started to tell us another tale about her young Pharaoh, as she liked to call Nuri. While she talked Becka and I picked everything up, washed the dishes and put everything away. We had picked up some pastries that Nuri said were his favorite from the bakery earlier at the market, we placed them on the table for dessert and tried to pour Abba a little more wine. She put her hand over the top of the glass and said,

"One glass is my limit. This will leave me several more evenings that I can enjoy your gift in the future."

We had a wonderful evening with the two of them. They were loving and so friendly toward us we couldn't help but feel comfortable and relaxed. I did feel a little guilty that the boys were spending the night in some terrible jail while we were here having so much fun with our new friends. I sincerely hoped it wasn't my fault they got in trouble the night before, when we disappeared into the caves.

The four of us talked late into the night, sharing secrets of our hopes and dreams. Abba and Nuri were very happy and didn't have too many dreams for their futures. Abba of course wanted many good and great things for Nuri and wished she could send him off to school, she feared his greatness would be wasted here in their current lives. We all agreed he was a gem and a young man of many talents.

Abba and Nuri had many misconceptions about America, Becka and I laughed and tried to explain to them, all Americans weren't millionaires. We told them many things about the states and what our lives were like back home. We told Abba how she reminded us of Becka's Grandmother and how much we loved her along with a couple fun stories about Gram, Mr. Mac and all our friends back home. It was almost midnight when we called an end to the party and found our beds, calling it a night. Nuri volunteered to sleep out under the stars in the back while we took over his room and comfy bed.

Becka and I woke at the first light of day. The boys would be getting out this morning and we had so much unfinished business here to try and get done. We had no idea when the boys would show up today but we wanted to be ready when ever they did. Abba was up too we could hear her out in the kitchen humming as she got things ready to start the day. Before we could finish combing our hair and getting our mess cleaned and picked up we could hear Nuri talking with Abba and then there was a knock at the door.

It was Shi and Bach, they were already out of jail and here. We rushed to get back into the main room to see them. Nuri was busy introducing them to Abba when we came into the room.

"Grand mother I would like to introduce you to Shi and Bach, Kat and Becka's friends."

"It's nice to meet you both I was just fixing some breakfast, are you boys hungry? There's plenty for everyone, sit down and we'll all eat before you leave. Nuri set the table and help me get things ready."

Becka and I both rushed over to help.

"What can we do Abba. Let us help you."

"You two can run out back and cut some fresh herbs for me. The first three pots on the right are the ones I need. Just cut off the top couple inches of about two stems from each pot and bring them back to me."

We went out to the back and were so surprised with the garden that greeted us on the other side of the doorway. Abba had pots of all shapes and sizes all over the small area she called her garden oasis. There were more kinds of plants than I would have imagined anyone could have in such a small space. It was a little like being Alice or someone who just stepped into the looking glass and found themselves in a whole new world on the other side. We hurried to cut the herbs and get back inside.

"Abba what a beautiful garden you have. I can't believe we've been here almost two days and we didn't see your garden before now. I've never felt more like a garden fairy than just now when we stepped into your garden." Becka said.

"Oh yes, my garden is my second love. Nuri of course is the first. Maybe if there is time after breakfast I can show you my favorite plants before I leave for the day and have to say goodbye." She answered.

The boys said they were so sorry to have gotten in so much trouble taking almost two days out of our trip. We all knew how much was depending on us for the future of the Merkids and possibly all of mankind. Before they could say more Abba started putting food on all our plates so we all started eating, talking and shared our experiences from our time apart. Nuri had the boys laughing with his stories of us all shopping for groceries for last night's dinner.

When everyone finished eating we told Abba we would clean up while she got ready for work. Nuri talked with the boys while we finished the dishes. They were telling him we needed to get back out on the streets, needed to get back to business. Nuri offered to help in any way he could. It wasn't easy for Bach to explain that unless Nuri could find the plant we needed, there was nothing he could do to help. That plant was our one mission and the only reason for coming to Egypt. He didn't feel he could explain the true facts to Nuri without confusing the issue even more. What would a blind boy in Egypt think if we told him the true mission of our trip, that Bach and Shi were Merkids from the lost continent of Atlantis and we were here trying to save the Merkids and ultimately the Guardians. Would Nuri think we were out of our minds? Or would he understand? Would he accept all our truths?

As those questions were swirling through my brain I saw Bach look my way and shake his head in the negative.

"We don't have enough time to find out. Can't take the chance Kat." Bach's thoughts danced through my brain. Had I heard his thoughts without using the opal?

The door opened and Abba came back into the room. She was dressed with her hair up and tied behind her head. She was ready to leave for work and we would have to say goodbye to our new friends soon. Becka and I were both going to remember this time spent with her and Nuri they had both been so kind and good to us.

"Girls, please come with me, for a moment" she said as she breezed by us and headed to the back door. She was already pulling one of the pots out from the back of the garden by the time we got out the door behind her. I couldn't see what she was doing but she was busy for just a couple minutes before she turned and handed Becka a small pot with a plant in it.

"It's my token of friendship to you both. I hope this is what you came looking for and it will do all you need it to do." She smiled as she pulled her hand away from the pot she had just placed in Becka's hands.

"OMG, how did you know Abba? This is the plant we have been searching for since the first moment we got here." Becka blurted out. "I can't tell you how much time we have spent trying to find just one of these and you've had them all this time."

"You can't imagine what this means to us Abba. Thank you so much. How can we ever thank you?" I asked.

"You girls I know what ever it is you're doing, it's for a great cause. How many strong, independent young women do you think we see traveling the world seeking and searching for such a sacred, ancient plant? I know you must have a very worthy need for it. I'm just happy I could help you end your search. I have treasured my Moon lily for most of my life and I only just recently did a couple cuttings to start new plants with. It was fate that brought you to our door. Do you believe in fate?" she asked with a smile.

"I will say my goodbyes now, I must get to my job and I wish you all a safe return to your homes. May Alia be with you my new friends," she said as she hugged and kissed us both on the cheeks.

She turned and passed by us heading inside and off to work. We just stood there for a minute or two staring at the plant in Becka's hands. OMG neither of us could believe what had just happened. We had spent so much time looking, traveling and searching all over Egypt to find this little plant. We had just about given up all hope of ever finding a plant to take back home with us to Atlantis and then Abba just drops one into our hands. We were stunned and couldn't move for another minute. When the shock started to wear off and the joy started to take over, we found our mobility and dashed back into the house.

"Look! Look what Abba just gave us!" Becka cried out. She actually had tears running down her face as she put her hands out to show the boys the plant she held. As they rushed to her side you could see the look of relief on both their faces. This was it there was no mistake about that. The fears of not being able to find the plant had just about done us all in but now the joy of having it in our possession was enough to take the weight of the world off our shoulders. I don't think I had ever seen Bach with such a big smile on his face before.

Nuri seemed just as excited as the four of us without really realizing what this meant to us. How could we explain? We couldn't and he would probably end up thinking us all crazy Americans once we were gone. Once the intense feelings of relief settled over us, we all started to realize, we could go home now. This journey was finally over.

We packed our precious package in Bach's carry pouch getting it ready for the sojourn back home, said our goodbyes to Nuri promising to write and keep in touch with him and Abba. I can still see him standing in his doorway, waving goodbye to us as we headed out to begin the journey home.

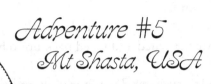

Adventure #5
Mt Shasta, USA

Saying goodbye to Nuri was the end of one journey and the beginning of the next, we still had the other plants to find and goals to fulfill. Becka and I returned home with no one the wiser for the time we had been gone on our search of Egypt and the mighty Nile River. As we started down our road we could see Ronnie was on his front porch waiting for us.

He headed down the stairs, waving some papers in his hand as he saw us approaching,

He must have found the pant he had been looking for.

"Hey girls, where you been all day? I've been watching and waiting for you for hours. I found my plant it's out west near Mt. Shasta. Sweet right!" he threw us his million-dollar smile as he waved his papers up in the air again. This time it seemed the plant we needed might be a little closer to home and that would be a nice change.

"Great job Ronnie." Becka told him. "That is sweet. Something closer to home might prove interesting. Ronnie had no idea how refreshing a location close to home sounded to both of us right now. Are you sure about the location?"

"Yeah. Look at the pictures side by side." He said as he put the two pages side by side for Becka to see. "This is your picture and this is the one I printed off the Internet. They're identical and the article said it could be found on the slopes of Mt. Shasta out in California. Turns out its some sort of ancient poppy. One article I read said this old poppy was one of the first flowers of ceremonial use as far back as Lemuria. Pretty cool they can tell you something that was used in a ceremony, on a lost continent everyone says is a myth. Like, who knows all this stuff?"

"Yeah, they used to say Troy was a myth too. Then one day they uncovered it and changed history." I threw in.

Just then Ronnie's mother stuck her head out the front door and called to him to come in for dinner.

"Got to go girls. Here you take the papers and I'll talk to you later." He handed his papers to Becka turned and raced back up to his house, disappearing inside.

"Wow, this time we didn't even get down our road and there's the next plant calling us to come get it. Four found and already back in Atlantis, one more on our radar and only two left to find. We might actually be able to pull this off Becka. I can't believe our luck so far. Isn't it amazing how each one of these have found their way into our hands?" I asked. "I'm still reeling from Abba handing us the plant we searched so hard to find and then bam there it is. What are the odds that she would have in her back yard the one plant we couldn't find anywhere in Egypt? It's got to be a zillion to one."

"Yeah really. What are the odds that we would meet her grandson, that he would give us a ride and offer to help us, that we would end up at his home and by chance they would have just what we traveled half way around the world to find? How did Abba know that was the plant we needed anyway?" Becka asked in return.

We were both shaking our heads in wonder at the miracle of it all. We did after all believe in miracles, heck we asked for them everyday of our lives. We asked but never had we gotten so many given back to us as we had since we met our new friends from Atlantis. Maybe there was something more to this higher vibration and the energy of the ley lines and songs the earth sang.

The kids were able to do things we had read about in books and they talked about it like everyday kind of stuff the sort of things all people could do. Maybe Bach, Shi and Mu were right. Maybe we let our minds keep us from doing all the same things they could do just because we didn't tell ourselves we could. Because we didn't remember, we didn't believe or know we could. Maybe it was because so many people told us not to try.

We went to Becka's house and put the papers in her room. We decided to have dinner and do the family thing until later. We'd spend the night together and contact Bach later about the latest discovery. A couple days in between adventures would be nice all this running around the world and searching could wear a girl down. I needed a couple nights of sleep in a nice soft American bed, my own or Beckas, it didn't really matter.

Mr. Mac teased us at dinner about the sunburn we had gotten that day.

"I'm surprised you two would get sun burned today. Didn't seem that hot to me. What were the two of you up to?" he asked.

"Nothing much grand dad. Just running all over Egypt, cooking in the Sahara Desert while we searched for a sacred plant for our friends." She answered him and laughed.

It was so funny. Telling the truth got a laugh from everyone at the table and no one thought she meant it. Mr. Mac dropped the subject of the sunburns and started talking about a project he was working on. We ate and tried to stay out of the conversation. Better to keep a low profile we didn't want anyone to put us on the hot spot and really have to explain where we had been. We said we would keep the secrets for the Merkids as long as we didn't have to lie to our parents. So far we hadn't but if they asked too many questions we'd have to spill the beans and tell the truth. Funny part was, we didn't think if that ever happened that they would believe the truth and we'd be in even deeper trouble.

The rest of the evening around the adults went smoothly and we didn't get put on the spot about anything. As we were asking to be excused to go to Beckas room her Mom reminded her they were all going to go visit their Aunt Grace for the weekend. That she should pack a small bag to take with her when they left in the morning.

Becka and I exchanged looks and waited until we got to her room to talk or say anything.

"Oh wow Kat, I totally forgot we were going away for the weekend. Now what are we going to do?" she asked. A second later she added, "When we contact Bach maybe we should ask if Ronnie could take my place. If not him, maybe one of the girls could go with you. I think it would be cool if Ronnie could go, he found the plant and he loves Indian things. This adventure would be right up his alley."

"Yeah I've hated not being able to tell the others about what we're doing. It was so cool to share the other adventures with Bunny and Amy. It'll be sweet if they'll let us tell Ronnie and see if he could get away long enough to go. Let's go see what Bach thinks.

We had just barely sat down and placed the opals on our foreheads when we both heard Bach's thoughts. He was willing to let one more of the friends be part of the next trip but asked that we secure his promise, to keep their secret just as the girls had to promise. In Ronnie's case, it wasn't would he be willing to promise, we knew he would. There was no doubt in our minds that he would and would love to go with us in search of the next plant, it was more an issue, if he could get away for the day and not get in trouble with his parents. As soon as we finalized the plans for the next departure based on Ronnie being able to go, I promised to meet Bach and the others on the beach at sunrise.

We'd have to talk to Ronnie and we decided it was better for us to go to his house than for us to call or ask him to come to Becka's. We went out the front and promised to be back in less than a half an hour. At Ronnie's house we went around back to see if the light was on in his room.

"The lights on, lets tap on the window and see if he's in there." I suggested.

"Okay but be careful we don't want to get him in trouble if his Mom hears us." Becka warned me.

I reached out and tapped lightly on the window. The blinds separated and Ronnie was looking through them at me with a questioning look on his face. He raised the blinds and opened the window.

"What are you guys doing?" he asked.

"We need to talk to you is it okay to talk now or can you come outside?" Becka asked him.

"I think I can get out. Give me a minute and I'll take Dinger out for a walk. That should give us plenty of time. I'll see you out front." He said before he closed the window and disappeared.

We met him in front of his house and walked with him and his golden lab, Dinger.

"So what's up girls?" he asked

"We've got something to tell you but first you have to promise never to tell another soul what we're about to tell you. We can't tell you anything without your solemn promise first." Becka told him.

"Sure, I'll promise. What could be that top secret? Tell me now." he bugged us.

"We know when we tell you, at first you're going to think we're nuts but we're not. Everything is true and we're not making any of this up. If you can do this, we'll need to leave tomorrow at sun up and you'll see for yourself. So for now just believe and trust us." Becka told him.

We tried to explain how we met the merkids and what had been going on for the last couple weeks. He looked at us like we were pulling his leg and doing a joke on him.

"Where's the camera? I know this has to be some sort of punking. Who else is in on this? He asked as he looked around to see who else might jump out of the bushes.

"No joke Ronnie. This is really, real. We're not the only ones who have gone. Bunny and Amy both have already been with us .Do you want me to call them and have them tell you themselves? I will. It all started when Becka couldn't go on the second trip so Bunny got to go with us. Then when Amy found her plant we asked if she could come. This time we wanted to be able to tell you. We didn't like not being able to tell everyone. We've wanted to tell you and share everything with you. This is the first chance we've had without breaking our promise to the merkids." I told him.

"This is the wildest thing you girls have ever told me. It's pretty far fetched and I think I'd be crazy to believe any of it but it's the two of you and I can't see why you'd lie to me. What exactly would I have to do if I decided to try and help you?" he asked.

"The biggest thing would be getting out of your house for the whole day. You couldn't call home or have your Mom trying to call you. It's a wild adventure sometimes and you have to put all your faith into the merkids. What ever they say they can do, they can. You might not think any of it possible but so far they have amazed us beyond anything you could dream up. Just know this, if you go, you'll never be the same again. This trip will change your life forever in more ways than one. You don't want to miss out Ronnie. What can you tell your Mom so you can have the whole day? Can you think of something so you can meet me at the beach at sunrise?" I asked.

"We have to know tonight. What do you think? Can you come? Do you think can you do it?" Becka asked him.

"After all that build up, how could I say no. I'll figure it out. Don't worry I'll be there. I'll see you on the beach at the crack of dawn Kat." He answered her.

"Okay Ronnie, the same place we always go. I'll see you at the waters edge. Wear tennis shoes and you're regular clothes but no watch. You can bring money if you want but nothing else. Okay?" I told him.

"Okay I'll see you there. I better head back and get Dinger settled for the night. Later Girls." He said as he turned and headed back towards his house.

"Well, there you go. It's all settled. Ronnie will go with you. I'll be thinking about you while we're gone, wish I could be there to watch Ronnie when he gets to experience it all. Save all the memories and bring them back for me" she added.

We walked back to her house deciding to call it a night. Egypt had been a revelation of emotions and insight for me. Who was I? Who had I been? Where was I going? What strange and wondrous things would be happening next? How much more could I handle? Egypt had been strange, exciting, enlightening, extremely tiring, exhausting and consuming. We both needed sleep. We needed to rest and recuperate on all levels mentally, physically, emotionally and spiritually.

Becka was snoring almost the second her head hit her pillow. I didn't last much longer, just long enough to see myself riding the barge on the Nile in that other lifetime. Feeling the fur of the two kittens touching my leg as they played on the end of the chaise.

The alarm went off at 6:30 and I didn't want to wake up. Becka turned it off and turned over to shake me.

"Wake up Kat. You have to go meet Ronnie in less than 20 minutes. Time to get up. Hurry so you can eat before you go." With those words she threw back the covers and jumped out of bed. I slowly opened one eye to see where she was and just wanted to cover my head and go back to sleep. I didn't think I was ready for another adventure so soon. I wasn't Wonder Woman after all just a teenager who wanted to sleep in.

I tried not to eat too much even though it was my favorite, pancakes. There would be another long trip ahead of me today. It wouldn't help if I were all weighted down by over eating now. If I could have taken a nap afterwards, I would have pigged out because I was still hungry even after the big dinner we had the night before. I thanked everyone for breakfast. I told them each to have a nice time during their visit with Gram's sister and then I gave Becka a hug before I took off.

"Later Becka. See you when you get back." I called out to her as I left and headed for the beach. My parents knew I was spending the night at Becka's and that I planned to go to the beach with my other friends for the day. They didn't expect me back until dinnertime. I hoped that Ronnie would be able to have as good a plan with his parents.

When I got to the beach Ronnie was already waiting for me. He waved his arm as he saw me come onto the sand.

"Hey Ronnie, what did you tell your parents? Are you good to be gone all day?" I asked him as I got close enough to talk.

"I did what you said to do. I didn't lie; I just didn't fill in a lot of the details. I asked if I could go with my friends for the day and promised to be back in time for dinner." He told me," I was surprised my mom didn't quiz me about who and what we'd be doing. She must have been tired when I asked but I think that helped me." He flashed one of his mischievous smiles and asked "So where are your merkid friends?"

I pointed and said

"There just look behind you." Out about waist high in the water was Mu. Shi and Bach. "Come on, we need to go out to talk with them first. Don't worry about getting your clothes wet."

We waded out, met the three of them and I make the introductions. Bach asked Ronnie a couple questions and once he was happy that Ronnie would keep our secret and knew what he was getting into, Bach was ready for us to take off.

Ronnie of course didn't really know what he would be getting into but he was up for an adventure, maybe even needed one in his life right now. This was going to be an experience he would never forget. I was sure of that. Shi explained the breathing gear as they handed us our pouches of food and water. Ronnie was getting a strange yet excited look on his face as they told him how everything worked and how we would travel to Mt. Shasta.

Bach said we'd take off for the coastline of Texas again and enter some old Volcanic tube like tunnels and swim out to Crater Lake in Oregon. From there we'd walk and hike down into California to Mt. Shasta, which was only about 145 miles south of the lake.

Once the talk and instructions was over with we all dipped into the Gulf of Mexico and started off on our next adventure. I was getting a little used to all the wonders of the under water gulf but I'd never get tired of looking at it all. I heard Ronnie think a couple wows at what we were seeing and mentally told him we could all hear his thoughts just as he would be able to hear ours. That was one thing no one had mentioned to him before we left the beach.

We swam for a long time while Ronnie and I both enjoyed the scenery. Hanging onto the waistband of the merkids, just taking a ride made it easy to gawk during the swim across the Gulf. There were several groups of dolphins and a shipwreck or two we passed but nothing too unusual this trip unless you wanted to count the big blob of oil we passed near the middle of the gulf. The water was warm and sparkling with lots of greens and blues along the coastlines. Out in the middle near the oil blob it was darker and didn't have the prettier colors so it was easy to appreciate them now as we neared the coast of Texas.

It was still amazing and uncanny how Bach could read an area and find just what he was looking for. The old Volcanic tube or tunnel had a medium sized opening as we approached and started to make our entry.

"Whoa….." was all I heard as Ronnie neared the tube and slipped in behind Bach. Mu went next and Shi and I followed. I couldn't help but notice I was in my least favorite spot again, pulling up the rear. The tube wasn't too dark and both Ronnie and I were happy about that. I never knew what these under world passageways would be like. The Tibetan one was darker than the Mayan or Peruvians ones were. I wasn't so worried this trip because I was getting used to Bach looking out for us and I trusted him. I just wouldn't get too close to him again if he was trying to talk me into something I didn't want to do. I think I learned that lesson in Egypt.

A few times as Bach wove this way or that the tubs would get larger and then return to the smaller sizes. I preferred being in the bigger ones myself, not that I was claustrophobic but I didn't especially like small places. So far this trip I wasn't worried about any fearful thoughts going out to the group. Ronnie how ever couldn't control his thoughts. His mind was going a mile a minute and he was full of wonder and amazement. I could enjoy his excitement as well as my own.

As we passed under Yellow stone National park Bach told us a couple interesting facts about the history of this area of the country in regards to Earth's early volcanic activity here. Glad I wasn't around back then. Who would be able to live with hundreds of years of no sun shining through the volcanic ash in the atmosphere? I had learned on several shows on the Discovery or History channels about the volcanoes in the park but passing them by now made it all seem so much more real. There were places you could feel the water temperatures rise from the heat of the lava, sometimes according to Bach, just inches away from us through the rock.

Ronnie was thinking so many questions the merkids took turns trying to answer him. He had a male twist on the kinds of questions he asked compared to Bunny, Becka, Amy or me and they didn't seem to mind his questions at all today. I'd have to tell him later how lucky he was. When I asked too many things the first couple trips I was told that a quiet mind is the way to enlightenment and too much chatter would take away from it.

You could tell the minute we entered the lake. The water got colder and the color was a cobalt blue. It was crystal clear and the purity of it was refreshing to your entire body and mind. I felt as if I had just taken a shower and washed layers of grim from my soul. I wondered if this lake was similar to the one in Tibet where they said swimming in the waters cleansed your soul of it's past life sins. I didn't feel anything like that in Tibet but today I felt something similar must have happened. I felt like a new me.

We swam to the surface and over to the rim of the lake to get out. The minute Ronnie's head came out of the water and he could remove the crystal breathing gear from his mouth he shouted out, "WOOOOOWHO!!"

The others looked at Ronnie like he was definitely over reacting and acting a little strange. They just didn't realize how free he felt at that moment. I wasn't sure if he had felt the renewing sensations I had felt coming through the lake. I'd have to talk to him later and ask my questions. I figured this was already the greatest adventure Ronnie had ever been part of and he was just expressing himself a little. They just didn't know Ronnie, if they did they would have understood and looked at him differently when he shouted out his joy.

It was a clear warm day and I was happy to get out of the cooler water. There was nothing but beautiful country for as far as we could see in every direction. Tall pine trees and lush forest surrounded the lake. The five of us stood together there by the lake taking in the new world around us.

"Blows your mind doesn't it Ronnie?" I asked him as I watched him trying to take it all in. Here we were, the other side of the country and it was a faster trip than even flying would have been. Seeing the merkids and how they functioned was a trip all on it's own, not counting all the rest that he was dealing with right now.

"You'll get used to it. Just trust the kids, what ever they say, they've always gotten us where we needed to be and they have our best interest at heart. It is pretty hard to take it all in at first." I told him.

"Yeah, nothing you could have said last night could have prepared me for this. I'm just happy you asked me to come and I didn't decide to blow the whole thing off as a joke. I did think about staying in my bed this morning. Can't tell you how glad I am I didn't." he told me.

Bach and Shi had been talking and getting their directions figured out. We all knew we had to head south and get down into California. From what I had read we should be able to see Mt. Shasta before too long once we got going that way. AT over ten thousand feet high Shasta should be like a beacon against the landscape once we got a little closer.

"If you're all ready we better get started and we need to go this way." Bach told the group in general as be pointed to the south.

So off we went, heading south into the forest. The temperature was warm probably in the 70's the sky was blue with a few clouds and a soft breeze. This beat just about every place we'd been so far for comfort. I couldn't help but think about the reports I had heard over the years about California having such great moderate temperatures. At least we wouldn't be cooking or feel like we were frying under a desert sun, Ronnie didn't know how lucky he was. Our clothes were dry before we hiked out of the woods that made us all a little more comfortable. I was enjoying the scenery, the great California weather and didn't mind hiking at all today.

We wandered through the pines for hours and came upon a paved road. My thoughts were, maybe we could hitch a ride and not have to walk the whole distance. I think Ronnie was thinking the same thing. The merkids didn't think the same way we did, they weren't used to cars and buses, so they didn't think about riding anywhere.

We hadn't walked very far along the roadway when a blue pickup truck with two men stopped and the driver called out asking us if we wanted a ride. We looked at each other but it was Bach who said we were heading towards Mt. Shasta if that's the way they were going, we'd be happy for the ride. The driver who was wearing a cowboy hat seemed like a friendly sort said we were in luck, that's the direction they were headed, just hop in the back.

With his pearly white killer smile he introduced himself as Bob Redford and his companion Song Bird. I smiled and almost chuckled out loud but caught myself. I'd never heard of a grown man being called

Song Bird. He looked more like a Kills Bears or Wild Pony. We didn't waste any time quickly climbing into the back of the pick up, happy for the ride. Bach wouldn't have talked with the driver if he hadn't gotten a positive reading off of him and the other man in the truck.

The ride was way better than some of the others I'd had while with the merkids on our little adventures. The wind was gently blowing my hair and I was enjoying the chance to relax and just feeling the warm sun on my face. Ronnie was still asking dozens of questions of both Mu and Shi, they were busy trying to answer them all. He looked like he had just discovered some great new magical form of insight. He was asking questions about the speed of light, inter-multi-dimensional travel and other brain twister type questions.

For me it all just happened and I was there but I didn't try to dissect it or understand it. I didn't really even know where I would start to come up with the kind of questions Ronnie was asking. He was a guy and I guess he wanted to understand how everything worked, for him it was like trying to take a car apart and put it back together. He just wanted to understand how it all worked. He was asking about the breathing gear, the ear crystals, ley lines and under world passages and how they navigated through them.

I watched it all from the back of the pick up, as the countryside was whizzing by. I was enjoying the differences from back home because this was my first time on the west coast of the United States and I wanted to see it all. We had crossed over the state line and were already in Northern California. Our cowboy driver host hadn't said how far they were going so I wanted to take in every mile of the scenery before we had to get out and walk again. The country was so beautiful, the rolling hills and mountains on the horizon. California was pretty brown, not near as green as I would have thought it would be.

Bach pointed up ahead of us, saying"

"There's Mt. Shasta."

Along with a few smaller hills, she was there dominating the skyline in front of us. You had to appreciate the beauty and majesty of her snowcapped slopes because there was nothing anywhere in the area that could compete for your attention.

"Mt. Shasta is a major vortex, I can feel its energy from here. It's the base chakra of Earth, which makes it a very important and sacred place. It's also some of the last regions of Lemuria that remained above water after the last destructions." He added a little running info for both, Ronnie's benefit and mine. We both sat up a little straighter so we could see the mountain better also so we could see if we could tell any of those things about it just by looking.

We rode awhile longer and got quite close to the mountain before our hosts pulled into a driveway with a gate and sign up over the it that read ' The Circle Double R Ranch'. The friendly driver turned his head around, opened the window between the bed of the pick up and the cab and said,

"This is the end of the road for us so unless you want to come up and get put to work. We'll have to part ways here." He flashed his handsome smile at us again just watching us until we started climbing out of the truck. We all thanked him and his friend for the ride. We were on the passenger side of the truck when we climbed out and it was the first time we got a good look at the other guy. He was Indian. His hair was long and mostly grey, he was wearing a cowboy hat as well and his face was lined with character.

Before we turned and started to walk away the Indian said,

"You're headed towards Mt. Shasta. You should be careful she's nothing like what you think. The old lady is full of surprises and she doesn't usually take to strangers. Be sure to show her respect and be careful."

Bach told him,

"We'll be careful, thanks again for the ride."

We were so close there wasn't much distance left to hike in. The mountain looked so much larger as we got closer to her slopes. You could sort of see the old volcanic shape of Shasta. Seemed strange to think of volcanoes with snow on them to me, somehow the two things didn't seem like they belonged together. She was a beautiful looking mountain but I hadn't seen too many mountains to compare her to.

Looking from where we were at the base of Mt. Shasta we couldn't see any flowers anywhere. I was hoping this would be another easy trip and we wouldn't have to go through too much to get the plant and head back home. Didn't look like it was going to be a slam-dunk this trip.

"So what do we do now?" Ronnie asked, "Should we divide up and start climbing up until we find them?"

"It's time for me to read the area and see if I can pick up anything. If I don't get anything we'll split up and start the search. I just need a couple minutes." Bach told him.

Bach tried but he said he didn't feel anything close so we decided to split up and do like we had in Tibet. Half of us would go one way and the others would go the opposite way. Shi said he'd go with us to the right, Bach and Mu would go the other way and we'd meet up on the backside of the mountain. I wondered how many hours of hiking that would take? No sense in wondering or worrying about it, better to just get going and try to find our plant.

The old boy scout in Ronnie must have been rearing to come out because he took the lead and Shi just fell in behind him as the three of us headed out. I didn't mind having the rear today, no dark shadows or closed in spaces for things to pop out of, I was actually enjoying myself. The sun was high in the sky and it was a great day for a hike so I just decided to get into it and have fun. We searched and found several flowers but not the ones we were looking for. There were little poppies and a few wild daisies. We had split up and each one of us searched an area about 15 feet wide at different levels on the lower slope.

We must have been walking for hours and it didn't look like we were half way around our half of Mt. Shasta yet. At one point as we got a little higher up we discovered a small cave. Shi suggested we leave it untouched no telling what wild animals might be back inside it. Better to leave Mother Nature alone today, last thing we needed was someone getting bitten by some wild creature. Wasn't too much excitement but it did create a little break in the afternoon.

We hiked on. Ronnie and I talked a little about how amazing all this was then Ronnie asked Shi a few questions about time bending and how they did it. He wanted to know if time was just an illusion of our world? Or did they change dimensions? Was that how they seemed to be able to alter our time away with them on our little adventures? He and Shi talked a long time about it plus a couple other things the kids could do. I enjoyed listening and hearing all that Shi had to tell Ronnie.

Shi tried to explain how many souls in the Universe were able to change from one dimension to the next at will. Third dimensional beings (all us normal human beings) could be raised up and taken with them if they could raise our vibrations enough. He told Ronnie that we were capable of raising our own vibrations but he added most of us weren't interested in applying ourselves even when we were told what we were capable of. It usually had to be a person who was more involved with spiritual advancement.

"The veil that divides the dimensions is a thin one but it also has a thick skin that holds many back. Kat experienced it for herself in Tibet. I told her she could step through to the higher dimension as long as she was with me. In truth she was capable of going on her own but she didn't believe and that lack of knowing or believing kept her safely locked in the third dimension of your world. Once you all begin to understand that you are a soul or spirit of vibration and not the physical body you have grown for yourselves, then you will be able to travel and see the Universe and all it's higher vibrations at will. Understand your vibration must be at a certain level to be able to achieve this but you, Kat and her other friends are all there. You just need to unlock your mind and release it from the third dimensional prison you choose to hold yourselves in." Shi told us.

"WOW, that's sort of mind blowing. To think that it's just our thoughts and our own minds that are locking us here on the Earth's plane. Guess we need to start thinking differently." Ronnie replied.

Shi continued on,

"Yes. Once you are able to transcend the dimensions you will be able to know and understand all things that are there for the few you call Psychics or Clairvoyants. The knowledge of the World and the Universe is there for all to see and understand it should not be limited to a few. You will be able to see and communicate with every spirit, to know life of the soul is ever lasting and all are one!"

"I feel like we should be writing this all down. You are saying things that sound so simple and yet are so hard for so many to understand and believe in." Ronnie bantered back.

I was following the two boys, listening to their conversation and enjoying how much Ronnie was opening up to Shi with his thoughts. Ronnie could be a little on the shy side when he didn't know someone and didn't always speak up like this. We hiked and we searched for our sacred plant as the afternoon slipped away with our interesting topics and conversation. Being with the Merkids was like being with some Guru from India or a spiritual Buddhist Monk. They were so insightful with the information they were feeding to us it never got boring listening to them.

Suddenly out of nowhere, Ronnie jumped and yelled,

"Did you see that?" then he started to run up ahead of Shi to the rocks in front of us.

By the time we reached the outcropping of rocks where Ronnie had pointed to, he had disappeared behind them somewhere.

"Where is he? Where did he go? What the heck.!" I cried out to Shi.

Even Shi looked puzzled and surprised. We couldn't see where he could have gone so fast to have just disappeared. Wait a minute.

"Where do you think he went Shi? Did you tell him too much about the higher dimensions? Could he have seen a gateway and stepped through?" I asked him.

"I don't think so Kat. I think I would see it too if he had seen a gateway. We need to look closer here, there must be a way into the mountain and we're just not seeing it yet. It's the only answer I can figure."

When Ronnie's head popped out from between the rocks I almost fell over from the fright of his reappearance.

"Come on, it's this way. Wait until you see what's here." He said and disappeared again.

At least this time we could see where he had gone. The way the light was hitting the rocks it didn't seem like an opening but it was. I could have walked by this place dozens of times and never realized there was an opening. I was a little unsure of following him inside but what the heck this wasn't my first time to enter a cave or underground passage. Once Shi and I stepped inside the opening was still there. No doors slamming shut behind us. We each reached in and put our beam crystals on as Ronnie had already done. It always helped to put a little light on things especially if they were dark caves or under world passageways.

"Look here." Ronnie said as he pointed to some cave painting on the rock to his right.

"Wow. I wonder how old they are?" I sort of speculated out loud.

"Hey that's not what got me in here. Did either of you see the figure I saw?" he asked us.

"I didn't see anything but you running up ahead of us and disappearing. Did you see anything Shi?" I asked.

Before Shi could even answer Ronnie said,

"Surely you saw him? It was a tall Indian figure. He was wrapped in a robe of some sort and he had a couple feathers in a headband around his head. I never would have seen this entrance if I hadn't seen him come in here. He can't be much farther ahead of us. Why don't we try to catch up with him and see if he knows where the plant we need grows? Besides, this is way too cool not to explore it a little farther."

Shi looked like he was deep in thought before he finally said,

"I guess we could try to catch up with him but if we don't we're going to turn around and get back out onto the top side of the mountain. I would think anyone knowing about this entrance would know Mt. Shasta well enough to tell us anything we need to know about it. Okay, lets go."

Except for the paintings on the cave walls, it could have been any cave anywhere in the world but soon as we continued further on into the cave we started to notice carvings in the walls and they were starting to look more and more like some ancient temple. It felt like we had entered an observatory of gigantic proportions in some otherworldly place. I even wondered out loud,

"Are we still in Kansas Toto?"

"WOW." Was all Ronnie was able to say.

"I believe we have found another one of your worlds myths. This must be the ancient home of the Lemurians who survived the last of the destructions. The markings you see here, these are the same as the ones our ancestors recorded and handed down to us in Atlantis. I have never seen them anywhere else until now. I don't know how to read them but I recognize them." Shi informed us.

"WOW, again." Ronnie piped in.

"So now what do we do? There's nobody here. How would we know which way to go next? Look it's like the maze of mazes there's at least ten different doorways." I pointed out.

What happened next almost made me jump right out of my skin.

"What in the world are you all doing here?" said a voice from behind us. It was Bach and Mu was standing beside him. How in the world did the two of them get here? Was magic happening or what?

"Look Bach, is it not amazing? This has to be where the Lemurians went after the final destructions of their homeland. Look at the symbols. Can you read them? I recognize them but I don't understand them." Shi said.

"I believe this symbol reads 'Remember and never forget.' That may be a simple interpretation but I believe it represents the true meaning." Bach told us.

If I thought the sound of Bach's voice a couple minutes before had almost made me jump out of my skin: it was nothing compared to the next thing that happened that almost made me faint dead away.

"Good, you are all finally here." The deep sound of the male voice on the other side of the room almost did my heart in. I was sure it stopped and would probably never start beating again. Holy cow, what next?

"That's him. That's the man I saw." Ronnie called out as he pointed towards the male voice. The five of us were all staring at the tall slender Indian wrapped in some sort of blue robe. Ronnie was right he also had a couple feathers in a headband around his head. He looked maybe half Indian and sort of Hawaiian to me.

Bach was the only one of us who didn't seem shocked or surprised by this mans presence. In fact it was Bach who stepped to the front of the group and asked the man,

"Have you been waiting very long?"

"For more moons than you could count," was his answer.

"What do you want us to do now?" was all Bach asked.

"I am Ramu. If you will come with me now I will explain everything soon." was all he said as he turned and headed back through the same archway he had come through just moments ago.

The five of us followed him as he wove his way through several passageways and then finally into another large room with a high ceiling. Once our eyes adjusted to the darkness of the giant chamber we noticed there were hundreds of others there. They were sitting around the outside wall of the circular room in several rows. Each one was wrapped in a blue robe just like Ramu's. As Ramu stepped forward, every seventh person lit a fire in front of them self and the room started to shimmer and dance with light.

"They are all here to witness the return of Lemur. We have waited patiently these many eons for her return. It is as the prophecy foretold. She has returned in time to face our final destiny together." Ramu explained.

Wow, prophecy, returning…destiny. What did all this mean? It certainly explained Mu's name, maybe Mu was just the nickname for Lemur. I turned to see what Mu was doing and how she was being affected by all this new information. She looked just as bewildered as the rest of us, except Bach, who seemed to understand it all. He always seemed to know what was going to happen. Is that how he and Mu showed up so quickly after we got here? Did Bach already know what was really happening here? Did he help get Mu here for what ever prophesy Ramu was talking about?

Before I could begin to figure out what was going on and guess what part Bach had in this happening, Ramu started talking again.

"This is the ceremonial room with a Lemurian Spirit Wheel in the center. This is our gateway to all the spiritual dimensions into the Universe and beyond. It is here Lemur must take her next sojourn to reconnect with her higher self and recall her place in the destiny of all. We are here to celebrate her return and to empower the energy of the wheel before she takes this journey of solitude tonight during the full moon. The lunar energy is the last requirement for the Spirit Wheel to open and let her connect with the spiritual dimensions and discover her destiny once again. The spokes of the wheel point out and represent the four directions and seasons of life as well as the rays of light from all the planets of the galaxy. The stones used to build the lines and paths are rich in crystals and gold which enhance and amplify the higher spiritual vibrations. One enters a wheel to make the journey of self-discovery and to connect to the spiritual dimensions. This has always been where our young men and women come to make their spiritual quest, to connect to the one and to read their own records of life."

I was surprised when I looked to see the Spirit Wheel he was talking about. It looked just like the Indian Medicine Wheels I had see in the history books and even on the Internet. Had this Spirit Wheel been the beginning of those Medicine Wheels made by the early American Indians? Now I even wondered if the American Indians were just descendants of the Lemurians? I wondered also if these people were third dimensional like us, or if they were some of those beings that could be in any level and were they really here physically or spiritually? Their bodies looked as solid as mine or Ronnie's but they also had another quality about them. I wasn't sure if I was looking at true spirits or real people.

"Wow. Can you believe any of this Kat? Is this real or are we part of some big play and you guys are just pulling a big one on me?" Ronnie asked. "If this isn't real, man I've got to tell you, it's about as real looking as it can get for me!"

The crowd started chanting and it began to sound like an Indian Pow Wow. The sounds of the chanting even began to make the hairs on my arm, stand up. Holy cow what was going to happen next? I couldn't help but wonder if Mu was ready for this. I was happy it wasn't anything that involved me because this was beginning to look and sound like some pretty heavy-duty stuff. I was way too young to be personally involved in prophecy stuff and I was happy to just be an innocent bystander. I wondered what the actually ceremony would be like. I hoped we got to watch and see what was going to happen to Mu. I wondered if enlightenment would change her much.

Ramu opened a box and lifted out some sort of jewelry, he raised the jewelry up high over his head and the chanting grew louder. He turned and showed the piece to everyone in the room then he started to walk towards us. I was surprised when he walked right past Mu and came up behind Ronnie. He lowered his hands and the jewelry piece passed down in front of Ronnie's face, as it did his eyes got really big and I thought they might pop out of his head. Mine must have gotten just as big. I thought I would stop breathing when Ramu tied the beaded, bone neck choker around Ronnie's neck.

Ronnie looked like he might turn blue he had been holding his own breathe so long. What in the world was going on? I thought Mu was the one this thing was all about, why were they putting this thing around Ronnie's throat? What did he have to do with what was happening? My mind was racing and I could see that little spark of fear suddenly in Ronnie's eyes. He was as lost as me as to what was happening here. We thought we were just bystanders. What was going on?

Two seconds later Ramu was answering our questions.

"You have returned Lemur and we have been waiting, destiny is fulfilling itself. It is good this lifetime you have returned as a male you will need the extra yang energy for this journey and spiritual quest. "With his last words he turned Ronnie around to face the rest of the room and removed his own robe and draped it over Ronnie's shoulders. When he did that the rest of the room went wild with their chanting and many of them stood up and started dancing near the fires on the floor around the outer rim of the Spirit Wheel.

The energy in the room was alive, you could feel it crackle, I could almost see the sparks of fire rising up from the auras of the people in it. Maybe it was their auras dancing and sparking with the inter actions of all the spirits coming together. I really wasn't sure what it was I was seeing but seeing it I was! The chanting and dancing went on for several minutes before Ramu moved Ronnie into the room where more could see him. He motioned his arms first up and then down for the room to be quiet. Once silence returned to the room he spoke again,

"Let us nourish the body and prepare the soul for tonight's quest."

With Ramu's words several groups started to get up and head off in different directions. Ramu motioned us to follow him and Ronnie as he turned and headed down a large passageway off to the left. He led us down several stairs and we worked our way deeper into the mountain and the old dormant volcano tubes, more stairs and before we knew it we had transcended three stories into the depth of Mt. Shasta to an open large dining room. Food had been prepared and they were ready for a feast.

I got to sit next to Ronnie when we all gathered at the table.

"Are you okay Ronnie?" I had to ask him.

"I don't know Kat. This is really wild and I will tell you when Ramu tied this choker around my throat, it felt like it belonged there. I almost felt like I remembered something but couldn't quite put my fingers on it. It feels like a shadow floating around in my memory banks somewhere. I really thought this was all about Mu and never had a clue he would single me out." Ronnie told me.

"Me too." I told him "I thought for sure this was all about Mu and her destiny. I thought your eyes were going to pop right out of their sockets when Ramu tied that choker around your throat."

As we sat at the table Ramu approached, sat next to Ronnie on his other side and started to tell him what he would be expected to do for his quest in the Spirit Wheel later when the full moon came up.

"You must start at the outer rim and follow the path slowly into the center of the wheel. You should stop and experience any of the revelations you might encounter as you work your way towards the inner and last circle. Once you are there, you must wait for your quest vision to be fulfilled. You cannot leave until you have the revelation of your destiny. You are there to receive the direction of your path, the path you promised to follow when you started out in spirit. To remember your quest and destiny in the Spirit Wheel will ensure the power of its future and fulfillment. Once you are centered and your destiny is sealed back into your heart you will know it is done and you will be ready to leave the wheel. You must remain alone in the ceremonial room within the wheel until you know your destiny and have the knowledge to leave and fulfill it. Your friends will wait for you here in this room. Enjoy yourself until the Moon rises, I will return for you then."

Ramu rose from his chair and left the room. As we watched him leave we realized we were all alone at the table. No one else was in the room with us.

"Whoa! Did that blow anybody else away besides me?" I had to ask.

Bach spoke,

"I understand our need to be here for Ronnie to enter his quest but we must ask the next time we see Ramu if he knows of the plant we are seeking. Each quest must be fulfilled on this trip but the plant is my most important mission and we must find our specimen before we leave this mountain."

"We will ask the minute we see him upon his return or anyone else who enters this room. Maybe while Ronnie is on his quest we could be retrieving our plant and preparing it for the journey home" Mu said.

Shi shook his head in agreement. Yes we all wanted that plant more than anything else. This quest thing was a total surprise but one we now felt we had to deal with. Who were we to stand in the way of prophecies? I still couldn't wrap my head around Ronnie being the soul this thing seemed to revolve around or depend on. Just wait until I got back and could tell the girls about all this.

It made me start to think. Could Ronnie be one of the seven sisters? At first I never would have thought about him being one of the sisters just because he was, a him, not a her. Did that all make sense? Did any of this make sense? I was still so overwhelmed by the events of the day so far it was hard to think about much beyond tonight's quest and where this was all going to lead us.

Especially Ronnie what could he expect to happen to him during his quest? What destiny and future was he expected to see or come to terms with? I worried for him a little. There were so many things that we had no concept about. Would he leave and go to some higher dimensions? Would he be able to handle whatever happened to him? He would be, all alone tonight could he lose his mind or worse, forget who he was and become this other person Lemur? If Lemur had been a woman, how would that effect him after the quest? It was making my head spin just thinking the thoughts that were jumping around in my brain right now.

None of us were really eating. Who could be hungry when so much was hanging over our heads right now? We really needed to find the plant and see where Ronnie's quest took him and then us. I really wished that Becka, Bunny and Amy could have been here. I really wanted to be able to talk to them about what was happening. I hoped I wasn't making a mistake by not trying to stop Ronnie from doing this quest. The word destiny seemed so large and consuming, how could anyone try to keep someone from discovering his or hers?

Ronnie certainly seemed ready willing and able. Maybe a little fear was lurking there inside his eyes but you knew this was something he was doing. Now that he knew what it was all about, he was in 100 percent. There was a new depth even in his voice now that he was talking about the quest. Ronnie had always loved everything about Indians. This Spirit Wheel was just like the Medicine Wheels of the American Indians and they had always inspired him. He loved dream catchers and he had a deep belief in the Indians love and understanding of the Universe and Mother Earth. This stuff was right up his alley of interest.

When we finally settled down and decided to eat a little something it was amazing how good everything was. There were some things that looked like fried flat bread, a vegetable dish that looked like corn, peas and lima beans all cooked together. Another dish looked like cooked fish and the last dish was some kind of berries and looked a little like cobbler to me. It was really good and after I ate a little I was surprised at how my appetite returned. I was almost licking my fingers it all tasted so good. Everyone seemed to enjoy the meal once we finally had gotten around to eating it. It wasn't too long after we finished eating that Ramu returned and told Ronnie it was time to go back to the ceremonial room.

Bach immediately asked him if he might be able to help us with our project and explained we were searching for a plant that was known to grow on the Mt. Shasta slopes. Bach showed Ramu the picture we had and he nodded like he recognized the plant.

"I promise to return as soon as Lemur starts the quest and enters the Spirit Wheel. I believe we have many plants that might interest you in our lower gardens." He told Bach.

Jeez I wondered where the lower gardens could be. We were already pretty low under the mountaintop, how much lower or deeper could this place go? I saw on television once a place in Turkey they said went five stories underground. The people had built an entire town with stables and wineries as well as rooms and homes for thousands of people. If I hadn't seen this place with my own eyes, I wouldn't have believed it could be here and in so many ways it was very similar to that place in Turkey. Why had so many people build so many places underground like this? Were they trying to escape the floods or other destructive forces of Nature?

It almost made me sad to watch Ronnie leave with Ramu. I didn't know if he was scared or not. He had on a brave face when he said "good bye, see you all later."

I wondered if he was concerned about what he was about to embark on inside the Spirit Wheel, this quest he was about to begin? I really wished I could be there for him. I would have liked to watch over him, I didn't like not being there just in case something went wrong. I know I wouldn't have wanted to go alone but maybe I'm a bigger chicken than Ronnie. I'd just keep telling myself, this is something he has to do on his own, all by himself and there's nothing to worry about.

I had some pretty weird things happen to me on these little adventures with the kids and I'd seen Mu go through a thing or two as well but we didn't march bravely into them the way Ronnie was doing now. They were things that just happened, nothing we planned or made a conscious decision to enter into on our own two feet.

It didn't take too long before Ramu was back, keeping his promise to show us the lower gardens, where we'd see if the plant we were searching for was growing. Ramu said we could take anything we wanted if we needed samples to take back. We followed him down even farther into the depths of Mt. Shasta. Turns out there were seven levels here and the lowest was the garden level. Ramu left us to search the gardens for what ever we needed telling us he would see us back in the dining area when we were finished here. For now he had to get Ronnie started on his quest.

It was a simple route and Bach or even I would have no trouble finding the way back. While we were hunting the gardens, which were very lush and bountiful Ronnie was up above us walking the circular path of the Spirit Wheel. I couldn't keep my thoughts from going back to him as I helped to look for the plant we came so far to find.

In the upper level, Ronnie stood, as straight and tall as an arrow when Ramu positioned him at the beginning of the spirit wheel. Before Ramu stepped away to leave Ronnie/Lemur to begin his quest, Ramu removed the blue robe from Ronnie's shoulders and recited some ancient words, which Ronnie neither, recognized or understood. As Ramu left the chamber Ronnie took a deep breath, took his first step into the circle and all the fires blazed a little brighter, the flames leaping a little higher. With each step he took, further into the wheel on his spiritual quest, he began to hear ancient whisperings of the past.

Down in the lower levels we had gone through several gardens and still hadn't found our plant.

"You would think if Ramu knew our plant, he would have said he recognized it and might have said which garden we could find it in." I said out loud to no one in particular.

"Perhaps he isn't familiar enough with the plants to know what is here and what isn't. "Mu replied.

"Well surely someone here knows and they could be here directing us a little. How many gardens do you think there might be? Bach haven't you, picked up anything yet?" I asked.

"It's here, I'm feeling certain of that. I think we're close." Bach answered me.

"Well that's a relief, I was worried we might be on a wild goose chase we should probably be getting back to wait for Ronnie. Who knows how long this is all going to take. He could be waiting for us right now." I just kind of rambled.

Ronnie was getting closer to the center of the wheel. He was dancing and weaving to some song no one else could hear. He looked more Indian than Lemurian as he did what looked like a rain dance into the very center. Once there he sat Indian style inside the circle of rocks and contemplated his quest and what part he might play in his own destiny. His face changed, he looked a little older and wiser as he began to receive the enlightenment he came for.

Images of the beginning of the world started dancing across his vison, the oozing mud and magma boiling and erupting, land building and forming only to shake, quake and break apart. There were shooting comets and sparks of stars speeding towards Earth. He astrally flew through the wormholes in the galaxy, visiting all the planets in all the worlds and dimensions of space, feeling and absorbing the energy of them as he went.

All seven colors of the spectrum were dancing and exploding, blending and moving to some galactic song weaving the understanding of the Seven Rays into his own Cosmic rays and chakras. Ronnie saw the connections of the Rays from his own body reaching out to connect to Earth, from Earth to the other planets and from the planets to the Universe and from the Universe to the other galaxies and beyond. The energies danced and sang to their cosmic song while sacred geometric shapes formed and multiplied, like a mixture of chakra patterns and astral kaleidoscopes.

The Akashic records and all the images of all his lives passed before his astral vision, the understanding of all the lessons and purposes encoded into his new awareness. Love was the light and the glowing awareness that surrounded each of the lessons he was given. The Ascended Masters were there by his side each of the seven gave him a lesson. Each Master showed him a energy and ray, the color and sound, a balance to the love and lesson they were giving him. Jesus gave him love, Buddha gave him compassion, Bob gave him Balance and harmony, Song Bird gave him wisdom and courage, the other four masters gave him, humility, trustworthiness, modesty and wisdom.

Several floors below the rest of us were still looking for that darn plant. We searched every garden bed and didn't miss a single one. Finally when we entered the last room and the second garden bed Bach cried out with the joy of finding our little treasure. Finally! I was so happy. Now we could get a couple plants prepare them for the journey home and get back up to the dining area to wait for Ronnie. Hopefully he might already be there waiting for us. It seemed like we had been down here forever looking for these two little plants we'd be taking home.

Bach was very meticulous with getting the specimens ready for the trip back. I found this part a little boring but I knew how important it was to the survival of the Merkids. So I tried not to act impatient. I was pacing a little and worrying at the same time, what could be happening with Ronnie? Was it all over for him? What was it like? Did he have any great and miraculous revelations about the world and it's destiny? I just couldn't wait to see and talk to him again. This was all taking way too long. I needed to get back up closer to Ronnie and the end of his quest. The girls were never going to believe all this.

Back up stairs Ronnie sat straight and tall like a beacon of light as his energy illuminated the chamber, his aura glowed pure white and flamed out as all the seven colors danced out from his body; the rays of the colors were like the northern lights dancing in the polar night skies. His body rose straight up while still in a crossed leg sitting position, rotating in a counter clockwise direction. His eyes were closed and he was deep in trance. While in the higher dimensions enlightenment just kept pouring in.. He was totally unaware of what was physically happening to his body as he entered the new higher planes of awareness. His astral body seemed to lift him as his physical body rose above the ground, high into the upper part of the chamber, he seemed to disappear as the fires died down and the chamber darkened.

Ronnie's body was up in the air about 25 feet over the center of the

Spirit Wheel and he was deep in trance. The vision quest he was here seeking was pouring into his astral eye. His third eye was receiving all the images of this destiny story and it was, a magical memory of the past that played across his mind now. He was a woman then. She was a warrior of peace and a spiritual leader of Lemuria. There were seven of them, they were sisters of the Universe, sisters of the Pleiades here on Earth to settle the new world and start life. He recognized them all.

They were there through those changes and the destructions of both Lemuria and Atlantis. They took the knowledge of their world and set out in seven different directions to start seven new colonies and begin the seven races of the new world. They were all leaders and set the standards for their people. They believed in the spiritual self and fought to keep their people connected to the oneness of the soul and the spiritual life.

Many times he saw himself coming back. Reincarnating numerous times as American Indians from Washington State, California, Utah, Wyoming and down through Colorado, New Mexico and Arizona. Always he worked to lead his people and instill in them the love of Mother Earth and the Father Sun, to respect and cherish the Earth and all she provided for them. He worked endlessly to keep them all connected to their spiritual origins and the energy of their souls.

He saw himself with the elders in spirit he remembered their teachings and the destiny he promised to fulfill. He knew now what he still had left to do. He gained the knowledge of the ages, the Universal power of One infused him and he became One with all again. He was renewed with the strength and knowledge to return to this life and join his sisters to help take them all to this final destiny together.

Once Bach was happy he had the two new specimens safely packed away he rose and said he was ready to return to the dining room. Finally. I didn't think we were ever going to get done with this and get back up to check on Ronnie and the progress of his quest. When we entered the dining room our meal had been cleared away and the room was empty. Darn I was really hoping that Ronnie might be back. Now we'd have to sit tight and wait for him. I wondered how long that might have to be? I couldn't wait to see him after his quest.

Back in one of the lower levels we were sitting there at the table, each lost in our own thoughts when I heard what sounded like a low roar of some kind. It didn't exactly sound like a train but maybe something like that. Then I started to feel the smallest, tiny tremor of movement.

"What the heck is that?" I asked.

Then the tremor started to get stronger I stood up and held onto the chair I had been sitting on. The chair started to shake and dance around on the floor then the table joined it. I was shocked and couldn't imagine what was happening. The others were standing now too. The whole mountain was shaking and quaking. Bach said,

"It's an earthquake. I can't believe I didn't feel this coming. I must have been too involved with the plants to stay open to the elements. Just stay where you are. We need to stay together."

"But Ronnie's not with us, what about Ronnie?" I asked.

"It should be over soon, then we'll try to find him and the others." He answered.

"What if the walls start to cave in? Are we going to be able to get out of here? I'm scared, I think we should run to get back up to the surface and out of this place. I don't want this to be my tomb." I cried out. The thunder of the quake was very loud and I had to yell to be heard. Underground the sound was deafening the roar had grown louder and louder. The louder it got, the more movement I felt and the more scared I got. It wasn't stopping it just kept going and going and going.

My fear was the highest I think it had ever been. I wasn't sure I could keep it together if this thing didn't stop soon. I wanted to be out of here and feel the warm sun on my face again. I wanted to see the blue sky and Ronnie again. I wanted to go home. Even Becka would never know what happened to us if we died here in this earthquake. That thought bothered me a lot.

The whole room felt like a roller coaster ride, it kept moving up and down and side-to-side. I expected any minute the rock over our heads would come crashing down on us, burying us alive here in the belly of Mt. Shasta. It was all I could do, not to scream my head off and run.

Suddenly I saw and heard a large crack in the wall in front of me. Our world was starting to come apart, this was the beginning of the mountain coming down on top of us, I could hear it and sense it was going to happen. My life was starting to move in slow motion. It wasn't passing before my eyes like they say it does when you're dying but everything went into a slow motion warp. I wasn't sure if this wasn't me losing it. Was the idea of being buried alive here more than my mind could deal with and it was shutting down?

Finally the shaking started to slow down. Maybe it would come to an end and we wouldn't be buried alive. There was hope. My mind snapped back to the present and I tried to will the rock over head not to come down, to hold and stay in place. The rocking and rolling under our feet slowed even more and I could stand fairly steady once again. Maybe Bach was right and it would end soon.

The rock dust was thick in the air but the world finally stood still again. There were several cracks in the rock walls around us but they were all still standing supporting the rock over head.

"We have to go find Ronnie. We have to go now Bach!" I told him. "Where is everybody else? Where are the others?" I asked. "Do you think they just left us here?"

"Try to pull yourself together Kat. Everyone is okay. I can sense Ronnie is well. We'll go back to the chamber room above and get him on our way out." Bach told me in his calm take charge, always in control voice.

Okay so lets get moving I want to see the sun and sky again. I don't want to hang around here just incase some of this rock decides to fall. I couldn't help what I was thinking, I just wanted to get out in case another earthquake hit or more damage from that one that just passed had a delayed reaction. I have to admit I was scared and I was still shaking inside even though the earth had stopped.

Finally we headed back up the passageway towards the ceremonial chamber. There were a few cracks here and there in the walls as we worked our way back but no real damage or blocked areas. Thank goodness none of the passageway had caved in. I think I would have died on the spot if we had found ourselves blocked and unable to get back to the chamber where Ronnie was waiting. I certainly hoped he was there waiting for us and hadn't left with everyone else. I still couldn't believe all the others left us on our own down in the belly of this place. Not one person came for us or called for us to follow them out. I was a little shocked and surprised by that fact. They all seemed so spiritual and so connected saying we were all one, they sure left fast enough when the ground started to move.

We got just inside the huge ceremonial chamber but I didn't see Ronnie or anybody else anywhere in the room. I looked and then I started yelling Ronnie's name.

"Ronnie, where are you? Ronnie are you here? Ronnie!" There was no answer to my cries. Where in the heck was he? Would he have left without us? I couldn't believe he would or did but he wasn't here. Then I saw it. There was a glow overhead that started to grow and it seemed to be coming closer down towards us from the ceiling area. What the heck was that? I looked up and had to rub my eyes. I wasn't sure what I was seeing. It seemed to be Ronnie, sitting Indian style floating down from the area overhead. I must be seeing things.

His eyes were closed and he seemed to be in a trance or meditative state. His body slowly floated down and softly landed in the center of the Spiritual Wheel. I think I was standing there in shock: I know my mouth was hanging open and I was sure I couldn't be seeing what I thought I had just seen. I had never seen anyone leviate or float down from above. I had read about it and I heard stories about it but never seen it for myself before. Even seeing it happen right in front of my own eyes, I still didn't know if I could believe what I had seen. It had to be my mind playing tricks on me.

I heard the words float though my mind,"I may have seen a lot of things but I've never seen an elephant fly," I don't know why I was thinking about the words I heard in that old Dumbo movie about the elephant that could fly, except this seemed about as wild an idea as that. I knew what I was seeing but I was finding it hard to believe what I was seeing with my own eyes. Actually seeing an elephant fly wouldn't have been any harder to try to process in my brain than seeing Ronnie there floating in mid air.

I wanted to rush in and make sure it was really Ronnie sitting there but I also felt that I shouldn't invade the space inside the Spirit Wheel right now. I didn't want to upset the energy or powers at work there. As much as I wanted to get the heck out of this place I also felt I had to respect the ritual and they said Ronnie couldn't leave until he had seen and received his destiny. I could only hope it didn't take much longer. I wasn't sure if I could continue to hold that respect if the earth started shaking again or if the quest lasted much longer.

"He will be coming back up from his trance shortly. I sense he had his vision and is just returning to this dimension now. Be patient Kat, it'll just be a few minutes more." Bach told me.

I think they all could sense my stress and the tension I was experiencing. Ronnie was one of my best friends and I felt responsible for him, especially on this little adventure of ours: I couldn't lose him or not take him back 100%. I did feel a momentary sense of relief with Bach's words. Then as I stood there, staring at Ronnie I could see the color coming back into his face and I felt even better. Then his eyes opened and he seemed to really be returning to us. He smiled and he looked so mellow and relaxed. The smile grew and seemed to reflect or project some kind of inner knowledge. We had direct eye contact and I knew. He had his vision and he was wiser for it. I got the message with just the eye contact we had for that minute.

It was like a source of energy traveled from his mind and connected to mine like a thought was shared by us on some other plane or dimension, I couldn't even explain it to myself. I felt like some form of energy connected our minds like a beam of unseen, invisible light might shine between two points. I felt like I could see into his soul and that he was seeing into mine. For that short minute all I could see was the shinning black pool of his eye's pupil. I didn't see his body, the other kids, the chamber or anything else. It was the most moving experience I think I had ever had. In a flash I heard the words, "the eyes are the window to the soul" and I knew it was true.

Ronnie just smiled and nodded at me. He stood and in a moment he looked as if he had totally returned back into our dimension and world. He walked slowly back around the wheel until he was back at the beginning, stopped and said,

"The others left via the astral planes when the earthquake first started. We should leave now too. There may be more after shocks coming and I think the entranceway we came in through may be blocked. We might need to find another way out. Lets go check to see if we can get out."

"I vote for that, let's get out of here as quickly as possible." I said.

"Yes, lets move out and check the way we came in." Shi added.

"I agree with Ronnie, I'm afraid that entrance way may be blocked and we'll have to find another way out but lets be sure first." Bach added.

So off we all went. Seemed like doom was hanging over our heads as we walked and prayed we could get out and the earthquake hadn't blocked our way. We didn't get very far before we saw the first of the rubble and rock. Real doom set in as we all realized we couldn't see past the rock and boulders. Unless there was another way out we were trapped inside. My heart sank. Oh crap, please let there be more ways out of here, at least one more anyway and let us find it.

"I think if we go back down to the third level we might find another lava tube that will take us back to the surface." Bach said.

Go deeper to try to get out. I didn't like the way that sounded but there weren't any choices. I was nervous and I guess it showed. Ronnie put his arm around my shoulder and said,

"Don't worry Kat, I'll take care of us. I know there's so much more we have to do, this isn't the end for us. Try not to worry, we'll make it."

The group was all heading back the way we had just come. Bach was in the lead with the merkids next and then Ronnie and I were pulling up the rear. Once again Bach seemed to know where he was and where he was headed. He read the area and was confident about where he was taking us. For a short time I felt positive again that things would work out. I mean, in Australia we had a tug of war with a croc, in Egypt we walked the scorching Sahara desert and lived, what was a little earthquake and another hike out from the underworld? I should be use to all this by now. Right!

We worked our way down from the first level to the second, through passageways and down again to the third. We worked our way from room to room. I was amazed with all the rooms and how many people it would have taken to build a place like this. Eventually Bach turned and started into what looked like a lava tube. We had to watch how we walked, the tube was more rounded and wasn't as flat a walking surface as the passageways had been. The tube wasn't perfectly round but it was definitely more awkward to move through. We lined up single file and tried to steady ourselves by putting our arms out to our sides to hold on and balance ourselves a little more. Ronnie fell in line behind me, which made me feel a lot better I never liked being the last one in the group at the back of the line.

We walked and climbed upward somewhat. I couldn't help but think, had to go down just so we could go back up again. We hadn't gone very far when the same sound we had heard before the earthquake came rumbling through the ground. Oh no, I hoped that didn't mean. Then the ground was vibrating and beginning to shake and take us back on that crazy roller coaster ride. I lost my balance and fell. After I bounced around a few times I managed to look up just as the merkids started to run ahead in the tube, then rocks and debris started to fall where the three of them had been standing just seconds before. The dust and dirt billowed up and both Ronnie and I started coughing. I kept trying to get up but couldn't for the life of me get back up on both feet. Suddenly Ronnie had me by the arms and was pulling me backwards away from the falling rocks.

As suddenly as it began, it stopped. Ronnie and I were still trying to breathe without choking on the dust rolling inside the tube where we found ourselves.

"Come on Kat, lets go back and get someplace where we can breathe. We need to let the dust settle in here and then see if we can dig our way out." Ronnie suggested. "I hope the others are all right. Did you see if they got out of the way in time?" he asked.

"They must have known what was coming and they managed to take off running before the rocks started to fall. I think maybe they're okay. I hope they're okay. I've got my opal, maybe I should try to connect with Bach and check on them. We're going to need more than a plan to get out of this mess."I answered him.

I didn't waste any more time. I dug through my pouch and wrapped my hand around the communication opal Mu and Bach had given me several days ago and pulled it out.

"I'll have to hope this works and Bach can answer me." I told him as I put the cool, smooth stone to my third eye.

I took a couple deep breaths and concentrated on Bach, mentally begging him to answer me. His voice was right there, instantly inside my mind. Thank God, they were all right and had just barely escaped the debris that fell. Bach estimated that at least twenty feet of rubble had fallen and it would be next to impossible for all of us to clear it out. He suggested that Ronnie and I back track to the spot where we had taken the tube to the right and take the other tube to get out. He said it would take us longer to get out but he read the pathway and it was still clear. He, Shi and Mu would try to meet up with us after they were able to get out of the mountain and work their way south to the point we would come out.

I started to explain to Ronnie what Bach had told me and he said,

"I know, don't ask me how, but I heard his words too. It was just as clearly as you talking to me. Is there anything they can't do with their minds?" he asked.

"Well I guess they can't work miracles or we'd be out of this mess and back with them right now." I said a little sarcastically.

"Well, I know the place he was talking about let's get started and see if we can't get out of here before there's another quake or after shock. I'm not too sure how long this place will hold together. I'd rather be up above looking up at the sun and blue sky too." He stated. Maybe he was reading my mine now too.

I felt a little more afraid not being with the kids. I trusted Ronnie and I knew he said we had a bigger destiny this wasn't going to be the end for us. Being here alone just the two of us made me less brave and I was feeling like a big chicken ready to run. I wanted to run but this tube was making that next to impossible. The angles were getting steeper in the second tube after we backtracked and made the turn. I could see why, if given these two choices Bach had chosen the other tube for our escape. I almost had to crawl to get up this thing. Sort of reminded me of going up into the Great Pyramid when we had to be half bent over just to get up the passageway in.

I tried to ask Ronnie about his quest and what sort of visions and destiny he saw but he said he'd rather wait and talk to all of us girls at one time. He also said he needed time to think about his quest and wrap his brain around it a little more before he would be ready to try to put the experience into words. He seemed more focused on us getting out of here and that was fine with me. I was for whatever it took for us to get out of this mess.

It seemed like days that we climbed and mostly crawled through that tube. I was so glad we had our water and the fruit in our pouches. I don't know what I would have been like if we hadn't had our beam crystals I would have been a real basket case if we'd had to try to do all this in the dark: I was definitely less confident without the merkids here being in charge. This was the second time I had gotten separated from Bach and Shi and it wasn't a very comforting feeling for me to deal with especially under the current circumstances.

We got into an area where we had to start to crouch down more and more as we continued on. I saw a movie once where the people in a cave had to crawl on their bellies to get through some areas. I remembered thinking when I watched it I hoped I never had to go through something like that. Now here I was getting close to being forced to the cave floor. I was starting to have some real panic set in. Ronnie seemed okay and none of this was bothering him, I was starting to get claustrophobic and I couldn't breath.

"Relax Kat, we're all right. We'll get through this. Bach wouldn't have sent us this way if we couldn't get through. Take a couple deep breaths. You really need to calm down. I don't want to have to deal with some freaked out, basket case, girlie girl. You are letting your fears and doubts run wild and they're disempowering you. Remember that old song Gram likes so well that says, 'I am woman hear me roar'? Let me hear you roar Kat. Come on, you can deal with this. We'll just stop for a minute, you try to center yourself, relax and try to breath slowly. I tried to find that empowered woman inside me, I think maybe she got left in Egypt but at least it put my mind to something else." He instructed me.

I tried to relax but it's pretty hard when you're having your first real panic attack and can't breathe. Ronnie tried to keep my spirits up and he teased me a little trying to get my courage back up. He even told me a couple jokes trying to get me to laugh. Once I asked him if he was afraid.

"I'll never be afraid again Kat. I saw things and I have this new sense of just knowing and understanding everything. Besides, there's nothing to be afraid of. You know that death is just one step back into the spiritual planes, it's not really death of the soul it's just like changing clothes and leaving your old ones behind when the body dies because the soul or spirit lives forever." He told me.

"Well I'm glad you're not afraid." I said, "because I think I'm afraid enough for both of us."

I did manage to get myself a little more under control. Ronnie continued to talk to me and try to calm my nerves. I think it was his steady calm voice that helped to get me where I could continue on again. After all, even I knew we couldn't stay here or try to go back.

As we moved forward our space got even tighter. I just closed my eyes and tried to mentally take myself somewhere else. With my eyes closed maybe I wouldn't see how tight the space was getting. At one point I thought I was stuck. Oh crap, how was I ever going to get out of this mess?

"I'm stuck Ronnie. I can't go any farther. I can't breath. I'm afraid we're going to die right here." I cried.

"It'll be okay Kat. You've got to relax and focus. If you can stop long enough to focus and just try to wiggle around a little I'm sure you'll be able to get loose. Come on and try. If you just try, you know you can do anything."

So I started trying to wiggle around a little, something had to give I just couldn't stay here waiting to die.

"That's it keep wiggling and you'll get through I'll be right behind you so don't be afraid.

I kept wiggling and trying to hold my breath exhaled and some how

I managed to get through the tight part. Now I worried would Ronnie who was a bigger built person than me be able to wiggle enough to get through too? Some how he did and as we worked our way farther away from the tightest spot and as we did our space inside the tube began to get a little bigger. We were able to crawl again, then to crouching down and being able to walk once more. Then much to my relief we could stand completely up and walk normal again. I felt like a re-born spirit, I could breath and the panic was easing away. The weight of the world had literally been lifted off of me.

"We'll be alright Kat. I can smell fresher air coming in, can't you?" he asked.

"I think we're finally getting close to the end maybe we'll get to see that blue sky any minute now."

Well that raised my hopes and managed to get my feet moving just a little faster. I wasn't sure if the air smelled fresher but hearing the words was enough incentive to get me going. We hiked on even farther before I could feel a little more movement in the air inside the tube and then I could smell fresh air and see a little light at the end of the tunnel up ahead of us. I practically ran the rest of the way I was so excited. When we came out of the tube and got our first look at our surroundings, I think we were both surprised.

"Where in the heck do you think we are?" I asked Ronnie. "This doesn't look like California or Oregon where we came in."

As I looked at the red rock and the towering rock structures I knew I'd never seen anything like this in person before. I'd seen pictures of the Grand Canyon and it sort of looked a little like this in color but not in the jutting rock temples I saw before me now.

"I think we're in Sedona, Arizona Kat. I was here once before with my folks when we visited Arizona a couple years ago. Remember when I told you and the girls about how incredible the place was and about the vortexes and energy they said was here. The Indians consider this a very sacred place. I can't believe we could have walked this far. In this time bending thing, do you travel farther? Is it possible we've walked this far? Is it possible that volcanic tube could have such a far reach? Where do you think the merkids are? Maybe you better try to get Bach again and let him know where we are," he suggested.

"Yeah, your right. I'll do it now." I answered him as I started to reach for my opal again. I sat down and looked at the beautiful blue sky over our heads and thanked all the powers that be for getting us here while I pulled the opal back out of my pouch. I put the opal back up to my forehead and just closed my eyes. I took a deep breath and as soon as I focused on Bach, his thoughts came pouring in again.

They were already on their way here. When they left the mountain they came out near the river and ran into Bob Redford and Song Bird fishing along the riverbank. Apparently Bob asked where the rest of us were and when the kids explained what happened they volunteered to help the kids come find us.

Bach informed us, Bob and Song Bird, a couple of the third dimensional beings were watching over Mt. Shasta, sort of like guardians. He and the cowboy were watchers and they sensed we were in trouble when the quake hit. Song Bird reminded Bach, that he had warned us that Shasta was a special spirit and a female energy that we needed to be respectful of. Bob and Song Bird tried to be where they thought we would end up exiting the mountain.

They were all in Bob's motor coach headed to Sedona as we communicated. He estimated it would only be a short time before they would be able to get to us. Who knew what that meant in our in between dimensions time with the merkids?

I sat the opal back down in my lap, trying to absorb everything Bach had just explained to me. Whoa!! This was a mind-blowing piece of information. I turned and looked at Ronnie,

"Did you hear all that too?" I asked.

"Yeah and on some level hearing his thoughts to you, inside my head that just blows my mind too. I am just so blown away by this whole experience. I'm not so sure about any of this, do you think I could still be home in my bed dreaming all this?" He asked.

"Nope, that's one thing I am sure of. You're not home in bed and this is no dream. Trust me, this is real no matter how unreal it might seem. It's real." I reassured him.

"Well what should we do while we wait? How long do you think they'll be?" he asked.

"I'm not too sure about that part myself. I don't know how to equate their time and our time. How about we just sit and relax. I think I could sit and watch the scenery for a while and just appreciate being out from under that mountain. I wasn't so sure we'd get out of there and I'm grateful just to be here, I'd like to sit and appreciate it a little longer." I answered him. "Let's just have some water and eat something while we wait for them."

So we sat there in silence for a long time, contemplating the beautiful scenery and the feeling of contentment that had enveloped us. Sedona was said to have special vortex energy, like many hot spots around the world. According to the American Indians Sedona was one of two positive hot spots for energy on the globe and Hawaii was the second one. I was a little curious about the energy and if either Ronnie or I could sense it. I was too happy about being out in the open air again to really care about anything else right then. Maybe I was feeling it already and this was how it was affecting me. I was just so happy to still be alive.

We sat for a long time before either of us started to talk again.

"Hey, how about we just take a short walk. Maybe check out the vortex energy for ourselves?" Ronnie asked.

"I don't know Ronnie, maybe I should try to check with Bach again, maybe they're getting pretty close and we should stay put." I answered him. "How about I check first and if it'll be a while yet, maybe we go for a short walk."

"Okay, sounds like a deal. See what Bach has to say." He returned.

I raised the opal to my forehead just as a large motor home pulled into the area near where we sat. Could it be them? It was, I could see Bob and Song Birds faces looking over towards where we sat. Yeah. We were back with the merkids and the world would right itself back again. We both jumped up and started walking in their direction. Relief was washing through my whole body. Now the weight of the world could sit back on the shoulders of the merkids and I didn't have to think or worry so much. We were above ground, free and soon we'd head back home.

They opened the door on the side of the motor home to let us in. I was so thankful to see them all again including Bob and Song Bird. As we entered the motor home I couldn't help but notice that Ronnie and Song Bird nodded towards each other, like some sort of acknowledgement between the two of them. Once inside Bach said he had talked with our newest friends and they were willing to give us a ride to Lake Tyler in Texas where we could take another underworld passage way back home. It wasn't so far from here and was the closest spot Bach knew of to find another passageway home. So, it was already decided and planned out. We were heading home and they were driving us to Lake Tyler. No more walking for a while I liked that part. Plus this time we were really riding in style. I couldn't believe their motor home. It had everything including a bathroom and room for all of us to sit in comfort.

I was a little surprised that the kids were talking about our business so openly in front of Bob and Song Bird. Usually we didn't let others know about the kids or what our little adventures were about. After meeting the spirits inside the mountain I guess it wasn't so surprising to find a couple of them outside the mountain. Spirit guides were wherever you found them I guess.

Bob and Song Bird are a strange pair in some ways but they were also very much alike. They were both spiritual guides and had been guardians of Mt. Shasta over many life times. Song Bird was entertaining us with the story of him and Bob and how they came together in this lifetime.

"I was on my own spiritual quest high on the mountain. I had been there for days with no food or water and in the middle of my vision came this white man who walked with the bear, the wolf and the eagle. I saw his face and it was not one I could remember ever seeing before. I knew my mission was to join with him and the wild creatures to protect and guard Mt. Shasta. There was a time when Mt. Shasta was the crown chakra of Earth and her energy was stronger and pure. I would join with my brother, the white man to protect and try to nourish her back to the glory of her beginnings.

When I left the mountain after my vision I came down looking for water and food when I was offered a ride by the face I had just seen in my vision. Bob likes to pick up and share the ride, with people of like spirit. I call him the Spirit Whisperer." He told us.

Bob just smiled and chuckled a little at the story. Bob had studied and traveled around the world he told us,

"You can tell when a man sees with his soul, when he knows the peace of the Universe and has found his passion for this life. I saw that in Song Bird that day he walked down off the mountain. I just wanted to share in the glory of his new awareness and I haven't been able to shake him loose since. We work our little ranch and watch over Shasta, not a hard life but it's a good one. It's a partnership of love for nature and the human spirit."

Bob drove on in silence after saying his few words but Song Bird talked to us more about the old legends of Lemuria and how the beings came to live inside Mt. Shasta. He called the inner city Telos, he said it means 'communication with spirit'. The Lemurians built Telos to be their strong hold and connection to spirit. It's the place they stored their records of Lemuria and Atlantis, the total history of the world is there, hidden deep inside her heart.

He knew all the same things the merkids knew of the destructions of the lands and the breaking up of the motherland and the sinking of so much of Lemuria. He talked of the times when the people went inside to escape the extremes of the climate and the troubles the world went through. He talked about the snake and ant people and how the American Indian always said they came from inside the Earth to repopulate the surface when Mother Earth found her peace once again. He said so many things that reminded me of the stories told by Cobar in Australia about the beliefs of the Aboriginal people there. He talked about the songs and vibrations of the Earth and all living things, and the sacred geometric shapes like the spirit wheel where spirit was stronger and easier to speak with.

He told us the story of the Star Woman, who was said to have come to Sedona from the Pleiades. She promised her people that she and the star people would return again some day when Mother Earth expressed her new energy and the dimensions of Earth rose into the heavens once again.

Bob said there was a really vast Universe of Galactic travelers out there and many had been to Earth and traded over the millenniums of time, for the resources they came to Earth to collect and they often left us with technology and spiritual enlightenment we wouldn't have if they hadn't visited.

It just couldn't be a coincidence that we met and were being helped by these two men. This was proving to be a long string of events and people who were helping us in our travels and search for the sacred plants we needed. I was starting to see a larger picture. There were energies at work here that I couldn't even begin to fathom. Gram always said, some things are just meant to be and one way or another, they always work themselves out. She said it was what was meant to be. It certainly gave me a lot to think about. Sometimes it was more than I could begin to put into perspective in my little world and I was happy for the scenery to distract me.

The drive down through Arizona was certainly an interesting one. I loved seeing the tall cactus all over the hillsides and there were a couple places where you could see what looked like cave dwellings high above the desert floor. Song Bird told us there were many ancient Indian ruins in the western parts of the United States, one just had to search them out. Americans seemed more interested in the history and ruins on other parts of the world than they did in the ones in their own back yards.

Bob was driving down Inter State 17 from Sedona heading towards Phoenix when we saw a car off the road with an over turned horse trailer. He immediately started to pull the motor home off to see if they needed help. When he pulled the motor home to a stop and opened the door both he and Song Bird jumped to exit the vehicle and dashed over to the woman and her daughter who seemed shaken and a little disoriented. You could hear the horse downed in the trailer screaming with fear. It was trying to get up apparently and couldn't. The trailer was bouncing and rocking from the horse's attempts to free itself. The five of us followed the men over to the site of the accident to see what we could do to help.

Bob yelled to all of us,

"Quick, we've got to get the trailer back upright before the horse hurts itself. Everybody get over here on this side of the trailer. When I say lift, everybody try to lift at the same time. Once it starts to go upright don't get caught underneath the trailer. Try to lift and push at the same time." He looked to see if everyone was in place and called out,

"Lift! Keep going and don't stop. Lift just a little more. Keep going."

The trailer was moving and slowly going upright again. The horse was crying out but maybe sensing what we were trying to do, it stopped thrashing around so much. The trailer rocked into its final upright position and came to a stand still. Then the horse started trying to rear up and you could tell it wanted out of that trailer. Bob immediately went to the back of the trailer and opened the gate. He started talking to the animal, trying to calm it down with just the sound of his voice and his hand on its body as he walked slowly to the front end of the trailer. You could see the horse start to settle down but still wanting out of the confines of the trailer. Who could blame it? It danced and pranced a little while Bob was talking softly to it before he started to back the animal up.

Immediately the animal started to settle down and backed up as Bob walked out of the trailer with it. Still talking softly to the horse, Bob was holding onto the reins and rubbing the horse's head. The horse and man walked, Bob kept talking to it settling the animal down even more. It actually looked like they were having a conversation: like the horse was telling Bob about the trailer falling over and being bounced around inside like a rag doll and Bob listening, understanding and telling the horse how sorry he was for the accident.

Song Bird turned and looked towards the five of us and said,

"I told you, it's with good reason I call him 'Spirit Whisperer'. That man could talk and settle down a full angry hornets nest in the middle of a tornado. He's been my teacher for many years."

It was pretty incredible how quickly the stallion settled down; it was almost immediate when Bob stood next to it, touched it and spoke softly to it. It was like Bob whispered some magical words and the stallion was settled down and totally recovered from the ordeal of the accident. I had never seen anything like it before. The mighty animal went from thrashing legs, flared nostrils and wild eyes to gentle animal. How could anyone have affected such a drastic and sudden change in an animal that was so shaken and panicked from the trauma of the nasty accident it had just been through? The trailer had taken a beating and it seemed pretty amazing that the animal could have come out of the fallen trailer.

Heck I was still pretty amazed that all of us had up-righted that trailer with the horse inside it. As soon as the stallion settled down the woman who had been driving the car and her daughter ran up to Bob and started to cry even more and thanked him for his help. Then they turned and thanked all of us. By the time Bob had the horse and the two women settled down, the tow truck that Song Bird had called showed up. Bob reloaded the horse into the horse trailer and we all said our good byes while the tow truck driver hooked up their car. Bob stayed with the horse in the trailer until the driver was ready to leave.

"He'll be okay, just take it slow and easy the rest of the way home." Bob told them as he exited the horse trailer. "Before you take off let us double-check the trailer hitch I better make sure it's not damaged or you could lose everything next time." He walked over, squatted down to do a careful inspection of the trailer hitch. After a couple minutes he seemed happy that it was intact and would hold for the rest of their journey home. We watched as the woman and her daughter got back inside their car and pulled away with the horse trailer in tow behind them.

Once we were back on the road again everyone talked about the miracle Bob worked on the frightened horse. He seemed a little uncomfortable about all the praise we were throwing his way.

"Life is a series of events, you just need to use your calm and inner peace to handle the situations life throws at you. The horse couldn't help being frightened and afraid. I just tried to convey to him my calm and he picked up on it. You might say we shared that same vibration once I was able to bring him out of the trailer and let him see the world was still flat and stable under him. It's not like I was really working miracles."

The miles whizzed by and before we knew it we had crossed into Texas and were getting close to Lake Tyler. Song Bird had kept us all entertained with his stories of the Indian myths and legends of the American southwest. We heard tales of Star Woman and many others. He pointed out how many stories had similarities and spoke of man coming from the stars.

In no time at all we were there, saying goodbye to our new friends. I for one was very appreciative of the ride and hated to say goodbye to two such incredible men. I was sure there was much, much more they could have shared with us and we could have listened to their stories for hours, days maybe even weeks without getting tired or bored.

Lake Tyler was huge and today the water was warm and inviting. The five of us slipped in, then under the water, heading home to Atlantis. This would be Ronnie's first trip into the famous city and I was looking forward to seeing his reactions and sharing it all with him.

This under world passageway seemed short compared to all the other trips we had made so far. It didn't seem like very long and we were reentering the Gulf of Mexico headed for Atlantis. Ronnie was doing good keeping all his thoughts to himself; I didn't hear a peep out of him the entire journey back maybe he had learned some sort of mind control during his vision quest.

It was with a happy and satisfied feeling that we all swam towards Atlantis. We had five of the seven sacred plants and only needed the last two to see if the kids could manage the cure they needed. It felt rewarding just knowing we had accomplished so much in such a short period of time. If I knew Becka, she and the others were busy searching for the last two plants. Even with her having to go out of town to visit with her Aunt, she would have her laptop and be busy searching every chance she got. The rest of the girls were helping Cookie to track down her plant too. I was sure by the time we got back to our beach we'd hear good news from one of them.

We entered the under world passageway into the city and in no time at all we were there at the steps entering the arrival chamber. Each time I entered the city the trip seemed shorter and shorter to me, it definitely felt like returning home for me too.

Ronnie looked mesmerized with the merkids tails disappearing again. It was rather hard to believe something so incredible could happen in just seconds. We were greeted by dozens of the kids as we climbed the steps into the chamber so that drew his attention away from their tails and to the group coming to greet us. Everyone seemed anxious to meet Ronnie for some reason maybe they knew something I didn't know? Mu made all the introductions then we were moving on out into the city.

First impressions are hard to beat but even for me, seeing the city of Atlantis, was magical every time and it never lost any of its magic or glow. In fact, sometimes I think I was able to see even more of the magic and be even more impressed. The air seemed so fresh and clean the beauty sparkled and glowed with more light and electrical charges with each visit I got. I say electrical charges because being in Atlantis made my skin tingle with some kind of energy I never felt anywhere else except maybe Egypt.

Ronnie's head was turning and twisting in every direction trying to take every thing in sight and lock it into his memory banks. I knew the feeling I got it every time we came here. When we stepped out onto the first terrace, where we could see the over view of the city, Ronnie took a long slow look from one end of to the other.

"Wow, this is exactly like what I thought it would look like." Ronnie exclaimed. "You have to tell me how it all works Shi, can we see the generator crystals? Is there time for that before we have to leave?" he asked.

"We will see how much time there is and if we can work it in." Shi promised.

First we had to deliver the plants to the hydra farms in the out laying area of the city. For the first time we all walked to an area I had never been to before and we boarded a small boat and we let the current of the channel take us out to the outer rings to the hydra farms. This was a treat I had never been on before. Unfortunately the ride didn't last too long and we were there at the farms. We docked our little boat and walked the dock onto land again. We were greeted by one of Shi's brothers and followed him into one of the large farm buildings. Once again I watched while the kids took the plant we returned with and safely unwrapped and replanted the specimen we brought them. The plants you could see were amazing. The vegetables were huge and you could probably feed dozens of people a meal on just one cabbage. Ronnie and I were busy taking in all the things we could see.

"Think they use Miracle Grow Ronnie?" I asked jokingly.

"Yeah, looks that way! This place is unbelievable isn't it?" he answered. We spent a little time looking around inspecting all the different plants. The food all looked like it had been grown under the midnight sun in Alaska. The zucchini squash was the size of logs, the fruit looked like the kind that would charm a snake down from the tree of knowledge in the Garden of Eden.

"Look at these strawberries Kat. Holy crap, can you believe how big they are? Wouldn't Gram and Mr. Mac be jealous if they could see them?" Ronnie called out. I stopped drooling over the giant tomatoes I had been looking at and joined him to see how big they were. Everything in the hydra farm was like that. You could feed a whole city with the things we saw growing here and they did.

When the kids were finished with things in the hydra farm we returned to the dock, the boat and headed towards the inner city again. Shi asked the boat driver to pull in at the power mines. We docked the boat and piled off onto the pier. Shi led the way and we followed, he entered an opening and took the stairs down. He led us down a long ways, probably at least seven or eight stories worth of stairs: this had a small deja'vu feeling with the stairs we found in Australia. They looked ancient and were carved in solid rock just as the others had been. Finally we got to the bottom and got our first look at the generator complex.

Never in my life could I have dreamed up anything the size of these crystals. They were the size of the Washington Monument and there were dozens of them. Ronnie and I looked out and down across the area where the crystals grew and worked. It was like watching thunderstorms dance around the clouds on a stormy night. I could see what looked like lightening shooting up and down the inside of the crystals only occasionally hidden from view by the cloudiness of the crystals themselves. It was a little like looking into the science project of a mad scientist.

It was hypnotizing to watch the light show inside the crystals. At times the bolts of electricity arched and displayed all the colors of the rainbow. There were what looked like explosions of color in the cloudy areas of the giant spears of crystal that reminded me of pictures I saw about the Universe and the colors of space. An old saying Gram has said more than once came bouncing into my thoughts "as above, so below." This certainly looked like a little piece of the cosmos right here in all these crystal spears. This was what lighted the sky of Atlantis, powered the air supply and made everything work and function so well.

Ronnie immediately started asking Shi all sorts of questions about how the whole thing worked, typical guy stuff. Their words faded away from my brain as I watched the electrical light show in front of me. What a magical place this was. This was so amazing and yet in some ways, so simple how it all worked. Simple science is what I first heard Shi say to Ronnie. If this was simple science, it was certainly on a grand scale.

We didn't stay too much longer before Shi said we better go if we were to get home on time.

"Don't want to be late and have anyone get in trouble this trip. Our time is starting to run out, we should go." Shi stated.

Ronnie's parents were pretty strict so it was a good point. There was so much I wanted to hear from Ronnie when we could sit and talk. I would go nuts if he got put on restriction for being late and we couldn't get together to talk. He hadn't uttered one word about what he experienced during his vision quest and I was dying to know what happened to him.

We both looked back as we neared the stairs where we wouldn't be able to see the crystals any longer. What a vision to have witnessed, I wanted to lock this picture into my brain forever.

The ride back to the arrival/departure chamber was quick and we were in the water and on the way back home in no time. The swim home was beautiful and a wonder to watch as always. We reached our beach, said our goodbyes, Ronnie and I watched the kids dip back under the water for their return home. We just stood there for a minute, trying to bring ourselves back to this reality. It was something of a cultural shock to come home after spending time with the merkids. They lived such simple, basic lives and didn't have all the noise and distractions of our world. They could have had computers and televisions like us they had the technology for it. They chose instead to meditate, read and work together in study groups or farm their food and keep their environment clean. They had every kind of trade and skill that we had and they used them in ways to better life for all. Everything wasn't focused around the bottom line or profit margins.

Ronnie and I slowly shook off the mellow gaze we had on the water in front of us and turned to head home. He didn't say much as we walked towards our street but once we were there he turned and told me,

"We need to get together with the rest of the girls. Cookie too this time, she's the seventh, missing sister. We all need to get together and talk. There so much I want to tell you all."

As we neared his house he said goodbye, ran over and up onto his porch and then inside. I heard the screen door slam shut as I headed towards my own house. I'd check in with Becka via phone because they were still out of town and see what was up with her plant search. First I would check in with Cookie on her search progress. Cookie was the only one of us at this point who didn't know anything about the merkids and all our little adventures. It wasn't easy keeping secrets but we promised the merkids we wouldn't tell others unless they allowed it.

Maybe I should check in with Bach and make sure it was okay before Ronnie had his meeting with all of us. Becka wouldn't be home for another day so I'd have to deal with getting Bach's approval on my own. As soon as I got home I went to my room, sat on the side of my bed and pulled out my opal. A couple rocks fell to the floor as I did. Wow, they must have worked their way into my pocket when I was stuck in the cave, wiggling around trying to get loose. I hadn't picked up any rock souvenirs this time so I was pleased to see a couple great pieces of lava rock to add to my collection.

As soon as I picked up the lava rocks and put them in my collection bowl I sat again with my opal and heard Bach's words, loud and clear, He said it was okay, to first get Cookie's promise of secrecy and then Ronnie could fill her in on what ever he wanted. He confirmed to me that Cookie was the seventh sister, Ronnie was correct in the disclosure he had made to me.

Wow, wait until we told the rest of the girls about Cookie being the seventh sister. This was going to blow Cookie's mind and I couldn't wait to hear what she'd have to say about it all. Cookie wasn't one to think about what she said before she said it. Things just popped right out of her mouth and she usually didn't ever regret what she had said no matter, how matter of fact or to the point it was. Plus she often had a sarcastic tone to a lot of what she said.

Next I needed to call Becka and see how her plant search was going, I'd call or go see Cookie later. I couldn't wait to talk with Becka, I hated it when we weren't together on these adventures: she was like my sister in real life we shared everything and didn't have any secrets between us.

When I called she answered by saying,

"Okay, tell me everything Kat. I've been dying, sitting here all day waiting for you to get home and call me. I love my Aunt Grace but this is so boring when I would have rather been with you and the rest of the kids instead. Its just adults all sitting around the kitchen table or out on the front porch talking about everything under the sun. I've been thinking, wouldn't it blow their minds if I could tell them what we've been doing lately!" she giggles as she finished her sentence.

"Yeah, it would blow anybody's mind but do you think they'd ever believe us?" I asked.

"Yeah I don't know, I mean I think they'd want to believe us but it would sound like a pretty wild story. I think I'd have to prove it to them." she answered back. "So tell me what happened and how did it all go?"

So for the next half hour I told her all the little details and explained we already had Bach's approval to get Cookie's oath and then let her into our little circle. I told her Ronnie wouldn't talk about his quest until we were all together but he said he had so much to tell us and I couldn't wait to hear it all. Then I asked her when she was coming home. Maybe we could get things lined up. Finally I asked if she'd had any luck with her plant search yet?

"Oh yeah, I found it early this morning. I was so excited to hear about your trip with Ronnie I almost forgot my other excitement. It looks like England is the next destination. It's the only place I could find anything about it. It was a plant used in sacred ceremonies back during the days when Stone Henge was built so it should be somewhere in the valleys near it," she answered, "We won't be home until tomorrow, late afternoon. Maybe we can get together with Cookie after dinner and then have the big pow-wow with Ronnie and the others. Talk to them and see if that would work for them and let me know later. Okay?"

"Okay, I'll take care of everything. Talk to you later Becka." As soon as I hung up I raced in to get a clean shower and feel the hot water washing all the dirt and grime off me. It always felt so good to get home. Things like hot water, a clean bath and bed to sleep in with fresh clean sheets, I never appreciated what a luxury they all could be.

After getting cleaned up I had dinner with my folks and watched a little television with my dad. Life was good and I had so much to be happy about. I never once sat and tried to ponder what I would be doing if we hadn't met the Merkids. I was getting wrapped up in something so much bigger than I could even begin to realize at that moment but I was happy for now and that's all that matter today.

The next day I got together with Ronnie, updated him on Becka's family plans and when we could try to get everyone together. Next I stopped to check in with Cookie and see if she had found her plant yet. She and the other girls were hard at the search when I stopped by her house. No luck yet but they were putting all their time and energy into the search. Bunny and Amy both tried to corner me and see what had happened with Ronnie and the trip to Mt. Shasta. All I could tell them was we'll all find out together. Ronnie's lips would be sealed until we were all together.

I didn't think the hours would ever pass as I waited for Becka to get home: I was ready to explode when I finally saw their car pull down the street. I was up and out of my chair where I could see their car pulling in before they could bring the car to a stop out in their front driveway. It was quickly decided we would all get together when we'd all had dinner. We planned to meet at Bunny's house because her parents were going out for dinner and we could talk without worrying who might over hear what we had to say.

Becka and I would go get Cookie and talk with her on the walk over to Bunny's. If we could get Cookie to believe us then promise to keep our secret then Ronnie would be able to tell us all about his vision quest and whatever other secrets he was shown that let him know Cookie was the seventh sister. I knew this was going to be a lot for Cookie to take in. We'd all met the merkids and been with them, seen what they could do, been on adventures with them and heard about the guardians. All of this at one time might be a little harder to accept and believe, especially for Cookie. Being one of eight kids, Cookie was used to just about everything that could happen with kids but this was going to be a first for her.

Becka started,

"Cookie I know you're going to have a hard time believing what I'm about to tell you but before I even tell you, you have to promise never and I do mean never, to tell anyone else what we're going to tell you. Even if you decide not to believe us, you still have to promise never to tell anyone what we say. If you don't give me your word, I can't say anything else."

"What the crap are you two pulling now? What do you mean I have to promise never to tell anyone a word of what you want to tell me? What is this suppose to be? Or maybe I should be asking, what in the heck have you two done? That's it, isn't it? You two have done something really bad and you need help to stay out of trouble?" Cookie asked.

"No it's nothing like that. It's just we know when we tell you, you're going to have a really hard time believing us but I want you to know we can't tell you anything unless you give us your promise first. It's easy. You know you can trust us. You know we don't lie, you can believe what we say. So give us your promise. Okay." I told her.

"Okay, I give you my solemn oath never to repeat what you're about to tell me with the penalty of death. How's that? Is that dramatic enough for you both?" she said a little sarcastically.

"Let's hurry and get to Bunny's so we can all tell her and get some help trying to convince her," Becka said to me. "I'm sure this isn't going to be easy."

She grabbed Cookie's hand and started to pull her in the direction of Bunny's house.

"Come on Cookie, the sooner we get there, the sooner we can try to explain everything to you." I told her as I grabbed her other hand and tried to help Becka get her going.

"You two are something else. This better be worth it or you'll never hear the end of it from me," She said as she finally started to move forward with us.

They were all there when the three of us walked into the room.

"Did she promise and give her oath yet?" Ronnie asked.

"Yes, I made the stupid oath and promised never to repeat whatever nonsense you all have to tell me. So this better be good. Spill your guts and spill them now." Cookie ordered.

Cookie was a little older than the rest of us and some times she treated us like we were children compared to her. This was one of those times. Cookie walked over and sat down on the couch. The rest of us gathered around her and we all started to talk at the same time.

"Wait a minute. How about one at a time you tell me what you have to say? Or one of you step up and just tell me everything," she cried out.

"Okay Cookie, I'll tell you how it all started and then the others can tell you their part." Becka told her, "Kat and I were at the beach one day and say two kids out in the water playing and splashing in the surf.

Suddenly we saw tails, you know, tails like fish have. At first we didn't believe our own eyes but Kat and I called out to them and we waded out into the water and talked with them. They were Merkids it turns out."

"Merkids? What in the heck is a Merkid?" Cookie asked.

"Merkids are half kid and half fish. In this case they were a girl and a boy from the waist up and a fish tail from the waist down." Becka told her.

"Yeah right Becka. What fairy tale are you trying to tell me?" Cookie asked really sarcastically.

"Well you don't have to believe me but I can take you to meet them and you can see for yourself just like all the rest of us have. They are willing to meet with you if that's what it takes to get you to believe. Each one of us has been with the Merkids and we have been on a mission with them to find and bring back the plant specimens we've been searching for. This whole thing with the seven sacred plants we've been trying to find has to do with a need the Merkids have to produce a cure for their last generation. I know,"

"Wait a minute, you said the kids are trying to find a cure? Since when do kids find cures for anything," Cookie asked.

"Well the thing is this, the merkids are from the lost sunken city of Atlantis and they"

"Hold on right there," Cookie almost yelled, "What's this crap about sunken city and Atlantis? Are you guys doing drugs or what? This is getting pretty wild are you all going to sit there and try to tell me you've met merkids from the lost city of Atlantis? I think it's time I head home." She stood up like she was getting ready to leave and Ronnie walked over and said,

"You really need to sit back down Cookie there's even more we have to tell you. You just have to know, we're not making this up. Surprisingly Cookie did as he said and sat back down.

"What else could you possibly say to top this one? "She asked.

"Well, maybe we need to explain a little more before we try to tell you the second part of the story. The merkids lost all the adults from some disease and that's why they need the sacred plants we've been trying to help them find again up here in our world. The kids don't have a lot of time left before they're all gone, unless the plants help them find the cure they need.

Each of us has been on a trip with the kids to find the plants. Nothing we could say to you now could prepare you for the things the kids can do and what they are capable of. They are able to bend time and lots of things like that we've all read about but always thought couldn't happen or didn't exist." Ronnie tried to explain.

"I'm just not buying this one you guys. What's the deal are you filming this for you-tube? I don't plan on seeing myself on America's Funniest Home Videos either." Cookie exclaimed.

Amy and Bunny both spoke up,

"We've seen them and been with the merkids too."

Bunny looked at Amy and turned back to Cookie to say,

"I didn't believe it at first either Cookie but trust us, life is stranger than fiction and there was an Atlantis, there still is but if we don't finish helping the Merkids it won't last much longer. There are hundreds of them but their time is running out. If we don't find the last two plants, if the cure doesn't work, it'll be the end of them and their incredible city under the sea."

"So why are you all telling me about this? Cookie asked.

"That's a tricky question to try and answer." Ronnie volunteered. "First I have to tell you a little story, about a vision quest I was on yesterday inside Mt. Shasta, out in California and before you start to say anything. Yes Kat and I were both in California yesterday. The kids bend time and you can go places with them and while you're gone, the time seems to stand still back home in comparison to the time it feels like you're gone. Bunny, Amy and Becka have all been gone on little adventures with the merkids while we've been home tracking down the sacred plants we've been helping them find.

While we were gone, I was told I had a vision quest I had to perform, which was somewhat related to being with the merkids. Plus, somewhat another entire story line and they were just part of the first story that got me where I needed to be for it to all happen. It's like puzzle pieces fitting together and with each piece bigger pictures emerge. I do know this sounds really wild and crazy but let me finish explaining. If you're still with me, I want you to know I understand the next part is going to sound even crazier and wilder than the first part did.

There was a time billions of years ago that the six of us, along with one of the merkids called Mu, were souls or spirits living in the cosmos. To be more specific we were living in the Pleiades, a star system in the constellation called Taurus. It was our decision as a group of souls to come to Earth to settle and begin life."

"OH YEAH. RIGHT!!" Cookie burst out as she nodded her head like she was agreeing with everything he was saying but not really.

"Cookie, this is as serious as I've ever been and I'm telling you, this is all true. Just let me finish." He scolded here." The Earth was very different then, the moon was so close to the planet our days were less than four hours long and the tides were monstrous. Back then we could go from the physical to the spiritual at will we weren't locked into our bodies like we are now. It took billions of years for things to get to the point that our main settlements Atlantis and Lemuria were falling apart and the new world erupted into seven new continents. Today in science classes they call that part Pangaea. It was at that point we each took some followers and set out to begin seven new settlements and the new world orders."

Cookie looked at the rest of us, as if to ask without words "Are you all serious?"

"A lot of this is new to us too Cookie. It seems Ronnie got more information during his vision quest. We've heard some of the prophecy from the merkids but not all that much yet." I told her. "It was on the trip to Tibet that the merkids started to explain about us all being the original seven sisters of the Pleiades and that there's some prophecy we all are meant to come together to do. We're having a hard time with all this prophecy stuff ourselves but because of all the other stuff, we have to wonder if it's not true. They know so much. Wait until you meet them and experience some time with them. You'll see what we mean. They're such an intelligent group and they're all young like us."

"Okay, so you're all saying you've seen and gone places with these merkids. They're from Atlantis, the lost sunken city of myth and fable. They can bend time and you've all been traveling all over the world with them searching and bringing back the sacred planets we've been looking for on the Internet. If they get all the plants, they will be able to find a cure for some strange disease that's been killing their older generations. Then to top it all off, they have some story about the six of us and some merkid girl being seven star sisters who have some ancient prophecy to fulfill but no one knows exactly what that is yet. Does that sum it up so far?" she asked with heavier sarcasm then before. "By the way, how do the fish kids go places with you? Didn't people notice their fish tails when you were on the buses or planes?"

"Don't be like that Cookie. The kids lose their tails when they come out of the water and they can walk around just like you or me. "Becka told her. "In the next day or two we'll be going to meet with the kids again. This time you'll have to come with us and see for yourself. Maybe if you can get away, you could go with them and see for yourself what it's like in the under world. They have breathing crystals and we swim all over with them, without a problem. We've been to Peru, Australia, Tibet and Egypt so far."

"So far you've been to five foreign countries and California and what's with the under worlds you're talking about? How did you get to all these places?" Cookie asked or maybe I should say demanded to know.

"Mostly we swam but after we get places we do a lot of walking." I answered her. "I've been cooked hiking in the heat of the Australian out-back, wrestled with a giant croc, fried under a scorching sun in the Egyptian desert, been lost in tunnels and bat caves under the great pyramids, almost died by dehydration when we got locked in a crystal chamber in Peru, just about got my body destroyed jumping between dimensions in Tibet and had to crawl my way out of Volcanic tunnels at Mt. Shasta. You don't scare me any more Cookie. If you don't want to believe us for now that's okay. You keep our secret and we'll introduce you to the kids so you can see for yourself."

The others tried to talk with her a little and finally she agreed to listen to the rest of what Ronnie had to tell us.

"I saw everything while I was in the spirit wheel. I saw the beginning of time, the Earth being born and evolving. I watched the destructions that killed the dinosaurs and the civilizations come and go all over the world. I witnessed and watched man forget who he really was and I traveled the cosmos.

I saw the Pillars of life, a place in space where stars are born. Can you imagine being inside the cocoons of the Universes butterflies before they spread their wings and fly? I landed on the rings around Jupiter and Saturn. I felt the heat of the red planet of Mars. I smelled the gases and followed the seven rays of color, the energy rays of the cosmos as they traveled from the other universes down through the black holes to each of our planets and through the stars and constellations down into Earth and each of us. It was like following the nerves or veins of the cosmos traveling and from one end of the Universes to the other. Each world was a world of it's own and yet they were all connected, forever forged together as one.

I saw the six of us along with Mu, in spirit form. I relived the events as we traveled from our home in the Pleiades to Earth and all the incarnations we've all had up until now. That's how I recognized Cookie as our seventh sister. Only part of the prophecy was revealed to me before the earthquake started. I know that we have a mission to start something new again. There are so many layers to the Universe and so many other worlds out there. I saw planets that no one has ever seen before and felt their pull.

I never believed in astrology as much as when I could feel the tugs and pulls of the planets and the energy of the seven rays. There are so many invisible powers in the Universe that we move to, sometimes only feeling and experiencing what only a few understand. You would have to have been there with me to understand because mere words can't explain it all.

"I wondered what you'd be able to tell us. I knew something big must have happened when I saw your body so high overhead levitating in the upper chamber space over the spirit wheel. You had a real vision like they always talked about in Indian legends and folklore. I'm so jealous right now." I told him.

"Tell us more about what you saw, what was the seven rays thing you were talking about?" I asked

"Everything is energy. Energy moves at different speeds and vibrations, the speed and vibration also creates color and represents music notes. The planets direct the rays through their own energy field feeding it and increasing it's power and force. The colors and rays of light instill into us its values and virtues. The seven rays are something like the veins or nerves of the Universe bringing us the energy from all the other forces out there on a daily basis. It helps to direct us and renew us. It's what keeps us going and energizes our own chakras. It's a connection to all and the one, through our spirit or soul. All the planets and stars out there also have a soul or spirit." He told us.

"Well, I'm still not buying all this, you guys are definitely up to something, there's been a few times lately that I wondered about you and what was going on but I think you'll have to show me if you want me to believe any of this crazy story you're telling." Cookie informed us.

"Okay Cookie, the next time the kids are here, we'll get you and go meet with them. If you see that part is true, maybe you can take the rest on faith and believe it all." Becka told her.

"Well, we'll see what we see I guess," she said as she stood up, "I need to get home so I'll see you nuts later. Don't go visiting any parallel Universes while I'm gone." She laughed as she turned and walked towards the door.

We all yelled goodbye to her and then turned back to Ronnie to talk and ask more questions.

We were still talking and asking questions when Bunny's parents pulled into the driveway. That was our signal it was time to break up our little group and head home. Becka and I decided to communicate with Bach so they'd know we found the 6th plant and we could make plans about when and who would go this time. We didn't know if we should ask for Cookie to go this time or not. Would she be ready to deal with all this yet? Even once she was able to meet the merkids and see their tails would she need some time to get things straight in her head? Cookie was the most bull headed of all of us. She might need more time to adjust to the new thinking she'd have to do before she'd be ready to go on an adventure with them. We decided to leave that up to Bach to figure out.

When we put our communication opals down after letting Bach know we had found one of the last two plants, we both sat for a few moments before we spoke. Bach wanted to meet first thing in the morning so we didn't have much time to get with Cookie. We needed to call Cookie right away and see if she could make it to the beach so early in the morning with such short notice.

Surprisingly she agreed but added a strict warning to us both,

"This better not be a wild goose chase or some silly joke you all think you're pulling over me, especially if I have to get up that early. You better be there, both of you."

You could tell, without a doubt she still didn't believe us. It was okay, in the morning it would be Cookie with her mouth hanging open. We'd see what she has to say then.

Knowing there was another trip we had to get permission from the adults to spend the day at the beach again. It was a good thing we were usually beach bums every summer or they might have been getting suspicious of us being gone so often. We did our chores and I got permission to stay over night at Becka's because that always made it a little easier to get it together in the mornings for the two of us.

The next morning we were up before the break of dawn having a little fruit for breakfast before we left. We both went to Cookies to see if she was coming. Just as we got to the front of her house she was coming out the front door to meet us.

She slowly closed the door trying not to make any loud noises and came down the steps towards us.

"I've been waiting, watching for you. So lets go meet your merkid friends or do you want to tell me the truth now before you get in any deeper with your joke? You could save yourselves a lot of grief if you fess up now and don't try to drag this out." She shot the words at us like daggers.

"Oh, you'll see, we're not pulling your leg or any jokes either. Lets just get to the beach and try not to be rude with the merkids. Bach and Mu will be there and Bach is not someone you should give a hard time to, he won't understand your sarcasm. They're not like us that way either." I told her.

Becka spoke up,

"We communicated with Bach last night. This morning will just be a meeting with you and them maybe the last trip for the last plant he'll bring you along, if you decided you want to go.

When we get back we'll talk with you more about the adventures we've all already had and you can decide for yourself what you want to do. While we're gone the others are going to try to help you find the last plant. No matter how long it takes, we've got to find the seventh plant because without it the kids are doomed.

Just remember no matter what you're thinking later after you've met the merkids you can't talk to anyone about what you see except Amy, Ronnie or Bunny. You have to keep your solemn oath of secrecy."

"Okay, Okay!! I'll remember!" she answered with a lot of disbelief and doubt still in her attitude.

We walked the rest of the way to the beach in silence. You could feel Cookies vibrations of disbelief. She was radiating with a' You're never going to hear the end of this' aura. The sun was coming up over the beach as we arrived.

"Okay, so where are they?" Cookie asked as she scanned the area of the beach on front of us.

""They will be here. Just wait a couple minutes. They don't wear watches and we just agree to meet around sunrise." Becka told her.

We stood and waited, watching for them to break the surface of the water out in front of us. The tide was on the way out so we walked a little closer to the waters edge to scan the horizon. Usually the kids were already here waiting on us. This wasn't helping with Cookie's doubting us, and what we had been telling her.

We had only been waiting about ten minutes when Cookie started getting irritated and she threatened to leave.

"Okay, I think the joke is over, no merkids! Time for me to go back to my warm bed."

"No, you can't leave Cookie. They'll be here. You just have to wait a couple more minutes. I'm sure they're coming. "Becka begged her.

They went back and forth for another minute or two before we all heard the sound of the water splash as three faces came through the surface.

We all stopped talking and turned to see what or who was there. Cookie looked the most surprised. We of course knew the kids would come.

"Hi guys." I called out to them as I reached around to take Cookies hand and start to tug her out into the water to meet them.

She hesitated but didn't fight me on it. She came out into the water willingly enough. As we approached the kids I told them,

"This is our friend Cookie. Cookie this is Bach, Shi and Mu the merkids we've been telling you about."

Mu giggled a little and splashed her tail, sending water onto Cookies arms. She did it just enough that Cookie could see her tail not to really splash her with the water.

"So, Cookie, it appears you are the disbeliever of the group. Let me assure you, we are, as your friends have told you, Merkids from Atlantis. That of course is a name they have given us. There are many ancient arts and knowledge we have and can use that your world has forgotten. We wished to meet with you, as there is a destiny we all have together and you need to awaken the knowing within you to perform your part." Bach told her and as he spoke, Shi and Mu handed us our pouches and crystal breathing gear and earplugs.

"With the crystal ear plugs your friends are able to communicate with each other and us while we are under water. The larger crystals create a small breathing mask so they can swim under water with us all over the world, through the Oceans or the under world passageways. With these crystals they are able to function just the same as we do."

Cookie stood there in the water with us and never saying one word back to Bach. She looked like she was shocked or stunned. She listened and slightly nodded her head as if to say she understood or followed what he was saying. Finally Becka told her,

"We've got to go now Cookie. We'll be back soon. Go find the last plant for us." Becka told her.

"Okay" she answered back. She didn't say or utter another word or even move.

The five of us dipped down under the surface of the water and started to swim away. Cookie stood there and watched us go. I was sure she could see the kids' tails even better as we swam away. She stood and watched maybe wondering if we'd have to resurface for air but we never did.

Slowly she turned and started to walk back up the beach. She didn't get more than 20-25 feet before she turned and looked back towards the water. Suddenly she collapsed, like the shock of what she had just seen had knocked the wind out of her. She sat there on the sand slightly shaking her head trying to sort it all out in her mind.

Seeing is believing!

Adventure #6
England

The five of us were shooting through the ocean on a mission. We had skirted around the Bermuda triangle again as we worked our way up the east coast of Florida and out into the Atlantic. The Ocean was a vast space with worlds all it's own. The water here was a little colder than the Pacific Ocean but no less interesting. We were headed for England and the 6th sacred plant. Today we swam with confidence and a feeling of coming to the end or close to the end of a long journey. Once we had the sixth plant we would only need to find the seventh and last one then we'd be done. We were all feeling confident from the other success stories we'd been able to achieve so far. Becka and I, both felt like soldiers in a war again mankind's survival and we were seeing the world, while we severed. How much better could it get?

As we approached the land on the other side of the world near Ireland, we started to swim over an area that reminded me of other places and some of the stories I had seen of lost and ancient cities now under water. We could see things that clearly showed straight lines, cut blocks and occasionally a carved design or two., worn well into the rock surface. I kept looking and wondering about what it could be. England, Scotland and Ireland were on the other side of the world and I knew very little about any of them and I was looking forward to seeing this side of the Ocean. There was so much history that took place in England and I wondered if we would see London or any of the cities.

I brought myself back to the ruins I could see in front of me now. Clearly this place had been something somewhere back in history. I couldn't help but wonder what it was or what they called it when it was above the water.

Bach answered me,

"Now, this is a place called Hy-Brasil by the people in the upper world. You may have heard about it in Celtic or Irish myths. The myths tell of an Island that rose from the mists once every seven years ruled by priests of unusual height. Many people believe it was a fairy island, others believed it was Atlantis or at least part of Atlantis. The latter are correct. From the earlier days before the final destructions, Atlantis was located where the two Americas and Europe came together. So all three areas were part of Atlantis before the first destructions. Not Atlantis the city but Atlantis the continent. Hy-Brasil formed and relocated from the first of the three major destructions that finally sunk our city. Can you feel the energy from the rock? This is the older, higher vibration of Atlantis hidden and lost here in the Irish mists."

Wow, I'd never heard of this place before. Never even heard the name Hy-Brasil. Who would have thought we'd swim over part of the old Atlantis while we were swimming near Ireland and headed for England? I wondered if Bach had been drawn here like a bird in flight headed home? Or maybe more appropriately, like salmon swimming back upstream. It was a thought that tickled my mind as I looked for more detail in the block and stone below us. Was this really an even older piece of Atlantis than the city we had visited so many times now?

Bach headed deeper into the ruins and seemed to be looking for something.

"This way." I heard his words and we all followed him. Apparently he was looking for something and had just found it, another under world passageway. So we followed him down and into the new cave network of under world passageways. I wondered if they had maps somewhere that showed all these under world entrances and exits? It was amazing to me how many passageways there were and how they connected back and forth across and through the Earth. Did all the grid lines mark passageways? Could Bach read them like a bird could read the wind currents?

"It'll be easier going inland through this passageway. This way we should be able to come up close to Stonehenge in the river of Avon. Stay close together this passageway has many twists and turns. It reads like a plate of spaghetti" he announced to our little group.

Well for my part I was holding on tight. It was up to Shi who had me in tow, to keep up with Bach and Becka. For a change it was Mu who had the last position in our little caravan of swimmers. The stone was almost black which made it all seem a little darker and the walls of the cave closer in. I couldn't reach out and touch the walls but it still felt like a small tight space and I never did like close places. Hopefully this part would be over soon and we could get back up on solid ground. England was a place I had never thought of going to or visiting but if I thought about it, I guess I had never thought of visiting several of the places the merkids had taken us.

This would be an interesting adventure. I had read a lot about Stonehenge and always wondered what it had been built for as well as how it was used. I liked all the theories I had heard or read about; some people thought only that it had some religious purpose others that Aliens had something to do with it and still others thought it had some higher consciousness purpose that the energy of the Earth's grid and Ley Lines empowered the place making it easier to attain higher spiritual awareness. That it acted like a gateway to the higher realms of consciousness and the astral planes.

Thinking about England now I wondered about all the old tales that had been read to us or we'd heard about in school. King Arthur and the Round Table, Sir Lancelot, the Druids and the mystical magical old wizard Merlin. When Shi heard my thoughts and Merlin's name he informed me,

"Merlin was once a great leader of Atlantis. He has been in many of histories most challenging eras. The stories about him were amazing. He was a master of the Universal energies and had a command of all the natural forces in this world as well."

"How do you know all these things Shi?" I couldn't help myself, the question just popped out of my thoughts, before I had time to think about it.

"Merlin's energy still lingers here and the Akashic records are there in the cosmos for anyone to read. Everything that has ever been or will ever be is energy and you can read energy, it never dies. The records are much like your radio waves. If you can tune into the right frequency, you can access all the information of all the ages, past, present or future. Bach is the best reader we have but I too am a very good reader. In your world I could compare it to you Googling something on your Internet. What ever you wish to know, you ask and the answer is given. All information is there for the asking. I'm sure you remember this as we have talked about it before. It's the same for me now. I'm just reading the Universal energy."

Wow, I thought, these guys were always making things so simple. If only it was that simple for us to tune in to that frequency.

"It is that simple, you need only to go within and listen. You fill your world with too much noise and activity. Few seldom make time to meditate or try to find the silence and space within. We will sit sometime and I will work with you to find your inner source. We will try to fine tune your chakras and turn up your spirit so you might taste the stillness and peace of the Cosmos. If you can do that, you can access the Akashic Records for yourself whenever you wish."

Mu chimed in adding her thoughts,

"Haven't you ever noticed being in nature seems so tranquil and you experience peace and comfort from the beauty and natural sounds of it? That is the first step to finding your inner peace and accessing that higher frequency. You must first quiet your own mind and ego to be able to channel into the higher dimensions of energy. Sometimes the vortexes and energy of a place can help to raise your energy. Remember some of the feelings we have all experienced in the different places we have been to together? The energy of some places is more closely matched to each of us. How do you think birds and fish can zero in on home when they must travel half way around the world to find it? With time you will learn to recognize the energy of the planets and the seven rays. You are starting to learn and you will learn more later."

It was a very interesting topic of conversation as we swam the last few miles and finally entered the river. We stayed low in the water not wanting to be noticed by the boats and travelers headed inland. Bach led us over to the side of the river once he found a quiet spot where we could go ashore unnoticed.

My first impression was that England looked like a beautiful post card picture. There were rolling hills and trimmed rows of trees with a few sheep and horses out in the pastures. I could see off in the distance what looked to be a town or city with the rooftops showing against the background next to the blue sky. There were spots of color here and there, mostly lavenders, purples and white. Everything I could see reminded me of storybook pictures I had seen. I wouldn't have been surprised to see an elf or fairy jump out of the bushes anytime.

This was a beautiful place with a very magical feeling in the air. I was already beginning to feel the sparkling sensation of electricity dancing across my whole body and I could tell Becka was feeling the same she was as busy as me looking and taking everything in but she also kept looking at the goose bumps on her arms and then looking to check out everything in another direction.

"I know this place Kat. I've been here before. The rolling chalk downlands are just as they were then. The valleys and vales are just as lovely, in fact they are more lush and beautiful than they were, time has been good to England. It was warmer here then even if it did rain more. I loved it here. Can you smell the lavender in the air?" Becka asked with a matter of fact sound to her voice.

"Becka, is it happening to you? Are you remembering the past and some other life or time?" I asked her as I watched the expressions changing on her face as she talked about what she remembered.

"I know I was a Moonraker, I just don't know who or when yet. I feel an electricity tingling my skin, is that anything like what you felt in Egypt?" she asked.

"Yeah it was something sort of like that until it all got strange and I started feeling the other personalities. I wonder if you'll get that too?"

Mu and the boys were taking in the surroundings and discussing which direction we would take off for next. They were busy and it gave Becka and me a chance to talk for a minute.

"What's a Moonraker?" I asked.

She turned and looked at me as if I had asked some stupid question.

"Well silly, it's a nick name for all of us from Wiltshire. It was a silly thing. There was a story about some smugglers who were hiding their barrels of brandy from the local constable in a pond and to keep him from seeing the barrels through the water, the smugglers raked the surface of the water, saying they were trying to rake in what they thought was a round of cheese, which turned out to be the reflection of the moon. The constable thought them mad or the very least, simple yokels. So began the nickname for the people who lived here. He thought us all daffy and crazy and started to call us Moonrakers." She told me.

"Were you a smuggler Becka?" I asked.

"Of course not silly. Well at least I'm pretty sure I wasn't. It doesn't feel like I was. I don't know for sure. Heck, I don't even know where that Moonraker story just came from. It just seemed to flow right out of some deep dark place I don't even remember. Now I'm not sure of anything."

Before we could focus on anything else, about how Becka was feeling, the kids said it was time to head out. We needed to get to Stonehenge and start looking for the plant. With luck, this would be a quick easy trip. It didn't seem like we could cook under this English sun or have to fight off wild, dangerous creatures: the wildest thing we should run into shouldn't be much more than a horse, cow or maybe a few sheep in this beautiful country setting.

As we headed north we started to walk away from the farms and cottages moving into an open area of flat land. There were rolling hills off in the distance but for now this looked like easy goings to me. I was really happy and excited about that because it sure beat climbing mountains and some of our other travels. This was going to be like a walk in the park and I was totally enjoying myself as we headed off to begin this leg of our journey.

We walked through open fields and talked a little about the Ley lines and the energy they held. I could feel the extra energy that Bach talked about as we walked the distance from the Avon to Stonehenge. It seemed to me to be getting stronger the closer we got. I kept watching Becka to see if she was experiencing anything strange or different. She seemed to be enjoying the walk and was smiling a lot as she took in the scenery. She looked and seemed very content so I tried not to interrupt her solitude as we walked. Stonehenge was up ahead of us and that thought gave me mountains of mixed thoughts to think about.

Now Stonehenge was a place I had read a lot about, even seen a few specials on it as well. None of that had been as informative as listening to Bach explain it all as we walked across the English countryside. He told us,

"Stonehenge is just one, of many places like it, found all over the world. The earlier civilizations did most of their gateways in the circular patterns, it adds to the energy and the vortex action. The stone helps to carry the sound and vibrations get intensified as they travel through it. Can you hear the hum?" he asked.

So you understand, even in Atlantis we built many things, including our main city in the circular pattern just for the extra energy it helped to produce, like negative ions in the atmosphere. The circle is a cosmic energy shape and one that appears throughout the Cosmos. It's the shape of all the stars and planets throughout the galaxies. It is in fact the shape of the galaxies, of wormholes and black holes. All energy rotates in a circular pattern. Circles are symbolic signs of power and higher energies at work.

If you then build your circular pattern with stone or surrounded it with giant stones, you would amplify the energy because of the crystal and gold in the stone. The more layers you add to the strength of a vortex area, the stronger the energy of the vortex becomes. The stronger the energy, the higher the intuitive energy inside it, so you can see the people who take advantage of this energy and live within it or even near it's pattern are the most open and naturally tuned into the Universe. If you then, build your temples and structures where the dragon lines cross each other or where there are lesser sacred tracks that cross each other you will build and store different energies.

Those were simpler times when Stonehenge was built and man didn't complicate things. Your world is so full of things that literally suck the energy right out of you; you don't realize all the little things that add up to a large loss of the intuitive and the natural energy of the soul or spirit. The spirit was much stronger back then, just as the aura of the planet was; now Earth and man are both weakening through abuse, of their esoteric energies and resources.

All vortexes are gateways to the other dimensions. Not all dimensions are horizontal they are also vertically inclined."

Bach's words and information, as always were a lot to take in. I was never great with higher sciences but somehow Bach made it all sound so simple and easy to explain. Most of the time I found myself shaking my head, at how simple he made it seem and I could actually understand it all. Maybe I should ask him to come help me with my class's next school year, it would probably improve my grades tremendously.

Becka seemed to be in a world of her own. I was sure she could hear our conversation but she didn't take part in it. She seemed to be lost in her own thoughts with a far away look in her eyes. I wondered what she was thinking. I remembered in Egypt how I felt when I was remembering and seeing visions of my past and I wondered if I had this look in my eyes then?

"Hey Becka, you okay?" I asked her as I nudged her shoulder with mine to get her attention.

"Hun? Oh yeah I'm okay Kat. Just lost in some strange thoughts, wondering where they're coming from." She answered.

"You want to talk about them?" I questioned her.

"Don't think I'm ready for that just yet. Let me feel this out a little longer and see where it goes. We can talk about it all later."

"Okay." I could understand and respect her feelings and knew she'd talk when she was ready. Maybe what ever was happening to her wasn't freaking her out as much as what happened to me made me feel. I hoped she could handle it, what ever it was but I knew she would talk to me, when she was ready.

I turned my conversation back to the merkids and gave Becka her own space.

"So back to the Ley Lines," I started. "The way you explain it all, I almost think the earth must have many bodies and sets of grid work that encircle it. There's one network that's sort of like our nervous system another one that is like our gland system and how it helps take care of our bodies. There's one that's like our circulation system pumping the life-blood of the planet. Some places are more like organs with the higher energy they produce and many of them connect to the others just as our organs connect to the rest of the body. Earths systems are all invisible to the human eye just like our auras are invisible to most people but no less real or powerful because of it."

"Yes, you're on the right track. Then once you understand this, think about the galaxy and all the planets working in a similar way, all the planets are connected by the seven rays which are pure energy connecting all that is." Shi answered me.

"All the worlds and galaxies of the universe and cosmos are connected. Man hasn't even begun to understand the worlds we live in. Your world is like a group of children in the first years of their education just starting to discover and understand. A time will come when more will be available, when you will be enlightened and understanding will follow." Bach added.

"So what do you mean a time will come? What do you know? Won't you tell us? We can keep your secrets. We've already been doing that, how about one more?" I asked.

"There is nothing I can tell you. When we have the cure and the guardians return, we will talk with them. They will have much to tell you." Bach returned.

As I turned my head forward again, I saw it. There was Stonehenge in the distance. You couldn't mistake it for anything else. It stood there alone, in its solitude with noting else in the field near by. My eyes stayed glued to the huge stones. Wow even at this distance the site was a marvel to take in. I could imagine on a cloudy, rainy, dreary day how strange and intimidating this place could feel. I couldn't wait to get closer and see if anything felt different and to see the ancient site up close. At first glance though I didn't see any color or flowers blooming. I wondered if we'd find our plant easily or this would be a major hunt?

We all walked a little faster, in silence now that we could see the stones up ahead, each of us lost in our own thoughts about the stones and this place. Becka had been especially quiet but I decided it was best to let her talk when she was ready and not try to push her. I was pretty excited to be able to see yet another ancient wonder of the world. This place seemed so much more primitive than many of the others we had visited. In fact I think this had to be the simplest and least adorned of any site we had seen so far. Even the Great Pyramid of Giza had layers and a complex of structures built around it. Not to mention all the chambers and passageways inside.

There were no carved designs, no soaring columns, no hieroglyphs painted or carved anywhere just plain solid, flat stone in a simple design and format. It looked more like something the cave man would have put together in its crude, simple, rough-cut design. None of the stones were precisely cut the walls weren't smooth but rough and irregular. I could almost see back in time, when a primitive people were here having ceremonies, detail wouldn't have mattered. It would have been the esoteric value of the energy and the vortex strength that would have been important. I read once that peasants used to bring their seed here to empower it, that it always grew superior plants from seeds that had not been placed in the Stonehenge circle.

Sadly they no longer let the general public go inside the circle of stones. They asked you to respect it with low ropes you could have jumped over but they only allowed special groups inside with permission. In the modern age it seemed more people wanted a piece of the site or wanted to leave their mark, vandalizing the stones in different ways. Sad that it comes to that and so few mess it up for the rest of us. I would have loved to get to the inner circle. I wondered if I could have felt any special energy or power?

I guess I just wondered about everything. I heard a saying or quote once that read, "Wonder and amazement inhabit here." After hearing that one, I always thought, that should be my mantra. I felt that everything was a wonder to behold and I was always amazed with things like this as well as simple things like a butterfly, the color of a leaf, the stars in the sky and just being alive, how it all worked and came into being.

Right now I was totally involved with the site ahead of us. The closer I got the more impressive it got. It wasn't like the great Pyramid of Giza or the Mayan structures I had seen but it was, in its massive size and crude, simple lines, a very imposing site. I wondered again if Becka might be having any visions of times here in her past. She still wasn't saying anything but didn't seem to be lost in space either. Finally we got up to the roped off area and were among a few other people enjoying a visit to the henge. We were all looking around none of us seeing any plants other than grass right now.

I have to admit; I was looking more at the circle and stones than I was for plants. How could anyone be here and not be drawn to the stone and wonder about it's use in the past? I wondered too, who built this place and what did they do here once they finished it? Had there been a time when there was more here and some time in history it was taken away or destroyed? My head was full of questions and I wished I knew the answers.

The boys got my attention back when they started making decisions,

"We'll have to walk out to the more treed areas across the clearing to search for the plants. Clearly there are none here. Maybe we'll get luckier over in the woods." Shi announced as he and Bach headed that way.

Becka finally decided to talk,

"Come on Kat. We've been here before lets just help the kids find the plants. You can come back and stare at the stones later after we find what we came here for."

I turned and looked at her.

"What the heck," I walked over and asked her,

"What do you mean we've been here before? Did you remember something?"

She didn't look at me but rather stared off into the distance and she had that lost look in her eyes again,

"I had a feeling or maybe it was more like a thought, not exactly a memory. I know we've been here. It was definitely a time when we were together. I think we were here when Stonehenge was finished. There were lots of celebrations and feasting, the henge was it's strongest and we were two maidens, dancing and living life to its fullest. I can't feel more than that or break it down more right now. I just believe you and I have danced inside the circle on more than one occasion. I can almost remember the feeling of the energy and I can see you. Your face was a little different than it is today but I know it's you. We were so happy."

"Well that's a lot. So did you get a feeling about what Stonehenge was built for? Can you tell if it was a gateway? Or was it a ceremonial place for religious purposes? Did you pick up what the real purpose of the stone circle was? Were the other kids with us in that lifetime? Did you recognize anyone else?"

She turned her head back again, looking toward the distance, a couple seconds later she told me,

"I know the vortex and energy of the place was stronger then but I can't quite pick up what we were all doing here. I know the energy here opened us and we found a vibration here that resonated with our souls. We were the happiest we could be and we were simple easy loving people." She looked around and saw we weren't keeping up. Watching her look away to remember and then turning her head back towards me to be in the present was trippy to watch. One thing I noticed was that each of us felt the past differently. It was never the same way for any of us on these little adventures. She looked at Shi and Bach walking away from us,

"Lets give it a rest and follow Shi before he has to turn back to come get us."

"Okay but you've got to tell me all the details you did get while we walk." I told her.

Following Shi, who was way out in front of us, we all hiked towards the line of trees off in the distance. During the short hike Becka tried to talk and explain her feelings, telling me many things about the energies she felt in the past at Stonehenge. She said we danced to a rhythm that matched the energies of the vortex and it opened our spirits to soar into the heavens. I wasn't sure exactly what that meant but it sounded wonderful. Sometimes I loved the sound of words as much as what they meant.

As we entered the woods Bach suggested we all stay within site of each other so we fanned out and made a long line to comb through the trees and the small forest area we had entered. Like a CSI team we searched for the plant like it was some lost clue to a murder at a crime scene. That was how we spent the next hours, going from one treed area to another searching. We beat the low ferns and grasses, looked high in the treetops; we rolled over logs and bushed the fallen leaves to check under them. This was not going to be an easy trip, so far no plant and no sign of them. We might have to start talking to the locals and see if anyone knew of the plant we searched for.

We spent the next hours checking everything all around the open fields surrounding Stonehenge. As we walked from each area both Becka and I found ourselves looking back to the henge, dreaming of its possibilities other times and where this adventure was going. We approached another wooded area and turned our attention back to the task at hand.

The trees were strange and different looking in this cropping, nothing like the ones we had seen earlier in our search. The bark was smooth and they looked like the roots of the tree had grown over and all around the trunks, strangling or hugging themselves. It was like looking at the clouds on a warm summer day, if you looked hard enough you could see things in them like faces or animals. It was a little eerie to see what looked like faces in the body of the trees. I almost felt like we were being watched.

"Look how strange and exotic these trees are Kath. Have you ever seen anything like them before?" Becka asked as she ran her hand over the bark of the tree she was standing next to. It was as if we were in some enchanted forest in this last stand of trees. The air seemed so fresh and clean you could almost smell the morning scent of the wildflowers still in the air. Even the light seemed to have more of a golden glow. If I let my imagination run wild, I would have said it felt like a fairies' magical home and the only things missing were a rainbow and maybe a unicorn or two. It was weird how everything about England kept making me think of fairy tales and storybooks I had seen.

"Pretty interesting looking isn't it? Looks like something from a storybook drawing doesn't it?" I answered back. "So far almost everything here in England looks like it belongs in a storybook. I keep waiting to run into some little people or elves. If one of them jumps out of the bushes, I'm going to run like crazy the other way."

Becka kept her left hand on the tree and started to walk around it. It looked like she was almost caressing and communicating with the tree as she walked around and inspected it. I don't think I had ever seen her so curious and intrigued by a tree before.

"Look Kat, what's this?" Becka asked as she peered into the dark inner core of the gigantic tree. "It's like someone left the door open. Look at this, have you ever seen a tree with a door?" She asked as she moved the panel back and forth. It did look like a door as if she was opening and closing it. How in the world could a tree have a door unless someone put it there? Pictures of elves and fairies started to dance through my minds eye again.

"Wow, look at that. Don't shut it all the way, we might not be able to get it back open." I warned her. The rest of the kids were behind us looking to see what we were talking about. I stepped back so the others could get around to get a better look.

"This is definitely a secret entrance to a larger place underground. "Bach announced.

It was Becka who asked,

"Can we go take a look? Who knows, maybe there's someone here who will know where we can find the plant. At Mt. Shasta you never would have found the plants you needed unless you had entered the mountain. Right? Maybe we're here to explore this place, whatever it is."

It didn't really look like the tree hollow was large enough to fit us all inside but as we looked a little closer, we could see there was a ladder going down deeper into the ground under the tree. What the heck? I was starting to wonder if maybe I was dreaming and speculated whether or not I'd wake up soon. This was getting weirder by the minute. If I saw the Mad Hatter or that crazy rabbit from Alice in Wonderland I was sure I would faint dead away.

"What do you think Bach? What should we do?" Mu asked.

I wondered what Bach would say. This was beyond looking like a fairy tale in this storybook land.

"Does this remind anyone else of Alice trying to decide whether or not to follow the rabbit into the rabbit hole? I'll be the first to say this at least looks bigger than a rabbit hole." I had to make a comment I couldn't keep myself from saying what was going though my mind.

Bach finally opened up and gave us his answer.

"I can read that there are other spirits down there and it appears to be safe. I sense they are waiting for us, so with that knowledge I believe we must go."

WHAT? "Others waiting for us?" What was he talking about?

Definitely I wished I had the same talents he had. I wish I could read an area and sense what was there and who these spirits might be. What these spirits might be. After going through dimensions in Tibet, I wasn't sure what kind of spirits we might meet. It was with curious anticipation I followed them into the hollow tree trunk and down a ladder into the unknown once again. Who would have thought England would have an underworld and it wasn't under London or some major city: this was going to be interesting to say the least.

Down the ladder we found a large area that had only one other way out and it took us deeper into the bowels of the earth. The walls looked like hard dirt that had been scrapped and shoveled out. It looked just the way the old mining tunnels were when men did all the tunnel work by pick and shovel. As we went into the actual tunnel it was shored up with timbers and made me think even more of entering a mine. There were lanterns with candles burning to light the way. There was someone here already waiting for us and they had lighted the way for us. I didn't know if I should be happy and pleased or worried and skeptic.

We walked in through the tunnel for at least 300 to 400 feet before we came to a larger area. As soon as we entered the large space we saw them. They were across from us sitting at a round table, yet another look into the past. They were dressed in full-length brown robes making them look like the old Druids from our history books. The hoods covered their faces so we couldn't see what they looked like. We all stopped as we got close to the table.

"Welcome." A female voice greeted us. But we couldn't tell who had spoken. The seven figures in front of us all looked exactly the same and it was a little eerie not being able to see their faces. The one voice we heard did sound friendly so I tried not to worry I just wished they would lower their hoods so we could see who they are. The others must have been thinking the same thing because next I heard Bach ask them,

"Would you lower your hoods so we might know who we are talking with?"

All seven lifted their hands and lowered their hoods. It was a group of seven very beautiful young women. There were, a couple red haired girls, two blondes and the other three had dark raven colored hair. They were all fair skinned and looked like fairy princesses from a children's tale I might have read years ago. What could these seven young women have to do with the merkids and us? I couldn't even begin to guess what connection there could be here. What in the heck were they doing down here under ground? This whole thing was beginning to feel other worldly and far from our upper world reality.

"I can sense you have been waiting for us. Is it possible you know of the plant we have come here searching for?" Bach asked.

One of the red haired girls stood and told him,

"We are the keepers of the sacred plants. You have arrived in time for the lunar blooming with tonight's full moon. Would you join us to feast until the moon rises? Then we will take you out and help you gather your plants. It will be our joy to assist you."

Well maybe this trip would end up being an easy one. We didn't find our plant yet but we found people who knew it, where to find it and the best time to harvest it, plus they wanted to feed us. These were my kind of people. I wondered what they would have to eat. I was getting rather hungry Becka and I hadn't eaten since we left home. I was sure it was past time to eat back in our time zone or dimension.

Becka had been pretty quiet but she was the first to walk over to the table and start to talk to the girls. They were all so beautiful and so fair I could see why the world talked about the complexions of the English and Irish women. If these girls were an example of the woman of the country they must all have a special beauty. Becka standing next to them in their group looked like she could easily be one of them.

The rest of us joined them, introducing ourselves getting to know their names. A couple of the girls left and returned with platters of food for the meal they invited us to share with them. It was good wholesome food, some sort of hot soup or stew, bread and some fresh vegetables. We ate and listened as the girls explained who they were and what they were doing in this space underground and how it came to be they were the keeper of the sacred plants. Elizabeth was the red haired girl who seemed to take charge and be the head of the group.

She started to explain that they were a group of spiritually minded women who over all the generations since time began had been the keepers of the sacred plants. They were descendants of the original Sisterhood of Lemuria and they practiced the use of the Seven Rays. This was the second time I was hearing about the Seven Rays, first the merkids and now these girls. She explained that the full moon would empower the force of the rays and they always did ceremonies on the full moons to take advantage of the extra power it gave the plants. She spoke very generally about all these things as if we would have already known them. She and Bach spoke about the location of the plants and how best to collect them. He was always a stickler for the littlest details and wanted to ensure the safe arrival back in Atlantis of the plants we were collecting.

Becka was speaking with one of the girls at her end of the table. I had to ask Katherine the girl next to me,

"I want to know how you happened to have such a interesting entrance to this little under world cave and is there any other way out?"

Katherine giggles and said,

"This was an old pirate smugglers cove and the other entrance goes out to the river. The tree became an entrance a couple generations ago when one of the members discovered the tree with such a large hollow in it and made the connection for a second route of entry or escape. It does make it all seem a bit like a fairy tale, doesn't it? It must have seemed odd to all of you when we left the door open for you."

"Yeah and how did you all know we were coming?" I asked.

"There was a whisper on the wind, an energy that surrounds all of you and your mission. We read your coming and knew you would need our services. We're all very tuned in that way. Are you not able to read the energy in the wind?" Katherine asked.

"No, I afraid I'm not tuned in like you girls or the merkids we're helping. I'm just a normal ordinary girl who's trying to get tuned in. My friend Becka knows some things but even she's not as psychic as the merkids." I told her.

"Don't be silly, we are all capable and have the talents. Some people just haven't tried to use them and practice to make the skill stronger. It's just like riding a bike or drawing pictures. You need to practice to get good at anything. Sit by yourself and just listen for the wind. Open your mind and try not to think about things, just listen. It'll come to you more and more. As the days and weeks and years pass you will get tuned in. It won't happen over night but it will happen. Once you find the way in you'll never lose it." Katherine made it sound so simple. Every time I tried to sit and meditate I had a very hard time trying to focus and not think about 100 different things. It's very difficult to sit and clear your mind. Maybe next time I'd sit outside and try to listen for the wind instead.

Everyone in the group were all talking and visiting with each other while we ate the most delicious meal. Funny how good things can taste some times. This was like magic soup because it tasted so heavenly and the bread was fresh baked with homemade butter. Just thinking about it was making my brain and my mouth water in between bites.

When we were done we all helped clean up and get ready to journey back to the surface for the full moon ceremony. This time we exited the cave in the other direction. The long cave ran a distance to the river where the opening came out in a rock cropping a short way from the rivers edge. The girls led us to a small hilltop over looking some wheat fields, nearby. We hiked up the hill through some trees and found a circular pattern at the top made from rocks, in the center of a clearing. It was a similar concept to the Stonehenge but on a much, much smaller scale. The rocks were just small ones lying in a circle, side by side, something more like the first circle of a medicine wheel.

Elizabeth explained,

"Depending on the season we do most of our ceremonies here or one other location up river. We follow the leys and work within the energy field they provide. Tonight we would ask you all to join us in the ceremony. The extra strength of your energies will help to guide the knowledge we receive."

How could we say no? It was Bach who asked,

"We will assist in any way we can. What would you like us to do?"

The girls all dropped their robes and stepped forward to form a circle inside the rocked circular pattern.

"Join us, we will all hold hands and I will led the group. Just do as I command." Elizabeth told him.

We all did as told gathering together with the girls in the power circle, joining hands, spreading ourselves out to form as large a circle as the twelve of us could. The sky seemed clear and the stars were sparkling overhead with the full moon beaming back at us from its heavenly spot. The girls looked like spirits in the wind. The breeze was lifting their skirts and long hair only adding to the make believe, fairy tale feel this adventure had. Was there such a thing as Wind Nymphs? That's what they made me think of as I watched them in the moonlight with their hair lifting in the breeze and their voices calling out to the heavens.

So there we were the twelve of us forming our energy circle, I wasn't sure what we were suppose to do next? Would we call out to the heavenly spirits? Try to bring down some special energy? Read the future? I wasn't sure what would be next.

Then Elizabeth summoned us forward. With their voices they all called us to come together closer, to join together in the center of the circle and as we stood there while Elizabeth called out to heavens above,

"We the Sisterhood of Lemuria, call out to all the spirits, the sun, the moon and all the stars above to guide us tonight in our transplanting of the sacred Miller's reed. Energize the plant with your rays to empower the potency of its seed. Lift up the power of the plant so it will carry the cure needed by our new friends."

They all started to back up to reform the larger circle next to the circle of rocks just as we did when we first entered. The wind picked up even more, the girl's skirts were lifting higher and their hair danced even faster in the stronger breeze. It was as if the words she spoke increased the power of the wind and in a short period of time it almost felt as if a storm might be brewing, heading our way. I could feel a static electricity in the air all around us. I had to question whether the girls were capable of pulling more energy into the circle with us or if it was all just my imagination?

As Elizabeth had us move forward again, the energy seemed to grow and I could almost taste it, even my teeth seemed to be vibrating with the power in the air between us. I looked to see if Becka was feeling the same as me. She just smiled and squeezed my hand a little tighter as if to reassure me that everything was okay. So maybe she was reading my mind and understood my look. Each time we moved forward we raised our arms high and as we moved back enlarging the circle we lowered our arms. I could feel the pressure inside the circle growing and I wondered how the girls were making that happen. Maybe they had something of a vortex building inside our human ring. I wasn't sure what was causing it I just knew it was happening.

By the sixth or seventh time we came close together in the circle some lightening and thunder cracked and rumbled through the sky above us. I jumped and almost broke the circle. Becka on my one side and Elizabeth on the other side both squeezed my hands tighter or I probably would have. Now I didn't really think they had summoned the lightening but I doubted what we were doing and wondered if this could be a wise thing to do? I didn't want to get struck by lightening and things were suddenly getting a little scary. I wondered what these young women were capable of. I didn't really know them, could they be like witches or some kind of wizards? After the meeting the merkids I wasn't sure if anything could really surprise me again. My next thought was, who are you kidding, everything that's happening right now is freaking me out and blowing my mind all at the same time. I was just about ready to jump out of my own skin.

The lightening struck again. The bolts were traveling horizontally across the sky over head. I had never seen it do that. All the lightening I'd ever seen shot up and down vertically not like this. It was lighting up the sky and suddenly there was something else happening. The lightening stopped and the clouds that had rolled in started to roll out, just as quickly as they had come in. I blinked my eyes and questioned myself. Surely this was some kind of optical illusion. I closed my eyes completely and shook my head a little trying to clear my head. I had to be seeing things or my imagination was getting the better of me, I wasn't sure which was happening. The sky was still except for one thing.

I looked to Becka to see if she was seeing what I was seeing. She was looking up and I was sure she had to see it. The other kids were all looking up too. They all had to see it but nobody was reacting. Were they hypnotized? Should I shake them? Or maybe I should yell and snap them out of the trance they seemed to be in. Was I the only one seeing and understanding what I thought I was seeing? I was getting nervous. I thought I might pee my pants. I wasn't sure what to do or if suddenly doing something might make things worse. Maybe I shouldn't bring any more attention to the group of us here on the open hilltop. I think I finally just froze in place and was stuck staring at the sky above waiting to see what would happen next. I was scared stiff. All the others had stopped too, that's when I felt sure we were all seeing the same thing and maybe each was wondering all the same things as me, what do we do now?

Then I even started to wonder if these girls, the descendants of the Lemurian Sisterhood, were summoning this energy and this encounter? They said these were ceremonies they did often and none of them seemed the least bit surprised with what was happening. The merkids didn't really seem surprised either. Were Becka and I the only ones looking up with shock and wonder?

I was seeing what I had to say was a UFO. It had shot in with the lightening and thunder and it was still there over our heads, not really all that high in the sky either. It was close enough that I could tell you it looked just like the ships I saw in the movie called Close Encounters.

The thunder and lightening seemed to disappear as quickly as it had come up. I could see it all so clearly. I saw the lights and I could hear the hum or vibration it was making. Except for the hum of the energy there wasn't another sound in the night around us to be heard unless it was my heavy breathing. I was mesmerized and scared at the same time. I was stunned and time seemed to stand still. I hoped they weren't going to take us up or steal us away like some of the movies showed. I didn't want to get probed or have things embedded in my skin or brain. That was the scary part, thinking what's going to happen now? I just hoped that I didn't pee my pants, if anything or anyone touched me just then I know I would have.

Becka seemed to be smiling, as I looked her away again. There was a blue glow on everyone's face from the lights on the UFO. It was a huge vehicle and I saw several different colored lights all around the bottom of it. Blue just seemed to be the main color showing right now. The lights were blinking and dancing in a pattern that seemed to be some sort of communication. At least I felt they were trying to communicate with us. The sounds of the night were all gone except for the hum of the ship above us the night was in total silence. If there was any sound I could hear there might have been just the finest little crackling sound, like electricity crackling and dancing around each of us. It wasn't the same hum that the ship was making.

One thought kept popping into my head, 'my dad would love to see this.' He was always saying he believed in UFO's and watched every show that came along about them. I wish there was some way I could tell him about this when I got home but I couldn't if I was going to keep my promise to the Merkids. Now I just hoped I would get home and they wouldn't take us away. My Dad would never understand or know what happen to me if they did.

The ship just stayed there, suspended in the air overhead, lights blinking and dancing and then swoosh it was gone in one heart beat. Holy crap, was I sure now about what I had just seen? I closed my eyes and then opened them to just question myself again. Did I imagine that? Was I hypnotized and it was never there? I looked towards Becka again to see what response she had to the sudden disappearance of the ship.

"I never in a million years thought we'd see something like that tonight. Maybe they're finally ready to meet us." Becka exclaimed.

So she had seen it all. I wasn't imagining and I wasn't hypnotized in to believing I saw something that wasn't there. I had questioned myself and doubted myself but Becka just confirmed it all. On one hand, what a relief but on the other, HOLY CRAP how was I ever going to process all this and put it into perspective in my regular life back home away from the merkids?

"I thought I was seeing things." I told her.

"Well, if you just saw a humongous flying saucer with lights blinking that almost hypnotizing you, we saw the same thing. I never thought I'd ever see anything like that tonight. Wouldn't your Dad go ape crazy if he could have seen it?" Becka answered me.

"So what does all this mean?" I asked the group in general. They seemed so unruffled by the encounter while I was still shaking and had goose bumps crawling up my neck and down my arms.

"Does this happen very often to you?" I asked.

"The Guardians are always coming and going they watch over us and the work we do. They are masters of energy and with their help we are able to enrich all the sacred plants before we harvest or transplant them. Have you never seen the crop circles in the fields? That is the result of the energy work they are doing. The patterns in the circle reflect the degree of energy they are working with and the frequencies they use. All energy has sound, color and vibrational patterns you just can't see, feel or hear a lot of it. "Elizabeth told us.

Katherine waited for her to finish speaking before she said,

"We should go now while the vibrations are still their purest levels and gather the plants before the moon wanes."

I don't know how long we had been there in the power circle before the UFO showed up and I wasn't sure how long it had been there but now Katherine said it was getting late so it must have been longer than I had first thought. I hoped the plants would be close by and this would be a successful adventure so we could head home safe and sound soon.

I was still having a hard time coming down from what had just happened. They didn't seem to think much of it and apparently were quite used to seeing the UFO's and I guess even Guardian Aliens. I knew and I heard the merkids talk about them but hearing it and seeing it for your self are two different things. I just couldn't settle down. I had just seen a UFO for real! I knew now, I would never be the same naïve teenager ever again.

I know I was still feeling a little edgy about that encounter. I kept thinking, did something happen I don't remember? I'd heard stories about people being abducted and not remembering for months or years because the trauma was too great to deal with. It was just this funny kind of feeling. Nothing I could put my finger on but it felt like maybe some time was missing for me tonight. Would I ever know? Maybe nothing happened. Maybe it was just the shock of the encounter even happening that I couldn't help but feel mesmerized and left wondering how much time had really passed. Maybe it was just the surprising turn of the evening and me trying to wrap my brain around the fact that I had just seen a flying saucer.

There was no guessing or wondering anymore, now I had seen it for myself and nobody could ever again tell me they weren't real. The merkids said they were real but, seeing is, believing: now I knew, no doubts, no more wondering. It wasn't something that someday might happen or even something to think about in the future. I had seen a real UFO.

The words kept echoing in my head, "I just saw a UFO, I just saw a UFO, I just saw a UFO." Was I the only one here who was freaking out about seeing the UFO? Maybe the girls were used to having their ceremonies joined by spacecraft but I wasn't and where was Becka? She should be as freaked as me but she looked pretty calm and at ease with everything that just happened.

Before I could get close enough to talk to Becka again the girls were all heading away from the circle and the hilltop.

"Come on Kat we've got to keep up and help them find the plants." Becka called out to me as she grabbed my hand starting to pull me in their direction. I jerked back on Becka's hand and she spun around and gave me a questioning look wondering what was wrong with me.

"What about what we just saw?" I asked.

"What do you mean? You knew the merkids said the Guardians would return and you knew that would mean flying saucers, ET's and UFO's didn't you?" She said it like what did I expect.

"Yes maybe so but aren't you feeling a little shock and awe? I mean I thought I might pee my pants when I saw that huge thing up overhead. How are you feeling so nonchalant about it all?" I questioned her. Usually Becka was the calm and cool one between the two of us but I still couldn't believe this encounter didn't have her a little more excited.

"I don't know Kat, it just all seems like the natural order of things. We're here with the merkids. We've both had memories of other lifetimes, we've seen treasure and temples and more hidden worlds than I could have ever imagined. The Guardians couldn't be any stranger or more unbelievable. Actually seeing the spaceship just seemed like a gentle greeting from them and it made we wonder what they would be like. I'm not afraid to meet them when the time comes, are you afraid now Kat? I don't think you should be afraid if that's what's wrong. Are you afraid?" she asked me point blank.

Before I could answer her she turned to see where everyone else had gone and said,

"We better go now. We wouldn't want to lose sight of the others. We don't know where they're going or how to get back to the cave. We better talk later and try to catch up now."

We both turned in the direction the others had gone and ran to catch up. As soon as we cleared the trees on the out skirts of the ceremonial circle we saw them down the hill just a little below us.

"Hey, wait for us." I called out to them.

We raced to catch up with the others and followed them down the hill. The girls were heading towards a valley just to the north of the hill. As we fell in step behind the group the girls started to sing a song. Their voices had an enchanted quality to them as if we were listening to the Angels of Heaven singing from their hearts and inner souls. The spirit of their words captured us in their spell and I felt as if we were flowing on the winds of time, as they carried us back to some ancient time. Every Celtic song I had ever heard was melted into this one and the vibration of their sound swept me away. The winds of the vale carried my mind to other times and places and I couldn't begin to capture all the pictures as they raced across my mind.

Were they putting us under some spell? Were they transporting us to these other times and places I could now see inside my mind? How could their words or even the vibration of the sounds they sang open some inner door inside my soul like this? I had read and heard of stories and tales of sirens who used such tricks to lure men to them. Were these girls, sirens of some sort? Or did they just know the keys to unlock some of our inner doors from the past? I supposed it was the latter as they seemed so harmless and helpful: I just couldn't suspect any negative energy or purpose from them.

We reached an area where the vegetation looked as if it had all been cut down and I heard the girls all gasp,

"OH NO!!! Someone has been here ahead of us and taken everything." As they spread out and carefully double checked the area Elizabeth stated again,

"Oh how could this be? Someone got here before us and they have taken everything. There's not one single plant left."

What? Now what would we do? How could this be happening to us again? I looked to the area and they were right, everything had been cut and probably just a few hours ago.

"Well there must be other places where the reed grows, surely we can find some somewhere else." I blurted out.

"Yes you're probably right but this was our source and I will have to ask for help and guidance from the nature spirits to locate any others. I know of no other location." Elizabeth answered.

"Well great, how do we get the help from the Nature spirits?" I asked her. What in the heck were Nature spirits and how could they help us now? This wasn't a term I had really heard before and I hoped what ever they were they'd be psychic and have the answers we needed now.

"We will have to ask for their help. It requires a special ceremony and chant." She replied.

"Well where do we have to go and how do we do the ceremony? How many of us will it take? We'll do whatever you ask of us, won't we? "I asked our group and everyone nodded approval and agreement.

"It's nothing you can help us with this time, they know our energy and will respond to it, if you joined us it might confuse them. Best we do this one by ourselves. Wait here and we'll get started." As she spoke the last words she and the other girls walked a short distance away from us and formed another circle. This time they sat and they put their arms out to their sides and wrapped their arms around the next girls shoulders. It was a tight circle and they swayed as they started their chant. We could hear Elizabeth calling out to the spirits.

"Devas of all nature and plants. Hear my call. Radiant ones we seek your guidance and assistance with your brilliant light please lead us to the sacred plants we desire to find." Then the others joined in and they all repeated the chant over and over. They called out the words and swayed to the rhythm of the chant.

The gentle breeze started to pick up a little, nothing like the storm that seemed to move in when the UFO appeared, it was just enough wind to lift the girls' hair and bounce their curls in the air like flames dancing to the sound and vibration of their chant. They must have been at it for more than five minutes before I started to notice what looked like lightening bugs in the air around them. It wasn't like I saw them fly in. They were just suddenly there dancing above the girls' heads like little twinkling lights of energy. At least I didn't think they were bugs.

It looked like there were hundreds of them. The lights glowed white with a soft golden halo around them. Were these bugs or were they the Nature spirits the sisters were calling for help? I had no idea what was going to happen when they started their chanting but I don't think this was what I expected to see. I read once that spirits could appear like sparks of light. As we all stood there watching Bach spoke up,

"Nature spirits are very powerful energy and they can be very powerful allies in our world of consciousness. It appears the sisters have a strong relationship with the Deva and often work hand in hand with them for the betterment of the world around them. I believe they will be able to help us find the plants we need. I have never seen them summoned like this before. I should talk with the sisters and discuss the chants they used maybe they would share with me their secrets. This is amazing energy work they have accomplished."

"If those are Nature Spirits, those things that look like big lightening bugs, you're right, this is all pretty amazing energy work." Becka agreed with him.

As we spoke, the sisters started to release each other and began standing up. The Devas were still there, all around and above their heads. The girl's hair was blowing and dancing in the breeze or maybe it was the force of the Devas energy lifting it, I wasn't sure which. Elizabeth looked towards us and calling out,

"Follow us! The Devas will help us find more plants."

As soon as the words left her mouth the Devas started to head out in at least a half dozen different directions so she called out again,

"Break up, go in pairs, quickly everyone follow them. Hurry!"

We never gave it a second thought as Becka and I darted off together to follow a group of maybe five spirits that flew off to the far right away from the rest of the group. We raced and giggled a little as we followed the dancing little balls of light. They seemed to lift, float and then grab a hold of the breeze and move forward even faster. It was just like chasing the lighting bugs during my summers back home when I was younger. So now it was with childhood abandon we raced to keep up with the Devas as they flew across the valley floor.

Once or twice they seemed to stop, as if inspecting a location. We never saw anything that looked like the Millers Reed we were searching for so each time as they moved on we followed them. We roamed across the valley for some time before the spirits seemed to pick up the scent of something and they made a b-line towards a crop of trees up ahead of us. There was a small cottage nestled under the trees with a little smoke coming from the chimney and a glow of light from a couple small windows.

Maybe this was the person who had beaten us to the plants earlier tonight. Otherwise, why would they lead us to this cottage? Neither of us knew what to expect, or what was expected of us now. The Devas seemed to surround the cottage and stand guard. We both just looked at each other. Now what?

To our surprise the cottage door opened and a shaft of light flooded the area where we stood. We looked at each other and slowly turned our heads towards the open doorway to see who was there. At first while our eyes adjusted to the light it was hard to see who or what was there. There was the outline of a small build person in the open doorway. We both waited to see what the person would say. Our eyes adjusted to the light and we stepped closer to see what she would say as we were able at this distance to see her face. I couldn't have been more surprised by the words that she spoke.

"I've been waiting for you. My name is Sybil please come in." She was a small petite woman, probably about 65 to 70 years old. She looked so serene and had a beautiful glow in her complexion. She looked like a lady you could trust and reminded me of someone's grandmother. Maybe that's why Becka felt we could trust her.

"Come on Kat, let's see what she wants." Becka said as she started for the open doorway. It was kind of interesting to see Becka be so bold and fearless on this adventure. I followed her inside and when Sybil pointed to a small table to the side of a fireplace we walked over and sat down.

"Let me make you some tea and we'll talk." Was all she said before she walked to the stove, picked up the kettle pouring the hot water she had ready into the cups she had on a tray. There were three cups set out, so clearly she was expecting two some bodies tonight. So many strange and 'mess with your head' kind of things had happened to us since we met the merkids, some how this didn't seem so strange tonight. I think we both felt comfortable with Sybil and wondered what she could have to say to us. Once she handed us each a cup of tea, offering us cream and sugar, she sat and made herself comfortable. She took a long slow slip and finally began the conversation.

"I can see you're both curious. I should explain a few things to you and then tell you why you're really here." She paused and took another slip of her tea. This might take awhile if she was going to sprinkle her conversation with these long slow sips of hot tea. Becka and I both leaned forward in our chairs to hear what she would say next.

"I am Sybil, we knew each other in another time and place. There was a time in history when we worked together in Delphi. I was a great oracle then, known throughout the land and you two were my daughters."

Another long slow sip of the hot tea and she continued,

"We worked together in that lifetime to try to bring the word as well as the message of the Great One to all who would listen. Many called me sorceress and they didn't listen or heed my words. I tell you this because it's clear to me in this lifetime you do not have your memories of that experience. I want you to understand that I have always been open and receptive to the energies of the Cosmos. I have been able to read the wind and the people around me, near or far away. I have always kept track of my two daughters from that Delphi experience because we had such rewarding lives in that time together."

She paused again and raised her cup to her lips. Another long slow sip of the hot tea and she set her cup down before she spoke again.

"I am an old woman now, so please humor me if it is taking a little while to get to the reason you are here tonight. I can't stress to you enough, how important I believe it is for you to heed my warning. I'm trying to give you some background regarding the time we were together in the past. A mother will always look out for her children and that is all that I am trying to do now. There is much that is expected of you and your group of friends. But I must warn you there are dimensions to all of this that you have no true understanding of at this point." She paused and took another sip, which gave me a chance to ask her my first question.

"Which friends are you talking about? The friends from back home or the merkids?"

"The merkids are the friends I'm speaking of right now. They have only the best intensions but there are powers at work here that even they are not aware of. You must be very careful in your journeys with them. You have already leaped through the gateway once and suffered only minor consequences. There are prices to pay for the transformation it takes to do so safely and without danger. It takes much training to be one who can control such energies and forces of the Universe. It is not something to play with and you should not go into such realms with such little care or regard for the forces there in."

As Sybil spoke the two of us sipped our tea and listened, wondering what in the world she was talking about. This was starting to sound very dramatic, a little wacky and maybe even a little scary. She was right about one thing what had we been thinking when we jumped into the next dimension in Tibet? Sybil was right we did that without a thought or care as to how we would or even if we could get back. Suddenly I could see myself, like the picture of a spirit locked inside the picture tube of the television, unable to get out, stuck and lost forever inside the static and white noise.

Wow that was a sobering picture and it brought me back to the present moment as we sat at the table inside this little cottage with an Oracle from the past called Sybil; someone who said she had been our mother in that lifetime. I wondered if other kids had ever had such bombs dropped on their heads as we had been having? First it was the existence of the merkids and the adventures with them then to ultimately save the Guardians from the disease they've been battling, the prophecy of the Seven Sisters and now this. My brain was turning cartwheels inside my head again. It was Beckas voice that uttered the next words.

"Are you saying we shouldn't be going on these missions with the merkids that we are some how in danger if we continue?"

"I can only warn you that there are forces that are stronger than you and your friends the merkids. Even they don't know all that is a foot in trying to save their generation and ultimately the Guardians on their return. You must start to open yourselves more so you can sense things for yourselves. Trust your instincts and intuition. Spend time in quiet so you may know yourselves better and increase your own power to read the wind and all that is."

Becka asked her,

"Do you see anything specific in the future that you are trying to warn us about? Maybe if you told us what you saw, we could be better warned and could take extra precautions."

"I don't know if I am blinded by my mother's love or if I am just getting old. I can only tell you to be warned that there are powers beyond your imagination that are at play in your future. I fear for your safety but you need to know I can only see shadows in your future and they scare me. Even though I couldn't see more than shadows, I knew I had to warn you."

Well I didn't know about Becka but I sure didn't like the sound of that little warning. How could someone, no matter if they were your mother in a past life, tell you there were dangers in your future but they don't know what it could be for sure or what direction it would come from? We'd have to look behind every door in our future and still not know what dangers we were looking to avoid.

I couldn't imagine what she could be talking about. Did we have to worry about the Guardians? Would it be something on the way home? This was really going to rattle my brain waiting and wondering what was going to happen and when. How could anyone tell you such a vague warning with no time frame to help you contain it? Well this was going to drive me crazy wondering and waiting for who knows what. I didn't know if I could live the rest of my life, how ever short or long it might be, looking for this unknown trouble.

"Well, now we'll have to live the rest of our lives looking over our shoulders until the bomb drops. What's with that? Can't you look a little harder and try to see what it is?" I asked.

"Kat. Didn't you hear what she just said? She can't tell what the danger is or she would have told us already." Becka answered me.

"Yeah but now we'll be the ones walking around afraid to go around the next corner for fear of what's coming. How are we going to live like that? I would have rather not known any of this. Now I'll be afraid of everything. How do you think you'll deal with this little bombshell of news?" I asked her.

"First off she didn't say a bomb was dropping. She just said be careful. I can do that. Can't you? Seeing shadows and talking about unseen forces doesn't necessarily mean total disaster for us. Besides it might not happen for years or even at all. Are you planning to live like Chicken Little the rest of your life? Just settle down and lets talk a little more. Maybe sometime in the future Sybil can tell us more. If more images became clearer to her later on maybe she could email us or call. We could try to keep in touch and see if she can pick up more later on. That seems the responsible thing to do. What do you think Sybil?" Becka turned back towards Sybil giving her a chance to answer.

"Oh most definitely. I will always be watching keeping track of the two of you. If anything becomes clearer in the future I would get in touch with you. Now that you've been warned there is little else I can do except enjoy you're company for what little time you have to spare tonight." Sybil answered.

"We probably should leave now." Becka told her. "We really need to get back to help with the search for the Millers Reed we need. The others may be wondering where we are. Sybil do you have any idea where we could find some healthy Millers Reed? You wouldn't happen to have any plants of your own would you? We only need one or two."

Sybil got a thoughtful look on her face and took another sip of her tea, which by now wasn't as hot, before she answered her.

"You know Becka I don't have any full plants here, only the ones I harvested earlier this evening. I believe I could help the Devas guide you to another location where I've been cultivating another crop that's just starting to reach it's fullest potential. How would that be?" Sybil answered her.

"Thank you Sybil, that would be great. As much as I hate to say it, I think we should be going. The others may be wondering where we are or what happened to us. We still have to find them, after we locate the plants and it's getting very late." Becka told her.

"If you get to the patch I have growing and it's not what you are looking for the only other place I know you can look is in Ireland. There is a more rare species that grows on the cliffs along the coastline. The two are alike except the flowers of the more rare species are purple, not the yellow of the ones I've been working with. Okay my dears, I loved seeing you. I can't begin to tell you how much this means to me. I know you don't remember me right now but you will some day. Take extra good care of yourselves and try to be more intuitive so you can sense when danger might be near. Here is my address and phone number just in case you ever want to contact me. I'll step outside with you and just have a word with the Devas before you take your leave." Sybil stood as she spoke and walked to the front door and we followed her outside.

Almost instantly the Devas all started to dance around Sybil's head. Their lights were dimming and glowing as if they were having some sort of conversation. They made me think of bees around the beekeepers head. Sybil just nodded her head and they started to move away as if it was time to follow them again. We each hugged Sybil and thanked her for both, her words of warning and her hospitality. She was the sweetest lady and smelled so good as she held me tight in our goodbye embrace.

The Devas started to dart away so we raced to catch up and waved goodbye to Sybil as we left. They were taking us farther away from the direction we had come from and I started thinking to myself, I hope they know how to find the others when we get that plant and need to head back.

It seemed like we followed them for hours, climbing up and over several hillsides often passing by open wheat fields and I wondered if dawn wouldn't be coming soon. It was hard to tell when traveling with the merkids how much time was passing. I was actually starting to get tired and we still hadn't reach the destination Sybil had sent us towards. I could only hope the Devas knew where we were going and we'd get there soon.

Finally we crested a small hill and could see several wheat fields full of tall grain gently waving in the soft breeze of the night. In the full light of the moon it was easy to see everything. Just to the side of the wheat field on our right I could see the Miller's Reed. There was a small patch of them growing in front of the wheat field. It was a much shorter plant and had a small yellow flower towards the top of the stem. That was it that was the Miller's Reed we were here searching for. I wondered if the others had found any or if we were the only ones to get lucky.

"We should let the others know we've found the plant and see if they've already found some and collected what we need." Becka suggested as she pulled her opal from her pocket and placed it against her forehead.

"Okay, you see what Bach wants us to do. I'm going to get a little closer and check them out." I told her as I moved closer to the little patch of reeds. Becka pulled out her opal and I turned to check out the plants. I thought it amazing how plants that might hold the cure to God only knows what, were here next to the wheat fields, growing like weeds. So far all the plants we had found were sometime rare but often just like weeds in whatever country we found them in. Could so many scientists in so many countries not realize the importance these plants seemed to hold?

At least here in England it seemed some people recognized the true value of the reed and were using it for medical and spiritual reasons.

I never had a chance to ask Sybil what she collected it for but now I wondered, did she have a different use for it and if so, what was it? Suddenly I wanted to go back and ask her a dozen questions. Once we got home again I'd have to sit and write her a long letter to see what she would say because there wasn't time to try and go back.

Becka joined me saying,

"Bach said they are some distance from here and he won't be able to get here until after sunrise. He suggested we try to sleep if we could. Think you could sleep if we tried? It seems like it's been a long day. I think I could get sleep if I just lay down someplace comfortable."

"Yeah right!" I told her as we both laughed as we looked around to find that soft comfy bed. The closest thing looked to be the wheat field we were standing next to.

"Maybe" I told her "if we pushed a small patch of the wheat over it would cushion us just enough to make that comfy bed you were looking for."

The Devas suddenly started to dance up and down in front of us again. It seemed they were ready to go and this time without us since we needed to wait here for the others. Becka and I just watched as they bounced around. We had no clue if they were trying to communicate and if so, what they wanted to say.

Becka finally just said,

"If you must go, then go. We have to wait her for our friends and have no idea what you are trying to tell us. Thank you for your help, we will always remember you."

I lifted my hand to one of the spirits and it seemed to hover just above my palm.

"Yes, thank you all. We couldn't have done this without you." As I said the last word they all just shot up about a foot higher into the sky above us and in a flash they were gone, back into the night, the same way they came.

"Well, now we're all alone again. Ready to try and get some sleep?" Becka asked.

"Yeah I guess but aren't you wondering about all that danger stuff that Sybil talked about? I don't know if I can sleep after hearing all that stuff. And what about those Devas? Wasn't that something pretty amazing?" I told her.

"Well I'm too tired to think about it anymore tonight. Lets make some sort of bed in the wheat and try to sleep. After Bach gets here I'm sure we'll be heading home and you know we can't sleep then." she answered me.

We stepped into the wheat field a few hundred feet trying to get away from the wind that seemed to be rising and pushed some of the wheat stalks over to the side, trying to flatten them without breaking the shafts.

"There, that's enough room for the two of us to curl up for a while." Becka said as she sat on the wheat trying to lie over to one side to make enough room for me to join her.

"Okay, I'll give this a try." I told her as I joined her in our little make shift bed. Once I was on the ground I wiggled and squirmed a little to get my spot a little more comfy. I felt something lumpy under by side and reached to see what it was. It was the prettiest little rock and without thinking I shoved it into my pocket. Surprisingly I don't think we were awake for very long, the worries of Sybil's warnings slipped away as sleep over took both of us in just minutes. Neither of us would have ever guessed the comfort we would find in our little wheat bed.

We were sleeping when the sound of the rushing wind seemed to call us back to reality. We both raised our heads to see if it was the kids already here. There was no one and before we woke completely sleep and blissful unconsciousness recalled us to their open arms. The sounds of the wind lulled us even deeper into sleep. Dreams seemed to take me around the world for what was left of the night.

The sun was already up when the sound of the kids all coming our way managed to wake the two of us. The seven sisters were singing again as they crested the top of the hill next to the wheat field. Becka and I both sat up trying to run our fingers through our hair and the sleep from our eyes. I wasn't sure if I had slept well or not but as I yawned, I tried to shake the cloudy webs from my thoughts, dreamland had to be put away to make room for the day ahead of us.

I had the strangest dream while we slept in the field. I felt energy raising Becka and me to some other dimension. I wondered if this could be some of the dark forces that Sybil had tried to warn us about? Could danger slip in while we slept? I didn't know what to think but the dream I had wasn't one I would be able to keep to myself.

"Do you remember dreaming at all last night Becka?" I asked. I was beginning to finally wake and get my head clear. Then I noticed some thing else as I took in our immediate surroundings. The wheat all around us was flat to the ground. Not broken or randomly thrashed about. It was all smoothly laid over and in the same direction. As I looked I found myself standing in the center of a large circular pattern where the wheat was laid in an orderly pattern and manner. When did that happen? How in the world could anything or anyone have done this without waking us last night? I knew for a fact it didn't look that way when we first arrived or when we made our bed to sleep on.

I looked at Becka who hadn't said a word in the last few minutes. She was standing there next to me, looking just as bewildered and confused by what she was seeing as I was. This just didn't seem possible. I mean I had heard the wind but wind alone couldn't have done this. If someone or something had done it, I just couldn't believe we could have slept though it. Had the UFO come back and we slept through it? We could see the kids on the hillside pointing and talking about what they could see as if they were as puzzled as the two of us.

If we could have seen the scene laid out before them, we would have known we were standing in the middle circle, of a multi circle, sacred geometric designed crop circle. I was still standing there taking in my surroundings wondering how this happened and we slept through the entire thing. Was this an energy force coming from inside the Earth? Was it energy of a Ley line? Had ET's dropped in and used their energy to leave us some message?

The crop circle had one large central circle with seven spirally arms reaching out from the center then each arm had seven circles reaching out in graduating smaller sizes. Each circle was touching and connected to the next smaller circle. I couldn't help but wonder if the seven arms related in any way to the seven sisters of the Lemurian Sisterhood whom we had just met, or if it had more to do with the Seven Sisters Prophecy that involved all of us. I couldn't stop thinking about it all. How did this thing just appear from out of nowhere and how did it relate to us?

As the others approached you could see they were excited and just as curious as the two of us. Becka and I were starting to move from the spot where were first stood and looked at the circle we were part of. I still couldn't believe anything this big could have happened. Last night when we decided to use the wheat to cushion us while we slept we had a full moon lighting and illuminating the entire field and none of this was here then. I think we were both feeling a little stunned that anything like this could be here now. It was almost impossible to try to imagine how any of this could have happened.

The others stopped short of entering the crop circle so we walked out to meet them. The sisters all started talking at once and surprisingly it wasn't anything about the crop circle.

"This isn't the right plant. We need the Millers reed with purple flower tops." Elizabeth cried out.

"This will never do, it's just not the same thing. Only the purple flower topped reeds will do. These with the yellow are not as strong and are a much less powerful plant." Katherine added.

"Well now what are we going to do?" I asked.

The girls all started to huddle together talking and brainstorming about what to do and where to look next.

"Sybil told us there was a rare Miller's reed that grew in Ireland along the coast. Could we go there if that is the right plant or do you know of a place near by?" Becka asked them as she worked into their circle.

"I can't think of another patch anywhere in the area. I think we'll need to contact the Devas again and ask them. They'll know if you'll have to go to Ireland or not. Give me a few minutes and I'll see what we can find out," with those words Elizabeth left the group and stood with her back to us about 50 feet away.

Becka and I looked back to the crop circle and were even more amazed seeing it from outside the center circle. We walked up the hill just a little to get a better look from a higher vantage point and turned to look back. It was just incredibly mind boggling to see this and realize it happened while we slept in its center. Other than hearing the wind last night we hadn't seen or heard anything. It just seemed so unreal to me as I looked at the miracle of it and it's design. I would have to burn the design and lay out into my brain so I could copy it onto paper later and study it's meaning if I could find one. All the sevens in its design had to mean something. I was sure of it.

Becka and I returned to the group waiting for Elizabeth to get her message and rejoin us with whatever news she had been able to receive. We all seemed to be watching her as she finally turned and smiled as she walked back towards us.

"I'm sorry to say, they said Ireland is the only other location for the more rare Millers reed you need. Can we take you back for a meal before you leave for Ireland?" she asked.

Bach spoke for all of us,

"I appreciate your invitation for another meal but we must leave and finish our mission as quickly as possible. Time is ticking away for us and we must go. Thank you for all your help and the wonderful dinner you shared with us last night. Did the Devas happen to say where we should look in Ireland? That would be most helpful if they gave you any specific direction for us to take."

"Yes, they said you should go to the Northern coastline near the Giants Causeway it's in Antrim County, north of Belfast," she answered. "You should look for my cousin Mary Todd if you need any help. I'll call and tell her you're coming that way. She works at the Causeway Inn, it'll be easy to find once you get there."

So it was settled, we'd head to Ireland in search of the sacred Millers Reed. We couldn't delay our departure, time was something we didn't have a lot of now, there was much left to do and we hadn't found the plant we came for yet. We would miss the girls they had been so helpful and such incredible people. Never in my life did I think I would ever meet people who could summon Devas and stand tall under the appearance of UFO's. There was no fear in them and they had secrets of energy that I could only marvel at. Their voices were something that would live forever inside my heart, mind and soul.

One of the girls told us the stones at the great Stonehenge were conductors of sound and vibrational energy. Their voices could be used to increase the energy inside the vortex circle of the giant stones, as the vibrations combined and increased it was like opening a gateway of a purer energy that could heal or enrich anything or anyone in the circle. She said it was much like the Kundalini rising up through the chakras of the astral body. The energy would be super charged and of pure sacred geometric design. She told us all sound is energy and when the energy of ones voice connected with you it raised your energy and lifted you closer to heaven.

Listening to the sisters singing while we were here with them, I had to agree she knew what she was saying: I seldom felt so lifted by someone singing but their voices did seem to make me feel better and we weren't even in the Stonehenge circle. I had to wonder what that might have felt like, to have heard them sing in the Henge. Would I have been lifted and how would it have felt?

Bach tore me away from my idol thoughts and back to the present moment. Time to leave and he was already heading away from the sisters after saying goodbye to them all. We followed his led and did the same, only we added a hug for each of them from both of us.

Bach thought it would be faster to return to the river where we had come from and swim from there to the Ireland coast line. I could get behind that idea, swimming was a lot easier than all the hiking we would have done if we trekked across England over to it's western coastline. I might have enjoyed seeing more of England but having seen the Stone Henge and some of the countryside, I was happy. Now I could look forward to seeing some of Ireland.

Just saying the name, Ireland made me think of wild legends and tales I'd heard in school and seen in movies. I wondered if we'd see any Banshee's or other Fairies there? I'd read once, Ireland had seven different kinds of fairies. Seven certainly was a reoccurring number in this world, which was another subject I'd have to turn my attention to at a later date. The seven fairies all had very interesting names there were Banshees, Leprechauns, Merrows and four others. Each had different domains they lived and functioned in.

I was learning that all parts of the world had similar stories about the spirits of the earth and the energy forces that sustain us. Each part of the world we had visited so far had pretty much the same stories they just called things by different names. What for example was the difference between a Ley Line, a Dragon Line, a Fairy Path or a Dream or Song line? They all had the same energy called by different names running through them. All these people talked of times when the energy or spirits were stronger and less polluted than they are today.

I wondered now as I thought about the fairies if the merkids were some how related to the Irish's Merrows? They had a lot in common it seemed as I thought about it now. Merrows were considered half fish with tails and half man or woman. They lived in 'Tir fo Thoinn' which, meant 'the land beneath the waves.' I was finding the world I lived in to be a much more closely woven puzzle than I ever imagined it could be.

It also seemed that many people around the world recognized there were good forces or energies and also negative or bad forces at work in the Universe. Some called those forces spirits some called them fairies or angles and archangels. I couldn't wait to see Ireland and to meet the forces of that wild and spirited land. Ireland had a violent history from some of its earliest days and I of course wondered about it's connection to Hy-Brasil and Atlantis. This could prove to be a real adventure for Becka and me.

It wasn't near as long as I thought it would be before we were back at the rivers edge and ready to start for Ireland. I had gotten lost in all my thoughts of Ireland and fairies. I hoped that Becka and the others didn't think I was being rude.

"Hey Becka," I asked," what have you been thinking about? I got lost thinking about Ireland and fairies."

"I kind of got lost in my thoughts too. Only I think I was remembering other times here. I didn't get anything too vivid or heavy but I feel like I've come home and there are times the goose bumps keep running up and down my arms and the back of my neck. It's like the thoughts and feelings are being acknowledged by my soul. I really can't explain it but it's kept me keeping my thoughts to myself."

We didn't really have time to say more than those few words and Bach had everyone in the water and ready to go. The water wasn't too cold as I dipped in and under the surface. I was looking forward to the swim and our arrival in Ireland. I was getting used to not always finding what we were searching for the first time or two we looked for it. That would be too easy and these adventure were more adventurous because of it. I was also hoping there wouldn't be any more disappointment and we would get what we needed and be able to go home.

It wasn't hard to tell when we left the river and entered the Celtic Sea because the water got a little colder and the color changed a little too. The current was also much stronger as we headed north towards Ireland. We saw a couple small Pilot whales as we worked our way through the Irish Sea. Later there were dolphins and even a few seals. I never got tired of watching the sea life we encountered. I also couldn't help but think about the stories I had read about the Selkies in Irish and Scottish legends. Selkies were seals that could shed their skins to live on land as humans. I had to wonder just a little, after all the strange and unusual things we had seen so far, if in fact maybe that could be something else that wasn't just a legend.

The merkids were strong swimmers and as we started to head a little more to the west and I knew we were rounding the coast of Ireland. The water was even a little rougher now. This had to be the North Channel and we were getting very close now.

"You're right Kat, we're getting close. This channel is only about 20 miles wide soon we'll pass a few other islands and then I'll try to take us in near the Giants Causeway. Once we make land maybe we should try to find Mary Todd at the inn and see if she can be of any help. Ireland has a long coast line and I wouldn't mind a little help to narrow down our search." Bach informed us.

I had no idea what the Giants Causeway was or what it would look like. The name was definitely creating pictures in my head. All the old tales of Ireland were filled with giants and little people as well, I was anxious to see what the Giants Causeway was all about.

Bach was listening in on all my wild crazy thoughts again.

"The Giants Causeway is the source of a great legend in Ireland but in truth it was created 60 million years ago as the result of volcanic action. More often, the legend is more interesting to you humans than the facts.

"Not true Bach, I love the facts and knowing what really causes things. I like knowing what makes things happen and how things work and there are lots of kids like me." I informed him.

It was Becka, who gave it back to him,

"Legends and stories are always interesting Bach but you, should know better than anyone, of all the kids in our school we are real seekers of knowledge and the truth. We're here with you now aren't we!"

"Well you'll get to see everything for yourselves in just a few minutes. We're almost there. Everyone should take care at the shoreline it's very uneven so watch your step. Here, everyone follow me." Bach ordered as he turned left and headed for the Islands edge.

As soon as our heads were above the water we started to take in the scene in front of us. My eyes widened as I focused on the most unexpected landscaped ever. I couldn't begin to imagine this was something formed by volcanic action. My mind was trying to wrap itself around the idea that a volcano could form all these hexagon shapes and then raise them like organ pipes in some areas and keep them flat like stepping stones in others. The only thing I had even seen with this form or shape was the honeycomb the bees make when they build their hives. Was it possible a lava-sluing volcano could form anything like this? I couldn't imagine it but here it was right in front of us and Bach said it was so.

As we walked onto the land we were all looking down at the Causeway stones. So many perfectly formed hexagons all interlocked. It did appear to be a Causeway of Giant proportions. The Causeway led from the land out into the sea and disappeared. But all around the landscape ahead of us were hills and cresting cliffs, all formed form the same hexagonal shapes. Some soared towards the sky and ran into cliffs others were smaller hills and I could understand why some of the names we learned were given to the different aspects were applied. They did look like organ pipes rising high towards the sky forming the nearby hills and cliffs.

The sight of all the stones and their almost perfect shape still made it hard to believe that it was the Earth and not man who created them. I wondered if I shouldn't have given the true credit to God? Who else could have formed so many sacred hexagon shapes and done it all with hot lava? All my thoughts led to my wonderment of this place and I speculated if we had landed in some strange and ancient land where perhaps there were Giants who walked this Causeway.

It was Becka who brought my attention back to the present.

"Isn't this unbelievable Kat? I almost can't believe what I am seeing. How did any Volcano form such a complex design as this?" she asked.

"It doesn't look to me like this could be some volcanic eruption. It does make me think of crystals they have this same shape and they grow high just not usually in such an organized design. I would suspect only Mother Nature or God could make something like this. I sure wish I had my camera. Wouldn't the others back home be amazed to see this? I guess we can look it up on the Internet but it's not the same as having our own photos." I answered her.

Looking down at the space in front of us, it was like looking at some interlocking pavers on a patio back home. Strange place for anyone to have paved a walkway but here it was. It was hard not to look and scan the whole area. I had never seen anything like this and I just kept looking at all the formations trying to understand how a volcano could do anything like this. My brain wasn't going to be able to even begin to understand how this could happen.

I walked looking down and then I'd see something else to one side or the other and I'd start staring off into the distance. I almost tripped as my toes caught on the edge of one of the slightly raised stones and that immediately brought my attention back to the walkway in front of us.

Becka laughed,

"You better be more careful Kat. I've never seen anybody trip over stuff as much as you."

"It's not that funny! I was looking over there. Look at that. Doesn't it look like some old organ pipes sticking up in the air?" I retorted.

She glanced in the direction where I was pointing to and said,

"Yes it does doesn't it, isn't this just the most unbelievable place you've ever seen? Well I don't know. After all the wild and strange things we've seen lately maybe this is just one more to add to the list."

"Yeah right. But I still find it hard to believe this was created from some volcano erupting. It just doesn't compute inside my head." I replied.

We were following the group as they worked their way up towards the top of the plateau. In some places the stones were all smooth and even in others they were all uneven and you had to watch your step. It looked like a rolling walkway running up to the upper land above the columns. Bach called them Basalts and told us the locals call them Giant's Eyes.

Bach picked up the pace a little after we reached the grassy hilltop. He was on a mission to locate Molly Todd to enlist her help. He read the area as soon as we reached the hilltop then started off towards the south. There was a path worn into the grass he told us it would take us straight to the Causeway Inn where Elizabeth said we could find Mary. Mary and Elizabeth were cousins and Elizabeth said she would call ahead and tell Mary to expect us.

The valley area below us was enchanting. There were sheep grazing along the grassy hillside and there were low stonewalls acting as fences dividing the land here and there. Some of the trees and bushes seemed to cut and make lines across the landscape as well. We had just stepped from one fairy storybook landscape to another and all in less than a mile. Enchanting just kept echoing through my mind. It was like being in a 3-d story I read about Ireland and all the pictures had come to life.

We followed the winding path as it wove its way to the Inn. It didn't take any time at all and we could see the cottages up ahead of us. They were white walled buildings with black roofs. There must have been at least four or five buildings surrounded by lush green hedges. This was Ireland and I wouldn't have pictured it any differently it was every bit as much a storybook looking place as England had been. Looking ahead to the cottages I could see a young woman standing in the yard. There was a soft breeze and it was lifting her long skirt she looked like she belonged in a bygone age. I was curious to get closer and see what this place was all about.

The young woman stood in the yard watching our approach. When we finally got close enough she called out a greeting,

"Hello there! Might you be Bach and the group my cousin Elizabeth called about?"

"Yes we are. How are you Mary Todd?" Bach asked and as we got closer he reached out his hand to greet her more formally with a handshake. "I hope you will be able to help guide us in our search of the Miller's Reed we've come for."

"First come inside and have some refreshments then we will talk." She told him.

We followed her inside one of the buildings that was set up as a large dining room with large wooden table and comfortable looking chairs. Story book time again. They couldn't have designed this any better even if they tried. It all looked as if we had gone back in time at least a couple hundred years or so. As we were looking around taking it all in Mary Todd spoke up,

"These building have been here for hundreds of years and we dress in the old style for the tourist who come and stay here. They seem to really enjoy it and feel it gives them a real Ireland experience."

Then she asked us all what we would like to drink as she set a large basket of muffins on the table in front of us.

"Here enjoy these they've just come out of the oven a few minutes ago. I'll get the tea and water and then we'll talk."

Becka jumped up,

"Here let me help you with that." And she followed her over to the cabinets to help Mary get the cups and tea.

Once we were all settled in with our tea and fresh baked muffins Mary sat and started to talk.

"I told Elizabeth the only Millers Reed I know of and that's if there is still any there. Is out along the cliffs and it's very difficult to get to. The cliffs are quite dangerous and many have fallen to their deaths out there. It's not a journey many would even consider. If you go, you will be taking your life in your own hands and you may not return. Millers Reed doesn't grow in the low areas. It seems it knows it's own value and makes sure it's a risk to try and retrieve it for any who dare."

The whole group sat there in silence for a couple minutes. We sipped our tea and thought about what she had just told us. Well, hadn't we been willing to come half way around the world for this darn plant? We couldn't stop now, this was too important and lives beyond our five were at risk. Heck the future of the world itself might be at risk if we didn't bring back this Millers Reed to Atlantis.

Before any of us could say anything, a tourist couple walked in the door and asked if they could get some tea and warm up. Mary jumped up and took them to the other end of the large table and hurried to get them tea. She served them and offered muffins from the large basket and came back to our group.

Bach asked,

"If you could give me an idea of where along the cliffs we might find the Reeds we can get out of your way and on with our search."

"I'll do better than that, let me fetch Charlotte to watch the Inn and I'll take you. It's not easy for anyone who doesn't know the way. Sometimes what you can see from the sea level you cannot see from above. We'll have to work from both levels to locate the plants. I knew you were coming so I made arrangements to have the day off. I'll be right back." she said as she left the cottage.

When Mary returned she was wearing her own clothes and another young woman came in with her to work in her place. Now dressed in her jeans and boots she was ready to hike the Irish coast and help us on our mission. She was also wearing a large sweater and asked us girls if we were warm enough.

"The wind will be blowing out at the cliffs and the sea breeze has a chill to it that seeps into the bones. I can get you something more to wear if you want?"

"I think we'll be fine but thank you for offering" Bach told her."

"Okay then, lets be on our way," as she said the words Mary turned and headed for the door with all of us behind her.

Outside the cottage Mary started on a worn pathway that headed back towards the coast but is a more southwesterly direction. We had been walking for a good ten minutes in my opinion when Mary said,

"We'll be taking the fairy path up past the Fairy Fort then we'll turn and head due west to the sea. I think that spot will be our best hope of finding the reed."

"I couldn't help myself, I had to ask,

"What do you mean by Fairy path and Fairy Fort? Do you believe in Fairies?"

"Doesn't everyone believe in Fairies?" she asked me back.

"Well some do and some don't, maybe more don't than do." I answered her.

"Well in Ireland we know better. The Fairies are part of our lives from before we are born until the end and then maybe even beyond: none have come back yet to say for sure."

"That's very interesting," Becka said, "Tell us about the Fairy path and Fort. I've never heard of them before."

"Well, a Fairy Fort in an entrance into the underground Fairy World. There are many of them in Ireland and you'll get to see one shortly. They are mounded earth in circular patterns and they're along the Fairy Paths. I think you might call the Paths Ley Lines. The Earth has strong lines of energy that make it easier for things of the supernatural to happen or materialize along. Fairies have more strength and power the nearer they are to a path or fort. They watch over all of nature, the water the trees the valleys and hills. Did you not meet the Devas while you were with Katherine and Elizabeth?" she asked.

"Yes and that was an amazing use of energy and consciousness. I would like to learn more of it sometime." Bach told her.

"We were all bewildered by the Devas and have never seen anything like it or them before. Do you also have the knowledge to summon them?" Becka asked.

"No, that level of knowledge hasn't come to me yet. I'm working on it but I'm not like my cousin Elizabeth. I know of the herbs and sacred plants, the fairies and energies that circumvent the globe. I'm just learning now how to read ones aura and chakra energy. Maybe the next time Elizabeth comes to visit I'll be able to learn more from her. She's a wonder isn't she?" Mary answered. "In the olden days she probably would have been called a sorceress or burned at the stake. She can summon way more than Devas, usually when she's here the hairs on my arm are always standing straight up from the wonder of it all." She wrapped her sweater a little tighter around herself and kept walking.

Soon we saw what looked like a couple of mounds in the hill just ahead of us. They were circular in design and very simple. There were actually two circles, inside a larger circles sitting side by side and the lines that defined the design were just the raised earth.

"I believe the ancients actually built their forts here and it was only later called Fairy Forts based on the Druids magical ways. There was many a tale that told of pots of gold hidden in them by the Leprechauns.

Today many still say it is the portals into the Fairy world and it's because of that they built here when the ancients started to use the energy of the sacred places to build upon." We had stopped while Mary explained the design in the ground and then she was ready to move on and we followed.

"Bach, what do you think of this place? Can you read the energy and tell if it is a portal into a Fairy World.

We were nearing the edge of the cliffs, the wind was picking up, getting stronger and she was right, colder coming in off the sea. Maybe we should have taken her offer for a sweater or something warmer to wear.

"Looks like a storm could be brewing off shore and headed this way. Maybe we should get a quick look and then head back because, if the storm does come in, it'll be too danger out here for any of us." Mary warned us.

It seemed with her words the wind slammed into us even harder. Off shore you could see a tempest brewing. The clouds were dark gray in color and churning like a war was getting ready to explode on the coast. The whole scene made me think of Florida and the hurricanes that tore into the coastline, all wind and thunderstorms tearing down everything in their path. This weather wasn't looking good for our mission; if this storm came any closer to the coast we would have to find someplace to take cover and wait it out. Unless of course we could find the plant we needed in the next ten to twenty minutes.

Personally I was thinking nobody in their right mind would want to get anywhere close to the cliffs edge, no matter what they were looking for or how important it might be. I didn't like heights to begin with but with the wind pulling and pushing around so wildly, I didn't want to have to look over the side for the Millers Reed we needed. So I just stood there waiting to hear what Bach would say about what we'd be doing next. I had to admit to myself, I was afraid to get any closer to the edge.

"I believe you are right Mary Todd. This storm is heading right for us and we should find a place to take cover. What do you suggest?" He asked.

"Come with me, we'll go to my house. We'll be safe there the old cottage has been standing for more of these storms than anyone from around here can remember. Let's get out of here before the storm blows any of us over the cliffs. Follow me and try not to fall." She ducked her head down as the rain started to pelt us. And turned to hurry back the way we had come.

When we got to the Fairy Fort she turned the other way and started to race down towards a smaller cottage we could see in the distance.

"That's my house over there. Hurry we're almost there." She yelled back to us.

We all raced down the hill towards the cottage and made it inside before the worst of the rain started. We entered a warm cozy living room with big over stuffed furniture that surrounded a small fireplace. Mary turned on a lamp and said,

"Come on in. It'll just take a minute of two to get the fire going and you can all dry off." Mary said as she started towards the fireplace.

"I can do that for you if you like. "Shi told her.

"Okay then, you start the fire and I'll put some tea on and get a stew started for dinner. The matches are there on the mantel." She answered him as she pointed up to a box sitting on the mantel.

"Let us help you in the kitchen, it's the least we can do if you're going to feed us." Mu told her.

"Well then, you girls come in and we'll get things started." Mary told her as she turned and headed into the kitchen. It was a small but again, a cozy room. Everything you'd need was there. It felt like the kind of place where nothing but great memories would be born and live on. All the pots and pans looked like they were well aged and used possibly by generations of Mary's family. The towels and curtains looked hand made and had the prettiest embroidered designs decorating them.

While we were getting warm and dry inside Mary's beautiful home the storm was throwing a ton of rain at the cottage, it sounded like drummers on the roof of the cottage playing their song. Mary hurried to turn on a second light in the kitchen and threw her wet sweater over the back of one of the chairs. Even the chairs at the table looked hand made and carved with love and care by the maker.

"Okay then, you girls can chop the veggies and meat while I make the biscuits. Here," she handed us each something to be in charge of, Becka got the meat, I was handed potatoes and Mu got the carrots and celery.

"Cut the meat into chunks about half an inch square. Kath, do the same with the potatoes and Mu make the carrots and celery about half that size. I want to be able to get this done in just an hour or two, if you cut things too large they'll never cook that fast. She handed out the knives and we all started peeling and chopping things. Mary started mixing flour and eggs to make fresh biscuits. We could feel and hear the fire in the front room as it started to take off. It looked like a family getting the evening meal ready and tonight it felt that way to me. Mary had taken us in and was clearly looking out for us.

She turned on the radio and tuned into a weather channel. When the weather report came on they said the storm had come in almost out of nowhere but would last through the night. Winds were going to be 75 miles and hour and gusting from there. Certainly was a night to be inside. I for one was really glad Elizabeth had her cousin Mary waiting for us otherwise I'm not sure where we'd be tonight. Looking around the kitchen I felt safe and warm and knew whatever this stew tasted like, I was going to enjoy it immensely. Mary looked like she would be a good cook and if her muffins were any example of that this stew would be delicious and with fresh biscuits and butter, it would be 'to die for.' Did I mention how much I love fresh baked breads and biscuits, warm from the oven dripping with butter?

Just thinking about it had my mouth watering and I looked to make sure I wasn't drooling on the table. The boys came in and suggested they could finish all the chopping and we could go dry off in the front room.

"Go on girls, we can finish this. You go on and dry off. Wouldn't do for any of you to catch the death of a cold while you're here." Mary ordered.

The cottage wasn't very large and we wondered if Mary lived here all alone or if someone else would be showing up. There were family pictures on the wall but they all looked old and more like antiques. I called from the front room,

"Mary, tell us, do you live here all alone or do you have family coming home tonight?"

"No, there won't be anyone else showing up. I'm engaged but not married yet and Brody is off to Dublin for a week. My parents are both gone and have been for a few years. It's just the six of us tonight."

The fire felt good, the three of us were standing close together absorbing the heat it was producing; we weren't all that wet so it didn't take too long to feel dry again. The warm and toasty feeling was really enjoyable and beat the rainy windy one that brought us here. Mary had started cooking the meat and the yummy smell was working its way into the front room. Getting warm and smelling dinner being cooked were two triggers that got my stomach to rumbling and both Mu and Becka started laughing at me.

"I can't help it. Doesn't the smell make your stomach want to call out too?" I teased back. "I can't remember when we last ate and you all know I like to eat and eat often."

They both just laughed at me again.

"What's so funny in there?" Mary called out from the kitchen. The girls laughed more and pushed me towards the kitchen.

"Kat's stomach started growling the minute she smelled you cooking the meat. She's the hungriest member of our group all the time."

"Well sorry Kat, this pot needs at least an hour to cook but I might be able to find another muffin if that would help hold you over until dinner." Mary laughed and asked the rest of the kids "Anybody else need a little something?" as she offered another basket of muffins to us. I jumped right in, took one and said "Thank You."

The others were a little less aggressively eager but they all took a muffin and thanked Mary. A long day and no time for meals made us all very hungry, my stomach was just the noisiest.

We sat and talked in the kitchen while dinner was cooking. Mary had so many fairy and Leprechaun stories she made us all laugh a dozen times with her tales. She wove her tales as the wind howled and the rain beat against the cottage, it howled and raged outside but we all felt safe and warm inside. The smelling of the stew was getting better and better as the minutes ticked by and it didn't seem so long before Mary said it was ready. We quickly set the table and after saying grace we all dove in to huge bowls of lip smacking stew with fresh warm biscuits and butter to make it feel like complete heaven.

We all asked for seconds and feasted like kings. It had to be the best beef stew I ever ate in my life. Mary seemed delighted with being the bell of the ball. We couldn't thank her enough or praise her cooking skills more. I think she enjoyed having us there. We sure appreciated being there and accepting her hospitality was like taking help from an old friend. I think she felt as at ease with us, as we did with her.

The storm was still going strong as we cleaned up the kitchen and listened to the weather channel again. The storm was expected to past the next morning so we had another night to get through before we could start the final search for the sacred Miller's Reed. Becka and I both thought it would be wonderful to curl up and sleep near the fire.

Especially when you could hear the wind and rain outside doing it's best to tear the world apart outside.

The weather channel on the radio said it was a hurricane that crossed the Atlantic. If we were lucky it would pass by morning and we could get on with the search. There could be a few minor rainsqualls off and on throughout the next day but the worst would be behind us. After hearing the report Bach was insistent that we try to go out again at first light, if the weather permitted. Mary seemed agreeable, weather permitting.

Once it was all decided, we all started to figure out where we would sleep for the night. Mary said she thought there was room in her room for us girls and the boys could have the front room near the fire. She got bedding for one of them to sleep on the floor and the other on the couch. Most of the bedding she brought out to them looked like old family quilts and hand woven blankets. The boys would certainly be warm and toasty for the night. She added a couple pillows to the pile she handed them and herded us girls into her room. She had two twin beds and a window seat in her room. Mu said she would take the window seat if Becka and I wanted to sleep together on the other twin bed, leaving Mary her own bed for the night.

Mary handed out her extra nightgowns and we all changed then curled up in our appointed spots. The twin bed was soft and oh so comfy. I didn't think I'd ever lain on such soft sheets they almost caressed what little skin I had exposed. Becka and I curled up close to each other, as there wasn't too much extra room in the twin bed. Mu seemed happy with her window seat she was stretched out with her head on a big fluffy pillow with a knitted blanket pulled up to her chin.

The wind was howling up a storm outside and it was so wonderful to be inside safe and dry. The bushes were brushing and scratching up against the windows and the sound was a little scary. Mary said the wind sounded like Banshees crying out their misery.

"What is a Banshee?" Mu asked Mary.

"Banshees are disembodies spirits or a ghost as most Americans call them. They tend to stay with their family generation after generation or until there are no more descendants to carry on the family name. They usually die with too many desires to watch over their families and that's why they don't move on. All of Ireland has different Fairies and such. Some say there's also a Watershee. They say the Watershees dwell in the lakes and bogs luring travelers with their sweet singing voices and once they have lured them in they devour their poor unfortunate souls. I myself am more into believing in the nicer fairies but I wear my cross and say my little prayers when I must go towards the lakes or bogs. One can never be too safe. When you have seen the things I have seen, you don't want to take any chances." Mary said quite seriously.

"Mostly we've heard of Leprechuans in connection to Ireland and Irish legends. Have you ever seen one Mary?" Becka asked.

"I can't say that I have ever seen one but I believe I have felt their energy a few times. They say they are 'quick as a wink' and can disappear in a second so it's not easy to spot them. The fairy you'd want to be watching out for would be the one they call the Pooka. He's a wicked character and the most feared of all the fairies. He usually comes out during the night creating his mischief in an assortment of disguises.

I would have thought you'd want to know about the Merrows. Seeing how they are the most like the merkids." Mary added.

Mu lifted and turned her head asking Mary,

"What do you mean they are the most like us?"

"Merrows are said to be half human, half fish and they are able to walk on land or swim like fish in the sea. The name Merrows comes from the Irish Muir, meaning 'sea maid'. Some say Merrows have been known to take human lovers if they happen to live by the sea. Maybe we should remember to ask Bach if he thinks they are any relation to you merkids." Mary answered her.

"Yes, I'll have to remember to speak with him about this." Mu said.

The conversation stopped and we were all thinking about what Mary had just said. Funny to think they had legends and tales of fairies who were possibly just merkids in spirit. That thought opened my eyes and my mind for a couple minutes and put more thoughts inside to bounce around. Nothing was impossible! I totally believed that now. I had also seen too much and been too many places lately to think there were any limits anymore.

The silence led us all into a sound sleep and the noises of the storm or Banshee's which ever they were disappeared from our consciousness. The night seemed long and restful. I woke about the same time as the others. I didn't know if we were finally tuning into Bach time or not but it seemed we all woke up that morning about the same time. Personally I thought "Bach is calling us with his mind and doesn't have to use his real voice anymore". He was our Bach-alarm!

Mary scurried to get dressed and make her bed before she went to the kitchen.

"We'll all need a little something to eat if we're going to be all over the cliffs today. I'll just warm some ham and scramble some eggs for us. Is tea okay for everyone? She asked.

We all dressed, did a little personal grooming since there was a real bathroom and then gathered and put up all the bedding. Becka went out to help Mary in the Kitchen and everything was ready by the time the rest of us got to the table.

"Protein" Mary said, "It's what we'll all need if we're going to be climbing the cliffs for your plant."

Everyone at the table devoured the breakfast, while the rest of us cleaned up Mary threw some things in a basket to take with us.

"What did you put in those eggs Mary? I asked "I don't think scrambled eggs have ever tasted that good before."

She just smiled and said

"Just a few herbs from my garden. I'm glad you liked them."

Bach got the group headed out and as we stepped outside the day looked to be calm with a clear sky. We got lucky. This wouldn't be easy under normal circumstances but if the wind were bad or rain was coming at us it would be next to impossible to climb anywhere near the cliffs. Mary had said more than one careless tourist had fallen to their death from the cliffs in Antrim County. None of us wanted to have a similar fate so we were thrilled to see such great weather as we climbed the hill headed towards the cliffs again.

This time the three of us girls took Mary's offer to borrow a sweater for the day. If the wind couldn't cut through you you'd get through the day a lot better and be a lot warmer she had said when she offered. Ireland wasn't all that warm a place, even with the sun out the wind had moisture in it and felt cooler than back home.

It only took a couple minutes and we were back to the Fairy Fort and turning towards the sea. The wind was getting a little stronger as we neared the top of the hill the water of the sea out in front of us was still rolling and cresting with more energy than it had before the storm, when we first arrived yesterday. The waves were crashing against the rocks below and it was quite scary trying to look down to see things. I wasn't great with heights so this was twice as hard for me to deal with. Maybe I'd stand back and let the others look over the edge for the Millers

Reed. I couldn't help but think, "How could any plant have survived the storm and the waves last night? The wind alone could have torn anything growing in the cracks or crevices out by their roots. "I know it sounded like the gates of Hell had been opened up as the storm made landfall so I wasn't sure we'd find anything there today. Maybe if we could have looked or searched yesterday before the storm but I had no expectations of anything living still being in the rocks this morning.

That thought of course put a real damper on my mood. If we had come all this way and couldn't get the Miller's Reed it would be a greater loss than anything I could begin to imagine. Bach seemed determined and was scanning the cliffs below like a hawk looking for its prey. That gave me hope. I knew if anyone could find it now it would be him.

After scanning the area with no results Bach told Shi to work his way back to the lower Causeway area and come back this way to scan from the water level. Maybe he would be able to see something from a different angle and advise us where to look. We all hoped if we found a plant we'd be able to get to it. Not many of the cliffs could be climbed from either direction. None of us could fly so I wasn't sure how Bach was going to handle this I was just hoping for the best.

"Maybe it's time to say a little prayer," Becka said as she nudged my arm.

"Yeah maybe so. I'm afraid to get any closer much less really look over the edge. Besides how could anything have survived that storm last night? It sounded like Hurricane Charley when it hit Florida and you know what that did to all the plants and trees." I answered her

We all watched as Shi headed towards the lower Causeway. Maybe once he could get a little lower he'd be able to see something and save the day. We said our little prayer and hoped for the best as we watched him disappear in the distance. It would take a while for him to get to the water and get back down to this area but he'd check all along the way for any sign of the reed growing anywhere. I prayed the purple flower would still be on the reed if there were any left out there, it might help Shi to see from the water such a small thing up among the cliffs.

Bach stayed busy trying to scout out the general area, some times even lying down on the ground so he could just stick his head and shoulders out over the edge of the cliffs. He made me think of an owl the way he was moving his head, he was scanning every nook and cranny from his position that he could. He was desperate to find the reed and so were we.

Mu kept asking if he could see anything as she too was craning her neck out trying to see to the other side of the cliffs. Even looking out over the edge was dangerous and I couldn't push myself to join them.

"Maybe we should go down to the lower areas and see if we can see anything down there. What do you think Bach? What do you want us to do?" I asked.

"Good idea, you girls could spread out along the lower areas, as Shi passes by you can help local the reeds if he sees anything from the sea. You could hold your placement if he indicates he sees anything near you. I'll come if he does so just don't move, stand as close as you can to where Shi says he sees a plant," he ordered.

Good I could breathe a little easier now, I didn't have to try and look out over the cliffs at the highest point. I was happy to move down the hillside to the lower levels and even happier when Mary said she'd stay at the next highest point and later Becka took the second spot leaving me the lowest level. This I could handle and immediately started to scan the balsalts, at all their different heights. Some were higher than others and at this level if I had seen a plant I might have been able to get to it without too much trouble or danger.

I hadn't seen Shi show up yet but he couldn't be much longer, surely he had made it to a point at or near the Causeway where he could reenter the water. The waves were crashing into the lower cliffs and the over spray of the waves was sending mists into the air above me. It was then that I saw Shi swim up he was trying to be careful as the waves were strong and they kept pushing him close to the base of the cliff wall.

I called out to him,

"Have you seen and plants at all yet?"

He yelled back to me,

"Nothing yet but I think I can see something green just up ahead. Walk along with me and let's see what it is."

"That was Bach's plan. We'll be your markers if you can see any plants." I called out to him.

"Yes I know. He's already informed me. Come on, let's see if we can find the reed," he answered.

So the two of us moved slowly along the cliffs. We had only gotten about halfway across the distance between Becka and me, when Shi started pointing and yelling to me. I couldn't see what he was pointing towards but it must have been a plant. He was too excited for it not to be.

The cliffs were only about 30 feet high at this point but the plant he saw was too low for me to reach, I couldn't even see it and apparently it was too high for him to reach. He tried a couple times to climb the balsalt columns and he would only get a couple feet high before he would slip or fall back into the sea.

Finally he decided to check for more plants along the way.

"I'll check the rest of the cliffs and communicate with Bach. You stay here and we'll get back with you. Don't move stay right there," he ordered me.

After he swam away I tried to see what he had seen but try as I might, I couldn't see anything. Some of the columns must have been blocking the view. He said it was the Miller's Reed and the purple flower was in full bloom. Unless they found another plant closer they would be back soon. When Shi swam past Becka and didn't find anything, she came down to join me saying,

"Well at least Shi found a plant. I saw him trying to scale the columns to reach it. Too bad this one couldn't have been an easy one. Can you see it, where is it? How hard do you think it's going to be to get to it?"

I looked back towards the edge of the cliff and told her,

"I can't see it from here, I kind of know, approximately where it's at. Maybe if we were cliff climbers we could get down to it. See if you can spot it." I told her.

Becka got down on her knees and started to lean towards the edge and scan the area below. She looked to the left and then to the right but she couldn't see it either.

"It must be more than 10-15 feet below us and if Shi couldn't get to it I'd say it had to be at least 10- 15 above the water level. So that means it's probably in the middle, not the best spot for us." She answered.

"Yeah and I'm no cliff climber either." I added.

"Maybe they'll find another plant somewhere up ahead where Mary or Bach are waiting that's closer and easier to get to. Let's hope that happens." Becka said

"Trust me, I've got all my fingers and toes crossed." I told her

We sat and took in the scenery, trying occasionally to look up the hillside and see what was happening if anything, with the other kids. The sea was starting to work up a little more, the waves seemed a little higher and the white caps were looking bigger. I hope this didn't mean more bad weather was coming at us. If a storm came again it would be too dangerous for Shi to be in the water that close to the cliffs and we might have to stop the search again. As we sat there contemplating the sea and the weather we finally heard the others coming down the hillside towards us.

"Shi said this plant is our best bet, all the others he saw were too far out of reach. This is our best bet. Can you see the plant from here?" Bach asked.

"We can't see anything but Shi said it was right below me. I stood exactly where he told me to and I haven't moved. I swear. It should be straight down from here." I told him.

He asked Mary Todd,

"Do you have any long rope at your house Mary? I think we're going to need some back up safety equipment."

"Sure, I've got rope. It'll take a few minutes to go get it and get back. Do you need anything else while I'm going? I've got some tools in the shed if you think they would help?" she answered him.

"Mu can go with you. Bring back what ever rope you have and maybe a pick and shovel if you have them. Oh and if you have one an ice pick." Bach told them.

They didn't waste any time, the two girls turned and headed back down the hillside. They took off at a slow run and looked like they would be able to hold the pace all the way down the hill to Mary's cottage. I wasn't sure what exactly Bach had in mind but I hoped it was one of the boys who were going to be using the rope to climb down to the Millers Reed. I knew I wasn't up to that challenge. I hoped they hurried back because the wind was picking up and the sky was getting a little less sunny all of a sudden.

Shi had worked his way back to the cliffs in front of us, where the water was getting rougher, making him bob up and down pretty wildly. He was trying to be careful and stayed out, away from the cliffs. He kept pointing towards the plant so Bach could try to hone in on it. He said there was a small patch of the Reeds tucked inside a couple columns about half way down.

"What's your plan Bach? Can you see where the plants are? I can't see anything from here." Becka asked.

"It's too far down to see from here, some of the columns are blocking it from view. From what Shi is indicating I think with the rope as a safety I'll be able to climb down to it and get back without any trouble. We'll find out as soon as the girls get back as long as the weather holds and doesn't get worse," he said as he turned and looked out to sea, accessing the weather I supposed.

I looked down the hill in the direction Mu and Mary had taken off in, I could see them coming back up the hill, headed our way. Mary had a long rope looped over her head and right shoulder and Mu was carrying a shovel and pick. Well now we'd have to see what Bach had in mind. The weather was picking up and it looked like some rain bands could be coming on shore soon. None of it looked as crazy bad as yesterday's weather but rain was coming for sure. If the wind picked up any more I didn't think even Bach should try to retrieve the plant yet. This might be a waiting game we'd have to play.

When the girls finally got back to the cliffs where we were waiting Bach said,

"I suggest if you girls think you can hold this end of the rope and be my safety, I'll go over the side and try to get down to the plant. The rope is more a safety net of sorts for the Miller's Reed. The rope is so I can get it back up the same way, safe and dry. If anything goes wrong a dive into the sea wouldn't be the worst thing that could happen to me. It's the plant we have to protect I'm not so sure it could hold up or live after a soaking in the sea."

Mary spoke up,

"What about the wind Bach? It feels and looks like some weather could come in from the sea, they warned of rain bands still coming onshore off and on today. Will you be safe?"

"I don't have a choice Mary, I need this plant more than you could understand and I can't give up over a little wind and rain. Let's just give it a try. Hand me the rope and lets get going."

With his last words she handed him the rope she still had resting on her shoulder. Bach started to tie himself into the rope, making a harness of sorts and tying several tight knots to secure it all. Then he tied a large loop on the other end of the rope handing it to Mary.

"Here," he told us," You're the tallest one Mary, you should put the loop over one shoulder and wrap the rope around you like this." He told her as he placed the loop over her head. "You are the main anchor and the other three will join you. I'm sure the four of you can hold me if need be. Just don't let any sudden movement take you by surprise. I don't want to see all of you coming over the cliff with me. Think you can do it?" he finally asked.

The three of us grabbed the rope and all of us answered him at the same time.

"Yes."

In my mind I was thinking, I hope we can anyway. This wasn't going to be easy especially if we were going to have to hold all his weight and bring him back up to the top of the cliffs. The rope looked strong enough but I wasn't sure of the four of us girls would be. This was one of those times where I guessed you'd just have to do what you had to do, if it came down to saving Bach and the plant we needed so badly. (I'd just hope and pray we could do it.) There wasn't a tree or old stump or anything besides the four of us to tie the rope to, the top of the cliffs and this hill were barren with nothing but grass growing anywhere. You would have thought with all those basalts columns everywhere that there might have been an extra one over here we could have used to help secure the rope but there wasn't.

Shi was still out in the water trying to hold his position while Bach started to descend the topside of the cliff wall. The way the columns were at different heights, some of the column tops would act as a small ledge here and there to help Bach make his descent and to have a foot hold to help him once he got to the level the plant was at. Once his upper body disappeared over the edge I think I felt my entire body stiffen, afraid I might suddenly feel his full body weight if he fell or lost his footing. I think we all braced ourselves knowing Bach's life was now in our hands and if anything happened it would be up to the four of us to save our friend. We couldn't see what Bach was doing or even where exactly he was. The four of us watched as the slack in the rope slipped over the cliff's edge signaling Bach's progress down the face of the cliff.

The wind was whipping my hair up around my face and there were times I couldn't see what was happening right in front of me but I was afraid to let go of the rope to push my hair back away from my eyes. We had lined up with Mary in the back and then Mu was in front of her and Becka was in front of Mu and somehow I ended up in the very front next to Becka. As I thought about my position I just hoped that I didn't get forced too close to the cliff's edge. I didn't like heights and I especially didn't like having to look down from up high and unfortunately that's where Bach was, down below us.

I hoped and prayed with all my might that Bach could get the Miller's Reed and get back up without any trouble. I didn't know if I was up to anything that might involve needing super powers I didn't possess today. I wasn't sure how strong either Mary or Mu was but I didn't think Beck and I were very strong even if we put all our strength together. Just as that thought was leaving my mind I felt the first drop of rain hit my arm. OH no. It just couldn't start raining now once the columns got wet they would be so much harder to stand on or get any really footing. Bach would be like a puppet on a string bouncing around the cliff wall trying to get back up.

The rope was drawn out the total length of it and Bach was tugging on it for us to move closer to the edge. He needed more rope to get to the plant. The first few steps weren't so bad. We had started back at least eighteen feet from the cliff face and now as we moved closer to the edge I was getting more worried. What would happen if the rope weren't long enough? We could maybe go another ten feet but any closer than that and I'd be freaking out. One thing I didn't want to do today was fall off this cliff.

He tugged on the rope again and we moved within a couple feet of the cliffs edge.

"That's as far as we can go Bach, we're on the edge now." I screamed down to him.

"That's good. I'm okay just hold tight and I'll let you know when you can bring me back up." he yelled back to us.

The rain was starting to spit at us now and the wind was whipping a little more strongly too. I hoped Bach was able to keep his footing and hold long enough to get the Reed placed safely inside his pouch before this weather got any worse. If the rain started to come down much more, the grass would get wet and our footing wouldn't be as strong and we were already dangerously close to the cliffs edge. I couldn't help myself all I could think about now was falling over the cliff to our death, all tied together in this giant noose.

From my place in front of the others I could see Shi down in the water and he was bobbing around more wildly as the storm seemed to be coming into shore. Bach yelled to him and I saw him wave off and turn to swim back towards the Giants Causeway where he had entered the water. I hoped that meant that Bach had the plant and was ready to come back up. I waited hopefully for his signal but nothing was happening. The rain began to fall as one of the squalls began to make landfall. It came in like a sheet had fallen and it was an instant downpour of rain.

The water was running down my face to where I almost couldn't see and I thought to myself, this is it, my life is going to end here and now. The rain was making such a clatter at this point I wouldn't have been able to hear Bach no matter how loudly he yelled. With the rain came even stronger winds beating at us. I didn't know if we could hold our stance and I was beginning to get a little freaked out by the intensity of everything happening at once. Bach's life was still in our hands and I felt as if I was here all a lone.

Finally Mu yelled,

"We've got to bring him up now or we could all end up over the cliff into the sea. Just back up slowly. Now!"

We all obeyed and started to backup. Becka's foot slipped out from under her and she started to slide under me and that action knocked my feet out from under me and I started to slip and fall on the wet grass too. The two of us slipping created a slack on the rope, which pulled the other two girls almost on top of us. I'm sure that Bach started to drop a little down the face of the cliff as the rope gave way from us.

Mu screamed as she and Mary almost fell over us,

"NOOOOOOOOOOOOOO!"

Somehow they managed to stop Bach's fall and hold the line while Becka got up and rejoined them in the loop of the rope. It took me a couple extra seconds to push my hair out of my eyes then get back to my feet and join them. The four of us started to slowly back up again. The grass was getting more slippery and our feet didn't want to co-operate with us and we slipped a little a couple times as we backed up the first four or five feet. The rain was beating at our faces and was falling in a wall pushing against us.

Then a giant gust of wind seemed to pick us up and sweep us all off our feet. It felt like a Three Stooges' skit from a comedy; except this was deadly serious. Bach was being jerked around and beat against the rocks by the same wind that was battling us. I felt bad for what Bach must be going through because of us, especially since he couldn't see what was happening to us anymore than we could see what was happening to him. We scrambled again to get up and keep the rope tight so we could keep Bach from falling anymore.

It seemed like we battled the storm it was a few steps back for us, then a win for the storm and we'd be down losing ground, then getting up and doing it all over again. It was just when I thought we'd gotten the best of the battle and we went down again. This time I fell back further than before as the wind gave the rain a helping hand and a gush almost threw me over the cliff's edge. My feet slipped and I was grabbing wildly trying to find anything to hold onto. Finally I found something and grabbed hold as tightly as I could. My body came to a sudden jerk as I stopped slipping and falling. It was the rope my hand had found and now I found myself dangling over the face of the cliff wall with just the rope between the sea and me.

I looked up as I heard a voice calling to me. It was Shi,

"Are you okay Kat? Hold on we'll get you back up." and then he disappeared from view.

Slowly the rope started to bring me back to the top of the hill. As soon as I was half way up over the face of the cliff Shi came forward again to help me get the rest of the way up without being dragged by the rope.

"Hurry, we've got to get Bach up before something happens to him." Shi said as he helped me get to my feet. We both pulled on the rope and this time we were winning the battle. The extra help Shi could give was making a difference. We were still battling the wet grass and the pounding rain now if the wind would leave us without another gust like that last one, we'd get Bach back onto the hilltop.

When we finally saw his face and he was smiling. He was probably just as happy to see us, as we were to see him. He was just as wet as the rest of us but as soon he was standing he patted his pouch in acknowledgement of the plant safely packed in it. We quickly loosened the rope from our bodies and gathered it for Shi to carry on the trip back down the hill. Bach grabbed the shovel and pick and we were off.

The rain wasn't letting up at all we were being beaten by the waves of hard rain, while we traveled down the slippery hillside. I slipped and went down twice, everyone else went down at least once before we got back to Mary's cottage. I was sure we'd all be black and blue from the beating this storm had caused us. I knew every muscle in my body hurt and all I wanted right now was to feel the heat of the fire inside the cottage.

Just as we reached the cottage the weather took another sudden turn and the rain stopped. As we looked up there was even blue sky peeping through. All I could think was, "right, now you stop!!!" The guys headed to the shed to put the rope and tools away. The four of us stripped down to our underwear and hurried into the cottage. Once we got inside Mary took us into her room and handed out dry clothes to put on. By the time the guys got back to the front door we were gathering up all the wet clothes to wash and dry.

Mary handed the boys a couple long robes and told them to go change. She'd wait for their clothes and we'd go start the laundry while they built another fire. Before she left to get the laundry started she asked Becka to stay and get the left over stew on the stove. We'd get a warm meal before we left and she wouldn't hear anything else about it.

"Warm bellies and dry clothes, it'll make you feel human again." She informed us.

I think she was right. I knew I was feeling a little beaten up right now and the bruise I could see on Bach's face looked like he got beaten against the cliff wall pretty hard. I didn't want to look at my arms and legs maybe it would hurt less if I didn't see any black and blue marks. At least that's what I told myself as I started to warm up by the fire as it started to grow. Bach and Shi hadn't wasted any time getting the fire going and I was thankful for the warmth. Just as all of us were warming back up the smell of the stew started to reach us in the front room. Mary went to check on everything and we all followed her to help out.

The meal was just as delicious as it had been the night before maybe even more so after all the rain and wind we had done battle with. It made me feel whole again as we sat there warm and comfy getting our fill. Bach started to talk about the trip home he wanted to leave as soon as possible. So it was settled, we'd finish our meal, change back into our clothes and after thanking Mary for all her help, we'd head home.

Mu, Becka and I all helped Mary with the laundry and cleaning up after the meal. Becka traded addresses with Mary to keep in touch later. We all thanked her for all her help and her hospitality. The sun was back out and the sky was only a little cloudy when we finally left the cottage to head back to the sea for the trip home.

I marveled once again at the basalt columns that lined the sea here and the Giants Causeway as we marched back over it towards the waters edge. This was certainly a wonder of the world I had never heard of or ever expected to see. I would never forget it either. This memory was burned into my brain as well as all the girls in the Sisterhood we met in England and Mary Todd who had been so wonderful to all of us.

Bach suggested that this time they would drop us off at our beach rather than going into Atlantis first. It would almost be easier than the other way around as we often did. He was hopeful too that the kids back home might have discovered the last plant we had been searching for. So much depended on the last plant being found now. The cure was possibly in sight for the merkids and then also the safety of the Guardians.

We all looked one last time back towards Ireland and the Causeway just in time to see Mary Todd waving from up on the top of the cliffs. We all waved our final goodbye and dipped back into the water. The water was a little cold but I tried to think about the warm fire we had just left behind to take my mind off of it.

As we swam we headed straight back over the Hy-Brazil area we had encountered on the trip in. I saw what looked like straight lines, maybe roads of stone. Nothing here looked like the ruins they had discovered near Havana Cuba with pyramids and courtyards surrounded by walls or roads and avenues. If this had been part of Atlantis the continent it was so old and under the water for so long, there was little of anything left. I wasn't sure if the Ocean here was so much rougher that it just wore it all down or maybe there was never that much here to begin with?

The way home was just as beautiful and we swam often with dolphins and other fishes from the Oceans. Once or twice we even saw whales when we were near the coastline of the United States. There was so much to see in the water world the Merkids shared with us.

When we finally approached our beach I can honestly say I was happy to be getting home. I wanted to sleep in my own bed and take a long hot bath after dinner tonight. Becka looked happy to be getting home again too. There was always the worry about if we were getting home late and how we'd be received if we were. We said our good byes to the Merkids and promised to get in touch as soon as we had good news.

As we walked down our road Ronnie came out to meet us.

"How did it go? Did you get the plant safely back to Atlantis? Tell me everything." He begged.

"Are we home on time? What day and time is it?" I asked.

"Oh yeah no worries there, I can't believe how long you can be gone and all the time you can be on the other side and it's only hours here. It's only 4:00 in the afternoon, you're home in plenty of time for dinner." He stated.

"Well we didn't go to Atlantis on the way home this time. Bach has the plant and will get it transplanted as soon as they get back. He's more worried about finding the last plant and being able to work on the cure.

We're so close now. I think he just wants to get that last plant. So did anybody have any luck while we were gone? Did Cookie or one of the other girls find it yet?" Becka asked him.

"No I didn't hear anything from any of them. I'm sure they would have told me if they'd found it." Ronnie answered. "Tell me about your trip."

"We're so tired Ronnie, can it wait until tomorrow. I just want to get home and get cleaned up. I'm hungry and tired right now." I asked.

Becka spoke up telling me,

"I know you're really tired Kat. You go ahead I'll tell Ronnie the facts and then tomorrow we can both talk with him again."

"Okay, I'm just too tired to even think right now. I feel like I ran the Boston Marathon and I need a hot bath my muscles are killing me. See ya both later" I told them and headed for my house as they stood there and talked.

Once I was home I headed for my room for a change of clothes and then the bathroom. My parents weren't home from work yet and I had plenty of time to take a hot bath and clean up before they would get back. I took the phone with me in case anyone called while I was in the tub. I set everything down, lifted the lever on the tub to plug it and ran the water. I saw a few faint marks on my legs that I hadn't noticed before but no big black and blue marks like I expected from my fall over the face of the cliff.

As I dropped my shorts onto the floor I heard a little thud and wondered what had caused it. I picked my shorts back up and reached onto the pocket and nothing was there. Then I tried the other pocket. As I wrapped my fingers around what had made the sound, it hit me, the stone from the wheat field the night of the crop circle. It had been dark that night and I hadn't gotten a very good look at it. I wondered now what kind of stone I had, so I pulled my hand out and opened my fingers to see.

It was a flat stone, about an inch and a half across with a smooth finish. It was brown and sort of shiny. I don't know what made me flip the stone over but I did and to my amazement, there on the other side was the exact design of the Crop Circle. I was stunned and couldn't believe my eyes. I was so blown away seeing the crop circle design it was as if the stone burned my hand and I almost dropped it. Was this some sort of message? Had it been Alien influence or a message from the Guardians for me? Clearly there were forces at work here that I didn't understand and wondered again at the warning that Sybil had given us. I placed the flat stone on the edge of the tub and dropped my shorts again. How in the world could that stone have the design of the crop circle etched on its surface? Was it on the stone when it went into my pocket or did it happen during the night when the circle formed?

Just thinking about the crop circle again gave me chills down my back. Then my thoughts went back to Ireland and falling over the face of that cliff. It was one of the worse things that had ever happened to me. With my fear of heights I think it was even worse than almost cooking in the crystal chamber in Peru. I joined in the tug of war contest with the croc in Australia of my own free will no one threw me into that fight. As I stepped into my hot bath, the memory of slipping and falling was too fresh in my mind. I just wanted to forget about it and never relive it again.

I was stretched out in the hot water relaxing to the point I had almost fallen asleep when the phone rang and brought me back to the moment. It only took a minute to focus and pick up the phone and get it up to my ear.

"Hello" I answered.

"Hey Kat, I just saw you and Becka outside with Ronnie but you took off before I could get away from my sisters so I wanted to tell you first. I found the last plant!!!" Cookie told me with a ton of excitement in her voice. "You'll never guess where it grows."

Suddenly I wasn't half asleep and needed to hear more, I was all ears and my mind whipped to attention. The next adventure would probably be very soon as Bach and the merkids were more than anxious to work on the cure and save themselves. A million thoughts were racing through my mind. This was the best home coming news I could have gotten. Once I hung up the phone I'd have to talk with Beck and see what our next move would be. We'd have to let the merkids know and plan the next trip right away. I hoped this time Cookie could go with us. I wanted and couldn't wait to see her face when she was faced with the truth and became a real believer!

Adventure #7
Bali

*W*hen I heard Cookie say the word, "Bali" I was pleasantly surprised. I could picture green rice fields, banana trees and beautiful palms on a South Seas island. Bali sounded tropically enchanting and I would hope to be one of the kids on the next adventure. It sounded so exotic and I could see all sorts of peaceful images start to roll through my head like the pictures of Bali I had seen when we studied it in a geography class at school.

"Wow that's so great Cookie. You found the last plant and it's in such an exotically beautiful place. I'll have to get together with Becka to contact Bach. I can't wait to tell him and hear the excitement it'll create back in Atlantis. I can almost hear all the kids from here. They'll go ballistic." I told her.

"Yeah, well after meeting the merkids, I have to say I am interested on going with you on one of the adventures. This might be the last chance for me. Do you think they might let me come this time?" she asked with a little hesitation, in her voice.

"I'll let you know as soon as we get to talk with him and see what he says. I promise I'll do what ever I can to get you invited. This is going to be so great. Maybe we'll make a believer out of you yet! Listen, I need to finish my bath before my parents get home. Let me call you back later, I think I'm starting to wrinkle up." we both chuckled and hung up the phones.

I could hardly wait to get out of the tub, get dressed and call Becka. Seemed like we didn't get much time to relax between trips but our purpose was so important there just wasn't any time to waste. I realized I had suddenly forgotten how tired and beat up I felt when I heard Cookies news. I could just imagine how ecstatic Bach and the merkids would be and I couldn't wait to deliver the news.

I hurried to get dried off and get into some clothes. I called Becka while I was combing my hair to deliver the good news.

When she answered the phone she laughed,

"What's up Kat? I thought you were ready to fall asleep you were so tired. I didn't expect to hear from you until tomorrow."

"Cookie called. She found the last plant. She said it's in Bali. She didn't call you?" I asked.

"No I haven't heard from her but I just got back in from talking with Ronnie. I heard your call when I was coming in the front door so I wouldn't have been here even if she tried to call me." Becka answered.

"When do you want to contact Bach and let him know? Cookie really wants to be able to go on the next trip if Bach will agree." I informed her.

"Yeah, that's kind of funny, Ronnie wanted to know if he might go the next time too. He wants another chance to see Atlantis and get out with the kids again" she told me.

"Maybe we should ask if we all could go. This has been a group effort to find and bring back all the plants maybe the final trip should be a group effort. What do you think Bach would say if we asked him?" I threw the thought out and waited a minute to get her feed back.

"I guess we could ask. I know I would love to go and be there when the last plant is found and brought back. It would be so great if we could all be there together this time. Let's ask and see what they say." She suggested and then added,

"Can you come over after dinner? We could contact Bach then. Otherwise I could try to do it after we hang up. What do you want to do?"

"I'll work it out and come over after we eat. I better go now. I'll catch ya later. Okay?" I answered her.

"Okay. Bye." She said and hung up.

I sat the table while I waited for my parents to get home. My Mom had called earlier and said they were bringing home Chinese food for dinner. I loved Chinese food, especially shrimp rolls and fried rice. Must have been a carry over from one of those former lives when I lived in China. I always figured I must have been a poor Chinese because I loved the basic Chinese foods but not the really fancy dishes full of things like squid, octopus and things with shells still on them, or eyeballs staring back at you.

I was no more finished with setting the table when I heard the front door open and they were home. The dogs were yapping and carrying on from the minute they heard the car door close. They were waiting at the front door and followed my parents down the hall, all three dogs jumping and bouncing around at their feet, looking up probably hoping for a taste. My Dad sat the bag on the table and said he'd wash up and be right back.

I opened the bag, pulled all the cartons out and grabbed enough spoons from the drawer for all the boxes. The Egg Foo Young was for my mother and the General Tao Chicken was for my dad and me. We'd all share the fried rice, shrimp rolls and Chow Mein. I placed two fortune cookies at each of our plates. The cookies were another one of my favorites and I always hoped for a great fortune.

We all sat and enjoyed our dinner together. They asked how my day had gone and I told them I had a great day. I told them about the Giant's Causeway that I had read about on line and told them how cool and incredible I thought it looked. My Dad said that would be one to go see some day.

I asked him what he thought about flying saucers and if he thought he'd ever see one. That got him going and we talked about all the stories he had heard that made him sure they were out there. I wanted so badly to tell him I had seen one with my own eyes but I couldn't. I was busting at the seam wanting to tell him about my adventure with Becka, the merkids and the Lemurian Sisterhood on that hilltop in England. I wondered if I did ever tell him, if he would believe me. Even I understood how wild and crazy it would sound.

I cleaned up the mess after dinner and while my parents went to watch television I asked to go over to Becka's for a while. After putting the left over's in the fridge and the trash in the garbage, I headed for Becka's.

I ran around to the back door, which was usually open with just the screen door closed to keep the bugs out. I knocked and Becka immediately appeared like she had been waiting for me.

"It's about time." She said and turned to head toward her room.

"Hey, I came as soon as we finished eating." I told her as I followed her down the hall to her bedroom.

As we went into her room, she closed the door behind us. Both of us walked over and sat on the floor next to her bed, pulled out our opals and placed them over our third eye. Usually whenever we needed to contact Bach we'd sit and use the opals they had given us and he'd hear us almost instantly. It was as if our thoughts traveled at the speed of light or sound, which ever was faster.

He was there in less than a second. He was so tuned into us I think he already knew. Like the minute Cookie told me, he heard it too. Maybe he even knew as soon as Cookie knew, I wasn't sure. He seemed excited but like he already knew. Becka didn't even have to ask if all of us could come on the last adventure. He suggested it. Bach said he thought it was time we all met in Atlantis to discuss the Prophesy. So it was decided, if all the kids could make it this trip, we'd all go on the Bali adventure together.

"Wait till we tell the kids." Becka blurted out as she lowered her opal. "That was a lot easier than I would have thought. I couldn't believe it when Bach suggested we all go on this last adventure. This is going to be so incredible but there's so many of us, we're going to look like some school outing."

"Well we better get busy calling everybody. It might take Cookie a day to figure out if she can get away, same with Ronnie I don't think it'll be a problem for Bunny or Amy, how about you?" I asked Becka.

"No plans for me that I have to worry about. Let's call the others." Becka answered.

So we made the calls and everybody worked it out. We would tell Bach we could go the day after tomorrow. We did the opal thing again and talked with Bach once more. So it was decided we'd all be there on the beach the day after tomorrow at sun up. I was happy thinking about being at home two nights in my own bed before the next adventure. Becka and I talked a little before I headed home. I was tired after all the excitement and was looking forward to hitting my comfy bed with the big puffy pillows.

When I finally climbed into bed I had visions where tropical islands were dancing around inside my head. Sleep came swiftly and I found myself lost in dreamland in no time at all. But in my dreams instead of beautiful tropical islands I kept seeing caves with huge deep holes and pits. Everywhere I looked the shadows of darkness seemed dangerous and scary. I tossed and turned as my dreams took me deeper and deeper into the unknown.

When I awoke the next morning I didn't feel as rested as I would have hoped. All the tossing and turning I did as I explored the dangers of the dark and scary cave must have kept me from getting the true rest I had longed for when I crawled into bed that night. I wondered if the dream was sparked by the shadowy warnings Sybil had given us in England. I was sure it must have been a factor in what created my dreams during the night. I might not have minded the dreams if they hadn't also followed me around the rest of the day. For some reason I just couldn't shake the feeling of darkness that kept creeping into my thoughts.

It was a busy day in the neighborhood we were all doing everything we could to get ready for the next day. There were chores to do and Ronnie had to watch out that he didn't get on the wrong side of his parents. He'd get axed from the trip if they grounded him for anything. There were a lot of times when we'd make plans as a group but Ronnie's parents would ground him for some small infraction and he wouldn't be able to go.

Ronnie told us he was going no matter what. He was still on his best behavior but he told me he wasn't missing out on this trip. He had changed a lot since the trip to Mt. Shasta and it was all for the good in my opinion. He was a lot more interested in science, history and everything metaphysical: after all who needed all the cable channels when we were living and seeing so many new things up close and personal?

After meeting the merkids, traveling with them in different dimensions and seeing the UFO all I could think about was how I'd never be the same again. Now I knew how small and limited we were saying the Universe was, how naïve we were, thinking we knew all the answers to Earth's history and how this all came into being. I had huge respect for the merkids and the battle they were dealing with and I was so proud of being part of the solution. I wished many times I could tell my Dad everything that had happen so far.

Somehow we all managed to get through the day and we were all free to spend the next day together at the beach. All the parents agreed we could have the next day off to spend together and we were all on the beach before the first rays of the sun peeked over the horizon. I think Cookie was the most nervous, not too sure about what to expect, where the rest of us knew what was going to be ahead of us at least to a certain point.

When the merkid's heads rose above the waters surface I was surprised to see both of Shi's brothers and Bach's sister Sheba with

Bach, Shi and Mu: the six of them, to partner up with the six of us. Mu introduced everyone and they handed out the pouches and breathing gear to each of us with instructions for Cookie.

Bach explained where we were headed and how he planned to get there,

"We will cross the Gulf of Mexico and enter the caves near Marita, Mexico. From there we will swim the under world passageways to Borneo. From the master cave on Borneo we will walk to the South China Sea and make the short swim to Bali and come back the same way. We need to stay close and work together as one. If you're all ready we should leave."

So with those last words we dipped our heads under and gave Cookie a couple minutes to get used to the breathing gear and the ear crystals. Having everyone hear your every thought would maybe take a little more getting used to than the breathing mask. I wasn't sure if I was really used to having to monitor my thoughts, they just slipped out all the time, it was a strange thing to deal with.

The morning sun was illuminating the water in the shallow depth we were swimming through as we left the beach. This was our largest group yet and it felt like a pod of dolphins to me as we headed out and into deeper water. Cookie seemed like she was okay. I think we only heard about a hundred thoughts bouncing around in her head as we started our Bali adventure.

"I was so sure you were all making this up. This is unbelievable. How is any of this possible?" Cookie couldn't help herself and I knew exactly how she felt, we all did. It was so cool to hear and share her excitement and things were just getting started wait until things really got going.

Borneo, even the name was evoking pictures of strange and mysterious animals and exotic Indonesian dancers. I loved all the colors and costumes of the exotic dancers around the world. I doubted we'd get the chance to see any dancers while we were searching for the seventh sacred plant but I could dream about them.

"Borneo has a rainforest that is at least 130 millions years old Kat. There are more than 15,000 species of flowering plants on the island. The Mulu Cave where we will resurface at the end of the under world passageway is the second largest cave on Earth. There are many wonders of Borneo that are far more colorful than the human dancers." Shi announced.

So many times when the kids had information for us they rolled it out as if they were walking or swimming encyclopedias.

Then Bach stated,

"When you see the diversity of animals, there are orangutans, elephants, rhinoceros, leopards, rare fruit bats and more species of animals and plants being discovered every year. Borneo is one of the most ancient rainforest and islands left from the old world. The Aztec called the cycles between the changes on Earth, Worlds. Borneo is from the oldest World. Its rainforest is older than the Amazon rainforest. There will be many plants and animals to draw your attention as we walk across the island from the cave towards the Sea."

In the meantime, the swim across the Gulf of Mexico was inspiring as usual. We saw a group of swordfish, hundreds of dolphins and lots of sea turtles. The smaller fish were always beautiful and as we swam into the more shallow depths, the colors of the fish stood out even more with the sun filtering down through the salt water.

The caves on the Mexican coastline were easy to find and looked like any normal cave you would approach while diving any warm water coastline. No hidden entrances or strange play of light hiding the entrance from view. This one was easy since Bach knew the way and could read the area in advance of our arrival. Only once or twice now had I ever seen Bach unable to immediately figure things out when it came to which way to go next. It was like he had some built in GPS system in his brain and he always knew north from south.

The waters here on the Mexican coast were the deepest azure blue yet. I loved the colors of the Gulf and the Caribbean Sea. Hawaii was beautiful too but those waters were more turquoise and lime green with a little sky blue mixed in. Tropical waters were all the prettiest colors and so incredible to see. I hated leaving them for the darker water inside the passageways.

The cave wasn't a large one but large enough for us to swim without being claustrophobic either. There were so many of us, it did feel like a school trip, as we entered the cave in pairs. Bach and Becka were in the lead and Shi and I fell in around the middle while Mu took up the last position with Ronnie in tow. Better Ronnie than me in that last spot and I was more than happy to fill in the middle of the parade.

The caves were similar to others we had been in. It changed a little from time to time. In some places the walls were smooth and light colored, in others they were dark and rough. The crystal lights were handy to have and I was happy any time we were allowed to use them in the caves for extra light. Cookie and the others seemed to be doing all right and the trip so far was going well. I think I was finally getting used to the under world passageways and traveling through them across the globe with the kids. It was like the long ride to my grand mothers house. When you were young, it seemed so far and took so long, then the more you went the faster it seemed to be over and you found you actually enjoyed the trip more.

I could tell we were starting to head back to the surface as the group swam more upward. Then as we reached our destination, in pairs we all broke the waters surface, inside the Mulu Cave on Borneo. It was HUGE and I couldn't see the top of the cave no matter how hard I tried! I turned my head to look from side to side and it was like being inside some giant reservoir, it was water, water everywhere.

I thought I could see a cave wall to my left but it was a long distance over to it and that was the direction Bach led our group towards. It was funny listening to the sounds inside the cave echo back to us as we swam to the side of the cave. I don't think any of us said a word as we swam across the surface of the water. Inside the cave all I could hear was the sound of our arms splashing into the water and the movement of the water as it rippled away from us.

As Shi and I swam up, we joined the others climbing onto the rocks at the waters edge and the others followed us. Finally we were all standing on the rock taking in our surroundings.

"Wow" Cookie said, "This is the biggest cave. I've never seen anything like this before, not even in books. Are all the passageways like the one we just came through? Or are they all different?"

Shi told her,

"This is one of the largest caves on Earth, you could put most of the other caves all together and they wouldn't fill this one or the one in Viet Nam. The passageways are all different, depending on what part of the world they are in. Many are similar, yet like people they are all individuals and different."

Their voices echoed inside the chamber of the cave where we now stood and it was so still inside, the vibrations of their words bounced on the cave walls creating an eerie sound effect as if the cave had no ending. I stepped a little closer to Shi as I listened to the sound of their words. For some unknown reason, I felt as if we had just entered the Twilight Zone. I had been in many caves and passageways with the kids, so I wasn't sure what was different about this one, to make me feel that way.

It was a little strange having so many in our group and the energy did feel different. Maybe it was just as simple as so many different energies vibrating so closely together, in such an untouched virgin setting of nature that made me feel so strange. I kept thinking when was the last time any human stood here or was in this place? Maybe it was the energy of the place and not us. I wasn't sure but I planned on staying close to Shi and not falling back to the end of the line again while we were here inside this place.

Bach took only a couple minutes to get his bearings and then the group was headed off towards the exit. We hiked for hours, each turn in the passageway seemed filled with different aspects of the cave, there were the usual stalactites and stalagmites but this cave had huge open chambers and areas where the rock had large ripples and groves worn into it from water rushing over it. As we ventured through her belly I wondered about this cave and it's name Mulu. Was there a connection between Lemuria and its nickname being Mu and the name of the cave? I'd have to check that one out when I got home. Maybe the Internet could tell me why they named it Mulu Cave.

I started to hear a sound, like rustling cellophane paper. I knew that sound. I had heard it more than once in Egypt when the bats came flying through the cave passageways. There was also a smell in the air that reminded me of the strong ammonia smell of Bat Guano. I noticed Becka and I both started to look up, as did the merkids: they had been in enough caves to recognize the sound of hundreds to thousands of bats coming their way. I think the rest of our neighborhood friends wondered what we were looking up for, then the bats came flying through. We all ducked and I think Amy, Bunny, Cookie and even Ronnie all screamed as they ducked and covered their heads with their arms and hands. I managed not to scream but a big part of me wanted to.

The smell was getting strong enough to gag you as we left the high-chambered area. It was hard not to get sick from the smell and we all covered our noses the best we could, trying to breathe through our mouths. As the odor grew stronger I could hear the sound of something else. I couldn't figure out the sound. Then I saw it. There were hundreds of cockroaches and beetles all over the piles of bat guano. Between them and the flies in the air, above the sea of bugs. I was sure I'd be sick but most of all I couldn't see how we'd get around them, without getting in the middle of them all and that horrible mess.

When Bach said there was no other way out, I thought I might even throw up from the thought of what would come next. The smell and the sound of them were almost more than I could handle. I just wanted to run the other way. I honestly didn't think I could walk through that sea of bugs and bat poop, without losing it. I hated creepy, crawly things and now they were all covered in guano. I thought the look on Cookie's face was worth a win, on America's Funniest Home Videos. If only I had a video camera to get it on film because I think she looked even sicker than I felt right then.

All of us girls were making faces and whining about the mess and the bugs when Bach spoke up,

"These are creatures, just like you and I and they are nothing to be afraid of. We will keep to the side of the cave as much as possible and just go slowly. Try not to step on them. They have a purpose in the cave and are a large part of its survival."

We started into the smaller cave single file. Bach was at the front of the line and the rest of us followed. It was slippery and the smell got worse as we got into the middle of the mess. I could hardly stand trying to place my feet in between the bugs and not step on or crush them. It meant my feet were on the ground way longer than I would have liked and they had too much time to start crawling on me.

There wasn't one of us girls from the neighborhood who wasn't whining, crying out and screaming as the bugs touched our skin and tried to craw up our legs. More then once I know I knocked a couple of them, off my ankles or calves. Honestly, I didn't care at that moment if they lived or died either. Not falling down in the middle of the slippery mess wasn't easy and a couple times I had to catch myself as my feet felt they were falling out from under me. A couple of the merkids were slipping a little but the bugs didn't seem to bother them at all.

Finally we were out of the mess with the bugs and cockroaches. The air was a little fresher and the worse seemed behind us. The new area of the cave looked like a sponge with random holes running along it's arched wall. Bach informed us the mountain was made up of sandstone and shale, that the water of the last million years had left it's mark in many places, in many different ways within the caves interior. He said there were sinkholes, pools and passageways that ran for miles.

The next part of the cave had the strangest floor. It looked like a riverbed that had dried up in the dessert of the southwestern states. I walked with care, half afraid that I would have pieces of it break away, under my feet. This part of the cave ceiling came down a lot closer to our heads but I could smell fresh air getting closer with each step we took, so I didn't mind too much.

The last off shoot and exit from the main cave was home to a giant colony of spiders and there were hundreds of spider webs all along the cave walls as far as we could see. I hate spiders, even more than bugs or cockroaches. How in the world would we be able to get out of here? Surely Bach wouldn't expect us to try and walk through all those spiders and the giant webs they had built. There just had to be another way out.

As if he read my mind, Bach said,

"Sorry girls, this is the only way out. We are going to have to get through this last portion of the cave to reach the rainforest. We'll go ahead of you and try to secure you a safe way through. I truly don't understand your negative attitude towards these smaller creatures."

"I guess it's just a girl thing Bach." Bunny told him

Personally I thought to myself, I think Ronnie hates spiders just as much as we do. So maybe it's not just a girl thing!

The merkids started into the cave with the spiders and gently tried to push some of the webs out of the way. Others they tore down completely to open a way through. It was just three of them working ahead to open things up and they called back for the rest of us to follow. This was one time I thought the back of the line might be the best place to be but jumped into the middle of the line near Becka. I just knew I didn't want to be the last one in line getting grabbed by the giant granddaddy of all spiders just like in the movies.

I had to hold my breath almost the entire time we were trying to slip past the spider colony. I followed the pathway the merkids made for us and tried so hard not to touch or be touched by anything. The spider webs were floating in the little breeze coming into the cave and occasionally a long thread of one of them would touch you or catch in your hair. It was all I could do, not to scream and run for the hills, knocking over anyone and everyone in my way. I hated the feel of the slightly sticky feel the web had, that helped it to capture its prey. I just knew some of those spiders were going to get into my hair or down in my clothes. Just thinking and worrying about it, I could hardly stand still.

Ronnie was in line right behind me and at one point I heard him gasp. When I turned to see what was the matter I let out a blood-curdling scream and almost passed out. There on Ronnie's face was a giant hairy spider. Ronnie's mouth was open and when he realized how close the spider was to his mouth, he suddenly slammed it shut. The look on his face was pure fear. The spider was hanging onto the side of Ronnie's face, stretched out over his ear and into his hair almost sitting on his eye. Every muscle of Ronnie's body was frozen and locked into place, except his eyes. His eyes said everything he was thinking and he was scared to death right now. Heck, I was scared to death. I didn't want to touch the thing and even if I did try to slap it off his face, what was to say it wouldn't bite us both?

Everyone had stopped to see what my scream was all about. Mu was the closest so she stepped around to see what was going on.

"Everyone be very still. This is a very poisonous spider and we don't want her to strike while she's on Ronnie's face. He wouldn't live another twenty minutes if she does."

Well, hearing that sure didn't help. I was sure I would pass out now. What if that thing tried to jump onto me? I was closer to it than anyone else right now and I couldn't have moved if my life depended on it. I was way too scared. I think if I saw that spider start to jump, it would be a different story and I'd be hell on wheels out of here.

Mu reached down and took off her little flip flop shoe and slowly started to move the sole of the shoe for the spider to walk forward onto.

"Come along little she spider. I won't hurt you so please be kind to me in return. Just come with me for a little ride and everything will be all right."

Surprisingly, the spider did just that and once it was on the shoe and off of Ronnie's face, Mu slowly moved her shoe and the spider away from us and towards the ground a couple feet away. I heard Ronnie finally take a breath again.

"Holy crap!" was all he said.

Mu stepped back to the group and suggested we move on before the spider decided to come back. She didn't have to say it twice. I was turned and moving as fast as I could, while watching twice as closely for other spiders as I had before Ronnie's little adventure. There was one part of my brain that even said to me, "I'm surprised you can even move after that." I had felt paralyzed but the desire to get the H, out of there was stronger than the fear at that moment.

It didn't take long to work around and under the rest of the webs and with no other incidents to deal with it didn't take too long to have it all behind us. I wanted to stop and have someone check my hair, just to make sure there were no hitchhiker spiders going out with me. Thankfully the light started to filter in from the mouth of the cave as we neared the exit and leaving all the she spiders behind us.

At last we stepped out of the cave and entered the Borneo Rainforest. The temps raised and the humidity dropped on us like a curtain. There out in front of us was the oldest rainforest in the world and it was breath taking. The birds and animals were calling out their greetings and the jungle was alive with beautiful colors, sounds and smells. All twelve of us stood there looking out at the rainforest in front of us, a monkey of some sort swung from a tree to get a closer look at our group and we heard the scream of some exotic bird as it took flight.

"It's not far to the coast we should keep moving. Everyone remember to stay close. We don't want to lose track of anyone in the rainforest below, there are dangers in any environment and this one has many including numerous poisonous snakes and insects. Watch where you place your feet and keep your eyes and ears open. The closer we stay grouped together the better, now lets go." Bach instructed us.

We fell in line and walked in pairs. Bach and Becka stayed in the lead, followed by the rest of us with Ronnie and Mu, once again bringing up the rear. I could have done without hearing about all the poisonous snakes and insects. Hadn't we just been through enough with the creatures in the cave? Sometimes I thought that, what I didn't know wouldn't hurt me and it would certainly make this trek through the rainforest a lot easier for me and probably the other girls too. Now with every step I took, I'd be freaked out about what I might step on or what might strike out and bite me. Not to mention what might be lurking overhead. If I was looking up how could I watch where I stepped and vise versa. I'd be a nervous wreck until we were out of this rainforest and in the water again.

It wasn't long before we had to walk single file but we stayed within arms reach of each other. Many times small animals could be seen scurrying away from our group. Shi reminded me that most animals of the rainforest would be more afraid of us than we were of them.

I chuckled at his remark because he didn't know how afraid I was, especially of spiders that could kill you with one little bite.

We were walking in a low area when I heard something overhead start to fall and tumble towards us from above. As I looked up, afraid of what snake or beast was falling on our heads I saw the most gigantic single leaf I had ever seen. Wow, who would have thought any tree, no matter how tall or what rainforest it was in, could have leaves that would be that big? Nature just always kept amazing me with her magic and displays of wonder.

I was so relieved that it wasn't a beast attacking us that I was finally able to breath again. I hadn't realized I had been holding my breath as I looked up to see what was coming at us. Funny too, because I realized that I had frozen in spot, when I heard the sounds coming at me, if it had been a beast of some sort it would have had me. I never even thought to run for my life, I was too afraid to move. What if it was another one of those she spiders landing on my face? I would have freaked and passed out for sure.

There were so many strange and wonderful things to see in the rainforest when your fear wasn't working on you. I saw things called pitcher plants and more bugs and insects than I ever would have believed could exist. The ferns on the rainforest floor were taller than most of us but the trees rising through the rainforest were at least 60 to 80 feet up over our heads. It was warm but not a lot of sunlight made it to the rainforest floor, if it had, the place would have felt like a pressure cooker for sure.

We trekked across Borneo and as we left the rainforest and got more into the lower plains we saw a family of orangutans. They were so human like except for their awkward body movements. It looked like maybe their arms were too long and their legs were bowed out a bit too much. Their faces were so expressive and they acted just like humans as their little group moved across our path. We stood and watched as they lumbered by our group about 50 feet in front of us. You could tell they had seen us but we stopped and let them have the right of way and hoped we weren't disturbing them.

They looked and you could tell they saw us as clearly as we could see them. They showed their interest by looking at us and watching to see what we might do. A couple times they stopped and just watched us, then they'd move on but kept watching us. I guess since we didn't make any aggressive movements they didn't sense any danger. Eventually they turned their backs on us and moved on.

It was times like this that always made me marvel at all our experiences with the kids. No Discovery Channel could ever be as good as being here, seeing all this for our selves. Cookie seemed speechless a lot of the time, I think she had been such a 'prove it to me' kind of girl that now, seeing and living all this must have put her mind into overload. Even for me and Becka, this was my seventh trip and Becka's sixth: it was so super amazing and words couldn't describe it most of the time.

I could have done without the spiders and insects everywhere but seeing the orangutans like they were a neighborhood family just out for a stroll was one of the most alive moments of my day. Surprisingly I hadn't been afraid. When we saw them a peace settled over me and I could see the rest of the group was affected as well. It was wonder and amazement at it's best. What incredible creatures they are.

We came up to a river we had heard for a good part of the last ten minutes and looked to see how we were going to get across it. The water was moving a little too rapidly to try to swim across, we would have been swept away in the current even I could see that. Bach assessed things for a moment and turned to head upstream.

We hadn't gone very far when we saw a rope bridge of some sort hanging across the angry water. It looked old and half worn out, not the kind of thing I'd want to trust my life on.

"You're not thinking about crossing that old thing are you?" Cookie asked.

"It appears to be the only way across this river. I don't see we have too many choices." Bach answered.

Cookie spoke up again,

"I'm not going over that flimsy thing. What if it breaks while we're on it? We'll all drown and end up in the sea dead!" she told him and she looked like she was holding her ground on this one!

I knew Cookie and she could be more stubborn than anybody else I knew but she didn't know how tricky the kids could be with raising your vibration level. Becka and I both knew first hand how that could change your actions no matter what your words were saying. I almost told her not to fight it but knew that wouldn't help so I stayed silent and let the boys do their work.

Looking out at the rope bridge in front of us I wasn't too sure about its strength either but I knew the boys would check it out first and Bach would read the area and if he said go, we should be safe. It was a strange looking bridge with a woven thicker section on the bottom and it wasn't a bridge with steps or boards, just the rope bottom that V'd out towards the top with the upper lines as rails that were tied and connected to the lower main line.

As Shi stepped onto the fixture the whole bridge started to sway and drip down towards the water. He took a few more steps and it all seemed to hold okay. We watched him tug and pull and even shake the bridge lines with all his weight to see if they held fast or not. They did and we all let out our breath that he hadn't plunged into the rushing river below.

Shi called back that he was going all the way across and would come back as a final test of the rope contraption he called a bridge. The whole thing was swinging in the air above the river a little more than I would have thought it would and it made the idea of walking across it on my own a more scary than I already thought it would be. Cookie was standing firm in her conviction that she would not cross the flimsy thing!!!

When Shi returned I think we all felt there was a strong chance we could cross and survive the ordeal. So one by one we started to climb onto the ropes and make the crossing. Bach and Becka went first with just a few feet of space between them. The bridge swung a little less with two people on it. Shi had suggested that we didn't push more than two at a time onto the structure for safety reasons. When it was Cookie's turn, surprisingly she walked right up and stepped onto the bridge. She didn't say a word but I was sure she would have a lot to say when she was on the other side and her vibrations were back to her own level. She didn't have a clue about what had just happened to her that made her do what she swore she wouldn't do.

Shi and I took our turn second to last with just Ronnie and Mu waiting to come across behind us. The bridge seemed to sway a little more as we crossed and Shi said something about the wind picking up. We took it slow and easy, Shi watching to make sure I did okay in front of him before he took any of his steps forward.

I was holding on for dear life as the ropes moved under me and seemed to bounce in the wind. My foot slipped and I screamed as I started to fall down into the ropes. I heard all my friends screaming from the other side of the river as they watched me falling. I heard the words in my brain screaming, "death here I come." Then before I felt the water and my body plunging to its watery death I caught myself.

I never let go with either hand, I'm sure that's the one thing that kept me from totally slipping through the ropes into the water below. Shi hurried forward as soon as I stopped moving and the bridge came to a rest. He hadn't been but two steps behind me and now he tried to help me get back on my feet and into an upright position. My next couple steps were very carefully taken. When I finally I reached the other side the girls all came forward to help me get back onto solid ground.

They all huddled around me as I stepped off the bridge telling me how scared they were and how glad they were I was okay. I was shaking a little from the fear that had shot through my body as I started to fall when my foot slipped off the rope. I chuckled through my fear as I heard Cookie. She kept saying she didn't know how they got her to cross over that flimsy thing. Becka told her, we'd explain it to her later. It was good to laugh at Cookie and shake off my narrow escape.

The next sound we heard was Mu's bloodcurdling scream. Everyone stepped around and turned back to see what had happened. Ronnie and Mu were close to our side when the ropes gave way or snapped. They were both hanging on for dear life as the racing waters of the river kept pulling on the fallen bridge ropes. We all rushed to the rivers edge and started calling to the two of them.

Ronnie was calling to Mu to grab his hand. He was hanging on with his left hand and arm reaching out to Mu with his right hand. She was trying to reach up to take his hand but she was a little too far away to make it.

"Hurry, if you can't reach my hand, grab onto my leg and try to climb up." he called to Mu.

Shi and Bach tried to reach down and take a hold of Ronnie to keep him from falling. We were all grabbing a hold of each other to make a chain to anchor Ronnie to the rest of us, if we could keep him safe, maybe he could save Mu from falling.

"Hang on Mu, Ronnie will help you." I yelled down to her. "Just do whatever he tell you to do. Climb up his leg, he'll hold on and we're holding on to him. It's okay."

"I'm trying" she called back.

We were all sweating it out could Mu climb up with so little to hold onto and could Ronnie's pants keep from slipping with her trying to climb up over him? Luckily he was able to wrap himself with the ropes and still had a good foothold in the ropes of the bridge that had fallen and failed them. It was just enough for him to be able to hold his own weight and support Mu's weight as she tried to work her way up next to him.

She looked like she was finally able to get her hands wrapped around the ropes again as she started to get up past Ronnie's knees. I think we were all working just as hard as Mu to get her up the ropes where Ronnie could help boost her safely up to the top of the riverbank and safety. They struggled together to get Mu up and over Ronnie's shoulders where Bach and Shi could try to help her a little more. Once Mu was up on solid ground with the rest of us, the boys turned their energy to helping Ronnie get up what was left of the rope bridge as it hung over the side of the embankment.

"I told you that was too flimsy and we shouldn't have crossed it. You're all just lucky nobody drowned and I still want to know just how you guys got me to do that? Did somebody hypnotize me? Is that what happened? Cause I want to tell everybody right now, if I can't trust you all, this is not going to be a very pleasant trip from here on out." Cookie declared.

"It's okay Cookie." Becka told her "the boys just raised your vibrations to reach a level of trust and when they did that you were ready to go and there were no issues for you to deal with anymore. You weren't tricked or hypnotized. I know because they did it to me before when I was afraid. Believe me, even though you might not think so right now you crossed that rope bridge of your own free will. I watched you and no one did anything other than stand close to you so your vibrations would rise to meet theirs. Can't you feel the difference being with them?"

"Well, I hope we don't have to come back the same way because that flimsy bridge is no more. So unless they can raise the vibrations of that bridge and make it reconnect itself to the other side, we're not going to be able to come this way again." Cookie declared.

As soon as she finished her tirade I saw Ronnie crawling up onto solid ground again and rushed over to see if he was okay. I couldn't believe that Cookie had pulled our attention away from Ronnie's fight to get back up the ropes. He seemed all in one piece and no worse for the danger he had just faced. In fact I thought he looked a little excited.

Everyone was asking him if he was all right and he kept saying,

"I'm fine. Is Mu okay?"

She smiled at Ronnie and said,

"I'm fine. Thank you for all your help. I apologize for being such a girl and screaming when the ropes let go."

Ronnie brushed the dirt from his clothes and told her,

"No problem I'm just glad you didn't get hurt."

Bach looked around and said,

"Maybe we should get going, there's still more walking and the swim to Bali. If you're ready we should get going." He looked towards Ronnie and Mu for their answers.

"We're ready." Mu told him.

With her words we all fell into line with our partners. The scenery was similar and yet different from anything I had seen back home in the states. As we trekked across Borneo I kept thinking this is Borneo and it made it all seem strange and exotic. Where else could a girl see orangutans and cross rope bridges? I chuckled a little to myself, where else could you go with this many kids and not be a school outing? I never would have dreamed it would be Borneo with all my best friends and a half dozen merkids.

These were the wildest adventures of my life and I loved every minute of them. Well maybe not every minute, there were a few times I could have done without, like the crocs, the crystal chamber and the burning desserts. Sharing all this with my best friends made it even better this time. We talked and joked and it helped to make the time pass a little faster as we worked our way to the Sea.

The water was beautiful when I could finally see it again. The horizon was painted in clear shades of blue and sea greens. The sun was shimmering off the waves as we approached the coastline and the beach of pure white sand. So much of the world had such intense and beautiful waters surrounding it but this was without a doubt one of the most amazing beaches I had ever seen. We all stood to admire it as we reached the edge of the sand and stepped away from the trees and the grassland behind us.

"What a beautiful place." Cookie exclaimed.

"I totally agree." Bunny added in.

"Come along girls, we have miles to travel and the clock is ticking." Bach reminded us as we finished taking in the view before us then we all fell back into line for the swim to Bali. Once we all had our gear on we entered the crystal clear water and slipped away towards Bali.

The water was cool and clear, filled with all the most colorful tropical fish. The corals were numerous and vivid in color as well. I loved watching the fishes in tropical waters they were so varied and swam in such large numbers. Many times I felt the fishes treated us like another of their species and noticed us very little. It was like swimming in a tropical wonderland watching all the under water vegetation sway and wave in the currents of our under water highway.

When we arrived on the island of Bali we came onshore near the Temple Pura Pakendungan, on the west coastline. The Temple was so serene standing out in the waterline with the waves lapping at its foundation. It reminded me of a lonely widow waiting and watching the sea for the return of a lost love. I don't know why the Temple made me feel such a strong emotion but it did. It was also inspiring to see it standing there in the sea, strong and steadfast in a land with so many varied beliefs.

The energy around the temple seemed so pure and clear I wondered if that was the energy that made Bali the purification center or gateway of the Earth. I remembered Mu telling us about the Dragon lines crossing each other in only two places on the planet, Lake Titicaca and Bali. She told us that Bali was the one place where the Earths blood was purified. She said there are four gateways into Bali where the final cleansing takes place and they are the four sacred mountains of Bali. One dragon line was the yin or female energy and was often called the Rainbow Serpent. The other was the yang or male energy usually called the Plumed Serpent or Quetzalcoat Serpent

If you wanted to know the true potential of the world you only needed to visit Bali to get a reading or understanding of the pure energy there. I could understand her words now as I ran them through my mind again. This was the most spectacular scenery. Bali was a land of volcanic lakes and mountains, tropical beaches, ancient temples and gracefully sculptured rice terraces, filled with a diversity of people. The Balinese people were of small build and as we watched some of them along the shoreline I was sure we wouldn't stand out as much as I had first been afraid and we might not look like a school group after all. We weren't as tanned as most of them but we might fit in nicely.

We didn't have any idea where on Bali we should start to look for the plant we came so far to find but Bach thought for now we could start here at the temple. Bach said,

"We'll start our search here. Better we leave no stone unturned. Bali is a small island but more square miles than I care to walk. Beware of the caves around and under the temple. There are poisonous snakes who guard the temple and I do not care to have a run in with any of them. Stay in pairs and look everywhere."

We stayed with our partners searching the land and plants growing around the island temple. We arrived during low tide and so the walls of the temples foundation were exposed and easy to check. Since we found our plant in Ireland on the cliffs we double-checked the sea walls of the island very carefully. I wasn't sure about anyone else but I kept my eyes open for snakes, afraid that one might slip out and find me when I wasn't looking. I wasn't a person who liked snakes much less poisonous ones.

Most of the others climbed onto the temple island to begin the search. Shi and I walked around the lower rock base of the temple island and at one point as Shi stopped to look inside a small opening, I stepped around him to find better footing and as I did I saw his arm swing out in a fast motion toward the opening on the cliff wall. When I looked and turned back to see what he had done I saw a long dark striped snake swinging in the air from his hand. I think I almost fell into the sea again as I tried to get away from both him and the snake he was waving in the air over head. I screamed as I started to fall, which got his attention back towards me and he stopped waving the snake around.

"Nothing to worry about Kat, just one of the guardians doing his job protecting the temple. No cause for worry he and I have had words and he will return to his station now." As Shi uttered the last word he lifted the snake back to the small opening he had been guarding and released him back into his cave.

I considered that a close call, much like the bridge when I slipped and could have fallen. I don't know why but for some reason all this suddenly made me think of Sybil's words back in Ireland. She spoke of dark shadows and forces at work against us, could this be some of what she was talking about? That was twice now that I could have had a very bad accident. It was something I'd be thinking about later when I could talk with Becka again. For now I just said a little thank you to Shi, my Guardian Angel. Then we climbed up to the temple to meet up with the others hoping maybe they had better luck than we had.

As perfect a place, as this would have been to find a rare and sacred plant, it wasn't here. We decided to move onto the main part of the island. We'd search for someone local who might be able to help us. We walked past rows of banana trees on the road into the near by village.

Once we got into the small village we started to ask about anyone who would know plants and were told to see a local medicine man. We seemed to fit in nicely, we just looked like another group of tourists and no one even gave us a second look. The medicine man's home was easy to find. It was a small village and Bach read it easily even though there were a few turns to get there. I was never very good at finding things when it came to following directions so I was always amazed with Bach's ability to know the way.

The medicine man lived down a small lane with a very interesting gate at the front entry. I loved all the carvings and designs on the homes we had seen so far. The entrance gate was called a spirit gate according to Mu. As you entered you would step through the gate and there would always be a small wall to block the bad energy or spirits from coming straight in. The walk way would go around both sides of the small blocking wall. So you would enter the gate and then you would enter the compound by going around the aling-aling, which is what they called the blocking wall. She said usually there were several buildings within any compound. The Balinese would also put a wall around their compound, if they could afford it, because they believed it also helped keep out the bad spirits or bad magic. Balinese life was one of a strong belief in magic and spirits.

Mu told us the Balinese people believed the home provided a relationship between life here and the cosmos. The home needed to reflect the balance of good and evil in the world as well as a balance of the magic and unseen forces that humans interact with everyday. One usually hired an "Undagi" to help layout and plan the home and he would act as both priest and contractor in making sure the home was spiritually appropriate for the family who would live there. It was understood by the Undagi that a person's home must be in harmony with one's own body. This ancient knowledge was called "Asta Kosaia Kosali".

The Undagi would measure many of the owner's body parts like how many inches from the fingertips to the elbow or the width of the fist etc. These measurements would in turn determine the measures used in the size of the compound. All things in Bali were alighted with the sacred Mount Agung, which is said to be the home to the gods and is the center of the island. Once a home is finished there are many ceremonies to be held which are said to chase out any remaining negative forces that are still there.

There was a lot more thought going into building and planning your home in Bali than in houses back in the states. It was interesting to hear the names of everything and have her explain about the many shrines in and around every home where the owners made offerings on special holy days. In some ways this all sounded a little like the feng shui of China but also a little different.

When we finally reached the inner courtyard area we could see three young girls all dressed in ceremonial Balinese costumes learning to dance. The girls were graceful and it was a wonder to see them. The music was softly being played as they did their morning practice. Their headdress pieces were golden and very detailed with elaborate designs that were very similar to each other. Their dresses or sarongs were more then colorful they were brilliant in their magenta and yellow colored bands. We stood, fixed in place, for a minute to watch the girls dance. They seemed to hypnotize our entire group with their exotic movements and hand gestures.

It wasn't until the older woman over seeing the girls turned to see us that we were set free of the hypnotic trance the dance seemed to pull over us. She turned and upon seeing us and asked,

"Hello, how may I help you? Did you come to see the medicine man Wayan?"

Bach spoke up and said,

"Yes we are in need of his help. Is he available this morning?"

The woman clapped her hands to get the attention of the three young, exotic dancers. They stopped in mid step of the dance and stood to face her awaiting her instructions.

"Madari show these young people to your father." She told her oldest daughter.

Madari immediately jumped down from the dance platform she was on with her sisters and came to guide us toward another complex building. We followed her across the courtyard and onto the front porch area of the building, she said her father was in, doing his morning meditations.

"If he hasn't finished just be silent and wait for him inside." With those words she left us at the open entry to the complex building.

Now, once again, we did sort of look like a school outing with the twelve of us going in single life through the entry into the cool room where we would find Wayan the medicine man.

I'm sure the others were just as shocked as I was to see this little

Balinese man levitating in the air about a foot off the floor. He was in the traditional meditation sitting posture, there seemed to be a glow around him and I gasped as I first saw him. This was the last thing I expected to see as we searched out the medicine man for his help. Some how seeing him levitating made me feel a little more confident that this man could help us. I mean how many people did you know who could levitate? Surely this man knew lots of secrets.

We all gathered close together trying not to disturb Wayan as he finished his meditations. It wasn't very long and his body slowly settled to the floor then it was another minute or two before he opened his eyes and saw us.

"Hello my new friends" he said "How may I help you today?"

"How in the world did you do that?" Bunny blurted out. "You were levitating weren't you?" she asked

Wayan looked at Bunny and explained,

"When all twelve of your chakras are open you have the ability to reside in any dimension. When I meditate I rise up to the astral levels, it just happens." He said with a smile.

"Twelve chakras? What do you mean twelve? We've always been taught there are only seven chakras." She bantered back.

"Five of the chakras are in the other dimensions or astral planes. You have two that are under your feet and anchor you to Earth and her energies. Three more are over the crown chakra and they connect you to the higher astral levels. Every medicine man and yogi has all twelve chakras clear and open. It is how we know what we know. Have you never heard of these before?" he asked.

"No" Bunny said a little bewildered "I've never heard of the other five before."

"We will talk later and I will explain it all to you. Now I must ask what you have all come to see me about today. I must assume it has nothing to do with learning about the chakras." he told her.

It was Bach who stepped forward to explain what we needed help with. He showed Wayan the picture of the plant we came searching for asking if he knew where we could find it.

Wayan flashed us all a huge radiant smile and told Bach he did in deed know where we could find the plant. He explained the plant grew on the slopes of the sacred Mount Agung, the active volcano on the northeast side of the island.

"I will send my son Wayan along to show you the way. I advise you do not take your plant until the moon comes into the night sky. The potency you need will not exist until the moon is high in the cosmos when the rays can reach down and empower the plants." He rose up from the floor, walked to the opening of the complex room and called to his son.

"Wayan." When he didn't see his son he called to the daughter Madari and asked her to find Wayan and send him to us.

When we heard foot steps coming up the two steps to the top of the platform we all turned to see if it was Wayan the son coming to answer his fathers call. I couldn't have been more surprised. Here was a young boy about our age, he had spiked hair and wore a t-shirt with the word SLACKER written across the front of it. Could this possibly be the son of the man in front of us? Could they have looked or seemed more different? The father was the old world Balinese medicine man who looked like he could have lived hundreds of years ago just as easily as today. The son in contrast was a typical American looking teenager. We would learn later that he was more a computer nerd and was trying to find the answers to time travel using his fathers knowledge with a modern twist put on it.

"Yeah dad they said you wanted me?" he said as he came into the room. He noticed us and stopped to check us out, probably wondering what we had to do with his father calling on him.

Wayan explained to his son what we wanted to do and told him he should act as the tourist guide for our group.

"Sure I can do that. When do you want us to leave?" he asked.

"Now, if you are to get to the other side of the island and have time to search out the plants before the sun sets. Find them but don't take them until the moon is high. When you finish retrieving the plant come back. We will meet again before you leave Bali he told our group." He flashed us that giant smile of his and turned to leave the room. Before he left, as he passed by Bunny he told her,

"We will talk more when you return," then he quietly walked out of the room.

"Well maybe we should introduce ourselves. I'm Wayan, son of Wayan the medicine man but you already know that. Why not tell me who you are?"

We each introduced ourselves. Surprisingly this time Bach went last and when it was his turn he started to ask Wayan questions about how far Mount Agung was and how he planned to get there.

"Well I have a bike. That would be a little faster than walking but I don't have enough bikes for everyone. I suppose we could borrow some that would get us there twice as fast. Lets go get a few supplies and we'll see if my friends are around to ask. We could probably get by with six more bikes if we double up. I'll ask the girls if we can borrow their three bikes and we'll be half way there." Then he flashed a smile that mimicked his fathers.

Wayan seemed like a good guy and friendly enough. I guess I was a little surprised by his t-shirt and the SLACKER label it put on him. So far he seemed far from being a slacker sort.

We walked across the courtyard again, to the complex building that served as the kitchen, where Wayan loaded fruits and water into his backpack. The girls walked in while we were there and when asked, said we could borrow their bikes for the day. Things were going well and soon we would be on our way. Things were looking up for the plant search and by the end of the day we should have our plant and be ready to head back to give our thanks and say goodbye to Wayan's family.

While we were checking with Wayan's friends trying to get enough bikes to start on our journey Wayan began to talk about his interests in Time Travel asking Bach and Shi if they had any theories or ideas on the subject. That sort of blew my mind. Who would have thought we'd meet someone on the little island of Bali who's father was a medicine man and he the son, would be trying to figure out the answers to time travel? My brain was spinning trying to sort out all the different aspects of Wayan the son, as he talked about computer programs he was working on, using mind energy or thought waves to enter the different dimensions of space.

"I figure it this way," Wayan said as we walked to a third house," thought waves are what makes everything work. I believe they are faster than the speed of light. The human mind is the key. It's like it's the computer that has Google access to everything. It's like the difference between physical and astral levels, astral is lighter and faster. Thoughts make the particles and waves open up and I believe that opens the dimension gateway to the Multiverses where time travel can take place.

There was a University group that came over a couple years ago looking on the slopes of Mount Agung for an ancient Lemurian gateway. They believed where the two dragon lines of the earth crossed here at Mount Agung the energy was it's strongest and purest. They were sure that with Bali being the cleansing vortex of the earth, it was their best location to find a dime gate from this world. I'm the one who named it a dime gate, it beats saying dimensions all the time and I kind of like it. Catchy don't you think? Any way they had old maps they said pointed to Bali being the location for the old Lemurian gateway. They came to find and reopen it but they ran out of money before they found anything. Hey if you want we could swing by the old dig on our way. I go by when ever I'm over that way. Sometimes I even stop and do a little digging of my own."

"Hey," Ronnie spoke up, "Bach can read anything. Maybe if we stop on the way he can tell you if the dig is in the right place or not. It's uncanny what this guy can do. If there is an old gateway of any kind he'd be the one to know."

Wayan turned and looked first at Ronnie and then to Bach,

"You psychic or something dude?" he asked Bach.

"Something, like that." Bach answered.

We finally rounded up enough bikes for all of us to ride to Mount Agung. You could see it from the little town we were in so I hoped it wouldn't take too long to ride there. The sea breeze was gently blowing and it kept us all cool for the beginning of our bike ride across the island. As we passed temples and towns Wayan pointed everything out to us. He and the guys were all having a lively discussion about time travel and Lemurian gateways.

I stayed busy watching the tropical trees and wishing for the hundred thousandth time that I had my camera to take pictures. The girls dancing had been so beautiful to watch and their costumes where incredible. The island was a wonderland of tropical landscapes and terraced hillsides. This was a true land of enchantment for me. The smell of blooming flowers was in the air and the people along the way were friendly and happy, so many great picture opportunities and me with no camera, again!

No wonder they call it paradise. The tropical breezes, the beautiful temples and the majestic palm trees all seemed to come together to make a very peaceful and serene landscape. We rode along, as if it was any other day back home, except we were passing by fields of banana trees and rice paddies. The road was narrow and bumpy and when a car approached you had to get as far over to your side as you could because most drivers seemed to think they owned the whole road. I didn't mind so much really, after all this was Bali: I was learning to adapt to my environment when I went places with the merkids. The breeze helped to make the trip very enjoyable and we were all talking and having a great time.

Wayan said we'd be going by the Pura Tirta Empul Temple on the way and suggested we'd have time if we wanted to stop, make offerings and take a dip to take advantage of the spiritual value of the cleansing waters. He told us that legend told of the god Indra creating it as a fountain of immortality and he never passed by without stopping, which seemed to be the Balinese way, when near any temple.

He explained the ritual took a little time but was worth it. There were four pools, the first had 22 fountains and it was the custom to pass under each one, in order, to perform the cleansing correctly. He mentioned that the pools were full of Koi fish, very slippery and the water very cold. He said it would be a refreshing break both spiritually and physically.

I was all for stopping and checking out the temple. There were so many beautiful places we hadn't time to see that I would look forward to this one. Wayan said there were over a million temples on the island, if fact more temples than homes. Everyone agreed, even the merkids, who wouldn't be able to enjoy the pool without everyone seeing their tails. They told Wayan they would use the time in the gardens to sit and meditate. Wayan didn't know they were merkids or the true story behind our adventure with him today and Bach didn't seem to want to enlighten him yet.

We only rode the bikes a little longer when we came upon an incredibly carved entrance to the temple. Everything looked so ancient here the stone was green and black with mosses and molds growing all over it. Wayan said a temple was built at this site in 926AD. So this one was really, really old or no one had dated the entrance and newer temple. I was impressed and all of us took a few seconds to inspect the carvings of the figurehead over the doorway to the temple grounds. The only slightly distracting things were the little souvenir vendors with carts outside the temple gate. It seemed where ever we went the local people were there, trying to make money off of the tourists1 coming to their special location.

Once inside we saw courtyards and gardens with several buildings with even more intricate carvings and statues. This was a Hindu temple so they honored Braham, Shiva and Vishnu here. I remembered studying India in school so I remembered the Gods and what they stood for or represented. I always thought the Hindu religion was more a way of life than a religion. The three main gods were actually all considered to be aspects of the one impersonal creator of the world. They each however, had their own look and personalities, as well as being the different parts of the whole. That was my understanding of it anyway.

Wayan explained, how the gates, fences and courtyards were to keep out the negative energies and spirits from the inner sacred areas. Which seemed to be incorporated into all the buildings and homes on the island because the Balinese were strong believers in the spiritual world.

Inside by the pools, there was an area where you could leave your personal belongs while you put on a sarong from the temple, which you needed to do before you were allowed to enter the pool. The merkids were making food offerings with us even though they couldn't go into the pool. Today there were too many people around for them to risk having their tails seem by the general public or Wayan. We hadn't tried to explain anything to Wayan so I think even he would have been shocked. I felt a little sad we couldn't have been there by ourselves so we all could have gone through the cleansing together.

This aspect, of the forces of nature, all being so important to the people of the land made me think of the Hawaiians we had met on Maui. They believed also that all water is sacred and holds the power to sustain life as well as purify it. Once again I was making the connections to all the people we had been meeting around the world who believed in the earth being a living entity: a living and breathing force that needed love and care from us whether you could see it or not. They all believed in holding the bounty of the earth sacred and giving back to it.

First Wayan said we must give our offerings to the gods. He brought fruit for us to give as and it had to be presented on a small basket like tray. He told us it was important to ask for the blessings of the gods and as we each made our offering we placed our trays among all the others, placed there before us. Some had incense burning along with food and flowers. Wayan said all things of god were good for offerings but food and flowers were the best to give.

Cookie was first in line when we were finally ready to step into the pool. She took the first step and stopped,

"It really is cold water. I don't know why but I just figured it would be warmer than this." She said and took the next step. The pool wasn't that deep but it was interesting to see the Koi fish swimming around with the people. Cookie even seemed to hesitate when she saw a couple big fish coming towards her.

Wayan turned and saw the look on her face,

"They won't bite, only nibble a little maybe." then he laughed. "Come on Cookie, I will show you what to do and you can begin your cleansing. Watch me and do what I do, then move on to the next fountain and do the same thing. You must pass and use water from each of the fountains to complete your cleansing and purification."

We all watched as he told Cookie what to do. So one after the other we took our turns. Ronnie followed Cookie then Bunny, Amy, Becka and I was last. The water was cold and seemed to get colder the longer we were in the pool. The fountains never stopped pouring out their cleansing, pure water. I wondered what made them run without any power. Wayan said they had been running for a thousand years since the pool was created and were fed by natural springs far beneath the ground, which also explained the reason the water was so cold. We all took the whole process very seriously. If we could cleanse our souls or astral bodies while we were here, we wanted to be sure and get it done and done right.

Wayan said he followed the ways of his father and knew he was right about his beliefs but the younger Wayan liked to try to incorporate a little newer modern knowledge with it. That's why he was putting so much of his time and energy into a computer program to use the mind to open the higher dimensions. He told us,

"Most people are too lazy to do things the old fashioned, hard way with meditation and silence." He thought he'd help the masses discover the higher truths with today's technology and get through to more people that way.

All made sense to us. Ronnie seemed very intrigued with Wayan's ideas and wondered how he could make it all work in a computer program. He was grilling Wayan with questions whenever Bunny left him alone long enough for Ronnie to ask his own questions. It was fun to watch Bunny and Ronnie battle it out to get their questions answered. I was sure that Bach enjoyed the break he was getting today because usually he was the one getting bomb-barded with all the questions. Surprisingly Cookie seemed kind of quiet, usually she was the first to speak up and say what she thought. You couldn't help but watch for her reactions since this was her first adventure with the kids. Personally I thought she was trying to act like it was all no big deal when really she was totally blown away by it all! I thought maybe that explained her silence.

It felt good to step out of the cold pool waters and begin to warm back up in the mid day sun. I watched as the goose bumps settled back down on my arms. Burr that water had been cold. We changed back into our own things and went looking for the merkids, in the outer courtyard, where they had stayed when we went into the pool area.

Wayan didn't seem to mind or question the merkids not joining us in the temple waters and he had been an excellent instructor for the rest of us. We joined up with the mertkids in one of the courtyards and headed back to where we had all parked the bikes. It was only a few minutes more and we were starting back out on our way to Mount Agung. It had been a very refreshing break at the temple and one I would remember always. The carvings and statues were ancient and inspiring only adding to the exotic feel of Bali I already had etched in my mind. What an amazing place this was.

We rode our borrowed bikes a few more hours before Wayan lead the way to the old archeological dig he had told us about. We were on the lower slopes of Mount Agung and nothing looked too unusual to me as I glanced around the general area. I don't know what I was expecting but what I saw was piles of dirt and what looked like some old spots that had been dug into along the walls of the hill side. There were a couple tools leaning against one of the open holes on the hillside where someone had been digging recently. Maybe that was where Wayan had been digging during his last visit.

"This is it. Park the bikes and lets check it out. I'm curious to see what Bach thinks." Wayan called out to the rest of us.

Everyone jumped off and parked the bikes. Bach was the first to walk over to the area along the slopes where others had been digging. Wayan watched Bach with even more interest than the rest of us. Except for Cookie, all of us knew what Bach is capable of and finding some ancient gateway was right up Bach's alley. Explaining to Wayan how Bach does it would be the hardest part.

Bach stood in front of each of the dug out areas and then walked over about 40 feet and just stood there.

"This is where you should dig. They weren't off by much, just enough to keep them from finding the gateway. It's here only a few feet from the surface. Grab the shovels and we'll uncover it in no time at all." Bach told us.

Everybody jumped to grab any tools we could find. The boys grabbed the shovels and the rest of us grabbed the few buckets we saw in the abandoned pile of dirt and a couple broken handles that we thought we could use to dig with. This was unbelievable we were attacking the hillside like we were trying to save somebody's life. It was exciting to think we could uncover a gateway that existed during the days of Lemuria. If Bach said it was there, it would be there! I couldn't help but wonder, what a real Lemurian gateway would look like. Wayan seemed to be shocked by our reactions to Bach's words but he jumped in there with us and we were all, feverishly digging away.

We were digging like mad men for at least 40 minutes when we all seemed to slow down and lose some of our fire. Wayan took one more, hard blow to the wall with the one pick we had and the rocks started to fall and expose open air. As the rocks fell and the wall finally gave way Wayan almost fell inside the new opening. We found it! Wayan would always have the joy and memory of being the one who made the final break through with the final blow.

I thought he would explode he was so excited. For a guy wearing a shirt that labeled him a slacker, Wayan was more like a dynamo. Once he knew he had really broken through and could see the open chamber area on the other side, he started shoveling the rock out of the way, by hand to make a bigger opening and started to crawl through the hole.

A lot of dirt and dust was flying into the air around Wayan as he disappeared into the hole he just opened. Ronnie immediately jumped up behind him and started to crawl through behind him.

Bach stuck his head up to the opening and called inside,

"Better be careful and go slowly. No one has been in there for millions of years, you can't be sure how safe it might be."

The rest of us just stood there. I don't know what we thought we were waiting for but in just a minute Ronnie was coming back out, pushing a few more smaller rocks, making the hole even a little bigger. Right behind him came Wayan and the two of them were covered in dirt and dust. The two of them, turned and started to push and throw the rocks out of the way, making the opening bigger. We all joined in carrying dirt and small rock away by the bucket load. After about five minutes they said it was good enough.

We gave it a couple more minutes to let the dust settle and then we were all going in. To my surprise it was Cookie who stepped forward to ask the boys what they had seen.

Wayan said,

"Inside is amazing in it's simplicity but this is it. It's a gateway of some sort no doubt about it. I can feel it. Let's go check it out."

He turned and headed back inside and this time we all followed him. We only went in about ten feet and there in the dim light we could see it. It wasn't huge like the star gates in the movies. This thing, what ever it really was, was kind of small. It was round and it almost looked like an old kids toy, some kind of top with a spinner inside it. It looked like the inside circle could spin in the opposite direction of the outside circle or band.

It looked like it was just big enough for two or three of us to huddle inside its inner circle. If this was a gateway, then either they were much smaller people back then or only a few people could go jump through the dimensions at a time.

Now not letting too many people jump at the same time made real good sense to me. One thing I never, ever wanted to feel again was how I felt when we came back from Shambhala. The human body wasn't made to go through such intense dimensional slams and you wouldn't see me volunteering to test out what ever this gateway thing was.

"WOW!!! Can you believe this? All this time this thing has just been inches away from being discovered and we found it. Thanks Bach you must be psychic to have zoomed in on it so well. I can't wait until I can tell the old man about this." Wayan was talking a mile a minute and was so excited. "Wait until the News Press hears about this. It'll be international news all around the world!!!"

It was pretty cool when you thought about it all. Here we were, the thirteen of us biking across Bali on a warm sunny day and by chance stop to check out something with a friend. Then "BAM" we do a little digging and discover something as old as time itself. To think this could be a gateway into other dimensions was almost surreal. I kept looking for carvings or inscriptions that might explain it all a little more. I wouldn't have understood it no matter what it would say or mean, who knew what Lemurian looked like? There were no records of it's existence must less what their writing looked like.

There were some markings on the surface of the stone but a lot of dirt would need to be cleaned away first so you could see it better. Wayan was reacting like a child on Christmas morning, who just opened the best gift he ever received. He was all over the place, touching and inspecting the gateway when he suddenly stopped and looked at Bach.

"Hey can you tell how this thing worked? What else can you do?" Wayan asked.

Bach had a very thoughtful look on his face, as if he was trying to decide what he might say in reply to Wayans questions. I think we were all watching Bach, wondering what he would say or do next. If anybody could figure out the gateway and how it worked, I was certain Bach could. But the real question here was, will he tell Wayan or decide it was information better kept to him self?

I could feel the tension in the air, as we all seemed to hold our breath, waiting to hear what Bach would say. Finally he turned and looked back towards Wayan and said,

"This is the gateway and it is older than anything else on this Earth. The first colonists used this as a portal to all the other dimensions and worlds but it was used during a time when humans could leave their physical bodies and travel in the astral. I don't believe this gateway was engineered to be used by souls in the physical it wasn't an issue back then. It was brought here from one of those other worlds and thoughts are the key to opening it, that part you've got right. Man doesn't realize the power of thought. In the beginning spirit ruled this world and it wasn't until millions of years later that the physical bodies grounded man and he could no longer lift himself above his human senses."

"WOW! Well tell me how does it work? What more can you tell me about the gateway and how time travel works?" Wayan begged.

We were all ears to hear what Bach had to say but at the same time we were all checking out the chamber we found ourselves in and the actual gateway itself. There seemed to be one main platform on top of the gateway, with smaller circular platforms around it at a slightly lower elevation, like one step down from the top. There was room on top of the platform for all of us to stand with lots of room left over. All the circles on circles made me think of a Star Trek transporter station. It made me think of the famous words, "Beam me up Scottie".

"I sense this is a gateway that has a simple key. Desire is the builder of all thought and I believe that you could just wish or desire it so and it would be." Bach told him.

"Maybe like in the stories of Aladdin. You just speak the command, "OPEN SEZME" and it opens." Bunny offered.

A few of us laughed at her words. I mean, maybe today, you could talk to your computer or cell phone and just give verbal commands but way back then? Or maybe it could be that easy? If they wrote such things in stories, maybe it was because they did happen and were real. It certainly gave you something to think about.

The twelve of us were all over the platform still checking out our new discovery when Wayan jumped down and walked back toward the opening to see the entire gateway area. I turned to see what he was doing when I heard him yell out.

"OPEN SAYS ME!!!" as he threw up his arms to make it happen, like a physical command.

It was the last thing I saw, or heard inside the cave. Then there was a really loud swooshing sound and I felt like I had been sucked into some giant vacuum tube. I felt like I was tumbling and turning and just being twisted and shaken at the same time. The seconds seemed to be ticking away, turning into minutes. Where in the heck was I and where in the world was I going? I couldn't see or hear anything or anyone else. It felt like some kind of void in space. I could only hope that wherever I ended up, I wouldn't be alone. That thought almost paralyzed my heart and for a split second I was afraid it had stopped.

Suddenly I was thinking about how much I loved my dad and the puppies and how much I would miss my old life if this were the end for me. If it was the end, well I guessed I could say I went out with a real bang. Meeting the merkids, traveling and seeing so much of the world and its history with them, and finally seeing a real UFO. How much more could you expect to put into a regular lifetime? If I had to go, if death was what was happening to me right now, I would come back and watch over my family and friends and try to be their guardian angel.

I wouldn't have too many regrets, except not being able to tell my dad what had happened and everything I had seen. I'd try to think positive and just accept what ever happened; heck at this point, I had no control over anything anyway.

That final thought was the last thing I can remember thinking, when WACK! I landed on something and it just about knocked the wind out of me. I was rolling and tumbling on something solid and hard that felt like rock and gravel under me. That seemed like a hopeful sign to me, at least if felt like my world, and I hoped I was right where I had been just moments before, on Bali in a cave with all the kids.

I cried out from the pain as I rolled and felt my skin being scratched and torn, on the little rocks underneath me. It was a hard landing and

I started to cough and choke on the dirt and dust that was clouding up around me. Except for the grunts and groans that I heard coming from myself, it was totally silent. Then I heard it. There was someone else landing and crashing back to the ground, crying out in pain pretty close to me. Then another voice and another, it sounded a little like cannon balls making landfall. When the dust finally started to settle I could see them all. The twelve of us were all here. Only Wayan was missing.

Still coughing and choking, everyone started to inspect their minor injuries and trying to brush the dirt off their clothes. Everyone was looking around trying to figure out if we were back, where we started or someplace new. Nothing looked like the chamber we had been in with Wayan, and we weren't inside a chamber now either; this was more like an old riverbed and we were definitely out in the open. I tried to look in every direction to see if I could recognize anything. The others were all doing the same thing. It was obvious that we were not in that chamber back on Bali and probably not even on Bali anymore.

"Where in the heck are we?" Cookie asked "and what just happened?"

"I believe, that Wayan with his desires for time travel and his excitement over the gateway, opened it without realizing what he was really doing." Bach told her. "As for where we are. I don't know that answer yet. I think we can all say without too much thought, we're not on Bali anymore. I think we'll need to check out the area a little better and let me see, what if anything I can pick up. If everyone seems okay I think we should go. Stay close together and will go see what we can pick up about our new location. I'd like to get to a higher vantage point. Let's try this way."

We were all together so I wasn't feeling too scared at the moment but I didn't see anything I could recognize yet. The sky was the strangest red color. I didn't think I'd ever seen a sky look like this before. It was a little eerie looking at the sky with such a deep red color and what looked like black clouds. It didn't feel like anyplace I had ever been before. I hoped with all my heart that Bach could read the area and we could get back to Bali or at least home from here. We still didn't have the last plant we needed and I didn't think Bach would want to go home without it. Depending on where we were now, it would probably help clarify that decision, when he figured it all out.

"Well crap, does stuff like this happen very often on these little adventures of yours?" Cookie asked Becka and me as she was still checking out her scraps and some little cuts on her arm.

Bach decided to head out towards a higher bluff area just off to our right. I think he wanted to get up above the gullies and find a high spot where he could read the area a little better, plus it would give us all a birds-eye view of our surroundings. So we all followed him, with a little more confidence in our steps than we actually felt inside. Our current surroundings seemed more like someplace in the southwestern United States. Things were dry, no trees but more brush and grasses. If I had to guess, I think that's where I'd say we were. At least if it was the southwestern United States, we'd be closer to home.

Cookie was doing a lot of grumbling about not knowing where we were or what would happen next. I think that was her way of covering up her fears. I was feeling some of that fear myself but I also had a lot of faith in the merkids and what they could do. I felt sure they could get us out of any mess Wayan had gotten us into. So I guess my faith out-weighted my fears, which helped me to move forward with the rest of the group and even, try to calm Cookie's fears.

"Don't worry Cookie, we've been in worse messes than this one. Bach always figures things out and saves the day." I told her.

"Yeah Cookie, We're doing okay. We'll get back on track in no time at all." Bunny added.

"It'll be alright. Just give Bach some time to think when we get up on the bluff and we'll see what he can pick up." Becka chimed in to try and add her vote of confidence to the conversation.

After what seemed like about 40 minutes of hiking across the landscape, we got to the steeper part of the bluff that Bach wanted to climb to the top of. We all started to climb and half crawl up the side of the bluff. The red clay of the rock was loose and it wasn't easy to get a strong hold anywhere. The red earth and rock seemed to crumble every time I tried to get a good hold, so I could climb a little higher up the bluff. Occasionally one or two of us would slip and slide-back down the steep slope and just have to just start climbing up all over again. I personally battled the steep bluff wall, longer than any of the others. By the time I managed to get to the top, they were all standing together, in silence, looking out in the same general direction.

What the heck were they all looking at? And why wasn't anybody saying anything? What could have them all so quiet? I stepped around the group past Becka and Shi to see what had drawn their attention.

"What in the world is that? It sort of looks like Mount Rushmore but those aren't any presidents I ever saw!!" I called out more to myself than to the group in general.

The scene before us looked like Mount Rushmore in the States but two of the faces carved into this mountain were more like a Native American and a Asian face. One in fact looked more like the ET's they called Greys. How could that be possible? To top it all off the one of the faces looked more like a woman's face. In what world would the faces of presidents be replaced with these?

Bach wasn't looking too confident and as I watched him look around at our new surroundings, I didn't feel too confident either. I think I felt my eyelid begin to do a nervous twitch. The blood red sky and the dark, black clouds in it seemed to foretell of a dark and foreboding future. I had to wonder if we were ever going to get home from here?

What would all our parents be thinking when we didn't make it home for dinner tonight? I couldn't help but wonder and I could picture them all frantically searching and never finding us.

Bach stood there and in a very calm, serious, steady voice he said,

"I don't think the question is, 'What in the world is that?' I think the question should be 'what dimensional or parallel world could this be? What dimension are we in now?' Clearly when Wayan cried out "open says me", with the power of his words he did open a gateway. Now the question is "what gateway, into which dimensional world and how do we get back from here?"

To be continued.....................